"Clarke masterfully captures the deeply human emotional longing for love and community, even amid violence and horror. . . . She paints this portrait well, never failing to remind us that through even the most grim circumstances lie a longing and camaraderie that ultimately draw us all a little closer together."

— Jennie Camp, *Rocky Mountain News*

"Calling all book clubs! Clarke, whose debut novel, *River, Cross My Heart,* was a 1999 Oprah pick, scores again with this Civil War–era saga, set in Washington. She tells the deeply affecting story of a family of freed slaves in an evocative, historically rich book that brings the turbulent period alive. The author neither averts her eye from, nor sugarcoats the truth about, the uphill struggle for dignity in this gritty town."

— *Time*

"A compassionate portrait of the terrors and hopes of slaves. With its slightly clipped period language, coolly measured tone, and rich supply of telling detail, Clarke's second novel delves into a compelling social panorama of black servitude in Washington, DC, as the Civil War begins. . . . Clarke's sensitivity and her lyrical, earthy narration bring a freshness to the somber subject matter."

— *Kirkus Reviews*

"Clarke's prose is intelligent, direct, and a voice of the times. . . . Clarke enlists the help of superstitious and unforgettable characters to show us readers the many faces of bondage. She depicts an unfathomable reality and achieves believability, empathy, and hope. . . . Experience history, a fresh look at slavery, and the Coats family's unwavering desires for freedom. Marvel at Gabriel Coats — the anchor in an impeding storm."

— Karla Mass, *Raleigh News & Observer*

"The language reflects the era in which the novel is set. And the African American family's emotional journey tugs and demands attention. . . . In the end, this is a love story in its purest form."
— Karen M. Thomas, *Dallas Morning News*

"Fans of Clarke's *River, Cross My Heart* will instantly recognize the author's poetic sentences and the powerful emotional scenes that leave us breathless." — Mika Ono Benedyk, *Essence*

"A fascinating look at the life of slaves, free blacks, and the country during the fast-changing period around the Civil War. . . . The story is one of a family's dedication to one another and to the dream of being free. It is about love, hard work, talent, heartbreak, and triumph. It is beautifully written [and] well-researched, and has a history lesson as an added feature." — Laura L. Hutchison, *Fredericksburg Free Lance–Star*

"A powerful story quietly told. . . . While much has been written about the physical and psychic abuse that was inherent in the institution of slavery, Clarke has mastered a matter-of-fact delivery that makes the cruelty immediate. . . . She uses deceptively simple language to pack an insightful, powerful punch. The resulting novel is one that takes the reader on an intense and memorable journey and is a fine follow-up to a lovely debut."
— Robin Vidimos, *Denver Post*

"Breena Clarke once again takes a clear-eyed look at her hometown's history of slavery and racism. . . . *Stand the Storm* is a fulfilling follow-up, written with the same restraint and sensitivity that made her earlier novel such a hit."
— Krista Walton, *Washington City Paper*

Stand the Storm

Stand the Storm

A Novel

BREENA CLARKE

BACK BAY BOOKS
Little, Brown and Company
NEW YORK • BOSTON • LONDON

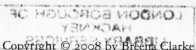

Back Bay Books / Little, Brown and Company
Hachette Book Group
237 Park Avenue, New York, NY 10017
Visit our website at www.HachetteBookGroup.com

Originally published in hardcover by Little, Brown and Company,
July 2008
First Back Bay paperback edition, June 2009

Back Bay Books is an imprint of Little, Brown and Company. The Back
Bay Books name and logo are trademarks of Hachette Book Group, Inc.

The characters and events in this book are fictitious.
Any similarity to real persons, living or dead, is coincidental
and not intended by the author.

Library of Congress Cataloging-in-Publication Data
Clarke, Breena.
    Stand the storm : a novel / Breena Clarke. — 1st ed.
      p. cm.
    ISBN 978-0-316-00704-7 (hc) / 978-0-316-00705-4 (pb)
  1. African Americans — Fiction.   2. Women slaves — Fiction.
  3. Slaves — Fiction.   I. Title.
    PS3553.L298S73 2008
    813'.54 — dc22   2007049805

10 9 8 7 6 5 4 3 2 1

RRD-IN

Printed in the United States of America

For my husband, my stalwart, my fancy, my Helmar
And for Popsi, always and for all

Stand the Storm

THERE ARE ENDLESS stitches to count. Handwork promotes calculation. Gabriel watched his mother pause in her knitting to rest her fingers for the briefest moment — a pause most observers wouldn't notice. He had always understood that her rest was a part of her work. It was how she could work so long and achieve so much.

As Gabriel made calculations in his own lap — upon his own work — he grew calm. His stomach, which lurched and talked up when he got to thinking about his freedom, would settle alongside Sewing Annie. For these were two folks on a rope. They pulled the same side together and they would never be one swamped by the other. They pulled together.

There hadn't been much need of Gabriel's small hands for fieldwork during the time of his babyhood, so he was molded to be a helpmeet for his mother. As he was a good extra hand, close by and circumspect, the Master and Missus allowed Sewing Annie to have her pup at her side.

The woman known as Sewing Annie at Ridley Plantation in St. Mary's County, Maryland, acquired her name honestly, as she had worked all of her life at sewing, weaving, knitting, and dyeing cloth.

"The woman that knits row after row never gets to the end like a dam that plants and picks down a row in the field. 'Cause when the light goes from the field they likely to let you rest. But a woman that works in her lap can keep on by candlelight and mostly they do. And mostly the mistress expect you to do," Sewing Annie declared flatly to any who envied her. She knew the field-working folks at Ridley considered her a lucky one who could sit on her duff and work with her fingers. They figured her fortunate on the account that her child worked close alongside. It could not be denied that Sewing Annie's fortunes were, in some eyes, enviable. She had Gabriel for the blacksmith and had brought a girl, Ellen, for the blacksmith, too.

But Annie did not spare the boy — her helpmeet. Rather she worked Gabriel hard to steel him and he came up a stranger to capering.

The child worked under his mother's command at hauling water in buckets and fetching and carrying bundles. He got to be good for stirring pots as well as preparing soaps. Aside from his knotted, sinewy upper arms, he was not muscular. Sewing Annie's Gabriel — as he came to be identified as he grew — exhibited a genuine aptitude for needlework. He inherited his mother's dexterity, crisp eyesight, appreciation of hue and balance, and quiet, steady manner. Gabriel's skills at dyeing yarn gave a considerable boon to Annie's output, as she could concentrate more time on making up the garments she worked on. She gave over handling the dyeing paddles as the boy progressed to the job of stirring the bath.

Gabriel was delighted by the concoctions to draw out and guide the coloring. His eyes would light up as the yielding and coaxing of tickseed, dusty miller, laurel, and lichens revealed the hues. His mother taught him to restrain his excitement, though. It was her strategy that he maintain his quietude so that he not be rebuked or punished. Gabriel came up to be a good shadow pair of hands, and Annie molded him to his tasks patiently but persistently. She was guided to build him strong and resourceful. She sucked each small finger and pressed it insistently, relentlessly to the jobs of sewing and knitting. She kept him at it even when she would have wanted to let him rest. And if she was loving with him she was not sweet. Many a time she switched him with her hand or a small strop to keep him stalwart — to keep him quietly hardworking and not inclined to lollygag.

When Gabriel gained the age of ten, Master Ridley thought to get more profitable labor out of him. He hired out Sewing Annie's Gabriel to a tailor named Abraham Pearl in town — in Georgetown. The tailor had advertised for a capable helper. Ridley, who often came to Washington to conduct business, thought the hire arrangement would yield some profit from a youngster ill suited for fieldwork.

Came the day and Annie would not let Gabriel mewl and cry. They would punish a crybaby. He must be firm and solid and do what they told him to do. The prospects for him were bright. This hire-out job would train him up and keep him out of the fields. The expendable ones were those who worked crops at Ridley. Season after season crops flourished or failed and Master Ridley had need of more or fewer workers. Thus he sold or bought persons upon his need of hands for the fields. Hands working specialized jobs were the last to go south.

When Abraham Pearl had arrived from Philadelphia to set up in Georgetown, he hadn't wanted anything to do with chattel slavery. His wife, Dinah, minded all that he was too busy for. She worked hard beside him and the two closed their eyes to the brutal business conducted throughout the town. Their plan had been to build the tailoring concern around the children they expected to be blessed with.

Together, man and wife made a good beginning. The business grew quickly.

A tailor needs an extra hand for keeping neat, for doing secondary work — setting on snaps and buttons and winding yarns and threads and reaching high and low when the tailor is with the patron. Dinah was capable if not artful.

In the early days of the marriage, Dinah was enthusiastic for the work. She was anxious to prove herself a better catch than her younger sister. She knew like every one else in her family that Abraham Pearl had initially been intrigued by Bessie, her sister, so dark-brown-eyed and milk-complexioned that their father had saved her for the attentions of some man more successful than Abraham Pearl. Dinah had the dark brown eyes, too, but had more time on the bone. She was reckoned a lesser catch.

Abraham and Dinah were blessed with compatibility, but no children.

"Aye, God is angry that we are so happy, he will not send a child," Abraham said with good humor. "Perhaps we should turn sour on each other."

"As I have not brought forth a hand for you, tailor, you must hire," Dinah answered. "The work is too much for a dry old woman," she continued, though she was just upwards of thirty. It became a business imperative for Pearl to get help when Dinah died of consumption.

The boy Pearl hired from Jonathan Ridley was not delicate or sickly, but he wasn't broad-built either. Pearl was relieved. He hadn't wanted a slave who would have to be subdued by force. He didn't have the stomach for whipping and beating.

The first night, the evening Gabriel arrived in Georgetown, he stood in the middle of the workroom with his eyes on the floor and shivered.

This child was unexpectedly slim about the shoulders but very well developed in his forearms, wrists, and hands. Pearl first examined the hands closely by turning them over in his own. To gauge his own power to control the child, he grasped him forcefully and exposed his palms. The boy submitted silently. He flinched when Pearl ran his fingers over the welts on his palms. He had received discipline here — more likely a mother's chastisement than an overseer's. Pearl removed the boy's shirt under witness of the broker to look for signs of gross punishment and found nothing on the child's back or chest.

At a nod from the broker the child unhitched his pants and dropped them off. He remained standing straight but trembled. He seemed to be approaching the end of his steady nerves. Pearl glanced quickly at Gabriel's smooth buttocks, his belly, the backs of his legs, and noted them unscarred. He did not indulge in any further curiosity though encouraged to do so by the leering broker.

"Take up your clothes, child," Abraham Pearl commanded gruffly. He was embarrassed at seeing the naked child and angry at feeling so. He gave the broker his fee and shifted from foot to foot impatiently. The man expected a cup of coffee or a biscuit or both to close the deal. But Pearl extended no welcome and the broker slapped his hat on his thigh and finally departed.

"Ah, the hooknoses have no manners! When the money has

passed the deal is done," he griped to his associate when he left the shop.

The gruffness covered Pearl's profound distaste for the process of hiring slave labor. He knew he must examine the boy — look at him to see if there were hidden signs of gross punishment or deformity. He had contracted for a smart, quick half-hand — a boy for fetching and training. He was nervous of getting a difficult, brooding helper. But he was not prepared to see a child stripped and shivering.

Pearl directed the child to make a pallet for himself in the corner. Certainly there was no need for him to fear his ability to control this slave. The boy could have been knocked to the floor with an errant elbow. The boy's face looked like a falling mud fence all during the first meal. Pearl worried that he'd not thrive — might not live even. He might crumble under the work and become a burden. Perhaps he had been too soon separated from his mother.

After eating and tending his wants with circumspection, the boy turned his face toward the wall and away from Pearl, who sat at his table and stitched on a commission by the light of a sputtering candle. Pearl intermittently looked over his glasses at Gabriel and wondered what this youngster was. He had been quiet and composed when he arrived with the broker from Ridley Plantation. But since the uncouth character had departed, the little fellow seemed to have lost his nerves and become tearful. When the boy began to snore, Pearl covered his shoulders with a blanket.

The boy's proficiency with needlework was clear from the first, and Pearl was surprised. Would Ridley have hired him out so reasonably if he'd known how skilled the boy was? He'd had practice with taking instructions and following steps to the letter and he was agile and accomplished at simple sewing. Pearl realized right away that this little Gabriel was a competent hand for tailoring.

Gabriel started in to learn the trade from Mr. Abraham Pearl and within a while of four years he graduated from doing the general work around the shop to accomplishing commissions.

After the first term of their agreement ended, Pearl attempted to convince Jonathan Ridley that his instructing the boy in the craft of tailoring should offset a part of the fee for Gabriel's work. After all, he argued, the boy had come to him in ignorance and was receiving an education. Ridley countered that the maturing slave boy was capable of more expert assistance, thus more valuable to the tailor.

When, after eight years, Gabriel's second term of service to the tailor came to an end, Ridley and Pearl negotiated a contract to employ Gabriel as a tailor's assistant. The increase Ridley proposed this time angered Pearl. The two men haggled and wrangled and tugged Gabriel between them.

Ah! It is prudent to be practical, Pearl decided. He was intimidated by Ridley's influence. And Ridley knew that he was now attached to the boy as well as dependent upon his assistance. True, Pearl had spurred the boy's development and felt pride in what he'd done. He'd shaped a son of sorts from this boy and did not want to lose his assistance in the shop or his companionship. He agreed to the steeper hire terms in large because of these feelings.

Pearl had seen Gabriel's eyes as he'd grown and thrived in the shop. Sometimes they were lit from beyond themselves. The boy had learned the work and a sense of himself had emerged.

Gabriel had listened to the negotiations regarding his hire fee. Abraham Pearl had bargained and cajoled to lower it — to keep hold of more of his margin of profit. He hadn't meant the disparaging things he'd said to Master Ridley — that the boy was of little use until he'd given him instruction. Gabriel knew he did not believe this. "Boy, you are well up to the mark!" Pearl had often praised him highly.

But from these discussions of his value — his worth — came the thought to acquire this sum for himself, for himself to be free. Could he know the sum and fasten his hope upon it and earn from his own commissions as Mr. Pearl had suggested that he might?

Out of the core of the arrangement with Ridley, another arrangement was created. Pearl agreed to allow Gabriel to earn money from work outside of his obligations to the tailoring shop. This knot, this plug of money, was his beginning.

The efficient division of labor in the shop and the rising fortunes of the region sparked a rapid growth in the tailoring business. Successful local men craved distinctive clothes. And those in government service competed to trumpet their tastes and importance. Pearl's shop catered to the increasing number of gentlemen aspiring to fashion.

As Pearl preferred not to shout commands or even to waste breath on repetition, he indicated much with silent signals, as had Gabriel's own mam. The boy's upright carriage with no touch of impudence was graceful and attentive. A beckoning gesture with the right hand was employed to call Gabriel from his post of observation and set him to measuring a client for a commission or briskly brushing his coat.

Late in the month of June on one of Gabriel's infrequent visits to the Ridley Plantation, Sewing Annie and her son sat together around the flagging nighttime fire in the cabin. The two engaged in lap work as they were accustomed to doing. Annie glanced over to her son's hands, gainfully employed with knitting, and mused on Bell. The boy favored his father about the eyes and around the nose and down the face. But Gabriel didn't have Bell's mallet hands. His hands were slender and dexterous.

"Keep your head about your shoulders," was what Sewing Annie said to Gabriel. She settled back and considered that she had formed him up well and she took pride from it. It was she who instructed Gabriel to figure on his fingers and to listen and be still and take care of what he said around the Master and Mistress. She credited herself for his fineness and appreciated her handiwork.

Gabriel held his chin down upon his chest and she touched it there. He faced her to say "Nanny," in much the voice of always.

Sparing as usual with their conversation, the mother and son worked rows on their knitting. It did tickle Gabriel to hear his mother's voice occasionally through the night. In Georgetown he sorely missed sitting up listening to his mother clack her teeth and her knitting needles about one thing and another. Talking in the deep dark was a stingy pleasure but a pleasure nonetheless.

Gabriel did some clacking and talking, too. He told his mother about the shop and about Georgetown. There were many things to tell, so his careful whisper was once or twice forgotten. "Nanny," he said excitedly. He spoke of carriages, cloaks, boots, elegant clothes. "Oh, Mr. Pearl's scissors will cut an eyelash, Nanny!"

She listened rapt, savoring the sound of Gabriel. "Master Ridley is but one among many. There are other rich masters in

Georgetown. And he is not one of the topmost either. And there are" — Gabriel lowered his voice, remembering to be cautious — "white men who do not believe that slavery is right. They fight for the good of slaves. There are even . . ."

Annie coughed a knot of phlegm and made a loud noise of expectoration. She shot a searing look of caution at the boy. Gabriel checked his words.

"Something went down the wrong pipe. Ain't nothing," she said to cover the silence.

On subsequent visits, Gabriel returned to the subject of freedom. "There's folks who help a slave to get to the free states," he said to his mother. He said no more. He'd let her think about the words and what he possibly meant when he said them. Then she'd consider what her own feelings were. Gabriel would wait for his mother — let her take her time to consider what should come next.

One

A CRUELLY COLD but bright sunshiny New Year's Day was when her mam was sold south to satisfy a debt incurred by the master. She and her mam had shared some honeyed cakes during the slack days at Christmastime. Both had enjoyed laughter and some resting. And then on New Year's Day young Annie's pallet was placed alongside that of Knitting Annie.

"Slaves ain't 'lowed to have shares of nothin' — no chick nor child," the woman said to the blubbering girl by way of consolation. "Master own it all."

Female slaves on Ridley Plantation in this time were generally called by a variation of the name Ann. The young girl apprenticed to the older woman who knitted was known as Annie-that-sews or Sewing Annie. She was thus called to distinguish her from the slave women they called Cookananny and from her mentor, Knitting Annie. There was as well the one known as Field Annie, lovingly called Fela, who led the gang of women that cleared brush for planting and harvesting crops.

As Sewing Annie grew, her reputation was gained mostly

upon her legendary skills at knitting rather than pure out-and-out sewing. But she kept the name Sewing Annie to thwart confusion.

Knitting Annie was the all-time leader on Ridley Plantation in production of knitted work. She far outstripped lengths accomplished by the eight other slaves who did knitting work and also Mrs. Clementine Stern Ridley, sister-in-law of the master and a needlewoman of repute. She also exceeded the production of Mrs. Mary Elizabeth Brackley Ridley, the master's wife, whose embroidery and tatting were considered of the finest quality in southern Maryland and whose hands seemed always to be occupied with threads or yarn. The closets in the main house were full of quilts, coverlets, counterpanes, and antimacassars, for the two Mrs. Ridleys assuaged their isolation with work on these favorite pastimes. Knitting Annie's expert needlework put her around the table at quilting bee time, working elbow to elbow with the mistresses. They greatly esteemed her skills. And it was surely the consideration of this that lightened her travails.

Knitting Annie and Sewing Annie were installed in the ground-floor room of a plank cabin they shared with a changing group of two or three other female hands. There the needlewoman and her charge slept upon a plain bedstead fitted with a straw mattress and a feather mattress. Knitting Annie guarded their mattresses and commanded complete charge of them. The morning after Sewing Annie lost control of herself and made water on the bedclothes, Knitting Annie only grunted and soaked the clothes in a bath of her own concoction. The sheets and covers were pummeled to sweet cleanness and the girl was cajoled not to soil them.

Knitting Annie covered their bed with a sweet old quilt.

This quilt was as plain as any other used by the slaves at Ridley, but its fineness was nevertheless indisputable. The back was made from feed sacks, as were all the others, but the top had a myriad of patterned pieces and bright solids of every kind. This was where scraps from whatever came to them as cloth ended up. Worn places were constantly, relentlessly patched, and it could perhaps be said the bedcloth — from patching — had metamorphosed from one thing to another. It was nearly a completely different coverlet than when it had begun, though it remained of one piece. It was old, old — had been done long before Knitting Annie was born.

The fineness of the old bed quilt was the underside, which was so flawlessly stitched and so intricate that to follow the spiraling stitches would hypnotize the eyes staring at it. Knitting Annie traced the intricacies, the whorls, with her finger. Sewing Annie fell asleep upon ruminations about where exactly the thread had begun its journey in this cloth, for each tiny nip and tuck of it appeared identical. However, this quilt cover did shun the straight. Its stitches were intermittently, deliberately broken to spoil the perfect. A needleworker of Knitting Annie's skill could come close to making it just so, but the devil would like that too much, the old people said. Thus the quilt had proper irregularity so that the devil would not grab up the two needleworkers in their sleep.

Knitting Annie often repeated, "The favored top for sleeping under, girl, is the Drunkard's Path. The devil will be sure to spurn it."

One such perfect quilt — not the Drunkard, but a complex beauty — was made at Ridley and caused no end of trouble in the night. It was said to entwine the legs of any who slept with it. Despite its beauty, Mistress disposed of the perfect quilt as a wedding gift to a young girl of middling favor in the county who was to go westward with her husband.

"Them threads was worked too sweet and even," Knitting Annie maintained as cautionary.

Knitting Annie was kind to her charge and looked after the girl as well as one who is a slave can look after another one who is a slave. It was her duty to pass to this young Annie all of what she knew about knitting and piecing together the knitted garments and the quilting, the spinning and dyeing, and what all else. She passed on all, as well as a few choice secrets having to do with which plants were best for dyes.

As part of the mushrooming prosperity of Ridley Plantation in those years, the needlewoman and her young assistant worked inside the loom house that Master built some few feet from the big house. Mistress Ridley prized hands that knew the needlework skills and the needlewomen were under her direct supervision. She checked output and recorded in her logbook detailed information regarding the projects the needleworkers undertook and completed.

The joint-aching chill of working in low-lying marshy areas on Ridley Plantation in January and February and oftentimes in cold, cold March was assuaged by stockings, blankets, socks, gloves, tunics, shawls, shirts, and pantaloons produced by Knitting Annie and her shadow, Sewing Annie. Knitting Annie had been born to the tasks in production of garments for the Ridley slaves. Her mam, a vague figure at the back of her thoughts, had labored upon a spinning loom. None in their line had ever known work other than the needlework.

"Hunt and peck and Ginny crack corn, and hunt and peck and two and three and four and . . . ," Knitting Annie singsonged to pass the time and set the tone. There was always the threat of fieldwork to keep them hard at their duties.

Knitting Annie carried needles and yarn in the deep pocket slit of her skirt and worked upon these consistently when her hands were not otherwise engaged. Sewing Annie adjusted the tempo of her needlework to that of her mentor. When Knitting Annie worked calmly and contemplatively she set a similar pace for the girl. The girl learned to speed her click-clacking when Mistress hovered, as Knitting Annie was wont to do. Sewing Annie learned her figuring — a series of tallies with her fingers — from Knitting Annie. Skilled tallying was the hallmark of Knitting Annie's work — nay, of any needleworker. So it could be said that she who had no aptitude for tallying could never rise as a needleworker.

At noon, Mistress Ridley retired to her boudoir for rest. The two Annies worked throughout the afternoon, though they allowed their fingers to move slowly during this time. This was the time of day for which the Annies earned their legend as the lucky ones who sat upon their duffs. Wary of being caught at a nap, though, the older woman stayed alert as the child was allowed to drowse. Knitting Annie dipped into the youngster's lap from time to time and worked some rows on the child's assignments. And if the youngster's work became knotted or plagued by runners, the older woman picked up her slack for fear they would both suffer. She had soft feelings for the little pup and nerves that craved after calm.

Mistress did not rest for long of an afternoon. She would emerge after precisely two hours' doze and begin a supervisory circuit of the loom room. She measured and counted the slave women's output to certify that time had not been wasted.

"She'll be watering the stock!" Mistress threatened when aging Knitting Annie's count fell. She said she'd put old Knitting Annie out in the barn to tote water for the animals were she to get so old she couldn't keep up. As the years passed, the maturing Sewing Annie picked up her mentor's slack when it came to it. She carried along the old woman's work that fell into her lap when the old precious slumped forward and snored. Some nights the bone-tired girl advanced Knitting Annie's work while she slept just as the old woman had done for her. She who had grown moderately tall and solid in the upper body and graceful and dexterous in the hands let the older one rest in a chair and blow gas. Sewing Annie worked ten more rows with her own eyes completely closed. The trick was easily done. It became her habit to go some little bit more after she had said, "Now is the time to stop." It strengthened her to push on — to leave the work well advanced for the next day before lying down to rest.

"My lap is bloody. I'm not expecting it. But my lap is got bloody. When I stan' up I see the stain a big, pear-shape, red-brown mess on the front ma' dress. A funny kind o' thing." Knitting Annie had never been a chatterer, but she was a dreamer and a dream interpreter. She had the habit of telling her dreams to Sewing Annie. She woke up one morning talking and unable to stay still. "Name ain't no Annie. Ma' name's Abiba — *Ah-bee-baa*," she said. Knitting Annie showed her gums, and her loose teeth clacked. She continued telling. "I was scared. Good right to be. I look down in ma' lap and I seen a white man's head. That what make the bloody stain and I thought it was the moon blood. I woked up then."

Sewing Annie thought that she ought not let the old woman

sit upright and sleep. She ought to be sure to lay her flat at night. They were tempting spirits to invade an old woman's dreams by leaving her upright through the dark night like she was a sentry. The old one was becoming chatty, slow, and unproductive, and she needed the night's whole rest.

Some months after the dream visited Knitting Annie, a blacksmith helper was brought to Ridley Plantation. Purchased to help the regular blacksmith, who had taken ill, he was a man of medium build with large shoulders and arms, at the end of which were hands shaped like mallets. These mallet hands were the main reason Ridley purchased him: "A nigger with hands like that will be useful to a blacksmith," he had said upon first seeing the slave in the Charleston market.

Knitting Annie died — wound down like a clock — on a stuffy afternoon in the loom room. The knitting she worked fell from her hands and her needles ceased sound. Sewing Annie felt all the air leave her body at the realization that Knitting Annie had gone. She sat and knitted a full five more rows before rising to call others to account for the old precious.

The old woman had in her prime been an expert gang leader for sewing and knitting, soap-making and yarn-dyeing. Her long suit was setting forth the steps to a task and pressing the workers to it. Over her lifetime she had forgotten more than the others had yet learned. Grief-stricken and shorthanded, Sewing Annie faltered and production fell off. Two girls, yet too small for fieldwork, became her assistants for toting and fetching. Neither of these children had aptitude for needlework. Thus the workload for Sewing Annie was punishing after the old woman's death.

Added to this was numbness and confusion. The old woman had been her constant and she felt like a stool that had lost

a leg. She was impatient with sitting at the weaving loom
and walked back and forth making a circuit of the room that
she'd shared with the old woman — a room that now seemed
shrunken. She stood at the doorway and worked upon her knitting. As it grew, Annie wrapped the length around her shoulders. She wore it as if it were her own shawl. Onlookers were
disturbed. They all believed it was bad luck for a needlewoman
to wrap herself in her own knitting while working on it.

Annie stood in the doorway and listened to the cadence of
the blacksmith's blows. She recognized a love of regularity in
the man who'd taken the place of the deceased blacksmith. Two
deaths — another one to come! The new head blacksmith had
a contemplative demeanor like hers. She heard it in the tone of
his strokes. He gained momentum on the regular and rising
movements just as she was used to doing. This was the technique that the old woman had taught her. He, too, could en-
dure for the long term, for he credited rest and recovery deep in
his work. He was productive as she was.

Old Knitting Annie had giggled when the young woman
told her about dreaming of a snake pit.

"You're wanting a man. 'Tis a plain dream of woman's longing," she'd said when the tale came out. With the old woman
gone, the yearning became keener.

"Your wrap is pretty, good woman," the blacksmith said,
surprising her. She started, then came to herself and saw that
she was standing in the doorway of the blacksmith's barn. He
did not halt his strikes, but only looked at her when he spoke.

When she came again to stand in the barn door and knit, he
was alarmed for her and also drawn to her. To protect her, he
made a show of interest. He knew she'd only come to listen to
the doleful hammer strikes. But Mistress was liable to think

her gone from grief and sell her off. Bell grinned at her, though mostly her head was hung down. It was an unusual court-ship — this first feigned interest.

"You're a pretty woman," he said after some days of looking at her. "Prettier than that shawl you're doin' up," he said, laughing. Indeed he brought out the bloom in her all at once with these words.

Permission was granted that the two could set up housekeeping in the cabin that Sewing Annie had shared with Knitting Annie. Until they joined Field Annie's gang, the two little girls who worked with Sewing Annie had to stay with them.

It didn't please Master Ridley for Bell and Annie to take up together. Some of his slaves he didn't want becoming permanent with anyone particular. It made it messier when the time came for a sale.

When baby Gabriel was born, fears began to fidget in Sewing Annie. As hard as she felt for Bell and feared a separation, she was ten times more bound to the babe. When Ellen came three years later, there was an increase in nervousness offset by a lulling into further happiness. The run of luck seemed to hold for Sewing Annie.

There were evenings of Gabriel as a bandy-legged toddler sucking on a sugar tit in the middle of the cabin floor. There were evenings of Ellen dandled on Bell's knee. There were hushed nights of Bell and Annie holding each other for dear life and true pleasure. There were stolen moments at first light or deep dark when Annie kneaded Bell's shoulders. There were secret suppers of corn pone and hog entrails and stolen delectables.

Bell yearned to formalize his relations with Annie. He wanted a marrying ceremony. He wished to stand up in front of the folks and proclaim that Sewing Annie was his woman and none other. He wanted to put a claim on his children. Much of this feeling was on account of being the blacksmith on the place. Working with the hammer was a point of distinction and it did raise Bell above other hands. He appealed directly to Master Ridley, who respected the man's abilities but was leery. Bell pointed out to Master that he and Annie had stayed together for a time and that they considered themselves to be good Christian folks. Bell would have gone on to mention the children, but he cut his appeal when he glimpsed the expression on Ridley's face. Days after, it worried Bell that he might have said too much to Master Ridley — that his reach had exceeded his grasp.

Sewing Annie had seen the face, too. She'd stood at Bell's left shoulder with her head inclined tight to the floor. She would not presume to enter the exchange between her man and her master. She turned herself to salt to remain there to listen and know. Her eyeballs swept from one side to the other without moving the lids, straining to interpret the faces of Bell and Master Ridley. She saw Ridley's displeasure and felt fearful.

Bell, expert at talking with the hammer, anvil, and bellows, was smart enough to know to clamp down and be dumb around the top folks. He said no more about marrying.

When Bell had his accident — accidental injury is what a blacksmith expects to meet him someday — the hammer rhythm stopped abruptly. His attention wavered? Who is to say? Bell lanced a great gash on his own forearm and the normally quiet man howled fiercely and ran out into the dirt yard in front of the smithy. The women working in the kitchen — they were closest — responded first to his hideous cries. The cook, running outside at full steam with a lard jar, slathered Bell's forearm.

Sewing Annie, nerves curdled when she heard the roar, ran out from the loom room, trampling her knitting in the dust. The two kitchen helpers, Annie, and the cook carried Bell to the cabin. Gabriel followed his mother. The toddling Ellen sat like a top in the dust staring at the women lifting, howling, and pulling and dragging to get Bell in the cabin.

Despite quick application of salve, Bell's wound festered. When the doctor was summoned, he told Ridley that the only way to save the whole man was to take off the rapidly rotting section of the forearm. Ridley agonized over maiming a slave blacksmith. There was money lost in destroying the arm of a blacksmith! "'Tis the same as chopping off several hundreds of dollars!" he exclaimed to the physician. Reluctantly, he agreed to the amputation.

The accident felled the blacksmith like a tree, taking him down in a series of deep, agonizing cuts. Bell survived the operation but did not regain strength enough to raise himself from his bed for several weeks. Defined by his arms and mallet hands, he was half a hand after the doctor's work.

The last and most painful cut was that Jonathan Ridley settled a debt for farm tools with selling Bell to Cyrus Wilson, a neighbor, who used him as a general hand to fetch and carry.

Two

BREEZY RELIEF CAME with the turn of season in the town. It was as if the breath that had been held all of the hot, stuffy summer was loosed. And the breath brought back all the wiry, lanky, rotund, and lop-legged politicians and profiteers to Washington and Georgetown. They came to the tailor shop in a flow, and the delicious uptick in business delighted Abraham Pearl and consumed every waking hour of his and Gabriel's days.

"We two bees will have honey, Gabriel!" Pearl exclaimed. "Honey is the reward for the hardworking bee and we two will have it!"

The log of commissions for suits of clothing burgeoned and Gabriel's output was the equal of Pearl's. Staggering their duties and spelling each other, they smoothly accomplished a good deal. As they had no time to cook up anything other than coffee, the two relied on fried cornmeal cakes and boiled potatoes for their sustenance.

In the ever-brisker air of October, minds were bent on pork as well. As was the annual custom, all Ridley hands hired out were called back to the place for the task of slaughtering hogs and filling the smokehouse. Since always, even the smallest child was given a duty to perform at hog slaughter.

Though Abraham Pearl tried to keep Gabriel in Georgetown, the young man could not hold against Jonathan Ridley or the pull toward his mother and sister or even the smell of singed hair and smoking pork.

"Mister Ridley, sir," Pearl implored when Ridley called at the shop to remove Gabriel. "I am committed for this boy's work." He dared not suggest how much indebted. "How will I complete these commissions?"

Jonathan Ridley allowed Pearl to wheedle a bit and implore him to let Gabriel remain at work. But he held his position and insisted that the autumn slaughter was inviolable.

"Mr. Pearl, I have told you this before. At hog slaughter, all of my able hands must join in. This one is no different. This year is no different," Ridley pronounced smoothly, assured of no further argument.

Gabriel was commanded to stop his work immediately and sit in the wagon. His countenance revealed no preference in the discussion. He was adjusted to Pearl and content in his duties, but there was a draw to Ridley, too. He sat dumbly in the wagon while Pearl gathered a sack of his things. He included some intricacies of topstitching that Gabriel was to sew upon while gone. These items Pearl thrust into Gabriel's lap and bade him quietly, "Come back." Not a request, it was a simple, urgent invocation meant to influence the fate of solemn-faced Gabriel.

"We've a delicious journey, boys." Ridley was gay and talkative when he drove out of Georgetown. He talked on brightly as if he intended to engage Gabriel and Mars, the driver, in his banter. Both Gabriel and Mars were clever enough to enjoy his levity in silence. Ridley spoke as if the hard days ahead of blood work and songs restored his vigor.

"We'll have chitlins, boys! Our guts will be full of them and fine it will be, too!" he exclaimed. Gabriel was surprised because he'd thought Ridley at a remove from the delights of pork.

Master Ridley, Mars, and Gabriel arrived still riding upon enthusiasm. They were three of Ridley at home to be counted and reckoned.

The job Gabriel had always had — since the dawn of his remembrances — was that of fetching the largest laundry pots to set boiling. When he was very small, his mother had charge of this task and he had to help her.

"Set the caldrons, boy," Annie cried in lieu of hallo when Gabriel's shadow fell across her threshold.

Sewing Annie turned and looked into Gabriel's maturing face.

"Hallo, Nanny!" he called excitedly.

"Set the pots," she said, and brought him back to his boyhood with a thud.

"Pity the hog in it all, for the work is cruel but we love the ham!" was Jonathan Ridley's sunup rallying cry setting each one to their duties.

At several days' end, after the slaughter and sausage-making and preparation for smoking, sloppy hog entrails were awarded to the hands. These were gratefully accepted and in each household chitterlings were cooked and appreciated.

"Stir up a pot of them things!" Master Ridley shouted to Cookananny when he came upon her in the kitchen with his own pail of hog entrails. Laughing and hoorawing took up through the house, as hog chitterlings had some reputation for aphrodisiacal powers. The familiar humor ringing throughout caused both the mistresses to be embarrassed.

Hog-killing time conspired to make Gabriel forget his uneasiness at Ridley Plantation. He wanted Georgetown and he wanted himself and his mother and Ellen to be for their own selves in Georgetown. He knew it was audacious and dangerous to be dreaming in this way. But Gabriel no longer doubted that the plan would form up. "Nanny, would you not be free?" Gabriel asked, and glanced at his mother's face in profile. He knew that she mightn't answer with words, but would give him the picture on her face.

"Keep shut, boy," she said warily. The thing she was always was wary. Sewing Annie was never a believer in the mystical efficacy of the hush pot and other widely held fanciful notions. The only way to keep the white people from knowing what was planned was not to talk in their hearing. Gabriel chuckled silently to think his mother did err on the side of caution. He'd not known Master or Mistress or any other to hear from so great a distance as between the main house and Sewing Annie's cabin.

"Nanny? If I come away, will you come?"

"To Canady?" she queried.

"Yes, Nanny, to Canada — perhaps," Gabriel replied.

"Is't where they all go?" she asked, and went quiet to consider. "What'll we do if we get there? Will we sew and mend for hire? Is there custom there?"

Gabriel was confounded at the clarity of his mother's thoughts and understood that she must have been thinking toward this. He yearned the more to talk to her.

Evenings at slaughter time were also productively spent with hands set to quilting. Nearly all of the women and a fair number of the men worked at quilting the tops pieced by Sewing Annie and the mistresses. Given a corner of the frame to work upon, each quilter was part of a four-person team. As the teams competed for prizes of smoked ham hocks, Gabriel, Ellen, and Sewing Annie were not allowed to form their own group but were circulated to others.

Teamed with three old sheep-shearing hands who were past strength for fieldwork, Gabriel worked his needle, as his mother required him. "You are your mam's boy," one old sheep-shearer had to say. Folks always said this and meant it kindly. Those who recalled Bell, the blacksmith, would say it often.

Young Ellen and her graceful, competent hands were put together with three old preciouses and their slower fingers. Ellen was sullen and silent, for she craved to trade gossip with the younger girls.

Sewing Annie circulated the barn and was manager of the quilting. From time to time she sat at her own corner and worked furiously to pull ahead of her partners.

"Nanny, you're a spinning top. Take a seat and rest yourself," Gabriel got bold enough to say when Sewing Annie had come again to peer over his shoulder. She was enamored of his stitches and they compelled her eye, though she did not say so. She only goaded Gabriel to work faster to compensate for the three old sheep-shearers. These old men laughed at Gabriel's impudence and began coughing and expectorating and halted their work. Gabriel's penance was his mother's good-natured thump upon the back of his head. As she stood close to him, her bosom pressed to his back, he regretted his words, for he would not have her move away.

Annie lingered behind her son and mused that Gabriel had stayed her right arm for far longer than she'd expected. She'd given him up for his own sake. Now she coveted him again. She wanted him back as her own right arm and not Master Ridley's. She saw the beauty of his stitches and the intricacies that he'd learned from Abraham Pearl.

Annie planned the last evening for Gabriel at Ridley. She drew an exquisite piecing of the Wagon Wheel pattern and bade Gabriel set it in the frame and take a corner to work. She seated Ellen, excited and full of love for her brother, at another corner of the frame. Then she took her own place. Some would call it dangerous for only three to work a quilt, for fear the devil will take the fourth place. But Sewing Annie scoffed at such belief and set her children to their parts. She had a method that used the three equally and quickly, and her children were well practiced. They happily stepped to the pace their mother set, determined to finish the work by the morning. The quilt would go back to Georgetown with the man who had come home calling himself Gabriel.

"Work fast, Brother Gabriel," Sewing Annie teased.

"Work faster, Brother. I can catch you," Ellen put in quietly. And indeed her fingers were so swift and lithe that he risked fascination by looking at them.

Sewing Annie slapped at Gabriel's hand to break his stitches. Even clear-eyed Annie held to the needleworker's superstition that disliked the perfectly straight. He smiled at her and accepted her compliment. Ellen had the tic of admitting a broken-stitch flaw in her quilting with such regularity that her work was instantly recognizable and of questionable efficacy in thwarting the devil.

When the sun came up, Sewing Annie slapped Gabriel's hands again. This time she roused him from sleep.

"Finish up your work, good boy," she said, and could easily have kneaded his face and his newly muscled body between her hands, exercising a mother's claim. But she cared not to crimp him or shame him or turn away whatever he would give her. Rather, she stood and looked at him fully and savored him.

Annie tied up a gift for Pearl and the quilt for Gabriel in a tight bundle. She boiled up their coffee and allowed Ellen to hang upon Gabriel's neck with some fondness before chastising her.

"Leave it, girl. Set to your work," she ordered finally. "You've come a masterful hand, Gabriel. You bring out the lovely," she continued, and smiled.

"Nanny, the Wagon Wheel quilt is the most highly prized in Georgetown," Gabriel spoke to flatter his mother.

"Sell it then," she replied, surprising him. She lowered her voice and repeated, "Sell it . . . and put the money by."

"Yes," he promised.

On a clear April morning that followed a rain-soaked day, Jonathan Ridley entered the tailoring shop tracking mud and debris on his boots. Gabriel left his sewing to swab up the street muck.

Abraham Pearl did not move hastily. He inclined his head when Ridley entered, but remained at his work. When Ridley slapped his gloves against his wrist impatiently, Pearl rose from his sewing machine and set Gabriel to a task of measurements while he attended.

Jonathan Ridley followed Pearl to the back workroom and abruptly offered him the opportunity to sell his business concern for a small bit of profit. The negotiations were brief, for the tailor had caught a whiff of this wind coming. Pearl would have liked to hold out against the offer to show his disdain for Ridley, but he was, in fact, delighted.

The population of Washington increased every day and the class of men in need of fine tailoring was growing. Pearl's reputation brought him many commissions that he struggled to fill even with Gabriel's help. The city was becoming crowded and Pearl had a lust for open space and more adventure.

Abraham Pearl was uneasy about the coming conflict, too. Everyone was predicting it. It looked as though the District of Columbia — trapped between two slaveholding states — would be in a vise. Pearl wasn't certain he liked the sort of men the conflict was spawning and the type of deals he'd have to make to survive.

Pearl wasn't squeamish and was of the opinion that a man was responsible for his own conscience. If a man could stomach the owning of another, then he was welcome to the practice. But the long ugly shadow of human bondage was becoming increasingly distasteful. Though the sale of slaves had been outlawed in the city, considerable trade still took place. And he, too, profited by the institution. He could never pay a free man to do the work that the slave, Gabriel, was being compelled to do. His conscience had never quite liked the bargain he had made. Why not have a buyer for his business and move farther west with his profits?

"I'm for the frontier, dear Gabriel," Pearl announced. "The shop and most of the tools are with you and your master. Don't keep with him too long, Gabriel. Perhaps the wind is changing even now," he said cryptically. "These will cut off an eyelash! Take care," Pearl said with a face of false jollity as he handed a favorite pair of shears to his assistant. The two had been a boon to each other these years and the parting was sad, but friendly. Gabriel wondered at Pearl's haste.

After the negotiations with Abraham Pearl were at an end and the deal closed, Ridley summoned Gabriel to implement a plan for setting up a trade in fine tailoring. Gabriel, the bondman, would operate the tailoring business and return all profit to Master Ridley. However, it was agreed that Gabriel could take commissions for additional work. Ridley gained much energy from the revelation of his idea to Gabriel. He became animated, marching back and forth in the workroom, gesturing with his hands for emphasis. The excitement added bulk to the man. He then lowered his voice and paused. The final component of his plan — the part that made the idea firm and filled with delicious possibility — was that Jonathan Ridley would install his late brother's son, Aaron, as manager of the tailoring enterprise. This young Aaron Ridley would oversee the operation, keep accounts, and supervise Gabriel's work without actually interfering with it.

"This will relieve you of the care. Aye, Master Aaron will do to keep the accounts, as no nigger can be trusted to look to the books," he explained.

The chance for Gabriel to buy his freedom! This was the jewel that Sewing Annie had been waiting for! They had been patient. They had waited. They'd teased little droplets of luck and now the bits were coming together. Annie remained still and applied herself to her own work. But in her mind she exulted. She gave herself the credit. She had trained Gabriel up. She had stamped him and made him currency!

Gabriel himself ruminated on this supposed good fortune. The binds of it did thwart any plan to leave for Canada.

"The two go on together, Gabriel. Put away the money to buy your freedom and start up flush," Sewing Annie counseled against his misgivings. "Go to the work with vigor, Brother Gabriel, and salt away the proceeds. Outwait the watcher. Put him to sleep with your click-clacking. Don't put your head down until his has gone before you," Annie said, exhausting her store of advice. She'd taken Aaron Ridley's measure and chuckled to think what little effort it would be to get around him. Master had put young Aaron there to watch Gabriel. Ha! As there was no real work in the shop that Aaron Ridley was capable of except the watching, he might become good at it.

Aaron Ridley, Master's nephew, had been brought to Ridley Plantation with his mother upon the death of his father, Nathaniel Ridley. Nathaniel, the younger brother of Jonathan Ridley, had died suddenly in a fall, leaving behind a young wife and a three-year-old child. There was no alternative for the widow but to put in with her brother-in-law and his wife. Her husband had built no fortune independent of his brother. The young boy was raised as scion in his uncle's otherwise childless home. Aaron Ridley, not known on Ridley Plantation for any particular talent or inclination, was accustomed to taking his cues from his uncle. Upon being informed of his new position, he was not enthusiastic but welcomed the chance to live in town.

Young Aaron did intend to keep some attention upon the running of the shop. But as far as the tailoring work was concerned, he could only watch that Gabriel worked sufficient hours on the shop's commissions.

Aaron Ridley was responsible for interacting with the white people who came to the shop to place orders or to inquire about one. He spoke with servants of the rank of butler, valet, and ladies' maid and with any white person who felt it beneath himself to conduct business with a Black. Periodically, he rose from his chair, crossed to the back room, and peered at his uncle's diligent slave.

The young master was given the rear of the second floor of the shop for his own living. Gabriel's sleeping quarters were on the level above the second floor in the half-height space just under the roof. The large back room on the first floor was the workroom and its table was used as well for meals. Abraham Pearl and Gabriel had eaten their vittles here. Aaron Ridley balked immediately at the arrangement. Averse to eating his meals upon the same table at which Gabriel worked and ate, Ridley took up the habit of going abroad to Pearson's Tavern for his meals.

Three

Dear Uncle,

I am in spartan circumstance in this shop. There is little for a gentleman's comfort here. The nigger is occupied completely with his sewing and is unwilling to undertake more. Forgive me, sir, but I must advise you that I am forced to toss my own night water, as there is no one to see to the duties of this like. I am required to go about to hire a woman for assistance. The available char are, I am told, mostly Irishwomen with diseases. It is a sorry lot to pick from. Advise me, dear sir. I am afraid that I will perish in this city's pestilential airs if my health is not attended to.

Your devoted nephew,
Aaron

The piglet was squealing so soon! Though he had raised this boy since infancy, Jonathan still kept the feeling that if the babe had been of his own body rather than his dreamy younger brother's, the boy would have come up with more stuffing and cleverness and grit. It was damnably hard to keep these young boys from indolence and pure silliness.

"It will take four hands out of your fields to replace her with the laundry," Elizabeth Ridley wailed when told that Sewing Annie would be sent to Georgetown to help in the shop. "There is no one of Sewing Annie's caliber for the needlework. The weaving will fall off. All of this because of a spoiled, lazy boy! Watch out, Master, your nephew will do you little good," she said, sneering. Her sister-in-law's maternal arrogance — the one bit of leverage the widow had always had over her — was, at last, under challenge.

But Clementine Ridley, usually cowed by her status in the household, spoke loudly in defense of her son. "If you are weighing him, Brother, then take your thumb off the scale. Give him the chance to please you. You've raised him as a gentleman. Doesn't a gentleman require a cook and a char in Georgetown?" she questioned.

It pleased Jonathan Ridley to set the two women against each other, for it reduced whatever influence they might combine to exert against him.

Indeed there was a sore need for Sewing Annie in the shop as the work at sewing engaged Gabriel's full attentions. He had come down to stirring up a pot of cornmeal mush to placate his stomach and leaving off all else but tidying his supplies and boiling coffee. The considerable all else that needed doing immediately became Sewing Annie's province.

As Aaron Ridley did not consider Sewing Annie's cooking talents up to his appetite, he continued to take his meals at the tavern and left the kitchen worktable to the slaves.

"Does a chicken give milk here?" Annie said to Gabriel, perusing the empty food casks.

"No, ma'am. I'll take you where is the milk and bread and

other things," he answered her sweetly, relinquishing the cloth he worked on and rising.

Gabriel had gained a measure of comfort in Georgetown through familiarity. He knew that the settling-in to town was daunting for the newcomer. On Annie's first morning there, Gabriel took his mam abroad under his wing with a market basket and a shawl.

"Nanny, mind the thoroughfare. Nanny, mind the patrollers. Mind to come and go." Gabriel pronounced lessons for newly arrived Annie. "Nanny, there are a great many harsh men abroad. You must be careful," he commanded her.

She answered with sucking her teeth, for she chafed a bit at his tone. The town, though, flummoxed her.

As he stood a head above her head now, Gabriel drew up appropriately straight though circumspect to the taste of the town for a colored man. He led her up and down the city's streets clasping his arm. He showed her through the alleys like a toddling child. Annie continued walking well past her strength the first day without acknowledging the tiredness, for she was eager to learn the customs and to see all.

A stop on Gabriel's circuit was Holy Trinity Church. The Reverend William Higgins, a blushing Catholic priest who greeted them at the door, was a particular friend to the colored. Daily delighted with flouting the church's rules, William Higgins drew Gabriel and his mother into the sanctuary and seated them on the oak pews in the nave.

"Hello, Mother," the priest cried out with unaccustomed respect. Annie did not look Higgins full in the face, though he smilingly sought to engage her. Undaunted by her silence, he continued with warm pleasantries and insisted that the rectory had laundry work if she agreed to undertake it. As they left the church, Higgins grasped Gabriel's hand and squeezed it familiarly. Gabriel was, as always, taken aback at Higgins's exuberance.

On their circuit, Annie noticed establishments that belched much music, much singing. There was piano-playing, mouth organ, and fiddles, and there was much laughing gaiety from these places. There seemed to be a policy of wink-and-blink among strolling law officers as highly dressed-out white women promenaded the thoroughfares at dusk.

" 'Tis a free and dirty place, this town," Annie said in a partly questioning tone that called for Gabriel to answer. " 'Tis a bit whorish with so many menfolk," she continued. She further mused that a consequence of this custom was a big call for laundry work and female doctoring.

"Nanny, . . . I," Gabriel stammered, greatly embarrassed by her inquiries yet determined to show himself an adult with his mam.

"Best to keep small around the lawmen in this town and around certain women running bawdy houses. Some free colored women and unattached white women are pressed to work the thoroughfare because they have asked the wrong person for bread and milk, Nanny. An equal number of unfortunate women are daily pushed into jail at the suggestion that they were abroad as a whore," he said with some bristling.

"Aye 'tis a town for a man's accommodation then," she answered.

"Aye, Nanny, a white man," he replied.

"A ripe place for laundry," she said, as if making up a plan.

At Sewing Annie's appeal, Aaron Ridley wrote to his uncle for permission to order four large casks to be made for the laundry operation. The new barrels rolled up Bridge Street from the cooper's workshop upon completion as if on parade, with each one handled by a man driving it on its side and pushing it. On their arrival in the backyard, Annie stood aside and insisted that each barrel be filled and tested for fitness, and they were. Additionally, Annie cajoled for a roof above the back doorway to the yard to create shelter from the weather. Aaron Ridley had suffered rebuke from his uncle when he balked at providing the barrels to Annie, and so he went along with all of the woman's ideas.

"Set me some rinsing water, Brother Gabriel," Annie charged her son as soon as he'd put down his supper. The old shoulder-to-shoulder working familiarity had returned. The young master had gone to supper and there was laundry to finish, and though Gabriel had worked the long day, for love she wrung more from him.

"Yes, Nanny," Gabriel said.

Some months after the sale of the tailoring business to Jonathan Ridley, Abraham Pearl sent a letter to Reverend Higgins that was meant for Gabriel. An important conduit for the exchange of information in the community of colored in Washington, Higgins received many letters at the church. Broadsides also passed through his hands linking colored in the town with others in the countryside.

Pearl knew that Gabriel could read and write, as he had assisted the young man in his pursuit of learning. But he was cautious. He would not risk addressing a letter directly to the young man. There was a penalty for such helping. Pearl trusted Higgins to take care and deliver the letter to Gabriel. Pearl's letter, which arrived at the tailor shop tucked with laundry in

Annie's basket, began with pleasantries and included descriptions of his journey from Washington to St. Louis. Pearl eloquently described his amazement at the passing show and assured Gabriel early on that he was happy with his decision to leave for the West.

Abraham Pearl continued his narrative for six long pages to discourage one who might pry into the letter. He guessed that if he'd sent a short, cryptic message, more attention might be paid to its content. A rambling travelogue would certainly bore a nosy soul like Aaron Ridley long before he'd gotten to the meat of the message. The information contained on the sixth and seventh pages was for Gabriel's eyes only.

Pearl revealed that a chest filled with army uniform buttons had been stored securely beneath the eaves of the shop's roof in an area that could be reached only through the garret occupied by Gabriel himself.

They were military buttons — army buttons! The chest held several hundred bright, unused regulation buttons. Pearl departed from the florid style of the first pages of his letter — full as they were with descriptions of flowers, trees, rivers, streams, and various animals — to explain simply that he had won the cache at cards with an army supply clerk. As a tailor with a view to future value, Abraham Pearl had taken the chest with contents in trade and had had the presence of mind to secrete them. Pearl claimed in his letter to Gabriel that he had simply forgotten the chest's existence when he'd taken off for points west. Anticipation of adventures had occupied his mind and he had not remembered to stow the buttons.

Pearl suggested that an industrious tailor might get a contract to sew uniforms and that these buttons might come in handy. Perhaps they would enable a clever tailor to make a smart profit on the work. Abraham Pearl finished his letter with advice to Gabriel to be careful who knew about the buttons and to consider the treasure to be a boon to his freedom plans.

Gabriel wanted to jump and whoop it up when he pulled the chest out of its hiding. The contents were as Abraham Pearl had said: shining brass army uniform buttons. There were several sizes mixed together, buttons for cuffs as well as buttons for coat fronts. They were each stamped with eagles and stars and they gleamed brightly.

Gabriel bowed his head over the chest and implored God to look after Abraham Pearl. He vowed always to include in his list of petitions a plea for his safety and happiness.

Annie cautioned her son. She was made nervous by the army buttons and she sought to take away Gabriel's excitement or temper it. She peppered him with questions. How would they explain having them? Despite Abraham Pearl's tale, could this be the boodle of a crook and they now a party to crime? Whom could they trust? The only thing was to return them to hiding.

Gabriel came around to agreement with his mother. The two satisfied themselves with counting them up and admiring them before tucking them back in their nest in the eaves.

Four

DANIEL JOSHUA CLAPPED eyes on Annie across the way — from back in the doorway on Bridge Street. "This partridge is got a nest some'eres," he muttered. A woman with so soft-looking a derriere must have a place to set it.

He saw she was a grown woman with arms fully muscled from her shoulders down to her wrists. He judged her arms for their strength because they would be to his purpose or against it. He saw her form despite her shawl and knew right away that she was a woman who toted water and wrung out wet clothes. A figurer, a ruminator, and a people-watcher, Daniel Joshua placed Annie as a free woman or a bondwoman with leave to come and go. He figured he'd have to chance that she would take care of the girl till he was sure he'd led the slave pinchers away. He didn't doubt he'd be able to find this laundrywoman again. He knew where this one and that one and the other one of his own people were likely to be.

The "pinchers" following Daniel and the girl had no direct knowledge of them. They had simply been lurking around the docks looking for whatever might be going on or coming off the barges. They were independent agents set to snatch their quarry as the opportunity arose. Every day brought some fugitive to tumble off a vessel and land on the dock bewildered. Mostly these were taken up by such pinchers. And they had spotted Daniel — him carrying a sack off a vessel. Daniel Joshua cursed himself for so carelessly arousing their curiosity.

Daniel made the quick decision to separate from the girl. It was the best chance for her survival — and his own. He supported her so she looked like she stood on her own legs. He moved swiftly to Annie's side and grasped the arm that had her market basket swinging on it. He transferred the dead weight of the wounded fugitive girl to Annie and spoke in her ear with great urgency. "Put your arm around her and hold her up! Say she's your gal. Say she's deaf and dumb. Say she's sick and can't stand up! Say it if they ask you."

Daniel's hot and fragrant breath blasted Annie's left ear. The man grasped her elbow and brought himself close — as close as he could get without standing on top of her feet. "Wrap your shawl 'round her! She needs you to help her," he continued. "It all depends on you now!" His voice was rough and direct, but not loud. He spoke, then left quickly with Annie's own basket on his forearm. Compelled by the man's words, Annie came to herself.

In her gut Annie knew better than to turn to face the man. It could be a life-or-death matter. His breath had been comforting on her ear, like it was a ladle of gravy on a fluffy biscuit. She was compelled.

The girl — the one he'd said was deaf and dumb — fell into Annie's arms. If Annie had moved or failed to grasp her, she would have fallen clear to the ground.

As it was, the girl fell onto her protector like a sack of potatoes. She didn't move. She was practically dead weight. Annie
sank to her haunches and cradled the young woman.

"Come on up, girl. Get on up now. Come on up, girl," Annie
pleaded. She was slight, but not a child. She was thin. Her eyes
were firmly closed and crusted. When Annie dared turn to look
after the hot-breathed speaker, he had completely vanished.
Annie turned her head very carefully, slowly, to look about for
him, not wanting to arouse suspicion by seeming to be hunting
anyone or to be confused.

"What's the trouble here?" A constable came up behind Annie and startled her. "What all you doing in the street here,
Auntie? What's this gal doing here?" he said.

Annie was grateful the cop asked more than one question.
This interlude gave her a chance to think. What had the mysterious man said? He had pressed her to grab the girl and to lie
about her. What was the trouble here?

"She got dropsy. She don't talk," Annie said dully, as if she'd
said this a thousand times. "I takin' her home. We ain't no
trouble, suh," she said, without ever having brought her eyes
level with the constable's face. She watched the buttons on his
uniform and held herself still, praying that he would become
too bored to ask more questions.

But what was Annie going to do with the gal? She thought
the girl must have the dropsy or be some kind of sick that kept
her from standing upright. Her lower parts were dressed in a
torn burlap bag and she smelled high. Lord, have mercy! Was
she nigh to death?

Annie brought her lips to the girl's temple and cooed and
whispered and hoped to bring her around enough to get her
away from the middle of the street and from the eyes of the

constable. There was no response from the girl, so Annie called on the Lord God, put her arms underneath the girl's rib cage and knees, and lifted her. She was surprised at the lightness of the pitiful thing's body. "Not more than a half a' load a' wet socks and under alls. She is a slight bit," Annie intoned, as if putting a benediction on the enterprise.

Why in the world had the man picked her out to take care of this odd gal? She appeared to be on her last leg. Annie struggled down four good blocks with her. She carried her high in her arms for some portion of the way, halted to rest beside a post, then continued. Who was the man who'd had the heavy warm breath that smelled like a bit of mint? Had he drunk a toddy or cup of tea before he spoke to her? This voice had a rich man's breath perhaps? But a poor man's stink had been upon him, too.

At the corner of Bridge Street and Jefferson, Annie slumped down to catch some air. The wet laundry came to life. The bewildered girl opened her eyes and looked at her protector seated upon a post catching her wind. The girl raised no question and, with great effort, tried to walk. Annie supported her the rest of the way to the back door of the tailoring shop.

"Keep shut and still — here," Annie commanded the young woman, and propped her on the handle of the backyard water pump. She repeated urgently for her to stay quiet and keep her heels down at this spot and wait until Annie returned.

Annie approached the front door of the tailor shop from the angle that afforded her a clear view. She well knew not to enter there.

Aaron Ridley sat yawning behind a newspaper with his coat off and his shirt collar eased open to make himself more comfortable. He thought it entirely hilarious that his uncle Jonathan had set him up as the manager of a custom tailoring business. Aaron disliked his uncle. He felt a slight, dull ache of displeasure in the man's presence and in his purview. Aaron's mother did not like her brother-in-law either, but she had not ever had the energy to make other provision for their livelihood. The two remained dependent and sulking under the roof of their benefactor and had always been forced to accede to his wishes and those of his wife.

The one aspect of the tailoring business that appealed to Aaron Ridley was the wearing of fine clothes. He delighted in dressing in well-made suits and did not mind demonstrating the quality of Gabriel's work. A fashionable suit emphasized Master Aaron Ridley's physique. Like his uncle, he was vain of his athletic form.

Annie stood outside the shop with her body turned on a diagonal from the front window so as not to appear to onlookers as too inquisitive or too bold. She saw the soles of Aaron Ridley's shoes propped up on the shop's counter. Master Jonathan wouldn't like it at all. He'd surely thump this boy on the head if he were to catch him at this. Annie studied the young man for a short while, deciding how to proceed. Aaron wasn't too wily, so she needn't be.

Annie was shot through suddenly with cold-fear sickness.

"Aye, God, the market basket!" Where was her market basket? She'd had a basket over her arm when she'd encountered the man with the hot whispered message and the girl who'd collapsed in her arms. Where had she left it? She was sick to think her several turnips and their lush greens had been lost in the street.

There was between Gabriel and his mother a secret "talk" that nobody had a handle on but the two of them and Sis Ellen.

From the first Annie had taught Gabriel and Ellen a series of agreed-upon signals that allowed them to talk around the white folks. Gabriel knew the moment his mam entered a room, depending on how her apron or head scarf was tied, what the lay of the land was. And over a distance — like from the outhouse to the porch — the way Nanny sucked the back of her throat and made a clacking sound could tell Gabriel to come or go.

Without a word, Annie approached Gabriel, who was seated at his workbench. She eased a tub to the floor, straightened her back, and tucked the corner of her apron into the waistband.

"Don't let them read your eyeballs. Keep them low and quiet," she'd lectured him since he was a babe. He knew. In response, Gabriel bowed his head once very briefly — nearly imperceptibly. Annie knew he would follow her to the yard.

When Gabriel reached the backyard of the shop two or so minutes behind his mother, he pondered the ease with which he'd just slipped out without being noticed by Aaron Ridley. He could perhaps keep going, walking — just stretching his legs into it. And he could be on the road to Baltimore and then keep on going to Philadelphia and be free there. Just get the wind at his back and walk all the way to free territory in Canada!

His mother had suggested it a number of times — a freedom walk. She said she could think of a lot of ways of giving him a head start. She would keep the Ridleys guessing awhile to give Gabriel time to get free.

But he had made a plan for his freedom and it included his mother and sister. They were all three to be free. They would all three pull together and be free that way. And maybe in truth — a thought he'd have rather pushed away — he just didn't have the stuffing inside that it took to run.

Gabriel allowed himself an expression of surprise and an inquiring twist of the eyebrows when he saw the emaciated young woman sitting propped against the water pump. He regained his composure, read concern and urgency in his mother's countenance. Gabriel reached between two planks attached to the corner of the house and removed a key. He opened the door to a root cellar that was three feet from the rear of the shop. Visible from the back of the shop, the cellar door was hidden from the alley by a sprawling bush. Gabriel and Annie lifted the girl down the three rungs of the ladder to the floor of the cellar.

"Nanny, who comes here?" Gabriel asked.

Annie's reply was a series of tooth-suckings. She shut him, but he was not satisfied and not complacent.

"Nanny, who'st you're bringing here?" Gabriel asserted, and stopped only short of demanding an answer from her.

It had been Annie's idea to behave as if the root cellar were overrun with rats. Shortly after she came to stay in the shop, Annie discovered the cellar and created a commotion of poisoning, wide-eye rolling, and shrieking. Master Aaron was encouraged to steer clear of the cellar.

In truth rats were plentiful in the low-lying areas near the waterfront in Georgetown. But Annie had hung a stinking pouch containing the musk of beaver in the cellar to fool the rats into thinking they were outnumbered there by others. They deserted this cellar and the floor was now dry and soft with straw and flour sacks.

"A sick girl came upon me in the street. We'll settle her here."

They helped the young woman onto a pallet. Annie closed the girl's hand over a wafer she drew out of her blouse. "Rest without worry till I bring you a cup of broth," she said. "Ain't a thing in here to eat you."

Annie and Gabriel closed the door to the cellar and replaced the padlock. Annie prayed the girl would be calm and quiet until they could return safely.

As soon as Aaron Ridley figured to have given a day's work, he headed for one of his regular alehouses for dinner and drink. The chief compensation that working in his uncle's tailoring shop afforded him was the proximity to ale and entertainment that Washington offered. To his delight there were plenty of amiable alehouses in Georgetown. At Pearson's, Ridley was becoming well known.

Annie let out a sigh as Aaron Ridley closed the front door of the shop and went off to his pleasure. It was a fortune of sorts that he was a young man of normal health and had interests that were appropriate to his age. Annie and Gabriel waited long enough to give Aaron Ridley the chance to go, return for something he might have forgotten, and take his leave again before going out to the root cellar. The two had studied him and knew his habits well. Tonight he stayed gone after the first time he closed the front door with a tinkling.

At the stove, working on her dinner, Annie thought of the lost turnips again and sucked her teeth in dismay. They would have put a solid anchor in her stew pot and she was doubly sorry because the pitiful thin girl would profit from a heavy broth.

When Annie brought the broth the girl fell on it. Her great hunger overcame any caution. Annie grasped the girl's left hand as she clutched the bowl in her other. She wiped the girl's hand to take off the dirt and blood. The girl drew her hand back to the side of the bowl, then surrendered the other for a quick wash. Annie softened her face encouragingly. The girl seemed trusting of Annie, though she looked anxiously at Gabriel, who stood in the path of the flickering light. This dancing light made the gentle Gabriel look to be taller, broader, larger than his normal self. His looming form frightened the girl. Annie motioned for him to squat and give the girl a chance to take him in.

"Brother . . . Brother Gabriel, you must sit," Annie said. He squatted away from the path of light.

Ruminating to the accompaniment of the thumping of a wooden mallet churning clothes washing, Annie considered the girl. The clothes she'd taken away were soaked with blood and crusted with man seed. She punched them into the hot suds. It appeared the girl had recently suffered rough treatment from a man. Was it the man who had breathed in Annie's ear? Surely, it was not. He wouldn't have tried so to save her getting picked up by patrols and policemen.

Sewing Annie's pitch-dark cellar, redolent with beaver musk, didn't scare Carrie. She recognized the smell and felt good on account of it. Ofttimes the old people had put a pouch of beaver musk to ward off rats in the fetid holes they'd made bed in. Rogers Spit — where she'd come from — was a stingy, meager place. She thought about the folks' tired faces and the damp smell and the smell of the beaver musk and the smell of folks who had worked all day — all of them crowded into a narrow cabin room.

Five

"SEND HER DOWN to market then," the woman pronounced offhandedly and returned to her house to change out of her bloodied clothes. Carolyn Ruane would have kept Carrie strung up and gone on flogging her if the overseer had not cautioned. There was possible monetary loss in continuing this way.

The blood upon Carolyn Ruane's bodice was flecked with bits of flesh, and her own infuriated spittle cascaded down her chin. Speckles of blood dotted her breasts. She shrieked when she saw herself and demanded hot water and soap.

Phillip Ruane's wife wanted her husband to see the pulpy, disfigured image of his slave mistress to thwart his desire. She reasoned she could not stop him taking what woman — white or black — that he chose. She aimed to spoil his cream with the ugly image before him.

But Ruane's overseer was reluctant to be wholly in the camp of the mistress. He became nervous that he could not adequately explain to the master his part in the enterprise of Carolyn Ruane's revenge. He ordered the girl be cut down and cared for by the old slave woman who was kept around for such as that. He would be questioned about it, he knew. And a man can go only so far against the interests of another man without coming to conflict. So he would have the girl sold off for gross recalcitrance and removed from the wrath of the mistress.

Carrie was, at first, happy that the master would be away from the place. She wasn't prepared for the fate that found her as soon as he left. She didn't have the time it would have taken to grab a kerchief. She was plucked from the field where she worked, pushed into the back of a wagon, and driven up to the main house. She was bound and strung up in the barn under the direction of Mistress and a flogging commenced, accompanied by epithets.

Rogers Spit was the farm John Rogers had given his daughter and her husband, Phillip Ruane, on their marriage. With the dower came land, two barns, thirty horses, saddles, miscellaneous farm implements, and forty-seven slaves. John Rogers was satisfied to be rid of his daughter and the Spit. He knew little about the man he'd contracted with except that he was virile enough to make good work of the girl, the land, and the slaves. The land was remote and hard to manage. This daughter, Carolyn, was third in a line of plain girls John Rogers had had to work to be rid of.

Carrie had been born at Rogers Main, the hub of John Rogers's landholdings. Her mother was sent to the Spit soon after her child's birth as punishment for her unwillingness to accept further visits from the Main's head overseer. As he had the authority to do so, this overseer rotated hands upon his own whim.

That fair yields were produced at the Spit was testament to Phillip Ruane's harsh handling of the people who labored there. The pitiful recalcitrants sent to Ruane's system were fed little and driven relentlessly. Carrie had begun in the rows as soon as she was able to carry a bucket and she remained a hand in the fields until she was taken as the master's concubine.

Ruane's once naive and frightened young wife became — under his influence — sly, cruel, and vengeful. While Phillip Ruane rode to Petersburg to oblige his need for gambling, Carrie was taken up and flogged and then taken away from Rogers Spit to an auction house in Richmond. She knew nothing of the landscape through which she rode, for she was bound with cloths to staunch the dripping blood and reduce the swollen skin, and the bandages kept her immobile.

In the Richmond slave pen, Carrie learned that all thus captured were slated for sale in the Deep South. Her companions keened and she moaned with the pain. She accepted some succor from the other captive women. All hope had left Carrie by the sunrise.

Before the slave women were to be brought to the auction stage, the guard attending them loosed their shackles so that they could clean up for the auction block. Each was prodded to wash off the mud and blood that was caked upon her body and clothes. The guard brought several pots of water and set the largest upon a stove to heat it.

A very short and thick woman of a mature age with three small children lashed to her waist removed her blouse. Slowly and tearfully she moved. She appeared to crave modesty in front of the young ones and she hunched over the small washbowl she'd been given. When the guard turned away to pee against the wall, the woman bent swiftly and picked up the iron kettle that was upon the stove and sloshed the hot liquid onto the man's back. He cried out, but she crashed the pot down on his head with so much force that only a strangled cry escaped him before he fell. His member was still outside of his drawers.

"Go. Scatter. Take yourself off, gals, 'fore somebody knows what has come about," the short woman exhorted the others, some of whom had started to chatter and whimper with fright.

Carrie took to her heels running. She didn't know what had happened. She had seen the pot come down and the man slumped with his thing covered in sawdust. The woman who'd done the deed ran past Carrie with the infant child tied to her chest in a sling and with the talking and walking babes one under each arm. She ran headlong down a street adjacent to the market square with the short, thick legs of her babes dangling at her back.

Carrie imagined with dread that the woman with the three babes would soon be recaptured. How would she keep running with the children weighing on her? But that woman had been determined. She had been the one who'd taken the chance. All of them were free — for the moment — because of her. She saw the woman's back slice through clumps of people and plunge headlong toward her freedom. These thoughts kept Carrie pumping her legs and sucking in breath and darting down passages. She eventually came to a dark doorway in a part of town filled with dark doorways and dubious passageways. The pungent smell of fish preceded a thwack on Carrie's head, and she dropped into unconsciousness.

When she came to, she heard some voices. The place — wherever it was — was dark and quiet. No light was visible. She smelled human stink and liquor. In the next moment a gaggle of men burst through the door and tied her hands and feet. They carried her onto a ship that set sail as soon as they came aboard it.

The men used her in turn. They stopped and withdrew only when she had fouled herself sufficiently to drive them off.

◆◆

If a watchful one stands back and takes his time he can discover a lot of what is going on without actually seeing it firsthand. Daniel Joshua was experienced with slipping around ships and was attentive to goings-on. The behavior of the three white men he observed meant to him only one thing: they had a woman in the hold of the ship and were taking turns with her. He wasn't close enough to hear precisely what they were talking about. But the odd word came clear. And it was a thing frequently done on vessels coming up the Potomac River to Georgetown.

When Daniel Joshua managed to get himself aboard, he was as if blind. The hold of the boat was unlit. He decided to chance a light and drew a tiny bit of candle from his pouch and the match to light it. His eyes scoured the area. One thing fell to view — only one creature — a black dark girl tied and gagged and lying on a pallet of bloody straw. Her eyes were wide, and when she saw Daniel it appeared they would shoot out of their sockets.

There was plenty of evidence of what had gone on in the hold. Clearly, several men had been about this business. Where had they gone? Likely they were sleeping off their ale and lust in a gutter nearby and would return to pick up where they'd left off.

Daniel held out his hands flat open. "It's stop time. I promise you it's stop time," he said to the girl before he dared reach to remove her gag. "Don't cry out. It's stop time."

She continued to moan. It sounded the louder after he removed her gag. But she didn't cry out. Her lips quivered and her eyes bore into Daniel. He put his hand across her mouth to seal her silence and she understood and made no more noise.

Daniel blew out his candle stump and grabbed up a sack to gouge out two air holes with the smoldering wax end. He tied the sack around the girl's naked body. He didn't want to scare her anymore, but he knew they'd have to make tracks to get off the boat. He covered her head and hoisted her on his shoulder. "Keep still and live awhile longer," he said, and bore her along like a sack of farm goods.

Daniel carried the thin girl across his back easily. He slipped off the ship and down into an alley on Water Street. A gush of sweat and the hackling nerves along his spine alerted Daniel to their pursuers. A pair of slave catchers had caught sight of them leaving the wharf. Daniel slipped into a doorway ahead of them and waited in silence. The girl made no sound and Daniel Joshua's guts settled down a bit to let him ponder. The best strategy for their survival would be to split up. He thought to separate from the woman and lead the pair of slave pinchers away up and down and through the labyrinth of gutters, cellars, and alleys that he knew like the back of his hand. He rubbed his palm along cobblestones covered with slime until he identified a loosened brick. This loose brick in this doorway on this block was the spot to turn sharply and duck behind a blind he'd made of planks. These planks created a slim place to stand and hide.

Daniel stood in the blind regularizing his breathing and trying to figure where to go next. The gal in the sack was naked and he could not take her far in that way. He stripped off his shirt to make a cover-up for her and he ripped and tied the burlap to make a skirt. Daniel hoisted the girl again and made for his next place to duck. When he climbed upwards to Bridge Street in early morning he put his eyes upon Annie.

Six

A MARKET BASKET holding three turnips was propped against the back door when Annie went out the first of the morning. She noticed it and turned her head around to catch sight of who had left it. But she knew she wouldn't likely see him 'cause the basket was doing the talking. She recognized this as her own misplaced basket and could see that whoever had had it hadn't eaten her turnips. And he was wanting a word with her.

Annie finished her duties in the yard and returned to the kitchen. She set about her usual morning preparations. From a barrel in the yard, Annie dipped up a pail of sweet water — her water that had stood still in a covered cask with peppermint leaves floating on its surface. She used this freshest water to boil for their morning tonics. Gabriel favored a cup of strong coffee to set him to his work. Annie brewed herself a bracing cup of tea. Aaron Ridley had become fond of a hot cup of coffee to sear his tongue and banish the taste of liquor from his palate when he entered the shop in the morning. Annie thus charmed him and became certain of him.

A day and a half it had been since the girl in the cellar was left leaning on Annie. How come she was here? How had the mysterious man gotten ahold of her? Annie sniffed the air and was sure that she wouldn't wait long to know what this situation was. There was a whiff of nutmeg or some such scent on the air when she stood at the back door and took in the springtime. She reckoned that this could hardly be the breath of the man who had left the girl. For only God's breath could be so pervasive as this fragrance was.

After she got a good fire going in the kitchen stove and the coffee was well on its way to done, Annie went to the yard to fill two pails with water to start her washes.

Daniel Joshua had stood behind a tree waiting for Annie to come for her water. If he knew anything, he knew she would come here and fill some pails to wash the dirty clothes he had seen her carrying.

Daniel Joshua dared not chance speaking to Annie in the open. He cracked a twig with his foot near where she came for water. He knew that she heard. He stepped from cover for a moment and let her look full upon him. Neither of them spoke. Annie nodded her head and Daniel slipped back in among the trees.

After Aaron Ridley left for the alehouse and they'd waited a bit longer, Annie rose to get her talking quilt from a place beneath the floorboards. She folded the quilt just so and set it over the sill of the window facing out back of the shop. It was the Log Cabin pattern with black in the middle. He would know the signal. If he had run and if he had helped others, he would know what the quilt meant to say. He would approach.

"You are welcome to share a turnip, sir," Annie said, to show their visitor that there was laughter in this house. Gabriel, who had risen when the man entered, extended his hand and said, "Come in, sir."

"God bless you, ma'am," the stranger said. "God bless you, sir." Daniel Joshua hesitated to sit down. He felt he ought to introduce himself before warming up their stool. "I call myself Daniel Joshua."

"You are welcome here. We are bondpersons — hired out. I'm known as Gabriel and my mother is Annie." The way Gabriel engaged the man as grown and equal surprised his mother some little bit.

Annie felt that this Daniel Joshua was like a small bear come in the room.

"Ma'am, I thank you for coming to my aid. I had took that girl off a boat and the pinchers was after her and me. I thank you."

"Where she going to?" Annie asked him after a long moment of silence.

"I can't say, ma'am. I discovered her 'board a ship and some men was using her. I beg your pardon, but I think you ought to know it in case she is run out of her mind because of it. I do not know where she has been or where she was going." Daniel Joshua dropped his eyes to the table.

Annie rose to the stove and poured him off a steaming cup of coffee. She returned to the stove and poured a cup for Gabriel.

"We will look after her in the cellar for as long as we are able and she has a need," Gabriel stated clearly and unequivocally. He had briefly considered what had been done to the girl. She hadn't said a word to him or to his mother about her travail.

Sewing Annie presented full bowls of stew with turnips swimming in them to the men. She placed a bowl with mounds of fried cornmeal bread at the center of the table. When she had served, she returned to the table with a bowl of stew for herself. Gabriel knew by the stiff way she held her jaw that his mother was amused and further pleased and on the point of laughing out. Daniel Joshua, though truly hungry, waited for Annie to come to the table.

"Eat up," she said when she did sit down. She burst to tittering then, for every soul born in the last long while knew that the bread she had fried was called "turn up" bread. This is what folks did to it in the pan to cook it. And everybody appreciates a clever cook's humor.

"Turnip, turnip. Live long enough and everything turn up!" was what the sage folks said.

"Evenin'," the girl said when she rose up from her seat at the table. She dipped her knees in a child's curtsy toward Gabriel as he entered the room. He pulled up short — startled. He said nothing to her, only walked to stand next to his accustomed chair. He stood beside his place at the table and did not raise his eyes from the floor until she resumed her seat. Then he seated himself and took up his sewing. She was freshly swathed and nearly swallowed up in the clothes. She was slight and hollow-eyed still.

The guest had emerged from her hiding in the cellar when dusk came on and Aaron Ridley was gone to supper.

"You are welcome to your vittles," Annie said with due politeness.

"Thank you, ma'am," the girl replied. Gabriel took no turn to speak, for he was flummoxed.

The hiding girl sat across from Gabriel and peeped at him in furtive fascination. She had seen oyster shuckers with practiced fingers fly through that work as if they could take to wing. But

Gabriel's speed and precision at sewing was a marvel. She tried to follow his movements with her eyes and could not.

"Sir, you stir the air up with your sewing," she cried out.

Gabriel looked up from his hands in alarm, looked to his mother, looked at the speaker, and then looked back at his hands. He did not speak.

Annie answered with pride, "He was born to this work and he is the better of most at it."

Gabriel's hands did falter at so much scrutiny, but the women could not detect the bobbling. He broke to have his supper dish filled by his mother. When he was done with it there was some competition between the women to take up the empty bowl. Confused by the atmosphere in his workroom, Gabriel expressed his pique by sucking his teeth and exiting. He went to the backyard for his constitutional.

"I been put to bad use, ma'am. But I come up a good girl," she said bluntly, for she feared Annie would think of present circumstance and judge her harshly. "Yonder the folk called me Carrie."

In the short time with them, she had caught a whiff of the relation between Sewing Annie and her son. The woman was deferential, solicitous, and worshipful of Gabriel, the tailor. She doted upon him and he was equally deferential to her.

Annie clapped her cup down on the kitchen table. She rose, turned her back, and poured off a bit of the evening's hot brew into the cup, then resumed her seat and her knitting. She took up her click-clacking work, brought her hands to rest in her lap. Then she started to click-clacking again — quietly, oh so quietly, but insistently click-clacking the needles. "Commence calling yourself Mary then. It will make a change," Annie suggested.

When Gabriel returned he picked up his needles and accompanied his mother. The consideration that he was unlikely to see this young woman again caused him to be melancholy. "She cannot tarry. She must not!" he repeated to himself. The melancholia came as a surprise to him. He had no truck to have feelings grow for this girl, but the feelings presented themselves.

"What is your business to be ruminating about her?" Gabriel asked himself.

Daniel Joshua culled an advertisement with a general description of one like Mary from a discarded broadsheet found in an alley on his circuit of town. He'd been looking to see whether the girl was advertised, and in the past few days of hauling dung about he had noticed several posts that could have described her. They were general and numerous and their generality could be dangerous. Others had been nabbed and sold south who had been many years free but resembled someone advertised. When these unfortunate were taken away, neither their word nor their free papers were accepted. Public life continued perilous for free people in this district, as well as for bondpersons. Being elusive is what Daniel had found to be the best protection.

Daniel Joshua was fast becoming a warm seat and regular in front of the fire in the back room of the tailor shop. Gabriel thought him tough as nails — reassuringly so. He was full of blustery, important talk and was very humorous. He did more laughing than Annie and Gabriel were accustomed to hear from the mouth of a Black man. The people they were most familiar with on the Ridley place did their laughing behind their hands and did not guffaw as a rule. Once or twice Annie was anxious that Daniel Joshua's laughter be heard in the workroom. But the sound of it was a comfortable joy to them.

From being companionable and boisterous around a warm fire, Daniel Joshua was mysterious otherwise. This was the first thing Annie and Gabriel learned about him. He came to sit awhile in the kitchen, then left the room like a wisp of smoke. He was abrupt in taking his leave, generally saying only, "Evenin', ma'am," and slapping his hat. He did not reveal to them the place where he rested his head. Nor did he let their eyes follow him as he slipped down the street.

And this is what he counseled Mary on the very evening he came to the back door of the kitchen with a notice specific to her. It was certain now that she couldn't stay in the root cellar.

Cold fear set in on the girl when she heard Daniel read out the description and the reward offered.

Phillip Ruane had been successful at his gambling and returned to Rogers Spit well flush. He had flown into a rage upon learning of the sale and subsequent escape of Carrie. Stung by his wife's actions, he endeavored to get his slave returned, though the expense was steep.

High upon her left flank is a brand — a wreath. It is a swollen crude wound — a raised design that does mark her as belonging to Mr. Phillip Ruane of Rogers Spit, VA. There is a $500 reward for recapture, for this is a prime hand.

Five hundred dollars was above Ruane's idea of the value of this slave to himself. To this must be added the fees for her recapture. But he spent the money mostly to discipline his impudent wife and reduce her allowance.

"You go hand to hand like many another has gone," Daniel

Joshua counseled Mary. He said known folk could deliver her, in company of others, from place to place until she had gained Ohio — Cincinnati, Cleveland, or as far as Sandusky. From these northern outreaches, she could go for Canada and the free air.

"You must be stalwart, girl. It's a per'lous journey. But it is been done."

The other side of Mary's ice-cold fear of Phillip Ruane was the shame — the return to shameful feelings that the description caused. Master Ruane telling it about her — under her clothes. Her heart became so fluttery at Daniel Joshua's reading that she would have commanded or begged him to stop except that she could not summon the words to speak out. She had feelings that were so warm for Annie and Gabriel now, and nested belowground in their cellar she'd begun to build upon pleasant thoughts. This reminder was a cruelty to her budding feelings for Gabriel.

It was raised and ugly and, in her imagination, prone to spread out and consume all of her skin. He had put this on her. He had taken a brass stamp with a raised crest from his writing desk and heated it and laid it on her. His causing her pain had fazed him little and he was often gentle upon her. She learned quickly, though, that Phillip Ruane was gentle only to titillate himself and would quickly revert to his brutal congress.

The group that had reached a cozy friendship wanted to resist Daniel's advice, but dared not. Phillip Ruane's conceit had spoiled their circle. She must now leave — to let her master have her back or scrabble toward the free north. She couldn't continue in the warmth of Gabriel, the colored tailor, and his mother and their back room. Phillip Ruane's advert changed that.

Mary slid from her chair, pulled her shawl to cover her head and shoulders, then pulled it close all around to obscure her tearful cheeks. She walked out of the back door as small and slick as a mouse.

To let the girl suffer alone did not suit Sewing Annie. Gabriel sat coolly. Butter would not melt in his mouth from the look of his face. Annie mused that she'd misunderstood him. She thought he had a hanker for the girl. But now he made no move or comment. After a few moments, she followed Mary.

Daniel Joshua said nothing because he was full of his own plan. He knew how to get from here to the next place for a person making a run. He was putting together a route for Mary in his mind — one that he had been working out in his head for the past days. It was the kind of escape Daniel Joshua liked, for it was planned and clever. He felt a warmth and affection for this particular young woman, too. He liked a good adventure. He liked outwitting the powers. There was some of all of that in it.

When Mary returned to their circle, pawing at her wet cheeks, Gabriel stared down into his lap and his feelings were contrary. Gabriel Coats did care for Mary in this short time and the loss of her would pinch him. If the plan unfolded, as it ought, this brand-new Mary would be walking in freedom in Canada! She would be lost to him forever. Maybe some word would get back to him or maybe he would one day be free and walk to Canada and find new Mary again. That much good fortune seemed unlikely.

Gabriel's uncharacteristic ill ease threatened to give away the leaving plan. For, in the days of preparation for Mary's journey, he became a restless, pacing man who made frequent trips to the toilet.

"Aye, Gabriel, has your old mam poisoned you?" Aaron Ridley asked with sardonic jesting on noticing his discomfort.

"Yes, Master Aaron," taciturn Gabriel replied with uncommon clever faces. "She has mixed up her dye pot with her stew pot and I am to suffer." Aaron laughed loudly, for he cherished a low opinion of Annie and was ever eager to express it.

Daniel Joshua knew a white man committed to his God and the cause of abolition who worked at a crossroads in the state of Maryland some miles north and west of the city. If Mary would get to this cooper, the man would take her up into the western mountains to join a group following bear trails all the way to Cincinnati. Along the string of trails were beads — people and resting places and some food and warmth.

"Brother Chester — do not say this name aloud, but know it to see it," Daniel said, and drew the letters of Chester's name on a piece of paper. "Brother Chester is a saint for the people and he will take you on further," he said to buoy her spirits. "He will deliver you, for he is on a firm footing with God almighty. Brother Chester and his woman will take you on."

Daniel patiently repeated the words to Mary and spelled the letters and impressed this all upon her. She was wanting so hard to stay with Annie and Gabriel that she was a reluctant pupil. Daniel was firm. He traced along the table with his sausage fingers, repeating the names of places on the route and the letters: *C-H-E-S-T-E-R.*

At dusk of the leaving day, Annie helped Mary to dress in layers of dry breeches and wrapped Mary's breasts and gave her three shirts to wear. She'd last longer on the foot trek if she wore the garments of a man. Annie cut away most of her hair. Plenty of gals would cry at losing their crowning glory. Even one with measly shreds upon her pate would balk at losing it all — or most of it. Mary didn't cry. She agreed to the sense of it.

Gabriel questioned his own resolve and his plan. Was he unable to gird himself for a trip like this one? He envied Mary's sturdiness. Mary had, in fact, no choice. She had to go — to run. Ought he to be going with her — to look after her, to make certain she reached?

At midnight, Mary and Daniel Joshua set out upon the path. Told to follow closely and silently, Mary sidled and crab-crawled through Georgetown alleyways behind Daniel Joshua until the cobblestones fell away under their feet. Threading through brush and tangles behind the cemetery for colored that bordered the creek, Daniel led Mary out of Georgetown. She breathed shallowly and quickly, and Daniel slowed his walking to steady the enterprise.

When they reached the Maryland side of the creek some ways from where they'd begun, Daniel dropped back to let Mary move ahead of him.

"Don't look back. Keep on a' goin'. Go all the way," he whispered at the back of her head. "God keep you, Mary."

Mary froze at Daniel Joshua's voice. She'd been expecting it. She knew he'd not go the distance with her. She knew he was bound to take her only as far as the District border. She knew he'd gone on a pace or two beyond that for sake of lookout and affection. She heard his words and was beguiled by them. "Go, Mary, go on." The whisper pushed her along and she followed the directive. She didn't turn to look back at him. She felt the urge to make water and to fall to the ground and wail. Her body quaked and dripped sweat. She settled her guts and walked on as she'd been instructed.

She went on solidly and surely — avoiding puddles and sharp sticks and loud crackling branches. She remembered that

Annie had cautioned her not to wet her feet if she could avoid it. She remembered Daniel's words: walk on cat feet, run like a rabbit, sly as a fox 'round the henhouse, chew the bear's paw. She remembered that Gabriel had simply held her hand and warmed it in his palm and held her eyes with his own. And she had savored his thirst for her.

Now there was a place to reach before her — a person. This was a steadying knowledge. She was going toward a place and a person and a refuge. She would get there.

She walked throughout the first night in the weak light of the waning moon. When light of morning came back, Mary's feet were still dry.

The sign Mary had been looking for — the ray of hope, the rest for her two feet — was on the horizon. It had come into view as she climbed the rise of a small hill. CHESTER COOPER- AGE COMPANY.

C-H-E-S-T-E-R.

Mary had repeated the letters in her mind for all of the journey. Daniel Joshua had drummed it in that she was to reach the town of Clearwater and proceed upon the road northwest of town to a crossroads where the barn with its sign would be.

CHESTER COOPERAGE COMPANY

Mary squatted next to a tree until the sun dipped down. The socks were no longer on her feet. She'd taken them off to keep them dry. Now she rubbed off as much dirt as she could and put the socks back on. Her legs and feet were weary and at the end of their day's strength, but she thought to present a decent picture.

CHESTER COOPERAGE COMPANY
Shooks, Barrels, and Staves

Daniel had assured her that the white man who owned and operated this concern on the outskirts of town was a friend of the runaway. This man was of the Quaker people and he and his wife assisted any who were fleeing from slavery.

"Wait out by the tree for the signal. If it be clear to come in, Missus will put a sign on the windowsill that says to come on in," Daniel had schooled her. "Don't be fearful of them. They're good people of God who can't abide slavery."

Mary kept her eye on the windows facing toward the hognut tree behind which she stood. When most of the light had faded in the sky, Missus did come to open the shutters on the window just to the right of the doorway. A woman who was nearly as wide as she was tall, Missus Chester placed a quilt on the windowsill. First she spread the cloth and shook it as if to rustle crumbs. The woman never raised her eyes up to look around. She made a careful fold in the cover to leave the full pattern clearly visible.

Mary's eyes fastened on the yellow at the center instead of the red carbuncle of the quilt. She could not so clearly distinguish much else of the pattern in the lowering light. But she did see the yellow center and knew it was the all-clear signal.

Still Mary waited for the sun to go down completely. The moment came. When she heard from the birds that call out the oncoming darkness, the running girl went to the back door of the house and scratched her fingers on its wooden planks. Missus appeared at the door and Mary removed her cap and bowed her head. Her body shivered and she feared the woman might hear that every bone within her body was clicking and clacking against its neighbor.

"Praise the Lord who has brought you," the woman said softly but earnestly as she opened the door. Conscious of what shadows and silhouettes and slivers of light can remain to be seen from a lighted doorway, the Chesters were careful with their lanterns.

"Come in," the woman said, and drew Mary into the room.

The woman held her lantern low so that Mary saw little of her face until she was well in the room and the door had been closed behind her.

Though not tall, Mary stood a head over Emily Chester, who might have been taken for a child if not for her womanly bosom.

Emily Chester was solicitous of Mary and immediately urged the girl off her feet. She seemed unsurprised at Mary's soft face, revealed when she doffed her hat. The woman brought her guest to a seat near the warm fire.

The Chester home was a small, sweet haven that served only to shelter and hold sway against the elements. It was a plainly furnished and sparsely decorated edifice that would never cause envious tongues to wag. There were only necessaries for work and simple comforts about the rooms. A spinning wheel and a weaving loom shared the small living room with four plain, straight-backed chairs and two stools.

Emily Chester brought a bowl of stew, a spoon, and a chunk of bread to the chair in which she'd installed Mary. As the white woman approached her, Mary leaped to her feet, then tottered a bit before collapsing back in the chair.

"Now, now, young one," Emily Chester cooed. "Rest and eat and settle your nerves. I shan't eat you. I have had my evening stew."

Matthew Chester joined his wife in her chuckling. He emerged from a darkened inside room as a man of typical height and breadth for his line of work. Matthew Chester did most of his business selling barrels to a local brewer of ale. This happy circumstance yielded his living wage and the perquisite of an ale belly.

Matthew Chester's workshop was a large structure appended to the barn. In the workshop, Chester had constructed a particular barrel that he used to transport those who must travel under cover.

Kind as he was, Matthew Chester insisted that Mary leave at dusk of the next day. His establishment was a way station only. It was not safe to tarry.

In a large barrel generally used for great stores of flour or rice or such, Chester had fashioned handles and a small platform upon which one traveling inside of the barrel might rest. Unlike the barrels made for his trade, this one had nearly invisible seams to allow air to reach inside. Also, there were holes whose bungs could be removed for more air and to see out. In this way, Matthew and Emily had transported former bondpersons out of the county and over the roads to the next stop on their journey. Some were frightened of the barrel and balked at being shut up. It was then that Missus Chester would implore and assure and swear that many had reached the free territory through hiding in this barrel.

"As God is my judge, you will arrive in one piece," she said. "Do not cry out. We are all in the hands of the Lord and upon the lips of the righteous!"

Rather than remain at home to give in to heathen fears and premonitions, Emily Chester accompanied her husband on the trips. There were no two ways about it, Pansy, one of the mares who pulled the wagon, was a finicky creature. She favored Emily's hand upon her reins and Matthew gladly allowed Emily to guide the team. They drove away from their place side by side, shoulder to shoulder, like the barrels in the rear of the wagon — the one barrel full of Mary, its twin filled with sorghum, and a third full of ale.

The band of patrollers — three men — came upon them and surrounded the wagon. The horses reared up at their sudden, noisy appearance and there was no possibility of cutting past the men. Matthew called out, "Quiet now!" The team settled and halted, but Mary knew he spoke to her. The horsemen circled menacingly.

"Ma'am," a scarlet-faced man said while tipping his hat mockingly. He reached and snatched the reins from Emily's hands. She would have answered him with a slash across his face with her horsewhip, for she was quick and strong. Matthew held her arm.

"I'll have what is in that barrel, sir!" The voice was loud and whiskey-slurred. "If it is flour, I will have it! If you are carrying sugar or sorghum for feed or cornmeal perhaps? Well, maybe you have ale in that barrel. Enough to wet all of our whistles." The fierce-looking brigands guffawed and the two Quakers foolishly relaxed their fears and laughed with them. These men were only out for drink. Matthew Chester cheerfully opened the ale barrel and invited the men for a drink.

The ringleader of the patrollers grimaced over his quaff and eyed the barrel that hid Mary.

"Whatever is in that barrel there will be mine unless you put down your life to keep it!" the man barked, and looked directly into Emily's eyes. He thought to unhinge her, but did not. The cruel knife twist of the man's voice unhinged Mary's courage instead. The runaway could not stifle a gasp of horror. Her voice was heard from within the barrel.

The patrollers broke open the top of the barrel over Mary's head and dragged her from her hiding place. They had found what they'd been tipped to look for: an escaping slave.

The men tossed Mary on the ground. The leader clubbed her at the back of the head to render her quiet.

The patrollers then used their clubs on Emily and Matthew and left them lifeless on the road.

Seven

DANIEL JOSHUA WAS accustomed to slipping imperceptibly down the labyrinthine streets and alleys of Washington. The city of snaggletoothed houses hunched up with just enough space between to sidle past and interspersed with alleys snaking and coiling was perfectly suited to Daniel's habits of skulking around unseen. Maybe he'd become slippery for having come to Washington and trying to stay free and helping some others. Maybe he found himself in Washington because he was the slippery sort. He and Washington were well suited.

Bending down a row of something growing and looked after by a man upon a horse wielding a whip is what Daniel Joshua had left behind. A plan had come to him and he had leaped and got free. He had stayed free through his wiles.

Daniel Joshua did not entirely inhabit the shadows. He earned his bread by day driving a dung wagon through the city streets. He was seen abroad. The work gave him good cover. Not many will look full at a man following horses and shoveling up their whatnot. The work was ever more steady and plentiful. More horses and their shit and their riders and carriages streamed into Washington and Georgetown each day.

"Is there news?" had become Gabriel's address to Daniel Joshua in these days since Mary had gone.

"None, Brother Gabriel," Daniel replied with gently mocking camaraderie. No news had come to them through the usual sources. But such information traveled precariously and took a meandering route through the mouths and households it passed. The time had been short.

Gabriel was eager for news of Mary and anxious to see his friend this evening.

"Sit to your supper, Brother Daniel," Annie said with her back turned from the bear come in from the outside. She paid him this womanly courtesy while he slapped dirt from his clothes and washed his hands and face in a trough of water. When he sat to the table at a seat that had become his own, she put a bowl of her stew before him.

There was an ambitious undertaking that needed Daniel Joshua's expertise in slipping and hiding. Gabriel had taken the audacious step of responding to a newspaper advertisement seeking tailors to work upon army uniforms for the government.

Gabriel presented himself, a sample of his skills, and an offer of his price to a sergeant at the army's Consignment Office. He had been scrutinized so thoroughly — the sergeant circled him and stared hard — that he'd feared he would be asked to remove his clothes. He had wisely maintained his eyes at the level of the floor and had spoken little.

"Show me yer hands!" the sergeant had demanded. "I cain't be fooled about a tailor's hands, you know."

Clearly one who knew the tailoring profession, the sergeant examined the colored man's hands and rubbed his own fingers along Gabriel's calluses.

"Either you got the right calluses or you ain't. You got 'em."

Though palmists are routinely ridiculed, there is a tale to be told in a man's hands. The consignment officer satisfied himself about Gabriel. Gabriel's price for the commission was rock bottom and the sergeant could not detect an offensive look or odor about him. He'd told the nervous tailor to deliver the completed uniforms in one week and to pick up the material at the Disbursement Office.

Secrecy was paramount. Aaron Ridley was not to know about this large commission. Sewing Annie closed her face against excitement at the prospect of the uniform commission and admonished Gabriel to do the same. She was rock firm in her admonition to Daniel Joshua. They must be quiet — careful if they would salt their mush.

Gabriel sighed and mumbled as the precious bolts of cloth were secured in Daniel's wagon at the Disbursement Office. Gabriel's poor digestion and nervousness at handling such cargo had him shifting his weight from hip to hip and rumbling low in his gut on the wagon ride.

"Aye, Brother, we've no ways to worry now," Daniel Joshua said as his companion blew gas nervously.

"Aye, Brother, but we are not yet home," Gabriel replied, sitting up tall in the seat next to his friend. He felt newly conspicuous and thus quaked a bit. But Daniel Joshua rested his shoulders and drove his nag and wagon through the streets comfortably. In fact, he spoke to a great many people. For at every corner there was a person who nodded or called out a greeting. Gabriel asked him outright how a man who had run away could live so openly in Washington. Daniel laughed and called himself a specter.

"Folks catch a glimpse, but when they turn I'm gone. Always keep two or three matches in your pocket and a flint or something to strike upon and when they are looking at your back going, you strike and flick a match head out and away from you and their eyes will follow it and leave your back and give you time and cover. I can be down an alley faster than the flicker. It is my invisible secret," Daniel said. "I know how to throw my whistle so it sounds like a bird. They turn their head and I flit off."

Daniel and Gabriel carried the five bolts of dark navy cloth into the back room of the shop at nightfall as though they were the blessed dead gone to glory. They were unobserved except by Annie, for Aaron Ridley was yet enjoying his supper and ale at an establishment on his circuit.

Gabriel and his mother decided on the pattern and what tricks would yield cloth enough and extra. Gabriel did worry over the care of the cloth now that he was fully responsible for it. The bolts were valuable and there wasn't the time to correct mistakes. He must deliver finished garments or pay.

Annie sharpened Gabriel's shears until satisfied with them. Gabriel then unfolded the first bolt and spread, rubbed, and smoothed the cloth. He stood back and looked and considered and rearranged. He draped his measuring strop around his neck. The measuring and cutting of the cloth approached ritual. Gabriel and his mother put Daniel Joshua in mind of a sawbones. They moved about the room readying their tools and eyeing the first bolt like it was a sick babe.

Gabriel lifted the shears and began his cut as Annie and Daniel held aloft candles to illumine his work. Annie guided Daniel Joshua's arms and positioned him behind Gabriel's right shoulder with his taper.

"Hold it high." She worried that an errant drop of candle wax would splash on the cloth and spoil it.

In the close light, Annie saw the pustules that ran down the left side of Daniel Joshua's face. These sores were made more inflamed and suppurating by his habit of wiping his dirty hands over them. A salve was what Daniel needed and she resolved to press it on him.

Annie positioned herself behind Gabriel's left shoulder and held the candlestick well above her own head. She breathed deeply and settled her arms into their duties solemnly. The seriousness of their expressions and the careful, deliberate way that Gabriel proceeded with his scissors would have caused an observer to bend her knee and bow her head and burble prayers into her chest.

When Gabriel finished cutting the first bolt of cloth, he felt the tension flow away from his shoulders and pool at his ankles.

"Go no further tonight, Brother Gabriel." Annie placed her hands upon his back to offer him comfort. Resolved to stop at this juncture and not risk the next bolt to his fatigue, Gabriel yielded to his mother.

He sat at the table and waited for a hot cup of coffee.

Daniel Joshua looked from mother to son in amazement. He, too, had been under the spell of the cloth, and every nerve in his body wanted to down a cup of the hot drink Annie was serving. He sat also. Annie put a plate of benne wafers on the table in front of the two men and looked at them and sat to a cup of coffee for herself.

" 'Tis beautiful, Nanny. And it cuts up well," Gabriel said.

" 'Tis you that cuts well, Gabriel," Annie replied.

"Nay, the cloth. You will have scraps and plenty odd strips left over for a quilt, Nanny," he put in modestly, for her praise made him uncomfortable.

The indigo cloth was a solid beauty! Annie was enamored of it. There was pleasure in handling it and warmth and joy in looking at the lovely color.

"Aye, Brother Gabriel," she said. "We'll make the Wild Geese Flying or some such?" She tossed the decision to him like a rubber ball.

"Yes, Nanny. We'll have plenty to make it up if I'm clever with the shears," he finished.

"Aye, every thread, Gabriel!"

When the three of them had downed their dregs, Daniel Joshua rose to take leave. Gabriel shook the man's hand and knew that his friend would slip out of the door and be gone down the alley at the back of the shop before one could whistle.

Annie was ashamed to recollect Ridley Plantation with pleasure. But working the cloth left a stain of bluing on her hands that put her in mind of spring at Ridley. She thought of spring and of the little girl who was called Blue Girl on Ridley Plantation when Annie, too, was small and working beside Knitting Annie. Little Blue Girl had come to Ridley just past the first of the year. She had seemed mystical to Sewing Annie because her arms were purpled from elbow to fingertips. Knitting Annie explained that this child had come from the Sea Island people — the people who dye the dark blue cloth. She'd been born to the work of indigo dyeing and her arms were stained. Folks wondered how she'd come to be at Ridley.

Blue Girl had given some of the other hands a fright. There were some who'd disdained to touch the Blue Girl or come near her at all. Worse was to have her touch you, they thought. Sewing Annie had worked beside her for the short while the girl was at Ridley. The two had been pressed to haul water for the extra laundry work entailed in spring cleaning. There seemed no end to the buckets of water put to fire. The two girls had lugged and dragged. Blue Girl did not last long at Ridley. She died just after Christmas that same year when the croup took off several youngsters.

Eight

THE MOLLYCODDLE WAS complete. Annie helped Gabriel out of his coat. She put her palm at his back and helped him to slough off worrying the shop's commissions. She took pains to feed him. She gave him his regular stew but added the fillip of powder biscuits and butter and honey.

"What, Nanny! Are we celebrating too early," he said boastfully — to tease her.

"Don't add to my weariness, Boy Gabriel. I have my own rows to work," Annie answered him in a familiar sparring singsong, and sat to her stew and biscuits and smiled.

"Aye, don't add to my weariness!" The phrase brought back recollections that were themselves trails toward bitter memories. She was betrayed by a fleeting lovely remembrance of the two of them together with Ellen on Ridley beside their old familiar hearth.

"Aye, don't add to my weariness!" Gabriel repeated. "You have always said that, Nanny — about powder biscuits. Whenever we called out for them at cabin you answered with 'Don't add to my weariness, boy.' You have gone toward weariness for me this evening."

"Go on, boy," she said, and clucked with her tongue to toss away his love. The boy was a prize and every day he grew dearer.

Annie set out his shears with ceremony and helped him to smooth the cloth. She traced a line across the drawn fabric with her fingernail, directing him, and was miffed when he gently brushed her hands aside and took up his shears. Gabriel was ceremonial in his preparation, too. As a preamble, he licked his left thumb and tested the blades of his implements. He was not satisfied that the blade of his scissors was sufficiently sharp and took up a file to improve it.

"Nanny," he answered to her surprised look. "I know the cut. I can make it with my eyes closed."

Gabriel showed his mastery with the cutting. Ah, his precision! When he had cut out the pieces for the entire consignment, there was one half of a complete bolt remaining.

"The babe is yours, Nanny. Do what you want with it," he crowed softly.

He was full of himself, but the work was splendidly begun. Annie put away her dear bundle and accepted a cog of the work. She began with sewing sleeves to the vests that Gabriel executed.

At the start, Gabriel set to quickly and quietly. He used Abraham Pearl's practiced stitches to assemble the garments and he used Pearl's practiced methods of measuring out lengths of thread and wasting none on biting and licking and sucking to gain a tip.

"You learned aplenty from Master Pearl, Brother Gabriel. I never taught you this or that," Annie purred, pleased with him and pleased to show it.

"No, Nanny. Mr. Pearl did not show me anything I had not seen you do before," he answered.

"Biscuits!" she exclaimed, and laughed out loud in sharp departure from her usual tittering and clacking. Gabriel joined her in loud laughing.

As a green youth, Gabriel had chafed at the constant suggestion from his mam and from Abraham Pearl that they alone were responsible for the skills and beauty of his needlework.

"You were always quick to pick up the thread of it, Son Gabriel," Nanny said frequently, as if no stitch had ever begun in his head.

Only Ellen was better than he with a needle. But Gabriel could best all with his scissors. He never made an ill-considered or careless cut.

Mother and son bent to their work and came up well at the end of the evening, which end came when Annie noticed that Gabriel was slumped and snoring — shushing and sussing and hitching his breath in rhythm.

"Brother Gabriel." She roused him and pushed him toward his loft and went to put away his work. But he would not let her do that. He awoke and cleaned off his work and climbed to his bed and urged Annie to her pallet as well.

When time came to finish the first of the uniforms, Gabriel brought out Abraham Pearl's hidden cache of buttons. It was the gift that made the deal. Saving the expense of purchasing buttons to finish his order would preserve much of the profit. Abraham Pearl was hailed furtively and fervently thanked.

The buttons came out of their hiding and gleamed riotously. Also hidden and brought to light ceremoniously was a doll dressed as an army man. It was a stuffed fabric figure in a small uniform, with a face of white bisque and delicately painted features. The lapels, pockets, and seams of the doll's clothing and the placement of the buttons were perfect. Gabriel used the figure to be sure of his work.

"Mr. Pearl's wife gave him this doll, Nanny. 'Twas their only babe," he said, smiling, fondly recollecting Mr. Pearl.

Abraham Pearl had decided to proceed with gentle firmness and gauge the result — thinking to train the boy up like a puppy. He made no apology for being disinclined to force and brutality. He had resolved to coerce the boy with kindness at the start. Working late by lamplight, Pearl had sat at his table gazing on the doll and scrutinizing the uniform. He had held it high and showed it to the tearful boy and smiled to cheer him.

"Aye, a clever man. Would that his luck will hold," Annie declared, and invoked a benediction for Abraham Pearl.

Nine

Sir:

I write to inform you of a matter of concern to you regarding these slaves of yours. I suspect that they have a plan of some sort up their sleeves. In the past two weeks the old woman has produced little or no knitted work. These items are especially popular with the folks here. There is a great call for knitted socks of the kind that the old woman can make. She goes about with her shoulders slumped and moaning. I am certain she is feigning aches in order to avoid work. She has produced far too few knitted goods in the last weeks and I am often without any stock to sell. Please advise if there is any action that I must take with this old woman.

Yours truly,
Aaron Ridley

In receipt of his nephew's missive about the output of Sewing Annie, Jonathan Ridley wondered how a young man who'd had as good an example of slave control could be so ineffectual. The stupid pup was afraid of Sewing Annie!

"It takes 'command' to make an impression on these creatures. I have given this boy the opportunity to show himself. But he does not take the reins. A child could see that there is no consequence to his displeasure," Jonathan Ridley said with a sneer to the boy's mother. "For this reason, madam, you ought to have left his upbringing to me! He is weak and dumb just as you are!" Ridley used this cudgel liberally to maintain control of the women. The boy's mother did not react. She only bore down more intently on her lap work, determined not to look at her smug, victorious sister-in-law.

Ridley decided he would get more work from the enterprise if he sent Annie's girl, Ellen, to join her mother and brother in Georgetown. Becoming known for her exquisite knitted work, Ellen could pick up the slack for her slow mother. Perhaps she might add her own distinctive work.

Ellen's coming to Georgetown appeared to be a fortunate turn of luck. So much a fortunate turn that Gabriel and Annie mistrusted it. Most often Jonathan Ridley's capriciousness frustrated them. This one time his whim had blown a breeze of pleasure toward them.

They deferred their joy until Ellen arrived.

Ellen came to Washington carrying the babe called Delia like an appendage to her left arm. She mostly held the twelve-month-old child on her left hip and grasped her as if she feared the baby would be snatched away.

The baby had a head of hair that was curly and copper-colored, thus her appearance arrested the eye. Ellen, concerned the child's looks caused curiosity, covered her head with a cloth. This head rag gave the baby the appearance of an old lady. Folk on the place cooed to her, calling "Ol' Maw, Ol' Maw, Maw,

Maw." They tickled her and capered, and most on the place came to do it — to call the babe Maw Maw.

Annie had heard about the goings-on at Ridley Plantation in her usual circuitous fashion. This one and that one told this one and that and the tale was brought to Washington in this one's mouth.

It remained to know what had happened on the Warren Plantation though. Right away Annie understood Delia was not the child of Ellen's body. She had drunk from that well. You can't make something so by just saying it.

"There's not one red-haired Ridley ever been seen," Favor Brown said knowingly, for she had born three for the master. "All of Ridley's yard children are sandy-colored with brown hair." It was true and it was incontrovertible among all at Ridley Plantation. Annie was reassured upon this fact.

Two seasons previously, a planter nearby the Ridley place had set an abundant crop of tobacco and had hired hands for the operation from Jonathan Ridley. Augustus Warren had wanted a gang of "soft" hands to work at topping off his tobacco plants. Dexterous young women were preferred, girls who could work fast and sure, pulling flowered heads off the delicate plants. Ridley had hired out a gang of five young women, including Sewing Annie's Ellen, to the Warren Plantation.

Jonathan Ridley had satisfied his curiosity of Ellen — pulling on her teats and plowing her haunches. He was certain now that he had not missed a delectable within his reach. He had not! Her coldness — her frantic resistance — was a damper on his desire and he regretted the trouble of her. Watching her come up a coddled little thing at the center of her adoring circle — Sewing Annie and Gabriel doted upon Ellen in their way — Ridley had made a plan. He thought she might be a saucy playmate.

But Ellen was no comfort, though she was soft from sitting and doing lap work. She was cool and tight and combative and unsatisfactory. He thought to ship her away.

Warren Plantation was a far larger enterprise than Ridley's, for Augustus Warren had several crops under cultivation on his several places and had scores of hands under the whip. The Ridley gang was housed in a large wattle-and-daub cabin and worked, slept, and ate together. The arrangement of keeping the Ridley slaves together was satisfactory to the girls as well as to Master Warren.

The driver of the gang of young women for tobacco topping was an experienced woman called Nancy. She had the technique for removing the flowers from the plant, and she instructed the green girls in how to do the job and save the plants.

As Nancy kept her gang productive, she was not much questioned in her handling of the girls. She was the undisputed authority and allowed no overseer to interfere with them. Nor was she upbraided for the confrontational tone often taken with the white bosses. She kept the girls at their work from sunup to sundown and well apart from the white men on the place.

Though they sometimes chafed under her, Nancy kept her authority with the topping gang. She brooked no laziness or insubordination and wasted no sweat on hurt feelings. She toughened them on the work — pushing and goading. The topping gang knew it was lucky to have Nancy to drive them.

At the complaint of one of the white men that a stick had been used on his back when he followed one of Nancy's girls into their cabin, Nancy was made to stand to charges. After an hour and a half of threats and one hard slap at her mouth while her gang stood idle and feigned confusion, Nancy was sent back to get them hard at it. The clever girls saved their boss a further beating.

Rather than break the whole crew for the noon meal, Nancy sent one girl to fetch the basket for the gang directly at the kitchen door. It was no honor or privilege or light work to fetch the gang's dinner. It was necessary to walk from the tobacco field, hoist two large baskets of the vittles, and carry both all the long way back to the field. The one who fetched would suffer the heated displeasure of the gang and of Nancy if she were too slow or too careless of the meal. Though the fetching was drudgery it was a change from the punishing tobacco work. The gang went to the field in dark and returned to their cabin in dark. This fetching afforded the briefest opportunity — on the way to the kitchen — to swing the arms freely at the sides of the body, to feel them dangle there, and to let the ache of fieldwork run off like an oil. When it was Mattie's turn, the food came quickly. She and Nancy drew off together and the others tittered over a hotter, longer supper.

On the hot afternoon that Ellen took her fetch day, the cook had ridden to town to have her tooth pulled. Ellen came into the kitchen as she was accustomed to and was no more surreptitious than was usual. They should have heard. Ellen saw the girl called Katharine who helped the cook. The cook herself never bothered with dishing up vittles for the gangs. Her grimy assistant handed out portions to the fetchers.

The girl certainly should have heard Ellen coming. She should have done something to hide the picture from view. But there they had been as plain as the nose on Ellen's face: Katharine with her bodice askew and holding Esau's hand against her breasts.

Because of the heat Ellen had thought momentarily that it was cool relief Katharine was after. But Ellen had seen the black hand on the girl's naked white skin. Esau had turned dead-calm eyes toward Ellen where she'd stood in the doorway. His face expressionless, his fat fingers continued to mash Katharine's untidy breasts.

Ellen froze. She put her eyes to the floor and did not move. She resolved to remain in this state brought on by the great fear in her until one or the other of them moved away. *Lord in heaven! What will happen? What has happened? What have I happened upon?* was the dialogue in her brain. She reflected upon what Jonathan Ridley had taught her when he'd come to the loom room while his wife was at her afternoon rest. He had grasped Ellen by the wrist and brought her to a corner of the barn. He pinched her face and pulled it toward a lamp. He pulled at her breasts and watched her face. He handled her so swiftly that his thrusting was not as painful as her mother had prepared her to expect.

Katharine broke the impasse when she snorted disdainfully. Who was a gal like this gal to be pretending she don't know nothing about what you do with menfolk? Katharine slapped Esau's fumbling hands away from her breasts and slapped his face. She adjusted her bodice and pushed out of the pantry past Ellen turned to salt. Katharine stopped abruptly, turned, and slapped Ellen across the face. The blow jogged Ellen from her shock. She assembled the vittles and hoisted and hauled the gang's meal back to the field.

It got to be a regular thing that Katharine and Esau went into the back pantry or the root cellar when Mrs. Clover, the cook, was gone for her rest and it was Ellen's turn to fetch for the tobacco girls. Ellen became complicit. She looked at them. And the looking fascinated and shamed her and caused her to feel she must stand on the secret. She feared if anybody found out about these goings-on there'd be a big ruckus and she'd be pulled into it. She knew that just knowing about this and not telling could earn trouble.

Katharine Logan was a girl who had been working on the Warren place for five years. She worked in the kitchen as a cook's helper and she served at the table. She was the oldest in a family of ten hungry young ones. Her mother had said gently but clearly that Katharine would have to go out to earn her bread. There was no help for it. The second oldest girl would stay and help Mama. Katharine was pushed out. Mother had arranged for her indenture to the Warren family to secure her meals and board and some useful instruction. And the family would receive credit at the Warren stores to get some blankets and mattress ticking.

Katharine Logan was on her own from that time. She considered herself fortunate. The Warrens were rich people — the richest of the rich from Katharine's point of view. For the first time in her life she had meals to count on and bedding not wet with the urine of some small child.

Katharine was brought on to assist the Warren cook, who was Irish like Katharine's own people. The cook, a stern, uncharitable woman, decided that Katharine was a low-class slacker as soon as she laid eyes on her.

Katharine was a physically developed girl who had not had the benefit of much advice, attention, or wardrobe. What clothes she had to cover herself were threadbare. Siobhan Clover complained against the poor girl to the mistress and said Katharine stank to high heaven. Mrs. Clover further huffed and snorted that she was above sleeping in the same quarters as this stinking slacker. She took it upon her own authority to banish Katharine from the sleeping quarters meant to be shared by the kitchen workers. The girl was left to hole up in a tiny slip adjoining the pantry.

As a rule, Mrs. Clover distanced herself from the distasteful supervision of the slaves. So she exercised her supervisory privileges on Katharine. The woman set Katharine to fetching and toting water, peeling vegetables, and carrying supplies. Katharine became skilled at avoiding Mrs. Clover. Eluding the woman was something of a proof against boredom for the girl.

Esau was a boy who'd been stunned by a blow to his head as a child. His dullness was confirmed by the expression he bore ever since. His face was as if suspended between a dull angry scowl and an attempt to smile. It was a perplexing visage and taken by most as a sign of Esau's idiocy.

Katharine kept her condition to herself right up to the time she was ready to deliver. Ellen, who'd been in on the situation from the beginning, pretended she didn't know about what was coming. Katharine hid herself under wide skirts until Mrs. Clover finally caught sight of her sleeping with her cheek resting in her palm, propped against a small apple tree in the backyard. Her wide skirts had fallen away from her stomach and the outline was plain to view.

It followed that Siobhan Clover berated Katharine for being an ignorant Irish whore — a slut. She threatened to tell the mistress to turn her out. Katharine mumbled to Mrs. Clover that an itinerant tinker had done the deed and begged to be allowed to stay to work out her term of service.

Mrs. Clover and the mistress weighed the trouble of discharging this girl and breaking in another hardheaded, red-headed whore of a kitchen worker. Self-interest won out and they allowed Katharine to remain at her job with the proviso that her term of indenture would be extended to cover the period of her lying-in and any expenses related to the inconvenience of the babe.

Mrs. Clover had doubts about the story of the itinerant tinker. She represented to Mistress that she believed the father of Katharine's bastard was one of the overseers, Jonas Kelly, a drunken adulterous lout whose manner was not sufficiently respectful toward the cook. Mistress and Mrs. Clover brought forth to Master that Katharine's pregnancy was evidence of Jonas Kelly's villainy. He was discharged upon their word.

Mrs. Clover ruminated on the true paternity of this babe. She didn't remember a tinker or any such, and figured she would have. She was more observant than the girl suspected. She had developed eyes in the back of her head as a child ducking blows from her own vicious family people. The cook had seen Katharine and Esau together and had caught the temper of the relation.

Ellen worried that Mrs. Clover had found out the true paternity of Katharine's baby. For Mrs. Clover sealed Katharine's punishment by arranging for her lying-in to be in the shacks used by the bondwomen working the tobacco. Her labor was to be attended by Meander, the slave midwife, a further insult arranged by Mrs. Clover. Could she have guessed? The ramifications of this birth worried Ellen mightily.

"She'll be seven years in the workhouse do this come out. Look at that child! It ain't no ways white! This a colored baby child! Look at her head!" the midwife brayed like a mule. "Dis why she brung her down here!" Ellen was frightened that the woman wouldn't keep her mouth closed. If word spread through the colored community and then to the white folks that a white

girl had given birth to a colored baby, Katharine would be sent
to the workhouse. The child would simply be taken and sold
south to the first trader who had the price.

"How this come about? You know 'bout who she been screwing to bring a colored baby?" Meander interrogated Ellen.
"What all is going on here, girl?"

Ellen looked at the copper-colored corkscrews on the babe's
head. The child's hair color was similar to its mother's hair,
though it was not slick and straight. Her skin was butter-
colored — a color often seen among colored folks. She'd never
pass for white, and Katharine would never be allowed to stay a
white woman and be her mama.

Ellen held a washbasin and pitcher for the old attendant and
the woman scrubbed away Katharine's bloody particulars from
her hands and arms. The foul pail was given to Ellen to pitch.
She was reluctant to turn her back on the old woman. It would
be easy enough to smother the babe and be rid of the trouble.
She sloshed the refuse out back of the cabin.

Ellen didn't know what to say to the midwife so she said
nothing — only looked at the woman and squinted a bit, as if
fending off a foul breeze of questions. She didn't have to do
much talking. Mrs. Clover soon swooped in the cabin and took
over the situation.

The first task she fell to was to upbraid the midwife for opening her mouth to croak at all. Mrs. Clover threatened to throttle
the woman if she talked to anyone. She put her arms akimbo
and convinced the other woman she was well up to the task of
beating her senseless. The midwife took low. She stood back
from the pallet where Katharine lay and calculated the value of
her silence. She recognized Mrs. Clover as a white woman, but
one who was surely scared. Only a dullard could miss that the

cook held herself culpable in this pregnancy. And Meander was no dullard. Siobhan Clover's fears were palpable. Mistress considered Mrs. Clover, because of her longevity on the place, to be the de facto supervisor of the white women who worked under her. She was to train them and keep her eyes on them for trouble. It was her responsibility to ensure that Katharine did not fall into just such a hole as she was peering out from. Mistress would see it that Mrs. Clover had shirked her duty. And the blame might splash upwards to soil the mistress's skirts if the master got wind of what had really gone on beneath his nose.

Katharine Logan returned to the kitchen within a day of her delivery of the babe. Mrs. Clover instructed Katharine in wrapping her milk-swollen breasts and gave her a clean dress.

For the first two or three days after the birth, Katharine sniffled and wept. The cook berated her. She harangued that a worthless slacker like Katharine should be relieved that she'd been saved the trouble of raising a bastard child. Mrs. Clover said plainly that Katharine's tears were unseemly, worthless, and tiresome and would not be tolerated.

The twisting, serpentine plot that Siobhan Clover concocted unfolded beautifully for her purposes. The disgusting lout Jonas Kelly was further accused in absentia of fathering a baby on the Ridley slave gal, Ellen. That explanation would silence all talk about color. Kelly's reputation for drinking insulated the accuser from the bother of substantiating her claims. He was getting his payment for his profligate eyes.

Mrs. Clover reasoned that though a series of lies such as these could not be easily excused, they did prevent the more extreme necessity of infanticide.

Ellen was told to take the babe and to tell no one of the child's true origins. Mrs. Clover threatened to knock her head off her shoulders if she raised an objection. And though Ellen did not object to taking the baby, Siobhan Clover did cuff her at the ears for standing stock-still with her mouth open in disbelief. Ellen was too shocked to utter a peep. She put her arms out and took the child.

Ellen squeezed goat's milk into the baby's mouth from a pouch, for there was no suckling woman to feed the child. When judged sturdy enough to travel, Ellen and the babe were sent back to Ridley with the attitude that the Warrens were washing their hands of the trouble of them.

On the morning she was to be packed off, Ellen narrowed her eyes, then lowered them beseechingly at Mrs. Clover and begged to be allowed to take the goat with her and the child.

On the road back to Ridley Plantation, the goat was more trouble than the baby girl. The child did not cry. She accepted her milk rag and slept. The goat balked at trailing behind the wagon, so Ellen pulled it in the wagon and held it tightly with a rope to keep it from bolting.

Master Ridley was told that Ellen was given a child by a former overseer. The Warrens as much as said that any idea that Ellen had been ruined during her time at the Warren place was compensated by the boon of the baby. Ridley was thought to be coming out ahead in the deal. The queer circumstances, however, made Ridley suspicious.

Suspicious he was, but nervous, too. He toted up the time that Ellen had been at the Warren place and wondered if she were bringing back something that had begun with him. But the cap of copper rings on the babe's head convinced all that this babe was not a Ridley. As well, the timing did not suit. Ridley chuckled to himself at sight of the young woman returning.

"Aye, this Ellen is a cold bargain. I credit the man who would tup her and give her a prize."

When Ellen returned to Ridley she resumed spinning, knitting, sewing, and soap-making. But there was a look from people that said she had been made a mule and was brought low. Ellen appeared to them a much different girl from the one who had left. People thought she'd been done to badly by the Warren overseer, Kelly. They blamed her lack of milk on hexing or some unspeakable horror. And people knew the regrettable involuntary of it, but nevertheless they thought differently of Ellen.

The news had gone all around the barn and back and had come to Annie and Gabriel in Georgetown from the lips of Dice, a bowlegged girl who traveled a circuit with a horse doctor. This horse doctor treated animals far and wide and Dice was the doctor's cook, bedmate, and assistant with the animals. She took considerable satisfaction in her abilities at carrying talk about the circuit. She was good at remembering and was well respected. She would tell a tale without getting partial.

What Dice told them was that Ellen had been brought back to Ridley Plantation with her head down, carrying a girl babe and pulling a nanny goat whose tits were more swollen than Ellen's own. She had slipped into her mother's former duties and was clinging to the child and the goat for dear life.

Ten

IN THE FIRST days after Ellen's arrival, the occupants of the house moved around each other warily. Gabriel had never been uneasy with his sister, but she brought a baby and altered the balance of his workroom and hearth. Having Ellen in Georgetown completed a circle, but the child confused things. Nanny had embarrassed him with the facts that were known and he felt a change in his relation to Ellen. The girl sister had gone and a woman whose heart was claimed by a strange child had taken her place.

Gabriel changed his sleeping place to the back room on the second floor as his mother requested. He gave her and Ellen and the baby the attic room. Considering the propriety of one sleeping arrangement over another embarrassed him and he let his mother make the decisions in this regard.

Ellen's arrival in Georgetown left little time for rumination. She arrived and had to get settled quickly. There was work for her to do. She began at once to cut into the backlog of knitted work caused by Annie helping with the uniforms at night.

During daylight hours, Ellen kept up the work on the knitted goods that were so highly sought at the store. As many pair of socks as could be knitted were sold to the government figures and vagabonds who now came in great numbers to the capital.

The young woman brought an inclination toward fancy patterns to the socks, scarves, and shawls. Gabriel cautioned her to maintain a plainer pattern for most. "Plain and simple, Sister. The plain and useful socks are the ones needed. There is much call for them." Ellen preferred to embellish with intricate decoration, but she held back at Gabriel's direction. "Produce volume rather than frippery and finery, Sister," he said teasingly. Ellen's skills had not diminished with doing fieldwork, but she was not as fast as she had once been. Her fingers were distracted by the demands of her babe.

Annie mused on her children and then upon Delia and the thought that this babe would follow them. They would soon press her to a baby's tasks — holding a spool of thread or knitting. Did she belong with them? Or would some claimant come after her? Annie's eyes dropped on the child's head below her on the floor and she bent to shove two ringlets under the babe's head rag.

A girl babe is yours if and until he wants her. The tough words sounded in Annie's ears again. "You will gauge her fortune and your own by how long he keeps her and how well or ill he treats her. When the master's done with your girl, her troubles and what's left of your girl are yours to keep," the Ridley midwife had said flatly. She was only telling Sewing Annie what she already knew. This was a well-worn path at Ridley Plantation.

The quartermaster drew a magnifying eyepiece from his pocket and ceremoniously examined the seams of the uniforms. He looked them over carefully — pulling an odd uniform here and there from the stacks of garments. On one coat he pulled on a loose button. Gabriel took the coat from him quickly and repaired it so swiftly that it was tight again before he'd finished saying it was loose. After his examination, Sergeant Miller looked pleased with his purchase. Gabriel was told where to deliver the uniforms and the sergeant gave him a signed paper with instructions to the paymaster for his fee. A nervous moment came between them as Gabriel's eyes grazed the paper. He was eager to read the words, but did not want for the quartermaster to know he could decipher letters. Gabriel had a prick of nervousness about his fee. He would not be fooled or robbed! But he should be cautious. The quartermaster and the tailor exchanged glances over their deal. Gabriel thought the sergeant's eyes were even and clear and that the man could be trusted. Sergeant Miller trusted in what he saw as well.

"Make fifty more. Drop these off and pick up more cloth and make more uniforms. Make fifty more in thirty days."

Once again Gabriel made a pact with Daniel Joshua to transport the bolts of cloth across town. This time they felt a need to be wary. Who might know the value of the cloth? Daniel Joshua's broad body was the sort that would discourage an opportunistic highwayman. If there were a planned attack, their wariness and craftiness might be their best defense. Thinking to discourage any kind of curious authority from uncovering the precious cargo and questioning the appropriateness of two colored men having possession of it, Annie gave up a mess of rags through which she had larded some chitterlings gone past eating and smelling high.

"Lay this upon a layer of straw and salt the cloth underneath it for to throw off the patrollers," she said. Daniel accepted this advice as sound and followed it, layering the foul garbage above dry grass in his wagon.

"Your ma is a clever one," he said to Gabriel. The son snorted assent and thought to himself that Daniel Joshua had yet seen little of her.

The men left the army supply office cautiously and well before dark. They regretted the wind at their back, for upon it the smelly rotten air blowing off the load went up into their noses. The odor would keep trouble back though.

Under cover of dusk, after sharing their supper, Gabriel and Daniel brought the bolts of cloth into the workroom. When all were seated around the table, Gabriel looked long at them. He pulled the bills of payment from a pouch tied under his right armpit. The money was brought forth and counted under the candlelight.

Gabriel spread the bills and offered them to his mother. She was made nervous by the gesture. She rose from her seat and fiddled at the stove for a few minutes before returning.

Gabriel gathered the money to himself and pushed several dollar bills across the table to his friend Daniel. Daniel grunted, and without looking or counting or answering, he pushed the dollars back toward Gabriel. There was no question of the outcome — that Daniel Joshua would accept the bills from Gabriel to pay for his transport. Nevertheless, the money was pushed and shoved across the table between the coffee cups and sugar bowl a few more turns until Daniel Joshua grunted again and put the bills in his pocket.

Gabriel gave the remaining money to Annie. " 'Tis our freedom, Nanny. Keep it hid. 'Tis our freedom."

Annie folded the money and swept it into a sack and put that inside of her bodice. As the money was off the table, the three chuckled and shook their heads from side to side. Freedom money was too serious a thing for them not to chuckle. It was all Gabriel could do not to holler. He did pound his heel on the floorboards for a number of whacks. Daniel Joshua sat quiet out of respect for his careful friends. It was all he could do not to jump up and dance a jig, for he shared their profound happiness.

Annie salted the bills next to her heart. It wasn't yet enough to buy their freedom, but added to what was already salted the sum was well on the way toward what was needed.

Eleven

THE BRISTOLS, PROMINENT Virginia landholders, were experimenting. Rich in landholding and cash poor in the short term, they happened on the idea of raising sheep for wool on their vast acreage of languid grasses.

Through judicious maneuvering Aaron Ridley managed to be invited to dinner on auspicious occasions at the home of the soft and lovely Violet Anne Marie Bristol. Aaron Ridley had a straightforward, healthy appearance. He had no pustules to mar his good face and his breath was fragrant, as his teeth were also good. Dressed in fashions tailored at the shop, he presented a figure of dash and charm. Though his uncle was cagey about plans for inheritance, it was generally thought that Aaron Ridley was scion of some wealth. He did warrant the consideration of Miss Bristol and family.

The elder Ridley recognized the wisdom of his nephew dining in the homes of Washington's elite families. Jonathan Ridley's hope was that his young nephew's social whirl would show him to advantage and bring him to the attention of a wealthy family with a marriageable daughter. This point was a place of agreement for the two Ridley men.

Sharing brandy in his uncle's hotel suite on a visit, Aaron ventured a bold and increasingly popular opinion expressed by his new social circle. "Sell the slaves to themselves! I advise you to take the money and get some profit from them. You run a risk that they will take a runner and you'll end with nothing. For you will have to pay to have them recaptured. These slave catchers don't engage cheaply. Let the slaves buy themselves and save you their trouble," Aaron cajoled his uncle. He was energetic with his elaborate plan and he promenaded about the room making flourishes with his hands.

Aaron's circuit brought him to his true aim in walking about his uncle's rooms. It was Bella Strong. Aaron came primarily to look at his uncle's mistress, the most compelling sexual being he had encountered. Jonathan Ridley was recently enamored of the dark-haired soprano and wooed her with prodigious expense and attention. The elder was happily exhibiting her to his nephew. She was beautiful, very ghostly white skinned with small touches of red-orange accent upon her lips, a thin line ringing her eyelids, and a small mole at a place high on her shoulder just beneath the base of her neck. Aaron imagined the tips of her nipples to be thusly tinted, and mused on her. Her eyes were a changeable color and went from light to dark as light reflected from her chestnut hair and was influenced by lamps about the room.

When Aaron tore his eyes off Bella Strong and spoke, his plan was simple. He declared that he had no love of the Negroes, but was thinking of the practical aspects of a manumission deal. There was cash to be had and the Negroes were nearly free in the District of Columbia as far as he could see.

"Uncle, the niggers come and go freely — as freely as birds, I tell you!" Aaron exclaimed. He continued on his point. He explained further that the infusion of cash from the sale would make a creditable investment in the scheme of the Bristols. Thus the cash would advance Aaron toward his goal of the Bristol girl.

"Uncle, the thing to fear is this: as Gabriel has risen in his own value, you must take pains he does not slip out from under his price. If he takes himself off . . ."

"If you watch that he does not, young sir!" the older man chided.

"Sir, they are not easily watched. He has a specialized skill that takes him about the town. And the women cluck about hither and yon."

"And these hens do bother you some, sir?" Jonathan Ridley said laughingly, showing off for his lady friend at the blushing boy's expense.

"He himself will pay you for his freedom. Let the slaves pay a top dollar for their freedom, for you'd not get top dollar for them on the market. They're not field hands. That Gabriel is weak and worthless at a market sale."

"Be quiet, boy!" Jonathan Ridley snapped. "I know Gabriel's worth. You go too far to convince."

"Field hands are most of what is wanted further south, Uncle — wanted by the traders. And the traders are taking a profit. Cut out the middleman!" Aaron spoke insistently, attempting to turn himself to the best advantage in Bella Strong's eyes. He had practiced to persuade his uncle, for he was eager to contribute a "scheme" of some value.

"Further, sir, with the abolitionist sentiment gaining strength, there is no guarantee that the District of Columbia will remain safe or profitable for slave-owning. Yankees continue to harangue about the appropriateness of slave-owning in the nation's capital. As if that matters! It's getting ever easier for the Negroes to steal away. There's a ring of white people mixing with roaming Blacks to aid runaways in this town." Aaron finished his point with passion and a snap of his fingers. "I tell you again, sir, this tailor will slip from under his price if you do not take care."

"Has Gabriel collected enough cash for his purchase? Where does this money come from, boy?" Ridley questioned, trying to bring Aaron down to earth.

Jonathan Ridley was indeed interested lately in securing an infusion of cash. As he was beginning to feel a sense of rising achievement, he was outgrowing the confines of his rural home. Ridley now preferred living as a town gentleman. He'd watched the popinjay cavort about the room with his ideas trying to beguile Bella. Yes, now may be the time Jonathan Ridley would liquidate assets to build his pleasures in town.

"They are calculators — all of them — they spend much time in figuring and toting up. Aye, they are limited by their race, but these are clever and cunning beasts," Aaron told his uncle knowingly.

"Aye," the uncle said. "Aye, and you are helpless to thwart them." This was a constant theme running between the two.

Know all men by these presents that in consideration of the love and affection I have for my people and the payment of the sums as listed
Gabriel, the tailor = $1,000.00
Annie, the knitter and laundress = $800.00
Ellen, seamstress and knitter = $700.00

The above-mentioned were slaves belonging to Jonathan Ridley of Scottsboro, Maryland, a gentleman and landowner, and are henceforth free. The three above mentioned further agree to continue to work and operate the tailoring concern of Ridley & Ridley with 75 percent of all profits after operational expenses from commissions of said concern to be payable to Jonathan Ridley as repayment of the investment in this business. Failure to operate the business, Ridley & Ridley, shall nullify this agreement and result in the swift imprisonment of said parties.

> *Whereof I do affix my signature,*
> *Jonathan Ridley*
> *September 18, 1854*

◆◆

The breeze that sneaked in the window stirred the curtains and dried the bit of perspiration on Gabriel's upper lip. It lifted the manumission paper from Jonathan Ridley's hands. He allowed it to float to the floor as if it were the most worthless piece of parchment he'd ever put pen to. Gabriel knew it gave Ridley a satisfaction to do this, for it shone on his face. Gabriel swooped to the floor to retrieve the paper and the movement was mostly a genuflection in honor of the long struggle they'd come through — all three. He, Sis Ellen, and Nanny were free!

Jonathan Ridley brought Gabriel back to it with his reminder that the child, Delia, was still considered a Ridley slave and her freedom would have to be purchased. Gabriel assured Ridley that Sis Ellen intended to purchase the child's freedom through her own industry at the earliest opportunity.

As Gabriel faced him with the paper dangling from his hand, Ridley walked toward his former slave. He approached close and Gabriel drew up straighter to meet him. Ridley commanded him — drilled into him with his eyes. These eyes of

Ridley's engaged Gabriel's eyes and the pair of dark blue jewels had a hold. The former master reached suddenly and grabbed the young man's scrotum and held the entire basket hard in his hand. The shock of it stiffened Gabriel's whole body, but he prayed to keep his cock soft. He made himself amused like a toddling child and the moment of urgency passed.

"You're a man, Gabriel, and hung well," Ridley said after a moment that he held Gabriel. He released his grip but continued to keep his hand upon the frozen-still young man. "I should have kept you on the homestead to give me more pickaninnies. Instead you've come to the town and been spoiled. Had I planned better I could have had another sewing pickaninny — one like Sewing Annie or your Ellen." Smiling at his former slave, Ridley relinquished his hold and turned away.

Gabriel left the sitting room of Ridley's apartment at the Whilton Hotel by bowing and backing away from Jonathan Ridley. He took leave in a formal, final way. Though his circumstance had changed radically, the terms of the manumission agreement also bound him to service to Ridley. He knew it plainly — soberly. But, still, it was not bondage! The three were free to plan — to look forward and to say how things could be. He and his mother and his sister had attained their freedom! It was a stumbling block pushed out of their way!

Gabriel placed the paper in his breast pocket. He walked out of the hotel and proceeded down High Street over cobblestones whose chill he felt upon the bottoms of his feet. Gabriel's shoes were thinly soled and they allowed his feet to feel all that was beneath them. Today he relished the contact. An aroma of horse manure hung in the air. But the air was also crisp and offered some relief from the city's myriad other stinking smells. Gabriel wanted to take off running and call out loudly. He yearned to celebrate his joy. He wanted to call out his mother's name and Ellen's name and his own — wanted to shout them out as loudly as possible. He wanted to toll the bells in the church tower. Think of that!

Eager to reach his home at the back of the shop, Gabriel moved as swiftly through the streets as was prudent.

Master — no, no longer. Now it was Mr. Ridley. He was just a man who had once owned Gabriel and his talents and labors and Gabriel's mother and Sis Ellen and now they were all free of him — or nearly.

Gabriel did still feel the grip of Ridley's hand on his meat and potatoes and knew the bond with this man was not severed. But he had wrested something — paid for and gotten something more than they'd had.

Gabriel brought a mood of alarm into the workroom when he entered. He did not speak at first, only nodded to his mother and then to Ellen. He sat and placed the parchment — the freedom papers — on the table. Annie put down a cup of coffee in front of him but did not interrupt his thoughts. She looked at his temple and noted that it throbbed. She waited to hear him speak — wanted to hear her son speak out as a free man.

Gabriel stared straight ahead as the others looked at his face and then at each other. Finally he parted his lips and made a sound that was like a groan of pain. Annie started. But before anyone made another sound, Gabriel began to hum and he built upon his humming until he was singing — though softly. He sang not to lift the rafters, only to commemorate.

Sewing Annie resolved to be Annie Coats in that moment and she joined her son in singing. Her voice was small and tinny but she sang out unabashedly.

Well used to drinking goat's milk from a cup, Delia climbed

into her mother's lap and pulled at Ellen's dry breasts and buried her face between them. Gabriel looked at her pawing at his
sister's bosom and felt some aversion spoil his joy at this picture. This child had no right to Ellen. And Jonathan Ridley
had not forgotten about her. Ellen added her voice to the singing and each of several familiar tunes made rounds. Only once
did Gabriel raise his voice as loud as was possible and he cared
not who heard him sing.

Gabriel put aside stitching on a commission when his mother
finally ascended to her bed. Ellen and the babe had gone before
her. Gabriel's restless hands took up his knitting as he mused
on the number of buttons sewed on to buy his freedom. For that
matter, what number of rows of knitting had passed his fingers
and his mother's to come thus far? It was quiet work — their
lap work — but it was furious and productive. How many rows
of knitting had his mother completed? It had been a many, oh,
Lord. It had been plenty! Gabriel considered that for his mother's sake, she ought never to take up knitted work again. She
could let her arms fall asleep at her sides. But he chuckled to
himself. It might be that his mother's arms would seize up and
become useless to her if she were to stop working at her knitting. Needlework was the thing she had done since she had
begun working — which had been so early in her years that
there could be no way to know when.

Gabriel imagined that when his mother had carried him her
arms had rested upon the bulge of him as they had when she
carried Ellen. This was in the long-ago time when their father
had been alive. He recollected his mother propping her arms on
her bulging stomach full of Ellen. He remembered seeing her.

And her hands were never stopped from knitting and what she worked upon rested atop the child's head.

Is that what makes Ellen so lively and sure at the needles? Gabriel thought, cheerfully recalling her early gifts. Ellen's lap work output was prodigious from her toddling. Her skills were so sure that the needlework seemed less toil than a beautiful undertaking that often couldn't be stopped or interrupted. She would knit smoothly for so long without breaking off that she seemed not to inhabit the body that worked. Gabriel remembered that he had used to think the same about his mother — that her soul belonged to her needles.

But he did, in fact, know better. He knew that both these women had belonged to Master Ridley and now they did not. Whether or not it made them happy or content to be so, it made them different. He mused on it — Sewing Annie and her boy, Gabriel, and her girl, Ellen, belonged only to themselves. Gabriel's vitals had a singular feeling when he considered the way they had all come. Yet there was the burr — the constrictions, the limitations. Again he felt the phantom grip of Jonathan Ridley squeezing his meat and potatoes.

At this thought, Gabriel's hands became still for the first time. They had moved constantly all the day. Even when he'd stood frozen before Jonathan Ridley, his hands had shaken and he imagined the bones in them rattling like dry stalks. He remembered his knitting and began again. Gabriel's weary fingers wanted to be still, but his thoughts would not allow it for long.

Mary — a tender, painful spot of worry for Gabriel. Where was she on this night? Had she reached Canada? Had she made herself free? Today Gabriel Coats was made free, but he could not fly.

Gabriel sighed and reflected that his work left him too much time to ruminate. He rose from the table to recapture errant pins and buttons and to wind threads. At last it was time to put up and go to bed.

Gabriel climbed to his room with a small candle end. At each landing, he paused long enough to catch a troubling sound if there was one. But the house was silent. There was nothing unexpected. He crushed the candle stub between his fingers and went to his rest.

Mournful boat whistles blew through the dusk as Aaron
Ridley left the shop to pursue his supper and his friends. Daniel
Joshua approached the shop's back door secretively. From behind a tree in the yard he looked for a signal that it was safe to
knock. Since Daniel had become warm with them, the Coatses
were a regular bead on his circuit of town. They had their signals between them. Daniel recognized Annie's signal in the
small square window of the kitchen workroom. A white curtain
tied in a knot in the middle told him they expected and welcomed him. His mouth got set for a bracing cup of coffee and a
pan of biscuits as he scraped his fingers on the back door. He
did wonder, though, how his friends would take the news he
was bringing.

When Daniel Joshua was inside and seated, Annie replaced
the knotted curtain with a square of indigo cloth that shut out all
light from the window. Not a soul else was expected that night.

Daniel took seat in a chair and paused only a few moments
before laying out the information he'd brought. "That gal that

you hid in your root cellar got captured and is brought back to be sold at the auction house in Alexandria," Daniel said. His words landed on their ears like a stone. There was no sound. Annie and Gabriel said nothing. They appeared to wait until all was said — until all had settled. Ellen looked at her mother's face and then at her brother's to discern the import of this Mary's name.

Annie and Gabriel hadn't had word of Mary in all the long time since she had left. They had been hopeful and prayerful for her safety. Now they knew her fate.

The oldest, most visceral lesson Gabriel had learned from Annie was to hold his water — to resist every inclination to react right away.

"No. No. No crying, boy," Annie demanded when he ran to her with a small, injured knee. She clutched him firmly, but with no indulgence — never that. "Be still, Gabriel," was her unequivocal command.

He had learned to guard his nerves. His cautious demeanor was his insulation against uncertainty and brutality — all of the painful consequences of revelation. Now, with great effort, he did not cry out or pepper Daniel with questions.

What consequence might come if he revealed to Daniel Joshua and his mother and sister the depth of his feelings in regard to Mary? He had an appetite for this Mary that he felt ashamed to reveal. He had nurtured this longing and fed it upon the thin hope of seeing her again. The time of separation had not dulled his ardor. He felt a fool to let his mother know his longing. And he felt a further fool to think Ellen or Daniel Joshua might guess his yearnings.

In the moment, Gabriel was a superstitious lover who imagined that his longing had brought Mary back to this jeopardy.

Cold reasoning told him that it was greed and cruelty that had thus tossed her like a handkerchief. It was chance that had placed her within his reach again.

Gabriel sucked sharply first at the air and then at his pierced fingertip. Annie sprang forward out of her seat and leaned toward Gabriel's wounded finger. He raised his hand and stopped her coming to his aid. His eyes flashed a rebuke at his mother's uncharacteristic fussing. She had bolted from her chair as if she herself had been stuck. What could she mean by coddling him when Mary was suffering untold horrible treatment?

The needle had pierced his fingertip with the same precise efficiency that it pierced cloth. Gabriel stared at the drop of blood and his own calloused finger. The painful puncture would thwart his work.

"She been through some several hands since the first. They've settled on to sell her deep south since she is a troublemaker — a runner. They intend to sell her for hard labor, though she don't look up to doing it according to the eyes that have seen her," Daniel said. He hadn't wanted to soften the words. He wanted them to have the truth. And naked truth went down best fast.

Annie spoke up more quickly than usual. She felt a trembling interest running through Gabriel. She sought to preempt him. "Is it anything we can do for her?"

"Had you the money you could buy her and set her to freedom — had you the money. She ain't to the taste of those that buy for the fancy houses. She done spoiled for that. They plannin' to do her like an ox and run her until she drop dead. Somebody puttin' together a work gang for cotton or rice likely buy her. Pitiful, poor gal!" Daniel said heatedly.

Gabriel winced some at Daniel's words and was poised dangerously at the top of his emotions.

Unexpectedly, Daniel Joshua was demonstrative of his feelings for Mary. His face was torn up with concern. He shuddered to think of what would befall her. He knew how things were done at the sale house she'd been put at. The man who had come to him with the descriptions and information was Bob Jackson, whose woman carried the meals over to the factors. He said Mary was hit and busted up a bit. This was the least of it, Daniel knew, for Bob Jackson's face unintentionally betrayed the ugly tale. They were selling her for a beast of burden and so they were not wasting care on her comfort.

Since Mary had gone away, Daniel had inquired for word of her from the usual folk who kept their ears to the ground. Until bowlegged Bob Jackson brought this news, there had been no reliable information. Daniel had heard it said that a Quaker couple had been clobbered into their graves and that the woman they were transporting was grabbed and taken back to slavery. This tale had been an unconfirmed rumor. Now it was stitching up a tragic story.

Annie rapped her coffee cup on the table several times. Gabriel dropped his needle. He clapped his hands together and rubbed them as if applying a secret powder.

"Nanny, I have failed the fire. Your coffee is cold," Gabriel said, rising suddenly. He went out of the back door to get sticks to stoke the fire in the stove and returned with one. He fiddled with the stove and stood to boil the coffee and pour for all.

Annie placed her flatirons on the stove and moistened a starched white shirt with a sprinkle of captured rainwater. Water from the pipes and spigots in town put blemishes on white shirting so that careful laundresses captured water in a barrel for their fine work. She took her time and let the irons sit on the stove, heating until their readiness was smelled. When she applied iron to cloth, the room became thick with steam. Clouds of it circled Annie's head and the hissing mist was tonic for her. She said nothing but simply clink-clanked the flatirons.

Reluctant to have the babe's gibberish spoil her mother's contemplation, Ellen scooped Delia up and put her to bed.

Gabriel peered at his mother through the steam and asked, "Shall we act on Mary's behalf, Nanny?"

"Yes, Brother, I think we must," she answered. Her eyes were still trained on the shirt that she ironed.

"I would move yonder mountain to help her, Nanny."

"Yes, Brother, I know," she said.

Annie stood upon the porch of the rectory of Holy Trinity Church and kept her head bowed respectfully. She knuckled down the center of the large, intricately carved oak door to call the priest's attention. She knew he was watching. She had seen him looking out the window.

Higgins opened the door. "Come inside, Mother, please. Come inside and we can speak," he said. Higgins stood aside briefly to allow Annie to pass through the door in front of him, realized that she would not accept this honor, and turned back into the house first. He felt her follow him down the oak-paneled hallway into the receiving room.

"Please sit down, Mother," Higgins said with gentleness and warmth. His manner always surprised Annie, coming from a pale white face with rosy circles on the cheeks.

William Dinmont Higgins, the young priest assigned to Holy Trinity Catholic Church in Georgetown, was an active antislavery worker. He was known in the circles of Blacks in Georgetown as a helper.

"Are you sent to me, Mother? Has someone sent a message?"

he asked cautiously, trying to ease the woman's nerves and get to the purpose of the visit.

Higgins was also the son of a woman held in slavery in Virginia and her white slave owner. Because he looked like his father, he'd succeeded well in passing as a white person. Occasionally he was disquieted by his own deceptions, but he was committed to using his color as cover to assist escapees. And he maintained the fiction of his color with all — white and Black.

Higgins would not stand out physically among men. He was not broad and he generally gave the impression of bookishness. He was, though, an active, aggressive man. He could be counted upon in a fight — having endured many pummelings in his youth. He usually finished the fray atop the one who started it.

Higgins looked long at Annie. This woman was not quite so old as he imagined his own mother to be. But she was apparently a woman whose every day was applied to the task of survival. When Annie entered the room and took a seat, the warmth from the fireplace caused her to unbend, and she loosed the many layers of her wrappings. A taller, younger, more vigorous-looking woman gradually emerged. Reverend William Higgins was mildly surprised.

Higgins preferred to refer to all colored women above a certain age as "Mother." He stoutly refused to call colored women "Auntie" for reasons that he explained to no one. His appellation was courteous without arousing the suspicions of those who might overhear.

Higgins thought he knew the travails of ones such as Annie from firsthand observation. He thought about his own mother's grief-stricken life and rebuked himself for his resemblance to the brutal man who visited his mother's cabin and ordered her children out the door while he raped her. The master cared not a whit for what the children saw, only that their hollow-eyed staring not distract him.

Higgins's complexion had always been his father's pale white with rose-red cheeks. His hair was also the master's, brown with red highlights, and was thin and wispy.

Again and again Higgins recollected the day his father whipped and then sold his mother. He whipped her before the traders took her. Why? To spoil her for the next man who would use her? Millie, as she was known on the master's record books, simply fell out of his favor. The boy received a kick to his head because he had the temerity to clutch his father's booted leg and beg for mercy for her. Aye, this was the tormenting nighttime vision William Higgins prayed against.

A short time after his mother was sold, William was sent to a Jesuit seminary to work for his keep and education. Years later he was not able to determine whether he'd been a slave of the Jesuits or a servant. He never knew fully what his father's arrangements had been. But he became a favored student when he excelled at his studies.

The other boys at seminary were ones like him who had fathers among the planters nearby. William was not the only one whose mother was a white planter's slave mistress. In fact, it was thought appropriate by some that the issue of these couplings should have the advantages of education. These offspring might bring about an improvement in the Negro race.

Some of the mulatto and octoroon boys the fathers had charge of were dusky-colored and had kinky ringlets. It was not until William Higgins was well toward completing his studies that he realized he'd been culled from the larger group to join the smaller knot of boys who, like him, were pale and could pass into the white world.

When William Higgins left the Jesuit seminary in which he'd grown and been educated, he left as a white man. Higgins's reflections and recollections of bondage came with him to the vestibule of the Holy Trinity Church rectory though. These pictures offered him no comfort, only contemptible familiarity.

He pondered the woman before him. What travail had brought her?

"Were you sent to me, Mother?"

"They commended me to you. A man that calls himself Daniel Joshua commended me."

"Yes, Mother, I understand."

"We've a girl that will be sold. She's come up to auction. She was one who escaped and has been caught and returned. They are going to sell her south! We want you to go forth and buy her. We want her to be free with this money," Annie said. She patted her breasts so that Reverend Higgins knew her to be honest and wise enough to keep her money where it could be defended with her own life.

"I have money enough if the price doesn't go too high," she assured the priest.

"This girl is your girl, Mother?"

"No, sir. She is a good girl known to me," Annie replied stoutly.

"Why, Mother? Why are you so determined to buy the freedom of this one? What is she to you that you do so?" Higgins asked. He did not doubt Annie's goodness or her compassion.

But the priest wanted to know why Annie had chosen to assist this bondwoman. He reached to grasp Annie's sleeve and she started.

"She drop in my pocket like a chestnut. I don't waste nothin'. I want her back," she answered.

"Whence comes the money, Mother?" Higgins eyed her levelly and inquired. It would behoove him to know.

"It has been earned, sir," she replied. "My son and I and my daughter have saved this money. This poor one is a chestnut we have known."

Yes, Mary's eyes were like those nuts. They were a simple, quiet dark brown that compelled the looker. They were not as dark as her skin, but were warm and round and took up most of the pool of her whites.

"Have no fear, Mother. I will accomplish the task. I will set myself to it. We will get your girl safe," the priest said with amiable conviction, as if answering her misgivings. His rosy red cheeks got redder still with his fervor.

Annie identified Mary to Higgins and he assured her that he had performed this onerous duty many times in the past and that he knew what methods ensured success.

As their meeting ended, Reverend Higgins suggested strongly that Mary would be safest if she left the area altogether after her freedom. Washington would not necessarily be a safe place for her. Annie said that her family was prepared to take Mary in.

Annie, who had never truly relaxed on the rectory chair to which she had been steered, rose up quickly to signal an end to the business and an eagerness to be gone. Reverend Higgins followed her to the door and closed it behind her.

◆◆

William Higgins never knew when he stopped being his father's slave and became a free man. He doubted his dreams would ever truly be free of the tormentor even though he'd exorcised him from waking hours. Higgins removed his cassock and put on the suit of clothes of a gentleman farmer. He had found that such a costume was the best guard against being identified as an abolitionist. A great many auctioneers would not allow on their premises one who was buying slaves in order to free them.

He patted his breast pocket for the purse containing Annie and Gabriel's money. It was secure and he prayed that the amount was sufficient to the purpose.

"Please, God, see to it the devil turns his attention in another direction today," he pleaded. Jesus would call him doubting Thomas were he to meet William Higgins, for the priest was so often asking for certain proof of God's agency. In fact, Higgins made an odd, questioning cleric. Today he fretted that he might be unable to purchase the girl and was chagrined that he would not be able to purchase any others. He knew that when he entered the pens and then the auction area, he would see many to pull against his heart. He must keep his mind upon only the good he was sent to do.

The auction house that offered Mary and others for sale was located across the Potomac from Georgetown in Alexandria — in the state of Virginia. Higgins completed his costume of a gentleman plantation owner by hiring a carriage to take him across the river to Whittier & Sons.

That which he had eaten to sustain the enterprise welled up in his throat on approaching the auction house. Odors off the fetid riverbank, whiskey smells, animal effluvium, and the fear and neglect of the wretched humans being offered for sale swirled around Higgins's nostrils as he dismounted the carriage in front of the auction barn. The test of his prayers would be the success with which he managed to complete his task and return to Holy Trinity with body and soul intact. He put the handkerchief that was part of his disguise at his nostrils.

The gathering crowd eagerly awaited a pitiful brace of sisters — advertised on handbills hawked about the auction house entrance by scruffy boys. When brought forth the two girls hiccuped as tears streamed down their cheeks. They were comely and well dressed, though their dresses were torn. Bidding for the sobbing girls opened high and was far out of the reach of the priest's compassionate funds.

In order to further excite the leering traders, the girls' bodices were torn to show them naked. Bidding soared. The trader who purchased the sisters handled them roughly and cared not a whit for their distress. William Higgins wondered if the two might not be free women stolen off the streets of a northern town as had happened to many colored. Their doelike faces indicated a complete lack of experience with the state to which they had been sent. Higgins could not hear the names they called each other, but burned an image of their features into his brain — one taller than the other by a hair, both nutmeg-colored, gone to a trader for sale to a fancy house — so that word of them could be passed along.

The woman known to Higgins as Mary, who was called Carrie, was presented some time after the hammer came down on the sisters. In contrast to the cowering girls, Mary had a wounded but rebellious look about her. She had been this way before today and her body was braced for the ill treatment that would follow the hammer fall. The auctioneer touted her as able to plow and carry loads. Mary's face was swollen and lacerated on the left and her shoulder was held hunched up to deflect blows to her head. The right side of her face was unmarked and she held it tight and still. The man who brought her to the stage turned her profile toward the bidding audience and raised his lantern for illumination. Mary's thin body was covered, though the dress she wore was crude and very soiled. Wisps of straw clung to her hair and she had no shoes upon her feet.

The bidding was light. Only a man making up a work gang to plant rice placed a bid for the thin woman. The planter dropped out at $125, shaking his head and muttering that the gal looked ill suited for specialized farmwork. The hammer fell to William Higgins at $150.

Upon completing the business and leaving the auction barn, William Higgins shoved Mary into the back of the carriage he had hired. The driver balked at allowing a slave woman to ride inside his rig. He insisted that she be tied outside of the carriage and made to run alongside. But Higgins objected to this and tossed a coin to grease the man's palm and shut his mouth.

Once seated inside Higgins removed the leather thongs that bound Mary's wrists. He turned his profile toward her rather than look at her head-on, hoping his propriety would put her at ease somewhat. He would need to explain the plan, what her new status was, what her friends had done for her.

Crouched in a corner of the hansom, Mary waited for a blow rather than an explanation from the man who'd purchased her. She kept her eyes low and could make no judgment on his character. She only waited upon her fate as one who knows that what comes next will be painful.

"Your friends Gabriel and Annie have given the money to buy you out. They learned that you would be sold here through the grapevine that the freed people have. Annie is the one who brought the money to me and who bade me buy your freedom as I have done for others. I will take you to a place of shelter and you can see your friends and thank them. Then you can do as you wish in freedom — once again, Mary," the man said kindly, smoothly. She started at hearing herself called Mary, as also her heart had leaped up at the sound of Gabriel's name. "Mary" was the name her benefactors had conferred on her when last they were her saviors. The tale this man told must be true. Higgins's words had a great deal of ceremony about them. It was a bene-diction — this freedom, this name.

Mary caught her breath and didn't know what to reply. Far back along the path of this travail, she had given up saying prayers. But if one glimmer of prayer had floated up to God, it had been that Gabriel might come to her aid. And he and his mother had done so. Perhaps she might once again be hopeful.

Annie and Gabriel allowed themselves exuberance as they rushed to Holy Trinity's cellar to be reunited with Mary. Annie entered the room and moved swiftly to clutch the young woman. She grasped Mary's shoulders and pressed her to her own chest. The older woman cluck-clucked with her tongue in a satisfied, maternal sound. Mary was startled some by the greeting. She was touched and somewhat incredulous at the fervor of her friends. After a few moments, Mary also smiled. In a sudden display of affection she brought Annie's hand to her lips and kissed it in gratitude.

Gabriel and Daniel Joshua stood behind Annie. They were

timid in their greeting of Mary and only thrust their hands toward her. She shook the hands of both men and kept her eyes modestly lidded.

Mary elected to stay in the church rather than to go that evening with her friends. She was uncertain of herself since she was free. Fearful of offending her benefactors by spurning their offer of a lodging place, she was, however, shy of "putting in" with them. Reverend William Higgins said she need not go anywhere with anyone since now she was free. And he stressed that she was not even beholden to her dear friends because they had given the money to facilitate her freedom. They had not bought her life. "No child of God can be owned by another," he said earnestly, with passion rising from collarbone to hairline. "You are ransomed."

Thirteen

MARY STIRRED HER stumps the next morning at the time a few birds outside began caviling about the merits of the dawn. She had not slept this first night of true freedom, but lay on her pallet in the cellar awaiting a cue to get up and go about.

"God bless you and God bless the new day of freedom!" Reverend Higgins said, and placed a chaste hand on Mary's shoulder when she came into the rectory kitchen.

The tawny-complexioned cook with hair and eyes of matching orange-brown color observed Mary dispassionately. She was accustomed to keeping her opinions behind a noncommittal mask. Reverend Higgins was made a bit uncomfortable by her, but had never found her a quisling to the cause of abolition. For her part, Winnie Wareham had figured out Higgins's passing secret and had sealed her lips on the subject. Wareham had helped herself to freedom some years prior and would not thwart another. Her lips dipped briefly to a welcoming smile. She prepared a plate of food like Mary had never known and seated the girl to the table at which she took her own meals.

The bright morning after her first night as a free woman —
when she'd filled her belly to bursting — Mary set out for the
back of Gabriel's tailoring shop. Reverend Higgins pressed a
basket upon her and bade her look as if hurrying about business
as she walked through the streets. Also anxious that Mary reach
her destination, Winnie Wareham wrapped a shawl about,
picked up a basket, and led the young woman down the cob-
bled thoroughfares to the shop. Winnie salted her directions
with warnings about the dangers of coming and going and the
two nimbly dodged expectorating men who gave no care to
soiling the skirts of colored women.

"You on your own to earn your bread. You got a job of work,
Mary?" Annie quizzed the young woman.

Mary set in to helping Annie as soon as she put her feet inside the workroom door. She hoisted a bucket and went out to
fill it with water for Annie's laundering. She returned and put
the water to heat.

Mary swiped her wet hands on her clothes and grasped Annie's hands as she'd done the evening before. She brought them
to her lips. "Give me a job of work so I can pay you for my freedom, ma'am." She turned Annie's palms upward and kissed her
hands as if they were her own mam's.

Mary's appearance had changed some. She'd left them as a
bald-headed figure shrouded in layers of men's clothes. Now
her face bore knots and welts around the eyes and on her cheeks.
It was saddening for Gabriel to consider what had been done to
Mary. Evidence was clear on her face, though she tucked her
chin next to her shoulder to shield it from view. He recognized
that much more could not be seen. But the woman they had
known was still recognizable. For that — and the luck of being
reunited — he was grateful.

Despite her weakness, Mary pitched in to work with vigor. Gabriel and Annie expressed concern for her strength, but she refused to be coddled. No matter what was said about who owed what and why, Mary was determined to repay her purchase.

It came down to the ease of coming and going and of attachments. Mary felt, despite Reverend Higgins's words, that she was beholden to the Coatses for their caring. Reasons like these were not bad ones to have for joining with them. She was no ways certain that things would continue thus, but a good beginning had been made and there was often good fortune in a new beginning.

"There is plenty of work here doing laundry and more if you can get it," Annie said as she slapped her washboard.

Between them it was decided that Mary would work a portion of each day for Annie Coats in repayment of the funds advanced for her freedom. The swift, tidy agreement was satisfactory to all.

Mary negotiated a room in the basement of the rectory of Holy Trinity. In return for the accommodation, she contracted to work for Reverend Higgins to swab floors and haul water. She so impressed the young priest with cautious, self-effacing industry that he left her to the tasks without worry.

New Mary quickly fell to the habit of rising well before light of day, fetching water for her own ablutions and tending to these. Then she put water to heat for Winnie Wareham, who rose after first light and was glad of the help. When this was done and the rectory floors were given their daily swab and polish, Mary set out for the shop of Annie and Gabriel Coats.

Trepidation, as well as chill, caused Mary to walk swiftly through the Georgetown streets to reach her destination. Congress abroad in daytime was new, exciting, and full of the potential for danger. There were agents about who would pull her from the thoroughfare and question her right to proceed. Some might challenge her outright. She must be sharply aware.

The temptation to lollygag was strong. For the streets through which Mary passed on the circuit between the rectory and the tailoring shop were chockablock with storefronts and were congested with all variety of people. On her previous circuit through Georgetown, she had not had the luxury of looking long at things in broad daylight.

In the back room of Ridley & Ridley Fine Tailoring, Annie was the driving hen on top and Gabriel was the rooster by way of his skills and the importance of his work. Annie took charge to organize those tasks auxiliary to Gabriel's tailoring duties. The others, Ellen and Delia and Mary, were the hens around the yard. Ellen, though she had status as a skilled hand, was nevertheless under the supervision of her mother. Eager to please her benefactors, Mary slipped onto the lowest rung for work as a general helpmeet in the Coatses' workroom.

Until being sold away from the place of her birth, Mary, called Carrie then, had been one of a field gang of women. She worked mostly with a hoe and had not the experience of much needlework except to mend a tear or sew a button. She'd not paid much attention to her hands heretofore. Now when she compared them to the swift, dexterous hands of Annie and Ellen, she considered them to be lacking.

In these winter months, there was the job of keeping the workroom warm and adequately lit as the light of day faded early. Throughout the first days Mary occupied herself with these tasks and with looking after the girl, Delia. She also accepted cooking duties to free more skilled hands for the myriad spinning, weaving, knitting, sewing, dyeing, washing, and ironing.

Mary shrunk into the lesser light near the stove, turned her back to the center of the room, and disappeared into the happy click-clacking from Annie and Ellen at Gabriel's entrance into the room when he left his duties in the front. Mary was unused to the company of men and his arrival caused a shift and change in her. This room became where Gabriel dominated, for Annie quickly relinquished it to him, swiftly going to his side to take his coat and brush it. She applied her stiff clothes brush to the collar and shoulders of her son whenever he made to leave the back room and return to face his clients in the front of the store, and she bade him remove his coat upon entering and sitting to his dinner. This worshipful ritual became a familiar preamble to meals in the back room.

Gabriel accepted Annie's attention — and Ellen's — with grace, yet high expectations. Brother Gabriel was never given the lesser biscuit or the lesser portion in this precinct.

Standing to the attention of the generally well-dressed clientele of Ridley & Ridley Fine Tailoring, Gabriel himself wore clothes that showed much wear yet were spotlessly clean. In this he again followed the advice of his mentor, Mr. Abraham Pearl. Pearl always insisted that the tailor must be clean but appear to be more concerned with his client's cut than his own. The tailor must not seem dapper, but neat and circumspect. Gabriel learned that this admonition served a colored tailor even more so. An important part of dressing well up to a standard for the well-to-do gentleman was knowing that not all could afford to do so. The customer must see the coarseness or plainness of one to appreciate the fineness of another.

"See the difference, sir," Pearl would say, draping a cloth over his wrist and comparing his own garment to the better wool. And so Gabriel developed a facade of quiet pleasantness to assure his clients of efficiency and competence. His quiet manner gave the proper odor of self-effacement and was well used.

It pleased Annie to make a fuss over her son and she was fortunate that his nature was without arrogance, for her attentions might have swollen his head. Mary thought that Gabriel would find it difficult to acquire a wife as solicitous as his mother. Only occasionally was his embarrassment at Annie's attention apparent.

Fourteen

DELIA SAT AT her mother's feet and mostly stared about the room at the adults. After a short time of trading glances, Mary urged the baby to toddle toward her. "We two babes in the woods. But we can learn, can't we?" she singsonged to the child under the notice of the other women. Mary grasped Delia's chin and cupped it in her hand, showed the babe a needle and illustrated her newly found technique at threading. Mary caught Ellen's eye. Sometimes dour when she worked, Ellen shared an open smile with Mary over the babe's head. Ellen's only vanity had become this tawny child and she was pleased that Mary cared for her.

The bright jot of the last several rainy days was that Annie's rain barrels would flow over. Because she was a superstitious one she'd stationed these two large barrels on the west side of the building. For she would not have the overhang of a willow tree above this captured water. It was well known that rain rinsed off a weeper would be nothing but hexing water and a certain danger. The patter onto the porch roof and the plopping into the barrels had become an annoying hum in these recent wet days.

Ellen, typically hard at a specific project requiring fierce skill and stamina, spoke little in the kitchen precinct, for she gave way to her mother and brother. As there was but one spinning wheel, Annie and Ellen alternated this duty to spell each other from weaving and knitting. At other times, Ellen placed herself next to Mary with Delia at her feet.

As sewing on buttons was easily mastered, Mary was seated next to Gabriel in the early part of the evening and assigned to attaching buttons to newly completed suits and shirts. Gabriel enjoyed this closeness to Mary. For him, the room was humming in contentment.

"If you would hold the button thusly, the work will go faster, Mary," Gabriel said, noticing her hesitation and the bobble of her hands. He leaned toward her and pulled on a button she struggled with. He controlled the temptation to pluck at her fingers as Abraham Pearl had done to correct him. It was often plucking that educated the fingers.

Annie coughed and shot a glance at Gabriel. Puzzled, he said no more to Mary. What had he done that was wrong?

When Mary rose to fetch water and finish nursing the evening meal, Gabriel regretted that these tasks took her from his side. Her face was pleasant and sympathetic in the low light. The outward signs of her ordeal were fading and her face seemed relaxed now. She did not yet smile at Gabriel. He felt that she was simply nervous about the propriety of it. And she had gotten away from the habit of pleasantries throughout her travail. But the relaxation and the bright sparkling of her steady eyes signaled him her interest and affection when she turned her face toward him.

Mary's obligations to prepare the meal dissolved into Annie's authority to serve it — to give it to her chickens. Annie did keep the duty and privilege of filling their plates and circulating the room to fill their cups with coffee.

"Nanny, come and sit and eat your supper. We need your salt," Gabriel cajoled her.

"Brother Gabriel, don't add to my weariness." She brushed him aside and did as she pleased about the room.

At conclusion of the evening repast, Mary cleared the dishes and lit lamps for the night work. It would be fine to see her as captain of her own, Gabriel thought.

Preparation for the night work was undertaken quietly — surreptitiously, as notice had to be taken of the comings and goings of Aaron Ridley. The group paused intermittently in their industry and listened for sounds of his leave-taking. Happily, Aaron Ridley's yearnings hurried him out of the shop. As soon as he departed all fell to the night work.

This night Daniel Joshua arrived shaking water from his clothes at the threshold. His face was not the usual cheerful moon. His forehead was knotted and his eyes dark and humorless. The dreary downpour outside the door drew the companions closer together. Mary pulled her stool close up to the table, hunched her shoulders, and drew her shawl tighter about. Her knees brushed Ellen's under the table and Ellen's skirt warmed Mary's and vice versa. The fire popped and sizzled as droplets hit it from leaks in the ceiling, for the several days' rain made the house soggy — pots and pans were distributed throughout to catch drips.

"Has come a cry to help a group from across the river. On a night like this!" Daniel fumed about the urgent message that had come to him.

"They are holed up in a pocket on the Virginia side," he explained. "They waitin' on a boat and boatman to give them a crossing."

His thoughts were plagued with worry regarding the group waiting on the Virginia bank of the Potomac. He'd been told that an indomitable woman had left a failing plantation with ten youngsters shortly after their master and his sons had fallen beneath a bout of croup. She'd heard the mistress talk of selling off the hands — children included — to a dealer. Then Mistress planned to move to be near her sister. The bondwoman had baked corn cakes, wrapped up the gang of youngsters, and taken off. Word came that the group was stranded at the river's edge — unable to light a fire and three of them with rasping lungs. They would need to move tonight, and Daniel was bound to row across and bring them to the Washington shore.

More than nuisance, it was going to be dangerous to get them to the shore in Georgetown this night. The water was choppy, the air chilly, and there was still driving rain. There wasn't a strong hand amongst them — them being a woman and some babes — to help with rowing and navigating. The woman had brought the children so many miles, but Daniel couldn't be sure she had much strength left to her. And could be she'd lost her wits. Worse come to it, could any of these travelers swim the river? Daniel doubted it. Daniel Joshua said out plainly that he needed a body to hoist a lantern on signal.

Mary bolted up from her seat at the table, tossing a lapful of buttons to the floor and striking her elbow in the bargain. "Mercy," she cried out. She scrambled to retrieve the buttons. Surprising the others, Mary presented herself and agreed to help without hesitation. She so wanted to be put to service helping other folks to get free. It was the opportunity she was looking for. Daniel Joshua accepted her and said she was to wait on the shore and raise a lantern upon his signal to guide the wayfarers crossing the Potomac River.

It did swell Mary some to be thought dependable enough for the task. Gabriel was surprised at her eagerness to sign on to this extravagant plan of Daniel Joshua's. He would have preferred a bit more reticence on Mary's part. But, he reflected, it was no concern of his what this girl did.

Except that it was a concern for them. The situation for freed people was precarious. And the race's women were judged immoral if they walked abroad at night. Gabriel preferred that a woman seen coming and going with his mother and sister be circumspect. His fervent hope was that Mary would continue to come and go with the Coats family.

Daniel Joshua's body was tense and active. He would not even sit to a cup of coffee. The usually talkative man only stared into a cup held in his hand as he paced about.

As surely as Mary felt Daniel Joshua's confidence in her she could feel Gabriel's fearful concern. She knew he wasn't afraid of doing the task himself, but was frightened for her to do it. Gabriel wasn't a soft man in case a person thought it because he sat down at his work. In fact, she had learned there was a lack of softness in him toward folks that was disturbing.

The women roused up. Annie began assembling blankets and thrust a folded stack at Daniel. Mary hoisted a pile of blankets given her by Annie for the comfort of the wet and chilled wayfarers. She stacked these and carried them upon the top of her head.

Annie turned to rummaging her larder for substance for a

pot of soup to feed the travelers. Ellen, too, put away her lap work, set her tot to bed on a pallet near the stove, and helped her mother prepare to feed the hungry.

"Go on and fill up my bucket, Brother Gabriel," Annie commanded. It hardly matters how grown you get do your mam take you down a couple of pegs. Gabriel put away his lap work for the night and covered his head to go out for the water.

The dark, wet night was cruel and unforgiving. The Lord who controls the wind and the waves and the drops of rain that fall, does, on such nights, seem to forget the birds of the air and the lilies of the field and the poor travelers stranded in bondage on the far riverbank. Gabriel was annoyed more than angry. The rain, the hardheaded women, and Daniel Joshua — who was certainly on the way to putting a noose around all of their necks — had spoiled his ease.

When Gabriel returned to the kitchen, his mother had already killed one of the rabbits she fatted for the pot and was skinning it and cutting it. The small hare would soon be lost amongst onions and vegetables. Ellen was hacking at carrots and turnips, and the sight of her ungraceful chopping and rough cutting made you wonder at the fineness of her needlework and fear for her fingers.

Mary ran to keep up with Daniel. He walked swiftly and dodged and darted in his customary surreptitious way as she labored behind.

Daniel turned down Water Street and disappeared momentarily into a doorway. Mary kept her head and proceeded in the direction she'd been led. As she passed close to a shed, Daniel reached out and touched her sleeve. She started but did not squeal. He fell in with her, holding a long-handled and bladed tool for chopping at underbrush. He also had a lantern that was not lit. Daniel again went ahead, and as they approached the river's edge at the end of the cobblestone pathways, he started to chop a path out of the tangled growth.

Mary grabbed at tangles in Daniel's wake and tried to yank them out of their beds.

"Save your spit for dying of thirst, girl. You'll need your strength to hoist the lantern. Follow in my stepping," Daniel said. He'd begun to doubt that he had the right helpmeet. Maybe this gal wouldn't be strong enough to raise the signal. But it was too late to change the plan now. He wished he had a cracker or some such now that they had walked so far and fast. He hadn't studied his stomach because of all the excitement. Now his belly was acting up.

"Here you are," Mary said to him, offering a piece of Annie Coats's hard tack. Daniel figured the girl had heard his stomach. He had better eat something or the patrollers would hear it, too.

The two squatted at the riverbank and chewed quietly on their crackers. The sky was uniformly black and the river was dark black as well. Rain continued to pelt. Upon finishing his cracker, Daniel put together a bit of shelter from trash planks and instructed Mary on where, when, and how she must raise the lantern. He walked off and left her under her roof.

From out of a bed of fallen branches and leaves some yards farther along the path, Daniel brought out his small boat. He couldn't tell until he saw the folks how many trips it would take to bring the whole group to the shore in Georgetown.

When Daniel reached the Virginia shore, the woman who had brought the gang off the place stood at the river's edge. Her hands were entwined and resting upon the top of her head.

She appeared peculiar. A body would think she had need to entangle herself to keep control of her arms. Perhaps the children were an unruly bunch. Daniel looked beyond the woman and saw that the children were huddled together and were as still as a mound.

Though she had packed some supplies to carry the group forward, they were at the end of these stores. The children were bitten by all manner of insect and by the rats that inhabited the low areas near the river's edge. The salve they had brought was all used up and the wounds had gone to fester.

Daniel feared they all would be discovered. The coughing could be heard a distance. Their intermittent rasps had guided him to them. As the two smallest children had succumbed to their fevers and their stomachs, there were eight children and the woman remaining.

"The babes lay unburied, sir," the woman said of the two small figures lying on a shelf of rock.

"Eh ah," Daniel said with a long sigh. "God rest their souls and let us go forth, ma'am." He put four of the smallest children in the boat and piled several blankets over them. One boy standing in the shadow of the woman looked big enough and able enough to row in a pinch or bail water. Daniel called him forth to come along and the boy hesitated as if reluctant to leave the woman's side. "I need his body to balance the skiff. I'll come back for the rest of you all," Daniel explained to the woman, who clutched the boy. She squeezed his arms and pushed him toward the boat.

"Make that he come back for us, you hear," she said to the boy.

The boy stepped into the boat. Daniel took his place and pushed the boat away from shore with an oar. The boy sat looking fearfully at the woman on the bank. They had been close to separation so many times since they'd left the plantation and even before — it was the fear of separating from this particular young one after so many had been lost to her that had prompted the woman to run off. She had taken all of the other children because without her there was no help for them. Throughout it all, her boy clung so to her that this small separation now felt horribly cruel.

The boy stayed upright and held bravely to the sides of the boat. The small babes lying along the bottom did not stir much. They quietly rolled side to side with the movement of the boat. The bigger boy's eyes were fearful milk-white saucers with tiny raisins at the center. But in the rocking back and forth he also made no noise. Daniel rowed until they reached a spot that was more than halfway to the Georgetown shore. At this point, Daniel Joshua blew upon a horn that was the signal to Mary to raise her lantern.

In response Mary removed the cover from her lantern and hoisted it. The comforting beacon shone out from the shore. It oriented Daniel in the dark blackness and he rowed toward it.

Daniel pulled his oars from the water, climbed over the side of the craft, and waded with it into shore. Mary greeted the travelers at the water's edge while keeping her lamplight low.

The nervous boy jumped from the boat and helped to get the young ones ashore. All the while, his attention was focused on the far shore from where they'd crossed. Daniel Joshua stood looking back across the water also, mentally putting himself through the paces of the next trip across. His arms and shoulders were weary from rowing. But he intended to cross again before resting them finally. Any rest would make his complaining arms believe they were finished for the night.

As Daniel Joshua waded out with the craft, the boy looked as if he would go back with him. Daniel stopped him. "I'ma fetch your mama and the young'uns. Better not weigh down the boat." He climbed back aboard and rowed away from shore.

Daniel got the remaining children and the woman into the small craft with some difficulty. The woman didn't want to leave the two dead children without burial. Her superstitions plagued her suddenly and she begged him to lay the bodies low. Daniel pleaded there was no time and nothing to accomplish the task. He had not brought a shovel and to dig them down and row the wayfarers across was asking too much.

The second crossing was unremarkable except that it was punctuated by a great many exclamations of "Lord!" "Oh, Lord!" and "Lord, have mercy!" The woman looked back to the shore she was leaving and moaned a great deal.

Daniel once again got out of the boat to guide it into the narrow pocket where Mary signaled and where she and the other children waited. Mary gently restrained the boy from wading out to his mother, and Daniel cautioned the woman not to jump into the water and soak her skirts in her eagerness to reach the boy. "Ma'am, you do well to keep dry and keep these other children dry."

She acquiesced and held back until reunited on land. After she had covered the boy with kisses she started to moan about the bodies of the two dead babes being left upon the spit of rocks. She agitated about auguries and kept up her talk even after they had reached where Gabriel, Ellen, and Annie waited with broth and blankets.

Both the woman and her son looked like hoot owls in the church basement with their heavily ringed eyes and vigilant stares. The wayfarers were to be secreted in the church's cellar until they could rest and be taken farther on toward north. Ellen and Annie fed victuals and ministered to the needs of the coughing children. Ellen took each babe in turn, wiped their faces, and rubbed them with oleo.

Callie of Greenbough Plantation is how the woman was called. She came into the basement at Holy Trinity Church and rocked and moaned about the two babes left behind. The children who had been rescued lay about the floor swathed in blankets and nearly as still as corpses. Only Callie and her watchful son remained awake after the first few moments of stew and warm shelter. Greenbough Callie, shocked to be alive after what she had come through, shivered, as did the boy, though they were covered with many blankets.

Gabriel's decision to row out in the darkness with resolve to recover the bodies of the dead babies surprised Annie, Ellen, and Mary. He sat with his head lowered nearly to his knees and fiddled with the contents of his pockets as he listened to Callie. His attention was hard on the woman's tale and her moaning. Suddenly he rose and prepared clothing to go out into the still constant rain.

"Brother Daniel, take me to the boat and I will row across for these babes," he said. He said as well that it would be best not to leave evidence that runaways had perched there. The bones the carrion birds leave would tell a tale.

"Will you raise the lantern for me, Mary?"

"I will take you to the boat. Brother Daniel can warm his feet," Mary replied boldly. She was surprised at Gabriel. She'd not known this man to plunge into action. But she had not known him long.

"Take care not to be seen and taken in, good Gabriel," Daniel called after them.

"If they take me, you will know where to come to get me, good friend Daniel," Gabriel replied.

Gabriel rowed out across the river to the place where the group had waited. The rain had abated and the sky was moving toward light. The bodies were easily found. The two small corpses looked like stone statues reclining. They were cold and the flesh was stiffly unyielding. Gabriel covered the small cold bodies with the quilt Sewing Annie had given him for the purpose. It was funerary — being dark-colored and containing a patch of the cloth of a dress belonging to old Knitting Annie. This patch was one that turned up in several of the quilts in the family's accumulation. It had the power of repetition and was the most they could do for these dead children. He rowed back with the tiny bodies wrapped in one package.

Guided by Mary's lamp, Gabriel came near the shore, waded in the shallows, and dragged the boat in.

"The dead must be buried, Mary. 'Tis just one of the things that must be done. We cannot leave the little babes to make food for carrion. We people got to cling together like it matters that we do. It's the only way we make it," he said. The intensity of the look in his eye commanded her.

As everyone knows it is unlucky for a childless woman to dress a body, Gabriel did not pass the bundle to Mary.

"Mary, go and tell Nanny that I'll bury the babies in the plot that some of our women have secured. It will suit them," he said, and walked away.

Gabriel returned home and stood in the yard, washing himself before entering. He removed his shirt to lave his arms and chest despite the cold air and the chilled water in the bucket.

Mary stood at the back door. She had waited. For the first time the sunrise would catch her here in the Coats house.

Mary looked at Gabriel's clothes and saw evidence of his digging the graves for the two babies. She considered the wisdom of digging the ground in the wet like this night. All this he had done in the dark and suspicious time — at great risk to himself. He was a puzzling man, she thought, and enjoyed watching him wash.

On the day that followed the daring boat rescue of the woman and her chickens, Daniel Joshua's chest filled with rasping noises and his body shook with chill. Once again Annie shuffled pallets and put Daniel Joshua to sick bed in her own sleeping place. For three days the man was laid low and fed broth to restore his energy. Aromatic clouds were circulated about his head and he was urged to breathe deeply.

Fifteen

"THERE COMES A time when a man wants to take comfort, Brother," Annie said, standing next to the outhouse. Between them existed no shame so that she spoke frankly to her son, who was taking his constitutional behind the door. Annie had followed Gabriel because she had not been able to cadge a private word with him in some days. She'd maneuvered to trap him in the toilet.

Gabriel was not a pacer, but had been visibly restless and ill at ease for some days. Because Annie had followed him to the toilet before, she knew his bowels were not locked against him, causing this discontent. He ruminated upon another concern.

"This girl is a good matchup. She's comfort and contentment, Brother. No doubt she's the tonic you need," Annie said with tittering. "Listen to your nanny, boy. It's a constant woman you're wanting."

"Go off, Nanny," Gabriel said, fingering his penis. "Leave me be."

"'Tis not good to worry, Brother. 'Tis not good to worry yourself either, Brother," she said, and laughed heartily. "Lay a claim before someone else," she finished, and quit the backyard.

Comfort and *contentment* — they were the words he would have used. Gabriel sat upon his seat behind the crescent moon and ruminated on Mary. He mused that she did give outward signs of feeling comfort and contentment around him and his family. Dare he hope that she would accept to stay with them and put in with them formally? Dash! Would she take him? Would she have him to husband?

Gabriel knew it to be felt amongst colored people and the main folk that only a married woman was a decent woman. A married woman would not get cutting sidelong glances from the strivers and the big colored around town.

'Tis an abundance of loose gals and disease among the other man's women in this town. Gabriel chuckled and hitched his pants and recalled the experiences of Mr. Pearl and himself. They had been circumspect, but they had occasionally availed themselves of the courtesies of the town's public women.

On the following evening, through a plan, Gabriel and Mary were left alone in the kitchen. Sewing Annie put down her work and went to her room soon after the evening meal. Ellen had also bid good night, scooped up her child, and been gone like a wisp. Had she gone to the outhouse? Had she gone to put Delia down to rest? The wonder crossed Mary's mind and she came to the realization that the women had left the spinning wheel idle purposely. It was an odd occurrence for the busy room and it set her on guard.

Gabriel alone remained and Mary had a sudden, timid fear that Gabriel had sent the other women away to press a hurtful purpose.

"I won't subjugate you, Mary. I won't take anything away from you that the Lord gave you," Gabriel said solemnly. "I would like for you to marry with me. It would be the most proper thing for us to do." As if to emphasize the rightness of his proposal, Gabriel sat very straight in his chair and placed his hands flatly on the table before him. This inactivity was arresting, for rarely in a day were his hands so completely still.

"Oh," Mary answered, as if the words brought forth an explosion from her. It was a dignified request. It was a sensible, practical arrangement for a woman who was free but unanchored. It was the stuff of a dream, but frightening in its implication.

"We might join at the church and take a ceremony there. We might have a fest, Mary." Gabriel spoke to buoy her and persuade her and to cover the long silence. "Nanny and Ellen will make a party."

Mary cried tears in answer and Gabriel was flummoxed. He was not so very vain, but he had thought she would say yes quickly. There was unease and there was more puzzling silence. Mary said her piece bluntly.

"I want you, sir, but I am afraid to disappoint you. You are wanting a good wife and I am no longer good. You are wanting a good girl to marry."

Gabriel went silent in his turn and became deeply engaged in thought.

"Mary, we want no girl here. I need a wife. You are a fitting cog and we will have you stay. It is best for us to marry if you stay. We will settle a home. I feel there is goodness in you . . . and more. I would have that goodness and more with me." Gabriel placed his hands to either side of Mary's chin and cupped her face. She shied from his hands, then could not break from him. "Mary, will you be joined with me?"

Mary mused on Gabriel's strong grip. Again and again she would discover that his hands were capable of many gifts: gentle, firm, authoritative, demanding, playful.

It was not lack of pure wanting but the fear of the measure that caused Mary to hesitate. She signaled her agreement by shaking her head, moving within his grip, and when Gabriel released her chin in joy, she said, "Yes, sir. I will."

Mary knew instantly that Annie, too, was in favor of this bond, for Gabriel would not have spoken if she opposed this. Annie was the chief here, but she was good and used all of them well.

Gabriel rose and walked about the room, coming to stand behind Mary's chair again. He exhaled near her ear. It was a rarity for Mary to feel the warm breath of someone upon the back of her neck — someone who did not mean to pummel her. Gabriel stared at her nape as he stood over her and spoke. His breath hitched and Mary felt the change in his warm exhalation. She was a tad startled by the man's cultivated gentleness.

His closeness unsettled her. Mary worried about her body. Her skin was not smooth and unmarked. There was upon her the perfect impression of Phillip Ruane's brand. Would Gabriel laugh at the sight of it or would he be sickened?

Mary sought out Ellen when the news of the nuptials was spread. She pulled her into the small store room at back of the workroom and bared her thigh and asked Ellen to gauge the ugliness.

Annie broke in on them. "I've seen you," she said to Mary. "I know you beneath your clothes, girl. There's nothing upon you that my son cannot bear. He is good and quiet, but he is not weak. I know his wants, girl. And you need a tree to stand under. Better a one like him." Annie paused. "You don't know much of men, though you have had your bad experience. Ellen don't either. Follow behind me. When they nature gets up, they don't start to quibble about what a'not perfectly pretty. It don't worry 'em." This declaration set the young women laughing and put a lid on the talk of ugliness.

Mary's curiosity about Gabriel's body was not chaste. What was beneath the scrupulously mended clothing that Gabriel wore? Had his life at Ridley Plantation been as soft and uncomplicated as it seemed? Did he hide Jonathan Ridley's fury on his back? Or had he escaped this ignominy? And if his front and back were smooth, where lay his scars?

Out of Annie's earshot, Mary did ask Ellen what was upon Gabriel's back that she had ever seen.

"'Tis as smooth as a babe's. Gabriel is Master's favorite dumb dog so he has no marks for disobedience," she said. At this, Ellen unlaced her own blouse and loosed it to fall at her waist. "I am marked, too, you see." She showed Mary a welt that ranged from beneath her left breast down her side and stopped at her waist. "The once I pushed him off he made me pay with his belt. Master Ridley was not pleased with me. Do not tell Nanny . . . or Gabriel," she implored.

"No," Mary replied. "I will never."

"I will make a nightgown for your bedding that will be so complex with tatting that Gabriel will be lost counting knots and will not notice much else until his nature is well up." Ellen laughed at her own humor and pulled Mary into it, and the two laced each other up with much giggling. They concluded with a kiss to seal their pact.

Gabriel Coats and New Mary stood up to declare themselves before the minister at Mount Zion Church on January 11, 1855.

A good-sized group of congregants joined to witness the nuptials, for it meant something that this couple was stepping up to formalize themselves. The puffed-up Reverend Noah Zachary was fond of expounding this point of uprightness and chastity. "The ministers are pressing colored for to marry. It is a good thing to say our people are coming out of slavery and doing things in a formal way."

Education, temperance, economy and moral rectitude, these were the virtues expounded upon at Mount Zion and aspired to by the town's free colored. The churches of the town promoted these simple ideals heavily. Aspiration above all was the air the freed people breathed in the sanctuaries and the songs they sang. These uplifting virtues were the drink for their great thirst. And beneath this banner, Gabriel did begin with his wife.

Annie ceremoniously brought bedclothes to the room on the upper floor that the newly wedded would share. Again Annie rotated the sleeping arrangements in the house according to the proprieties. The married couple was to have the topmost room.

Annie placed the linens on a stool just inside the door to the small, irregularly shaped room. She freshened the bed with a mattress of good straw and grasses laced with some cinnamon shavings. A lovely cloud of aroma redolent of Christmas rose from the bedding as Annie fluffed and punched and arranged it. Several lit lamps embellished the warmth and disseminated the spicy smells. Mary, who shyly followed Annie up the stairs, took a place near the door. It embarrassed her, this fussing — especially as Annie grinned despite her pretense at solemnity.

The sheets to cover the mattress were as white as a whisper and the pillow shams were bordered with Annie's finest needlework. Pillow shams! Embroidered pillow shams! The pattern was a needlewoman's favorite — the Cornucopia. It was thought a charm for the most fortunate to have linen worked with the Cornucopia. Annie set store by the way she could execute the intricacies.

Annie made her way around the bed, pulling and tucking and clucking her tongue with satisfaction at the work. Mary came forward to take a lofted end of the sheet — to assist — but Annie waved her away and smoothed the sheet herself and tacked it with precision. It was a delight for Annie to look at the sleeping pallet with the starched and stiffened covering that was smooth and unwrinkled like butter. Ah! She enjoyed the feel of this cloth and was proud that Gabriel and his good wife could begin with each other on a bed of fluff and comfort.

When she was done with her bed-making, Annie smiled at her new daughter, who stood with her back at the wall. The girl was nervous, she knew. Annie might tell her that Gabriel was good and gentle, but he was a man. Mary would learn him for herself as every wife learns her husband. After earnest consideration Annie did say to Mary, "It is sensible to keep the man satisfied. It ties him to you. Do as he says to do. Learn him."

Early on that morning Annie had taken nervous Mary — leading her by the shoulders — to the front room of the shop. She had put the girl in front of the mirror and presented her own picture to herself. A reflex caused Mary to shy from the glass. Annie held her firm in front of it. She was made to see that she was lovely in the dress Annie and Ellen had made for the day. Ellen had festooned the white cloth her mother had sewed with lace trim of great intricacy. The dress suited Mary's form perfectly. She was all-over lovely. Ellen brought forth a secret undertaking — a shawl of knitted whorls that she'd worked unobserved by the others. The shawl was worn on the head and it draped across Mary's shoulders and the bodice of her dress.

Young Aaron Ridley good-naturedly insisted that Gabriel make a wedding suit for himself from the stock of the shop. He offered up a fine black wool cloth. Gabriel graciously allowed Ridley to take some measurements. It pleased the young white man to be, in some manner, a benefactor of the couple. Gabriel had already put aside the brushed beaver pelt that he would apply to the collar of his wedding suit. If it were not the most fancily decorated garment, it would be the best made of all the great many he had sewn.

"You will make a splash, Gabriel!" Aaron exclaimed. "There is no nigger to match you!"

Gabriel was excited by the upcoming wedding ceremony at Mount Zion. The colored tailor's rising popularity appealed to church members and they wanted him amongst them. Likewise, Gabriel wanted to claim a place in the town — among the free colored. There was a splash to be made for a tailor. For his big moment at the church, Gabriel skimmed his hair close and oiled his head with lard. He wanted no woolly stuff. His shirt collar was a perfection of white. It was high and starched stiff by the expert laundresses in his household. It framed his handsome, unmarked face — no mustache, no chin hairs, and no scar.

Winnie Wareham, who had become an especial friend to Annie and the Coatses, promised plentiful yeast rolls for the wedding party fare and brought them. Daniel Joshua, surprised at himself to be in such genteel surround, brought sacks of sugar and tubs of cream for the wedding coffee.

After the repast, the assembled sat and sang the familiar songs. There was a harmonica and an able woman called Sally

Matto to play upon it. There was a singing, warbling saw blade played by Nathaniel Booker that was the very blade his papa brought out of slavery. A tale told over and over was that Nathaniel's papa risked all to take the saw blade away from the cruel place they had been. He said it sounded like his own mama in the mournful way it sang. Hake and Jake Leonard played horns fashioned out of a dead bull. They had taken the end off the animal's horns so as to be able to blow on them. And they had made some very fine horns.

The saw blade rose in full-throated celebration and Nathaniel was tireless upon it. Hake and Jake followed him. The others came on their heels and singers joined in. Nathaniel played "I'll Fly Away" and they sat and sang many a verse of the song. And though it was a joyful celebration, there came a time the souls of the dear departed seemed present in the room. The people sat around and sang round after round of the popular pieces.

> *Hush, hush, somebody's calling my name*
> *You may call for your mother*
> *Mother can't do you no good.*
> *Crying, Oh, my Lord, what shall I do?*

After the ceremony, when the wedding couple had left the clutch of well-wishers at the church, the Coats family returned to their workroom hearth to boil coffee and eat fancy-made sweet biscuits. Annie, Ellen, and the babe, Delia, ate heartily and happily. They licked sweetness off their fingers and doubled the cream in their coffee before settling back to their needlework. The stunned married couple sat beside each other without speaking and little eating. Gabriel waved off cream and drank a dark cup of coffee and doused his biscuit in the cup. Mary took no repast.

"My mother is pleased for you," Aaron Ridley said ceremoniously, coming to stand in the doorway between the shop and the back room. Gabriel and the three women were startled and rose. Each one upset a task on the table and the general confusion caused Aaron to retreat a few steps.

"My mother and I give this to you . . . in celebration." He held out a large paper-wrapped, tied bundle, but was unsure of whom to hand it to. Annie came forth and took the bundle with a curtsy. She inclined her head and said for all, "We thank you, Master Aaron. We thank your mother heartily."

Aaron Ridley stood still longer, basking in their thanks with his arms dangling uneasily. "Well, ah," he said. "Gabriel . . ."

"Sir," Gabriel answered, proffering some new prestige to Aaron Ridley. He stood straight and expectantly.

"Well . . . be of good cheer," Aaron said with some surprise, and turned to exit.

"Sir, my wife and I and my mother and my sister do thank you and your saintly mother for your favor. It does mean much to us," Gabriel Coats, a man with a sprig of wedding flowers in his lapel, declared.

Aaron Ridley had obtained this gift, a quilt his mother had amongst her stores that was the lovely Double Wedding Ring, on one of his periodic trips to Ridley Plantation. It was a treasure. It did make Annie Coats become Sewing Annie at the sight of it — as it tumbled out of its paper and was unfolded. Her mentor, Knitting Annie, had worked upon this beautiful quilt from Ridley. This is one quilt her fingers had not been allowed to touch in her childhood. And now it had come to her son and his wife!

Gabriel, too, recognized this quilt. It was Nanny's teaching quilt. She drew it from the linen closet at Ridley again and again to show him the stitches and the placement of pieces. Whispering during Mistress's naptime, she would put his small fingers on it — having scrubbed them herself — to educate him, to teach his fingers the stitches of Knitting Annie, to show his eye the placement — the strict, unerring sense of the pieces of the pattern. There was a beautiful, meaningful account in the stitches, in the quilt. He remembered the lessons, though he'd never seen the old one Nanny talked of. The old one was dead before he had come, but she was his teacher. Nanny pressed him to this quilt and began his education in counting and piecing. She had risen in her own estimation when she had, upon the death of her mentor, become the caretaker of the quilt.

Young Knitting Annie had made it to be part of a dowry for a weakly related girl in the Ridley family. The mistress swapped it at the last moment and wrapped up a lesser quilt for the relative. Mistress and Knitting Annie savored this cover and used it as a teaching tool. Sewing Annie was trained up with it and Mistress's sister's girl learned lessons from it.

Annie opened the wedding package to show Gabriel. She unfolded the quilt by layers, gasping as it lay out revealed. Large tears fell from her eyes.

"Nanny, all has come home at last," Gabriel said to his emotional mother, well pleased that his wedding had brought this treasure back to her.

In the wake of Annie's ceremony in the bedchamber, Mary was sorely agitated. She had never contemplated a bed of linens and sweet-smelling grasses and a man. She felt her cheeks become hot with anxiety. She sat and continued to sit. Finally she recognized a silent exchange of pointed looks, and the other women left for their beds.

Mary then rose and went up the stairs to the husband and wife's loft. Gabriel dillydallied over his buttons and scissors and snuffing candles to give Mary time to take care of the womanly things. He did not want to scare her by following too quickly. Above it all: his dread of frightening her.

Gabriel did mount the stairs in lighthearted anticipation. His member was excited, but lost its nerve on the climb in the cold air. Ellen had been mistaken. Gabriel did not eye the gown Mary wore at all. His eyes did not come to a single spot when he entered the room. He lifted the gown over Mary's head where she sat shivering upon the bed and tucked her beneath the covers to keep her from chill. Loathe to crease or muss the counterpane, Mary remained still in the bed. Gabriel put out the candles, removed his clothes, and slipped under the cover.

He stretched stiffly beside her. He felt an obligation, but his member lay still. It had always come up merrily, but was stalled now and his stomach was uneasy. Upon a sigh — Gabriel did not know if it was his own or Mary's — his member did rise. He pulled her body beneath his, parted her legs, and put himself in before his prowess flagged.

AARON RIDLEY CREDITED a changed demeanor in Gabriel immediately following the wedding. He put the change down to the contentment of wedded constancy. "Any mutt is constant with a bitch at his own hearth." Aaron repeated to his uncle the accepted alehouse wisdom. So it clearly was with Gabriel. But Aaron Ridley told his uncle that he suspected there was more. He regretted his wedding day camaraderie. Gabriel, still obsequious enough for even the most demanding customer, was lately more upright in his bearing. He'd developed the habit of trading looks and expressing unsolicited opinions in a way that smelled of arrogance.

"The air I must share with these beasts is noxious, Uncle. Will you permit me to take rooms, sir?" Aaron pleaded. He held that his position in the tailoring business had necessarily changed after the manumission agreement between his uncle and Gabriel. But in view that the concern still would be called Ridley & Ridley, Jonathan Ridley insisted that his nephew continue as manager. He considered that he had made an investment and that a hefty percentage of the concern's profit was to be paid to the Ridley family. As realists, neither Jonathan Ridley, Aaron Ridley, nor Gabriel Coats believed the business could flourish without the management of a white gentleman. They would lose an advantage with tradesmen and suppliers and their profits could not stand. As well there were a great many of their customers who wouldn't abide a colored man about their person no matter their respect for his skill.

In a lather from his appeals, Aaron did win from his uncle the concession that he might move away from the shop and establish living quarters under another roof.

Like pegs set well down, there was stoutness and resolve about the Coatses now. They had the freedom! The value of it seemed illusory — to be mostly in Gabriel's chest, for he felt only a small difference in his daily going about in the city. The temper of the town was to put restrictions on the movements of the free people — to question their intelligence, their honesty, their decency. The Coatses, as they were now widely and generally known, could all come and go as free people. Yet still they were liable to be set upon by hooligans or constables or soldiers.

Gabriel started to cultivate as clients — and this was the main cog of his plans — the growing number of successful free Blacks in Georgetown. Word of his exceptional talents with cloth and his willingness to accommodate certain customers in their own homes circulated on the vine of household help and among the congregation at Mount Zion.

"If opportunities for free men were fair available," Daniel said, "a colored woman could play the lady."

Disgruntled when the talk between Gabriel and Daniel went to pontificating about "our" women sitting at home, Annie sucked her teeth loudly. "Huh! Never the chance for a colored woman to sit on her duff if the house would all eat," Annie said.

Indeed a colored woman was fair vulnerable as she went about the streets of Georgetown and Washington in her work. The white matrons who employed colored women in laundry and general char favored women they deemed upstanding, not loose, unattached adventurers. And so they judged appearance and behavior very sharply. A laundress seen in the wrong circumstance might lose her customers.

To cart laundry about the town was to rub shoulders with a flock of other colored women. The great many bordellos generated a copious amount of washing and ironing work. Some of the more elite of these establishments advertised themselves upon the feature of clean sheets and lace and accoutrements. There were syndicates of laundry women helping one another in handling customers and covering when a member could not keep up her customers because of a babe or other hardship. Syndicate members also helped others to a turn at the public water hydrants and elbowed out strangers. These arrangements kept newcomers from pinching off good customers.

Mary hoped to move into one of the syndicates and looked to Mount Zion Church. A good many of the free laundresses were members of this house of worship. Mary's religious instructions had been stingy. She had a few precepts and some few stories from the Bible. The formality of the Mount Zion worship had its draw for her. Gabriel little shared her blossoming interest in the church, but he did not impede her, for he recognized the practical wisdom of it.

The Ladies of Olives of Mount Zion Church, a syndicate of

colored laundresses, became the linchpin of Mary Coats's aspirations.

Annie was skeptical of the fees and the joinings. Mary, who had become a true daughter and claimed a daughter's affection from Annie, had some trouble to convince her. Though Gabriel had agreed to the expenditure, Annie claimed the right of supervision over funds earned at the laundry trade. She stood upon the idea that the barrels had been her insistence and she had shaped the concern.

"Nanny," Gabriel conceded with his hand raised behind his ear, "you are the captain."

Mary cajoled that the few coins in membership fee for the Ladies of Olives were put to good use and in no danger — for there was burial and bodily protection attached. Paid-up members of all of the laundry syndicates could expect to go abroad unhindered by other laundresses and with confidence that upstarts would not encroach. Encroachment, stealing, overturning baskets, dumping baskets, spitting on baskets of clean laundry — an unfortunate fashion among the coarser element that lived in the alleys — or attacking the person of a syndicate member would result in a severe pummeling by the committee of sinewy, hardened, and salty women who exacted and kept the syndicate's bond. Mary had suffered such on a day when she boldly approached a bordello on Congress Street. She had naively inquired at the back door, received dirty sheets, and left exuberantly. Set upon at the mouth of the alley behind High Street, she was warned and pounded by the fists of the committee.

These vigilantes took no turn in the broader pond of attackers of colored women. They were circumspect as a rule, though they once came to the aid of a member set upon by rapists in an alley. On that occasion, the committee of the Ladies of Olives administered a thrashing soundly and thoroughly, massing themselves with wooden mallets and pails. As the miscreants in this case were Blacks, there was no response from the authorities. In a similar incident with a white man, the woman caught standing over him with a bloody mallet was summarily taken to Maryland and hanged by the neck in a barn.

That Mary had been married at Mount Zion Church and was the wife of the very excellent colored tailor was a great boon to her membership in the Ladies of Olives. Unmarried Ellen was quite shy of joining. She was loath to test the women's Christian tolerance of her, but became a member upon the wings of Gabriel and Mary's luster.

As accounts must be kept, permits maintained, and price guidelines strictly adhered to, the Ladies of Olives required literacy and promoted it. Mary's education — her learning to read and to figure — occupied her and kept her in the kitchen until late at night. Annie had urged her to attend lessons at Mount Zion Church with Ellen and Delia. Gabriel sniffed at Mary's industry, though, for he was jealous to lose her company for an evening. But he did consider her improvement and was pleased.

Considerable numbers of alley-dwelling Irishwomen sought work as laundresses and there were syndicates amongst them, too. A good deal of fighting and competition existed between the Irish groups, such that they had little energy to fight with the colored women. The occasional incident was generally resolved tit for tat.

Seventeen

THOUGH HAPPY IN her marriage — being tucked within the family — Mary was skittish with Gabriel. And though roundly pleased, Gabriel was tentative with Mary. He worried to be clumsy or cruel unintended. She could not prevent herself from starting at his touch, however gently he approached her.

Mary felt herself marked and unfit. And because nothing in Gabriel's manner had convinced her otherwise, the new husband and wife shrank from each other.

Respectful, dutiful attention was what a wife owed to her husband, Mary thought. A decent and pleasant man like Gabriel, who was watchful against offense and slow to express anger or vexation, was a good partner.

Gabriel was not used to taking and wrenching congress from women nor did he know the art of pretty persuasion. His experience of the pleasures of women was from several brief, instructional visits to a Georgetown bawdy house with Abraham Pearl. Pearl had felt he was obliged to guide Gabriel in discharging the pent-up energies of youth lest a virtuous girl would suffer for it.

"Boy, do not let your manly humors build up to a pitch. Release them in one way or another," he'd instructed. Slave or no, Gabriel was a youth come to manhood under Pearl's influence.

On several occasions, the two shared the time of a bawd who would have them both. She was not averse to well-formed-up Gabriel nor to moneyed Pearl. She enthusiastically and quickly worked them and had her pay. She was not reticent or skittish.

Gabriel was uncertain of how to press his cause with Mary. He did long for her. He was not so much a child that he did not recognize himself. Ought he to grab her and assert a husband's privilege? The thought of this made him shamefaced and spoiled the feelings of excitement that arose when he came close to her. She was a small, lovely woman. It pained him to sense her heart flutter with trepidation when he approached her, even as his blood cavorted in her presence.

Daniel Joshua, who himself appreciated the womanly attributes of Mary, counseled Gabriel to be forceful. "She will thank you after all is done," he said.

"I would not frighten or vex her," Gabriel answered.

"Aye, but this one is no new penny." Daniel bluntly delivered the observation. "You cannot spoil her."

"Do you insult my wife, Brother Daniel?" Gabriel bristled at Daniel's free tongue and prepared to make a physical challenge.

"Make her your wife, boy. Then defend her honor," the rough man countered, and turned his back.

Gabriel's own ways of gentle persistence and watchfulness were best after all. Upon an evening when the moon was not quite bright, Gabriel watched as Mary spun at her wheel. This wheel was fast becoming her especial skill after washing and ironing. It was a mundane task, he thought, but suited to her even, plodding temper.

The light from the candles got low and still she worked — bent forward a bit. Gabriel rose and stood close to her, wordlessly reached toward the spinning wheel, and began to turn fibers between his own fingers. Mary drew in her breath and focused her eyes upon her work. She kept her face at right angle to her husband and inhaled the air between them.

Gabriel left her side briefly. As he moved from the circle lit by the two candles he disappeared in the room. Mary sighed regretfully. She wanted him near, though she was confused about what to do with his nearness.

Annie and Ellen were vanished from the room. These women were happy to come and go upon Gabriel's whim. *'Tis always Gabriel's wants that are first here,* Mary mused. How lucky he was such a pleasure to his women!

Gabriel returned to her side with a stool and placed it near her. He sat on the stool and touched the spun yarn — gazing upon it. He said nothing and touched only the wool. After a few moments of stroking the yarn that was spun, Gabriel took up knitting upon some socks and sat silently next to Mary for the rest of the length of the candles. The tongue of his finished work fell between his legs, and when the last candle faltered, the two rose together and put up. Gabriel drew aside the small window curtain and let in the moonlight to illumine their final chores. They ascended to their bed in the upper room.

The next evening, Annie and Ellen again rose early from their evening work and went to their beds.

Surprised at the uncommon quiet of the house, Mary continued at her spinning. Gabriel again placed a small stool near Mary's stool and sat beside her at the wheel. Now and again he would touch the spun yarn between his sensitive fingers.

"It is silken, Mary," he said, and rubbed a hank of yarn near his nose and eyes. He laughed and sneezed, and she was taken aback by his boyishness. He pulled closer and whispered praise for the fineness of her work.

When sufficient yarn was spun, the two rolled it into balls. Gabriel faced Mary on his stool and gave his hands to the task. She rolled balls and scooted closer toward him. Her heart lightened as the work progressed and she regretted the end would come.

Gabriel dandled the made balls like babes upon the knee. They were without chaff or small sticks or anything to make them scratch or chafe. He smiled at Mary, though she did not raise her eyes to his. Playfully he touched one of the fluffy yarn balls to the shy side of her face. It was puzzling that since their marriage Mary never turned her face full toward him. She had become reticent where she had once been somewhat bold. The feel of the yarn and the childlike abandon with which he touched her cheek caused Mary to smile broadly and face him. For a few minutes they relished the softness of the yarn. Finally, they grasped each other's hands.

The two gained the floor to their loft hand in hand held tightly. Mary tended the candles that they'd brought and busied herself about the room with her back turned from Gabriel. She heard the collar of his shirt as he unbuttoned it. Her trepidation was then replaced by some other feeling — some delicious anticipation. She heard his collar scrape at his neck as it was brought off. She turned and saw Gabriel's soft skin slowly revealed for the first and was affected with a possessive passion.

The delicious one was hers if only she would accept him! His tobacco-brown color continued evenly to his shoulders with the hard knots upon them. The whole front of his body was covered over with unbroken, smooth skin and dotted with kinky hair that disappeared below his waistband. His arms were sinuously lovely. He pulled her to his naked front and held her face against the bristling hair of his chest.

Mary did not remove her shift. Gabriel gained her beneath the cloth and the pleasure of the congress was doubled by friction and the swathe. Dim candlelight colluded to reduce their shyness and build their comfort.

Watching her sleeping husband, Mary studied his body in the moonlight entering the room. Gabriel's soft face was a liquid brown tonic in sparse light. His sleepy lips were slack. His shoulders, arms, fingers — these muscles always so busy, always so tensely, authoritatively, expertly moving, were now still, flaccid. His soft penis lay resting in a warm nest against his thigh. All over his body was resting and replenishing itself. Wind puffs burst from him — from mouth and anus — and the air was full of the smelly, benign things that had been inside of him.

Gabriel's body odor was sharp, incisive, manly, though not hot and frothy like the sweat of a man who labors out-of-doors. His was not the reek of manure or of the thoroughfare. Gabriel's skin smell was coupled with soap and the starch of his clean shirts. This was Gabriel. The aromas of the chests and drawers and the stacks of Annie's laundry and her quilted stores and yarns were the aroma of Gabriel and the Coatses. These scents were palliative. They were now the familiar, the comfortable — that which Mary associated with happiness.

The newly discovered joy that Gabriel and Mary felt with

each other was evident in the new smiles between them and their affectionate touching. Annie disapproved slightly of so much for others to look at. It was plain in her eyes when she caught them at it. But when she retired, she did not always sleep. She sat on the side of her bed, muffled the noises of her needles by moving them slowly in her lap, and listened to the sounds overhead. She had brought this all together and felt satisfied and was shameless in her vicarious enjoyment of it. Perhaps they would bring her a babe before long.

Eighteen

IT OCCURRED TO Daniel Joshua that his feet had gotten stuck in Annie Coats's kitchen. Since his experience of the croup, a keen sense of companionship had developed between Annie and himself. Most every evening he was found in her orbit and other companions had missed him.

"With happiness and respect, Miss Annie, I will take up with you by the book," Daniel Joshua intoned solemnly, standing close to her on the lip of the back porch. Annie brushed past him and put her rain barrel between them so as to discourage him from touching her.

Since it was the spring, the herring in nearby Rock Creek were swimming practically right into the frying pans. Folks said that a herring loses his mind in springtime with swimming every which way, and it was said that a man will do the same.

Earlier in the day, Daniel had taken Annie's elbow and gone to the shallows in Rock Creek. The two used a net to catch a herring dinner. Fish thus caught in this season were considered sublime and were eaten greedily and taken as a treat. The popularity of the herring run among the colored had given the colored settlement near the creek its name, Herring Hill. Some women caught up the jumping and wriggling fish in their skirts, and there was a good deal of ankle and calf visible to the eye at netting time.

"Let's us get a place to us — off from the others," Daniel suggested to Annie. "I can keep you as good as your son. I can fix up a pretty place for you. I can keep you in a respectful way."

Annie was shocked — instantly struck with panic to consider this. To leave Son Gabriel's house? She had always planned to work alongside him and build with him.

"Daniel, I cannot go from Gabriel. Gabriel is like my right arm. I would stay attached to him. I work beside him. Would you drive a wedge between us?"

"Are you stuck on your son, Annie?" Daniel Joshua inquired carefully. He'd taken a lot upon himself in asking her this, but claimed the right to do so.

"I am stuck to build the business with him. He can rise high with my hand to help him," Annie answered without even a small sting of pique.

"You covet the boy? He has a wife. He has the one you gave him. You ought not to want him, too."

Annie thought to sling the pail of fish on Daniel, but was loath to waste them. They were still wriggling and fresh and she was peeved that this conversation was delaying their preparation. She stood and imagined that the front of her dress had grown cold, wet, and that Daniel had slung her with fish guts. His words had the smell of rotten. And it had just come to her what he had meant all along. Had she never considered the way she held to Gabriel — how it did look? It was just that the footloose, orphaned Daniel Joshua had never known a hearth like hers and Gabriel's. It was in Daniel — dumb Daniel — that the shame lived.

"You're a pretty cork, Annie. I can do you some good," Daniel put it explicitly. "For that I'm better than your son."

"Aye, I'm sure you can," Annie declared. "But I will stay in this house — his house."

"Ah, you want me for a fancy and him for a husband! Shame on you, Annie Coats. I'll keep my shoes elsewhere, girl," he said without rancor.

"I want a constant son and a sometimes man," Annie said. "It's what I want plain and simple. And I know I got it," she added confidently.

Daniel Joshua was wounded. He would maintain his secret abode. Annie could not make a house dog of him. But when his pride was salved he intended to come back to put his shoes beneath her bed.

"Such as that is a nasty sight, whore!" a woman barked at Ellen. Her voice was low-pitched and gravelly, but thrown out loudly across the expanse of the street. Drawn up to a height that was a head above Ellen's, she stood in a yard on Prospect Street across from the open lot.

Ellen and Delia, their identical shoddy skirts stirring in the soft rustling morning wind, were pulling up wild dandelions with two slung bags over their shoulders. At the sound of the woman's coarse voice, Ellen raised her head from contemplation of her gatherings. The woman's eyes were upon her and Delia. Most pointedly it was Delia that the woman gazed upon with harsh expression. She pointed her finger menacingly. Startled, Ellen cocked her head to one side and curtsied with subservience. The sudden movement caused her to drop the greens.

She pushed Delia's head down and tugged the kerchief to hide all the girl's red ringlets. The two remained bowed and frightened — altogether stilled. They shielded their faces as if deflecting blows until the woman turned from watching them. Both retrieved their spilled and trampled dandies under duress of the woman's stare.

Ellen's body shook long after the woman had gone. She pulled her shawl up around her neck and impatiently shoved Delia through the streets to return to the back of the store. When they arrived in their yard Ellen's heart was throbbing and she was at pains to catch a breath. Delia, too, panted like a small animal, for she had been marched ahead of her mother and her strength was taxed.

"Say nothing, girl!" Ellen commanded, and twisted up the girl's locks. Gabriel was so nervous of their coming and going through the streets that he often cautioned her irritably. Ellen knew that Delia's looks and circumstance were the source of his ill ease. And Nanny was uneasy, too. If her mother found out about this trouble on the street, then Gabriel would soon know. She tied a kerchief so tight around Delia's head as to cause the child neuralgia.

Nineteen

"AYE, GABRIEL, WILL you drink coffee?" Mary said aloud, and rose as her husband entered the workroom. All eyes were upon her as she rushed to remove his coat from him for a brushing. It had taken a long time for Mary to overcome her shyness and use her husband's name aloud before the others. But when she said it now there was a smug and knowing flavor to it. This new possessiveness did delight Gabriel. Her industry and her womb gently tugged him away from his mother's authority.

When the baby girl came, there was a shift of affection in the entire household and the new babe became the center of all. Gabriel gave over to exuberance and fascination and playfulness in such a way that those who knew him were greatly amazed.

"Mother, is this baby needing something?" he so frequently asked his wife that she rebuked him good-naturedly.

"Gabriel, she has all the riches in the world. She has your heart in her pocket," Mary said.

"Aye, Brother Gabriel. This love has the flavor of ribbons and geegaws. It is not good to spoil a girl. We will not be able to have her hand in work if you indulge her so," Annie chastised him, with some waggling of her fingers at the child. "Na, Na, Na, Namama," she urged the girl to say. In the pleasant breeze of Mary and Gabriel's joy, Annie indulged herself, hoisting the baby above her head and twirling around and singing a nonsense song.

"Mother, has this girl got small, beautiful hands? She will be good for fine work like Sis Ellen," Gabriel effused dreamily.

Mary, consumed with caring for her babe, was brushed glowing with her husband's excitement.

Gabriel renewed his passion for Mary and his dreams and he had them both as a tonic each late evening. So if the two parents were not equal up to now, they had become so with the birth of Naomi. Now they had the pull of sharing this child — each possessing the other within the child — each able to love the other with caring for her.

Before the first-year anniversary of Naomi another was coming. The parents, used to unmitigated happiness, were lighthearted in waiting for this one. She came and was named Ruth because Mary and Gabriel had become members of Mount Zion Church and had become enamored of Bible tales. This sealed a bond between the sisters.

"Another clutch of pretty fingers!" the father exclaimed, and examined the new girl's tiny hands. Gabriel betrayed no disappointment that the children were girls. Instead he did the unthinkable: he wished upon them. He made plans for their future.

"Brother Gabriel, restrain yourself," Annie said at the birth of the third girl, Pearl. "We have proof of you. You are a man and we know it now. We are at some pains to take care of all of these children."

"Nanny! I'm no child in your lap!" Gabriel cried out indignantly.

"Aye. Like I said, we have proof of it!"

"Nanny!" He chafed at her advice and her teasing.

"There are other women abroad the town, Brother," his mother said knowingly.

Young Delia gave up her place to the newer children. The grown women shifted and adjusted duties to fuss over the small ones. Even Ellen was lost in the finger-waggling and cooing attentions on the babies. She accepted her rung in the household. She clung to a place in her brother's orbit, for he was ever in the orbit of their mother. She clung to Delia as her only jot of happiness. And now she applied herself to helping care for Gabriel's children.

But a blister rose between the siblings. Gabriel was no longer warm toward Delia, nor even inclined to credit her presence. He no longer spoke to the girl except to upbraid her or give her a command.

Delia became silent when her uncle came into the room. Mary and Annie and Ellen danced around, attentive to his requests. Turned full face toward the stove, she greeted him with a slight genuflection then turned back to her chores. Unless he spoke to her, she did not speak. Long ago Delia had stopped trying to match her mother's needlework. Nothing she had ever produced even reached a level with Ellen's mistakes. And nothing that she had fashioned with her seemingly unlikely hands had ever reached the standard of her uncle's expectations. The Coatses' expectations were high. They wanted the beautifully cultivated precision needlework that came from Annie. Mary accomplished it by dent of great industry. Ellen was simply endowed with it. But Delia struggled.

"She does not have your blood, Nanny. She is no girl for fine work like your children are," Gabriel said to his mother.

The girl heard him because she was well used to standing in the dark pantry listening to them. They were secretive and complicit, Gabriel and Annie. She felt justified in ghosting on them. They were the planners who decided upon all between them. And it was they who dragged the others — Mary and Ellen and her and the babies — along. It was good to know their plans. Delia stretched herself across some sacks of rice and heard all.

"She has the blood of her mother. She has the tempers and infirmity of this woman. She has the blood of a slattern and this may, in some way, be catching. It is possible that a bad girl can infect others while they are yet still good. They might catch a fever of wantonness from her and be pulled away from what is proper."

Delia had always known there was a stain upon her even though she did not know its character.

When she saw the affection that was lavished on the infants, Naomi, Ruth, and Pearl, she realized fully what she had lacked. This unrestrained love, this affection that was unashamed, was gleefully given to the babies — was so much more than the shadow of care that the Coatses had for her. Not Ellen! Only Ellen, her mother, had truly cared for her.

Mary was quietly sympathetic to Delia's aches. She knew the girl was not included in Gabriel's grand plans.

"Gabriel, she has given you no cause to condemn her. You must not turn her out," Mary said. "She is a pure girl and we must keep her so. We will keep her at work with us." Through familiarity Mary had grown sure of herself with Gabriel and did not hesitate to appeal to him.

"We need her help, Brother Gabriel. You have given us so many babes to keep. We'll need the girl's help," Annie said finally and flatly. She did not love this gal either and was nervous, too. But Ellen must be considered and they needed her hands as well.

Gabriel's instinct was to argue with his mother and with Mary. But he governed himself. The women were softhearted and shortsighted and would be proved wrong, he was certain. They pushed him forth to be leader of their band, but sometimes they were in league against him!

"Would you send Ellen's babe away from her now that you have these of your own?" Annie spoke quietly.

Ellen came to wonder in what position to place herself. She felt Gabriel's wife was her ally, but she was wary of coming between a pair in love as Mary and Gabriel were. Gabriel! She had always owned his affection. Ellen and Gabriel had not fought over their mother's breasts. He had delighted in her when she was a babe and continued his love for her as they grew up. But now he was becoming harsh and uncompromising! Ellen agreed with her daughter. It was good to know his plans — their plans, her brother's and her mother's. The umbrella of their lookout was in some measure uncomfortable for Ellen. She, too, floated to the periphery and realized the two were most attentive to their own interests.

Twenty

THE WOMAN WHO came into the tailoring shop was a surprise to Gabriel's eyes and nose as soon as they fixed on her. The fragrance that wafted through the doorway ahead of her was indelicate. It was a foul amalgam of crude perfume and careless hygiene. Gabriel's eyes darted up and down as he tried to take her in quickly. He had developed the habit of squinting — a mannerism that allowed him to make more complete observations of white people than a colored person was generally allowed to get because of the custom that a colored person, bond or free, must cast his eyes to the floor in the face of a white person. It was impertinent in the extreme and punishable to be caught gazing into the eyes of whites. Though Gabriel's work put him in daily, intimate contact with white persons, he was extremely careful to glance at them indirectly. His squinting manner was a cover that afforded him a chance for a good look.

Right away Gabriel realized this woman was not his typical customer. Her clothing was cheaply made. The velvet material was coarse and in need of a stiff and vigorous brushing. And the woman did not wear it well. The length and weight of the fabric of the skirt overwhelmed her and she hoisted it rudely with each step. The faded yellow dress flattered neither her red hair nor the eyes that were the gray of a dreary day. Further, Gabriel opined that the high red color on her cheeks was a result of more drink than was the general habit for a lady.

Gabriel wrestled mentally with how he must act toward her. She was no lady — white or not. She looked like a cheap woman and he didn't want her to be seen in the shop.

The nine years since Katharine Logan had given birth to her babe had been harsh to her. She had endured cruelty from Mrs. Clover for one more year after the birth. Then she had left the Warren Plantation in the company of a cock of the walk called Joe Bungate. The two had begun a romantic liaison that took them to several states deeper south. By the time they reached New Orleans, Katharine's illusions were as an overturned pot of gruel — all spilled out and going cold.

In the course of her traveling love affair with Joe, Katharine had revealed the secret of her bastard child. Ever on the lookout for a moneymaking scheme, Joe Bungate had hatched a plan to lay claim to the child. He figured the two could make a profit by selling her to a house that had want of a young mulatto car-rottop.

"Let her grow up as a char in a bawdy house. We can hire her. 'Tis how my mam began. Let her take her place when the time comes. We can take the profit in setting her up so well," Joe said convincingly. This was an old game and a sure one.

Joe Bungate's scheme seemed reasonable to Katharine. No fledgling maternal feelings had survived her vilification by Mrs. Clover and Mistress Warren. In a turn of luck for Bungate and Katharine, they had managed to locate the old midwife, Meander. Put off the Warren place for getting old, Meander had made her way to Washington, too. And for the price of a bag of flour, a sack of cornmeal, and a block of salt, Meander had agreed to speak up to Master Ridley about the birth of Katharine's child.

"A gal that calls herself Ellen has a babe that ain't her own. I want to know where that gal is," Katharine said to the colored man who'd asked her what help she needed.

Gabriel's ears received such a shock at her words that his startled reaction was visible. He fought to regain control of his facial expressions.

"Missus, I do not understand," he said most unctuously, surprising even himself.

Katharine caught his fleeting look and was indignant at the disrespect she read in Gabriel's face. She continued sharply, "I know this gal is your sister. I have word that she is living here. Call her out. I want to talk to her about the babe."

"I would ask you what business you have with Ellen. She's hard at her work and cannot come forth, Missus," Gabriel said.

"She is keeping a girl that belongs to me. She took her and I'm here to get her back. I will take it up with Mr. Jonathan Ridley himself. I have the midwife that knows the story. You tell Ellen that Katharine Logan says to give up the child!" She built up to her forceful conclusion, gaining courage and conviction as she spoke.

Gabriel's reply was interrupted by Aaron Ridley's entrance into the shop. Walking through the door briskly, he stopped short at the sight of Katharine. There was a brief moment when he was unsure what lady had graced their shop and thought to spruce up to meet the challenge. But Aaron Ridley, too, made a quick assessment of the badly dressed woman and drew his conclusions.

He said to Katharine, "We have no need of a char. We have our own people. Good day, madam." Aaron Ridley then held open the door for Katharine to leave and the bell atop it jangled. Katharine was too flummoxed to do other than look at Gabriel briefly, curtsy with a jot of humility, and go back out into the street.

Gabriel bowed his head with a quick dip toward young Ridley and moved to the back workroom. He continued out the back door to the center of the yard after having signaled with an inclination of the head for Ellen to join him.

"The woman who bore your Delia and the midwife who witnessed intend bruiting about the child's birth in order for the mother to lay a claim to her. They are going to testify to their story to Jonathan Ridley — to get him to turn her over." Gabriel spoke plainly. Ellen stood still with her face locked in fearful grimace. The thing she had finally stopped being afraid to consider had happened. Nothing in her sphere of knowledge suggested that Katharine Logan would come to claim the child. Nine years! Nearly ten!

"Now she comes?" Ellen gasped. "After all of this time she would come to say this child is hers? Does she dare it?"

"I believe there is another behind the scenes in this. What will you do, Sister?" Gabriel's manner was stern, but not unkind.

"I saw her born and they gave her to me — to cover up the shame. I was not allowed to refuse her. I 'tend to keep her with me," Ellen declared.

Katharine, Meander, Mrs. Clover, and Mrs. Warren — all of them, with Ellen included — had come up and told a lie. All of them had been in it and they weren't going to go back on it now. A feeling got trembling inside of Ellen that said to stand against all and hold on to Delia.

"Brother, I am on this rock and will not budge off it," Ellen told Gabriel, and prepared herself to face his displeasure.

Gabriel only shook his head to say that he'd heard and understood. He turned back to the shop. Would that they could take advantage of this opportunity to be rid of her, he thought.

Neither Gabriel nor Aaron Ridley was impressed with the cut of Joe Bungate when he came to the tailoring shop with Katharine the next day. He had, at least, used a brush on his coat and trousers and had worked up some spit for his boots. He'd been attentive to the whiskers on his chin, too. Just after sunrise at the transient encampment west of town where the two were temporarily settled, Bungate had set up his mirror and lathered himself with no assistance from the slattern. She had been told with the back of his hand to keep her mouth closed and do as he instructed. She had cut him a wide berth and only looked at him slantwise.

Bungate waited with his foot hitched on a tree trunk, then entered the tailor shop when the window shades were raised.

"I call to see Mr. Jonathan Ridley!" he exclaimed with thumbs screwed in his lapels. Bungate's dull brown hair was slicked to his head and shined like the surface of his boots.

"I act for my uncle, sir. May I help you with a suit of clothes?" Aaron answered, with a polite expression that nevertheless could turn off quickly.

"I come to speak to Mr. Jonathan Ridley. Is he about, young sir?" Bungate chose to say.

"As I have said, sir, I act for my uncle in this precinct. Will you tell me your business?" The young man's manner deflated Joe Bungate a hair.

"I do not come about a suit of clothes, sir. So run your monkey off as 'tis a business for white men," he said, eyeing Gabriel.

"State your business, sir, or take your leave," Aaron Ridley answered, and gestured a nonchalant flourish with his hand. Gabriel held his tongue and the ground upon which he stood.

" 'Tis a slave child you're holding that is rightfully a babe belonging to a white woman name of Katharine Logan," Bungate began uncertainly. "This girl is no slave of Mr. Jonathan Ridley. She is the product of unfortunate circumstance. We would relieve you and your people of the responsibility of her." He bowed obsequiously, having sputtered out his tale.

"How is it that you know of these facts, sir?" Aaron Ridley inquired.

Bungate turned and spoke to the front windowpane as if actually he intended that passersby would read his lips. He did not look directly at either Ridley or Gabriel as he spoke.

"Aye, this Katharine yonder was but a helpless girl ravished by a beast of a slave on the Warren place. 'Twas used ill by the missus there and the head cook. These two gave the child to your Ellen," Bungate continued. "The child is being held illegal and away from its best interests." The rough-edged man turned from the window, though his eyes were trained on the floor at Aaron Ridley's feet and his thumbs again pulled at his lapels. He fidgeted and insisted that Katharine's claim was bolstered by evidence from the attending midwife, Meander. He finished his speech with a nervous demand: "Hand over the girl to her rightful circumstance."

Not the least moved by Katharine's travail as presented by Joe Bungate and having been accosted by Bungate on the way to his morning meal, Aaron Ridley was no longer polite.

"Sir, this is a questionable claim. However, I will inform my uncle of it." He felt early-morning irritability and was impatient for his coffee and biscuits. He told Bungate to return in a week's time to inquire.

"Return at the rear door, my good fellow. It is only gentlemen who enter at the front," Aaron pronounced with a recently cultivated hauteur.

Aaron did write to his uncle. He described the situation as presented and the parties involved. He included his own opinion that Joe Bungate and Katharine should be horsewhipped for their audacity.

The unpleasant facts came as some relief to Jonathan Ridley because they confirmed his own suspicions. He'd doubted the story that Ellen had borne the child. Her body had had no swelling left from carrying the babe and no striations on her flesh. Her breasts had still been meager and adolescent and she had brought with her from Warren a goat for baby milk. And no woman he'd ever known who'd borne a child was still so tight and narrow between her legs. It was this blissful tightness that was Ellen's only appeal, for she had been more sullen and unwilling when she had returned from Warren with the babe.

Ridley's azure eyes gamboled when he confronted Katharine and Joe in his rooms at the Whilton Hotel. He was merry, for he knew he could win his cause. Both of the miscreants were too nervous of soiling the opulent furnishings in the Whilton to accept a seat even if Jonathan Ridley had offered one. And Ridley certainly did not. He would not show them a fig of courtesy.

"I care not at all to whom the child is connected by birth. It returned with Ellen and has been fed and clothed by me. I am given the story that the child is hers and that is firm and firmly known. When it comes to proof, a slave midwife's word means nothing." In answer to their sputterings and protestations, Ridley raised his hand and commanded their silence.

"Quiet! You will go to jail for your part in this fraud, good fellow." He waved away Joe Bungate's protest.

Then Jonathan Ridley upbraided Katharine Logan for daring to suggest congress between a white woman and a black slave.

"If this ignominy had befallen you as you claim then, if you were decent, you should surely have killed yourself before the child was born. You are making a false claim!" Jonathan Ridley said. He raised his hand to the side of Katharine's head and struck her. The hard *thwack* landed on her temple as Ridley pronounced that she was lucky to be thought merely a liar. The blow was tepid in comparison with what she'd become accustomed to from Joe Bungate, but the vehemence of Ridley's power frightened her.

"She will stay with us, but 'tis in Master's pocket that she lives. 'Tis only we poor ones who feed her." Gabriel angrily interpreted the proceedings, which had been reported to him by Aaron Ridley. He had held on to a tick of hope that Ridley would concede the girl to Katharine, her natural mother. Ellen would be pained to separate from the girl — but pained for a while only, Gabriel thought. They would have been free of the bright nuisance of her!

Ellen stood facing Gabriel. Never frightened of him, she was always a head shorter and looking up into his eyes in adoration. "Brother, I love this child. She is my child. I . . ."

"Yes, Sister, but you have taken a clod of dirt that is disputed between dung beetles." Gabriel's words sliced at Ellen with an unaccustomed sharpness. "Sister, you should take a husband and bring your own children. This girl is an impediment to you."

"I will pay for her freedom. As agreed, I will save the money for her papers. Master Ridley has it that I will bring him the money. My heart obliges me, Gabriel," Ellen insisted. "We can offer him a good price and buy her freedom."

"Her looks are a premium upon her value. He will command a high price," Gabriel said.

"Nanny, will you take Delia's bond?" Ellen confronted her mother.

Annie sat quietly. For the first time she did not impede her children's voices and she did not intervene. Ellen pulled her into it. "Nanny, does this child mean nothing to you?"

"We are feeding her, Ellen. And she remains in Master Ridley's pocket. He is yet making plans upon her. You may depend on it. He will not sell her to you so cheaply as before."

"She does not eat so much. I will halve my own portion and give it to her if it will matter. I will take what remains for me and halve that and give it to you, Brother, to make your belly bigger!"

"Be quiet!" Gabriel commanded her. "They have given you something rude and ill fitting for yourself and you have tried mightily to make a whole of it. But what starts out badly ends badly!"

"Let her loose now, Ellen." Annie's words startled, though she patted her daughter's shoulders to make them seem kinder.

"Nanny, you wrong me. You bought a wife for Gabriel and you will not buy this daughter for me?" Pitiful tears poured down Ellen's face, unrestrained.

"Take hold of yourself, girl!" Annie grabbed Ellen's shoulders and shook her. "We bought Mary low. She was sick and broken and they sold her low. This child will sell high and Ridley smells it now. Mark me, it will not be long."

"I will cut her face. None will want her and he will sell her to me cheaply."

"Aye, that would bring her low. But it would not cancel her value to the ones who could use her. And perhaps you would ruin a chance for her," Gabriel put in. "If she is to the taste of the rich gentlemen, then let her to it. It would be a soft life." The women were silent in response. Neither guessed that Gabriel was so cruelly knowing.

Harsh as it was, though, Annie did feel the same as Gabriel. The girl didn't belong to them and carried a mark on her nature. She could likely come to trouble. And the trouble would be for them. Why not let Ridley's trading factors take her? And Gabriel had the point that Ellen might form up with a man and have babes of her own if this troublesome child were out of the way.

Annie had wishes for Ellen just as she had for Gabriel. They were more vague from the outset and had now become uncertain and filled with disappointment. But still she pictured a hardworking man and some natural children for her girl, as any mother would.

"Listen to Gabriel, girl," Annie said. "He knows a man's appetite better than you."

Gabriel felt the bristle in his mother's words, but he spoke coolly to finish the debate. "A man that wants a fancy with buttermilk skin and red hair might give Delia a life of some ease and rich belongings. This would be preferred to being taken up rudely and sold away. Consider the unpleasant possibilities, Sister. Even if you bought her you could not easily keep her free in this town. Do not be rash. With her clumsiness at fine work,

we cannot use her. She'll be hoisting buckets to make a living."
Gabriel pressed on to show Ellen the picture. "With a lovely
face, perhaps she will appeal to a gentleman of taste who will
treat her well. Let her stay pretty awhile," Gabriel said. He
grasped Ellen's two hands between his, lacing her fingers with
his own. "And let Master Ridley take her when he comes for
her. He is the one who will decide, Sister." He kissed Ellen's
fingers and sought to work her to his opinion with the appeals
of his affection for her.

Twenty-one

SEWING ANNIE COATS was no child to go to bed when told. She let Gabriel have the crowing, for a rooster needs the exercise. She only gave him this leave because he was an infrequent storm — not usually one to fuss and argue at the top of his lungs.

"Nanny, please go on to bed," Gabriel said. "Please take your leave and let me be. I have a sour stomach and I can't bear company this evening. I must wrestle with this, Nanny." He said "Nanny" in his way of customary childlike respect and affection and this adornment blunted the rudeness of his command. The others had left without word or questioning gesture. They accepted that he could command them.

Gabriel had ordered Mary to put the children up and go to bed. The tense atmosphere had chased Ellen from the room and Delia had followed her.

Sewing Annie remained behind the others and looked at her son to take his temperature. Tonight in the workroom his eyes betrayed a deep shock and fear. They lighted nowhere, only flickered from one hand to another, one wall to another. She could not engage his eyes — pin them and probe them for an explanation. He rubbed at a spot an inch from his heart. Annie feared he was stricken with an infirmity, but the rubbing caused a sound of crackling and she realized a paper was in his breast pocket. He rubbed it over and over.

Reluctant to engage displeasure, Annie went to her bed. Gabriel insisted he wanted to agitate the problem alone. Let him be alone then!

Annie sat on the edge of her bed. She listened to Gabriel scratching on paper and blowing breath with exasperation. She, too, agitated. She pitied her son for what she saw from the upstairs window. Back and forth he went to the outhouse. The evening's stew would not stay with him. It was Gabriel's point of greatest vulnerability — his gut. It was where his fear and anger lodged, but would not settle. A cup of tea might help him. But his puzzling annoyance was potent. She'd like to brew tea for him, but would not test his nerves or her own.

Annie sat upon the side of the bed wearing her night shift and shivering some despite the stiff, hot summer air. She rubbed absently at her breasts. She strained to hear Gabriel and she pictured his moves about the room below. Aye, tonight he was as impatient and disagreeable as the mother had ever known him.

Annie rose, dressed again, and wrapped herself in a shawl. She descended the stairs, went to the front of the shop without a lamp, and left by the door that opened onto the street. She did not come and go by this front door in daylight, but would claim some action this evening. She chafed at being barred from the kitchen workroom by Gabriel's fulminations.

There was a short, wide tree stump of little consequence a

few steps from the front door of the tailor shop and Annie sat on it musing. A dim light on a pole beside the stump illumined the night.

In summer, in Washington there is always the fear that the thick, humid air carries illness to swirl around the heads of residents. Little relief comes with the dimming of the sun, for the haze thus caused produces a miasma. Inside the constricting house at Bridge and High Streets, it was as though one was facedown in straw and suffocating.

Annie looked out from her seat on the prospect overlooking the riverbank, pulled on her bottom lip, and deposited a dollop of snuff there. She brushed the powder from her hands. She circulated the snuff in her saliva and considered the scene. She spat and watched. Around the clock, the thoroughfare was choked with outbound men and provisions. Inbound the wounded and the detritus flowed.

In step with soldiers and frightened bondpersons lumbering into town was a legion of rats. These were heartier than most of the folk walking, plodding, and trudging alongside them. They were fatter by far. They were as well mud-covered and dragged their long tails through copious puddles and piles of garbage. Stubborn vigilance had once driven them out of Georgetown. But they were returning now with a bit of impudence in their demeanor.

The rats sought transport on any moving thing crossing the river away from south. Likely they were escaping a frying pan in Virginia. Since the conflict had begun, much news of starvation in the Virginia countryside had reached Georgetown. Even rats were clever enough to know that there was now more edible garbage on this side of the Potomac River. Carts, wagons, and small skiffs hauled wounded soldiers back from the battles and rats rode on the litters to dine on gangrenous limbs. In barrels and haversacks they rode and leaped ashore as soon as they reached the shallows. They'd been seen riding atop bodies floating downstream. The nearly dead and deadly exhausted humans the rats accompanied into town had little spirit to fight with them. Some of the wounded were so grievously hurt and dosed with laudanum that a rat's bite went unnoticed. Escaping from Confederates emboldened the rodents or as likely had culled the weak from their numbers. And these rats, devouring rotted flesh, could be said to perform a good service as the number of soldiers' bodies brought from battle lines to the capital far exceeded the capabilities of the town's embalmers. This was true even though the number of morticians had swollen with the war.

Uphill the rats climbed from riverfront to the pavement at Bridge Street. Annie pondered the many in their limitless army she had fought and displaced in the root cellar of the tailor shop. She'd chased them with burning tapers and had clubbed, knifed, and hung pelts to drive them out — to gain the place for the family's own hiding and provisions. The rats had left the cellar to her superior vigilance, as there were places to go where people cared less. Now, when the women and Gabriel might need to go down for shelter and safety, the rats were returning to reclaim their precinct.

Cold winters on Ridley Plantation had been instructive. Annie thought to set a trap for these Georgetown rats. A time might come when they would be a delicacy.

Frogs, too, had become numerous. Frogs at the riverbank, an ordinarily sonorous group, now croaked at their loudest and most constant until the air was full of them. The sound was raucous and was rattling to the nerves and sounded as though a fear had taken hold of them. The practicing artillery fire, the stomping and marching that rumbled the ground, and the frantic, nervous people had frogs harrying the quiet. The hopping fools should have been more careful. Folks were reminded of "frogs in a pot, frogs in a pan" and the croakers' numbers would, in a few hungry weeks, be vastly reduced.

Sewing Annie had reckoned hundreds of the beasts before she realized for herself what she was doing. It was habitual to count — to tote up, to reckon things. It was the habit of her labor and her son's. In fact, she mused with some humor, between them all it was the thing they mostly did. The stitches and the buttons and the lengths and the bites and measures — the whole box and dice of it was their occupation.

There was this, too: the perfume of baking bread in the air wafting regularly as the wind blew it from the direction of the downtown. A seat high and dry was good to catch this aromatic bread breeze.

Ah! There was much competition for stinking up. The increasing number of horses in town perfumed the air considerably and the diseases that plagued them and numerous mules and the odor of gunpowder and machine oils and rotting flesh were bundled together. The smell of cook fires, too, pervaded and the smoke from these stung the eyes. Most any animal that had lived within the city's limits could be found on a spit above a fire now. In back of every thoroughfare, a crude encampment with crude cook fires was burning fetid fuel. The fainthearted could not stand it.

Annie surprised herself with longing for Ridley Plantation. She missed it. It was air she missed. Even on the most stifling days in the loom room at Ridley, the air was not so stagnant as here; rather, it was sweetly redolent of clover. It contained clarity of fragrance that the tumbled-up city of so many people could never have. Though Annie had been shut up at Ridley and not inclined to sit upon a stump and muse, she had been able to spread her lungs without coughing and peer through a window and see far afield. This exercise — encouraged by her mentor — had relaxed the sockets of her eyes, so strained in close work.

Annie's eyes got moist when they succumbed to tiredness. She mashed and rubbed them. Recollections of her years beside the old woman Knitting Annie came and buoyed her. This city living would have flummoxed the old one. She would have had no idea about this place. She had been a sweet old blossom and her resting back at Ridley is what kept the place dear to Annie.

Annie drew knitting needles from the slit pocket in her skirt. She pulled them from deep in the needlewoman's hiding sleeve — a place every daughter of Dorcas would cut into her clothing. She settled and ran her fingers along the needles before employing them. These were especial ones made of bone that had been given to her by Gabriel. He had saved aside to give her a fancy present of carved bone knitting needles. Ah, they were beautifully cut! And they were rubbed but still untempered, and she drew them out for rubbing throughout the day. Her fingers glided into the work and oriented her. Her fingers were about their accustomed business and the exercise regulated her breathing and clarified her thoughts.

What was plaguing Gabriel?

Turning a sock on the needles in her hand, Annie pondered the noisy paper in Gabriel's pocket. She trembled a bit to consider a paper that could cause such a change in her constant son. Why hadn't he confided in her as he'd always done? But of course it had come, Annie thought wryly. A day comes — a moment of realization. The son has gone over to his nature and is no longer yours to guide and influence.

And what of the so-called contrabands — those slaves following the Union soldiers into town? Every artery in and out of town was choked with them. Their faces showed profound relief when their feet touched the town. They considered it done and well done when they reached Washington, the capital and Father Abraham Lincoln's home. They hoped — their eyes were full of it! — they had reached a home for themselves.

Annie's eyes got moist for them with knowing how long their travail. Who blames a drowning man who grabs at anything floating? She snorted ruefully that grasping would cause a piece of floating debris to sink and take the one who grasps with it. The city of Washington was, for these ones leaving slavery, a precarious log in an agitated sea.

Destitute was how most of them arrived — trudging, slogging, and dragging. Descriptions in the papers of slaves fleeing at the advance of the Union army sounded like an account of dandies on parade. They were said to be preening themselves and promenading down the thoroughfares of Washington decked out in frothy skirts, scarlet frock coats, and gray hats festooned with feathers.

But the true picture was something else. The women trudged with their arms tugging at stumbling children, and children taller than a hickory stump were carrying babes on their backs. A common sight was a man who had made himself into a mule by putting a strap on his forehead so that he could carry his old grandpa or granmam on his back. Step upon step he would lug the old one, who was yet mere bones sparsely covered with skin. If they had worn a fine coat when they left, it had been stripped away long before reaching the banks of the Potomac or the

Eastern Branch. Even if they came from lands nearby, they had likely crisscrossed these places again and again — hiding and running from combatants and hostile irregulars. Most that Annie saw arrive were barely clothed and a long time away from their vittles.

Annie was ashamed to think that she had feelings of longing for the Ridley place. But the most joyful times she and Gabriel had known were the brief forays in the clear air to the upland knolls at Ridley to collect plants for their dyes. Then, if mother and son had managed to reach an open stretch with no one watching, Annie would release the boy to run and explore and fill his mouth with laughter. The two would dare to plunge their faces into beds of plants and smell and look aplenty and satisfy themselves with the beauty of the places. Their strong bond was nurtured on the collecting trips that were few and far between the long days Gabriel spent holding and dyeing yarn and spinning it to balls alongside his mother.

Going back in her mind she recollected when, as a child on the place, there was much production of wool yarn. Sheep were raised at Ridley Prospect, an inland hilly farm that Master kept for the purpose. The beasts were coddled in their own meadow. Their yearly shearing was a fearful excitement that all the hands watched. Some festivity was attached to shearing and much liquor got passed around. Luxe wool from the back and shoulders of the sheep was separated from the dirty wool on the animal's undersides and was spun to ultrafine balls by the needlewomen. Stomach wool was combed free of whatever clung to it by the needlewomen and wound to balls, too. Wisps of detritus clogged the nostrils of Annie and the other small girl combers. They were stuffed with holiday vittles and they became nauseated and dizzy. They were also festive, happy children at sheep-shearing. A clutch of stomach wool would make Annie recall it in deep detail and long for it.

Gabriel sat with pen and paper but couldn't keep his seat. He would not sit in the chair. He cared not to sleep. He sprang up and paced about his kitchen workshop in the dark. He allowed himself only one short candle's worth of illumination as he struggled to compose his letter. Unlike some who fought to find adequate expression, Gabriel Coats struggled with an excess of words for his plight.

Above all Gabriel wanted a calm, quiescent freedom — to work at his trade. Many thought it unseemly for a colored to embrace a calling. He had persevered against that tide. In his workroom — his sanctuary — a piece of paper had stolen the calm.

Gabriel cringed at recollection of his own loud voice sending dear Mary off to bed — shouting at her tender attempts at ministration. His sharp words and tone had frightened the babes and set off a brief tizzy. Ellen and Delia scattered like chickens as well and he felt compunction.

But he could not have them before his eyes when he studied this document.

KNOW ALL MEN BY THEIR PRESENTS THAT I, William A. Eberly, am working on behalf of Jonathan Ridley in the matter of compensation for former slaves.

The following persons formerly held as slaves in the District of Columbia and having been manumitted by edict of the Congress of the United States shall report to the offices of Eberly and Co. for inspection and valuation.

◆◆

Gabriel yearned for a cup of drink, but the fire in the hearth was too low to boil water. During the time of his apprenticeship, his most important evening duty had been to keep water at boil for Abraham Pearl. The man was fond of a hot drink at night.

Gabriel Coats's solemnity was exacerbated by the darkness of the room on this evening. He had lit a single taper and had this near his elbow. It brightened only the page he wrote on and a small circle outward from his hand. The rest of the room disappeared into a netherworld beyond the candle flame. Gabriel was superstitious that full illumination would give the pernicious, official paper the more power. He removed it from his breast pocket and pushed it nearly to the edge of the table — far away from the light. His own writing seemed weak — powerless beside it. It was a commanding document. It was a document for taking away from himself and his women — his family — their souls, their lives in freedom, their dignity. They had had none — he had purchased it or a semblance of it and now this document would take it back.

Gabriel's stomach burned to think that his former master, Jonathan Ridley, believed he could perpetrate this fraud. Did he mean to take the government's reimbursement money for freeing slaves he had already manumitted by written agreement? Tales of fraud in connection with the new decree were circulating the town. Others had enriched themselves by this method. Folk who were long ago legally freed through purchase were being called up and claimed by their former masters. It was a circle of viciousness!

Gabriel exhausted a portion of his anger in writing a letter to Reverend Higgins. He had some influence in the town that he exercised on behalf of colored. He was the only white man liable to help them. The agitation threatened to unhinge Gabriel as he tried to keep the situation from the others.

Of course, this evil news would soon be known as any vinegar that is spilled from an overturned jar is known for what it is. It pained Gabriel to imagine how the others would receive the news. And the children! What of them? They were compelled to report for examination! Compelled! If they did not submit themselves, the authorities had leave to come and bring them. From this Gabriel worriedly sought to protect them. Just that! He had pledged to Mary that being free they both would bring free children and keep them free through earnest toil. And now this had come!

His chickens were to be taken up! If not lost or damaged then handled and bandied about, and it hurt him to consider it. He imagined the look in their mother's eyes — a look that would strike him mortally if it were a bullet. What would Mary think? Gabriel had seen the expression of deep devotion and possession on his wife's face. This feeling that gives way to fear when the child gains her feet and begins walking away from the nurturing arms. Often he'd seen it in Mary and had felt the same and wondered whether it was so clearly read in his face. Jonathan Ridley would steal the profit of these children when they had never been his bondpersons! They were capriciously in his thrall! No law or edict or promise came out to benefit the colored man.

Disquietude was the enemy of Gabriel Coats's stomach. He went to the yard and heaved his misery onto the ground yet again.

It had been decreed that slaves residing within the boundaries of the District of Columbia were free. But this was a stingy and ugly decree, for as a consequence a slave owner was eligible to receive monetary compensation. Eager to beat the six-month deadline for filing a claim, Jonathan Ridley had hired a representative to secure his compensation.

The lie! Aye, there it is! Jonathan Ridley is not entitled to this compensation. Because these people mentioned are free people. These are the people whose freedom had been purchased by Gabriel Coats and his mother. They had worked to pay Jonathan Ridley!

"These daughters — my daughters — are free girls from a free purchased woman, my wife!" Gabriel slammed his fist on the top of his mam's laundry barrel. It thudded like a sour drum. "Mary's freedom was secured after purchase at an auction. He has no right to claim that she or her daughters are his bondpeople! They are free-born children!" he exploded.

Still they were mentioned and would be considered and valued for his money! The freedom meant nothing then, for the white masters would make the freedom into slavery just as sweet milk would turn to clabber in the sun.

Ah, sweet milk — sweet girls! Would they turn their innocent eyes on their father as they were led away? Would he stand impotent to help them? What would become of the father protector who could not save a daughter from this humiliation? If he rushed against the man who put a hand on them, would he not risk his own death? And if he resisted physically and put down his life, could he rise from the dead to care for these daughters? Could he then coddle them and train them and give them over to some good and strong husband? Would they not fall into poverty and a life of drudgery without their father? He could not relinquish his daughters' freedom to support the lie. He would resist this on their behalf and for the other women.

If this lie lived and flourished, then all along the freedom had meant nothing. Ridley could have come at any time and told these lies and taken them away? This was a cold thought that Gabriel had not entertained till now. Had Mary considered this possibility? Oh, what would become of this woman who had placed so much assurance upon the fact that these girls belonged to none but their parents?

Gabriel knew that Mary waited for him upstairs. His brusqueness would put off her questions. He needed to mull before he could explain this tangle to her. He wanted her comfort though. He wanted her to ply his face with kisses but not know what wounds her kisses salved. He would not tell her yet.

Annie returned to her bed and was comforted by the familiar — as always the familiar familiar — the same old same old things. She pulled a quilt to her chin. She lay beneath it and considered her children. Listening to Gabriel and Mary rustling about in their bed, she finally rested.

Twenty-two

GABRIEL KEPT THE brutal document next to his chest. It irritated, yet he was afraid to put it away.

. . . shall report to the offices of Eberly and Co. for inspection and valuation.

When the day was hard upon them and Gabriel was no longer able to bear solitary torment of the decision, he lay out the matter to Mary, Annie, and Ellen.

It was egregious — the deceitfulness of Jonathan Ridley! It proved his worth that he would violate a document to which he had put his hand. Could the Coatses prevail if they challenged him in the court? And if they did so — or even tried to redress — what effect upon the business agreement? This babe, too, they must protect and nurture. Could they all survive if they did not have his leg to stand on?

As Gabriel feared, the impact upon Mary proved the most severe. She clapped her hands against her eyes and wept into her palms as he laid out the travail.

"Husband! Husband! No!" she exclaimed.

Ellen listened and said nothing. Her face was immobile, though dripping water.

Annie became impatient of the crying and begged Mary and Ellen to gain control of their feelings.

"Hush and listen!" she commanded, though her own voice wavered.

"There is the examination to determine a value . . . ," Gabriel said, his voice trailing off to quiet. Mary's sniffling continued.

"They have . . . ?" she asked.

"Yes, they have mentioned the babies — the children — as if they were not born free. It is the reason I have kept the news in my chest. Mary, I am sorry for this." He grasped her shoulders in a steadying gesture and swept her against himself. Mary sobbed with renewed vigor and stood close by the simmering fireplace with her face pressed to Gabriel's body.

Annie's face remained dry. She was not indifferent to sorrowing, but she feared to have them all buffeted by these fears and be unable to forge a strategy. Aye! They were in the tow and how would they proceed — how to go forth?

"All he wants is the money." Annie hit upon the chestnut hard and flat and the nut came — from considering and from knowing Ridley so well. "When he longs for money, he thinks about us. We are his money in the bank. Let us give him money — match what he is liable to get from the government and settle with him." This was no woman who wasted time with crying. Mary was taken aback at her mother-in-law's stern practicality.

"Nanny, we cannot match it. We do not have enough for all mentioned," Gabriel replied.

"Ransom the children then. We will argue Mary because she is no slave of Jonathan Ridley. We will stand upon the paper that says we bought her freedom. You will argue with him. Brother, you and Ellen and I will stand the test," Annie said, and tossed the pledge as a laurel and looked at him evenly.

"Nanny . . . can we?" he asked haltingly. His mother had said they could if they must. But he further questioned her as if testing the pain of a sore. He pressed her. Could they stand if they must go without Ridley — or against him? She was stalwart in her opinion. She said yes.

"Pup, what makes you doubt me?" she shot at him.

Gabriel wore his good-quality brown frock coat.

"Sir," Gabriel called out without demur as he entered Ridley's sitting room. Startled, Jonathan Ridley turned and faced him. It was an affront to be called to by a monkey — though it was his beloved monkey, Gabriel.

That Ridley appeared braced for a challenge was, in itself, an advantage to Gabriel.

"My babes are . . . not yours to claim. We are all put down as your property. This cannot be, sir! You cannot let this proceed!" Gabriel spoke directly to Ridley's full face, daring to meet the man eye for eye.

Ridley raised his hand and struck Gabriel soundly. He took back his hand quickly as a parent does who chastises more harshly than intended. Ridley was momentarily frightened of his own actions, though Gabriel was not. He stood with his hands clasped at his back and offered his chest and face to Ridley.

Ridley wondered whether he was to be forfeit of his life at Gabriel's hand. A downtrodden being who once raises his head is liable to chance anything — any bold move. Would Gabriel raise his fist in retaliation — in defense of his pickaninnies? Ridley twitched a bit and controlled himself with great effort.

Gabriel stood his ground and waited until the air in the room became quiet again.

"What you want is money. That is it. What you want is money." Gabriel's calm was plainly impudent and aggressive. "Sir, this reimbursement — is to put a brick upon the heads of my children. For my own value I would not flinch to suffer the humiliating examination and valuation. What do I care that a fraud is perpetrated?" At this remark, Jonathan Ridley drew up indignantly and moved as if he meant to flog Gabriel, though he had no whip. "My mother would not flinch either if that were all of it. But by your false testimony, you cause my daughters, who were born as free people, to be examined by a slave trader. These beloved of their parents have had no part in your commerce. My wife! She is not bound to you. They have never been your property. To strip them naked and expose them to the perusal and calculation of a slave trader is abominable, and yet you would make it a feature of their lives for a small sum of money!"

"Ah, you have hit upon it, dear Gabriel!" Jonathan Ridley clapped loudly. "I want the money they are paying."

"Twice you want to be paid?" Gabriel spoke defiantly but very quietly. The exact measure of Ridley and his wants came clear. "We have money," he continued. "We will pay to keep the children unspoiled."

Ridley laughed. "I will accept your offer and more. There is a trader who has made an offer to purchase the girl, Delia, and go south. It is still legal to make this contract, for she will be held in deep south. There is money to be made."

"Do you traffic in women, sir?" Gabriel controlled himself, but bile rose into his mouth. He swallowed and felt ill, yet remained standing, faced toward Jonathan Ridley.

"Take care!"

"Sir, you must take care," Gabriel countered. "There is your name to consider," he said, and took a second blow to his cheek.

"Impudent scoundrel!" Ridley yelled.

"As you say, sir," Gabriel pronounced, and was poised to receive more blows.

"I traffic in niggers. The trade is lucrative. I will take cash for your mother, your sister, yourself, and the pickaninnies. I will sell off the girl, Delia. Thus, I will relieve you of the trouble of her. It is a simple bargain."

"Can you not allow one such to raise her head from shame? You propose a moneymaking scheme on the head of this girl?" The words pinched.

"You are above your station," Ridley replied.

"Do you imperil yours, sir?" Gabriel came back. "Please consider this." He then turned to go without taking leave from Jonathan Ridley.

"You are an arrogant!" Ridley shouted, and his tone halted Gabriel, who struggled to regain the picture of his beloved chickens and their mother and the others. His wind of confidence and resolve was tested. He fought to put all of their faces back into the forefront of his mind. Delia's visage, too, appeared before him, and Gabriel rebuked himself for the ease with which he would bargain with her fate. Had he betrayed the girl? Had he been uncaring to an innocent? But he must ransom his own chickens at all cost.

"I will not relinquish that one," Ridley said.

"Sir, please, for my sister's sake."

"She is for the trader. The arrangement is made."

Delia's murky situation gave Jonathan Ridley a wedge and he used it. The legality could not be questioned.

"Will you turn her over or will I send a sheriff to arrest her?" Ridley finished.

Gabriel left the rooms. His body was rigid and felt full to bursting with pus. When he got out of the hotel, he walked blindly. How high must you stand up to clear the head? Where is the cooler air — the air fit to cleanse the lungs and pacify the stomach? Gabriel squatted at the lip of an alley on Olive Street and retched.

Many lives are saved because murder at hand is hard to accomplish. Gabriel squatted over a gutter and dreamed of the weapon that would accomplish Jonathan Ridley and knew he could not wield it whatever it was. He lacked the iron to go against this man. But he would have plunged himself into the act of murder if he'd had a knife or a pistol in the rooms at the Whilton Hotel. In that room with Ridley had been an atmosphere of ferocity that would have been the better of him.

"Husband." It was Mary's face he encountered first of them all. She was waiting for Gabriel in the yard behind the shop. She stood and blocked his path.

"What has happened?" she asked with unaccustomed firmness. She was planted and would know all before the others. "What will become of our girls?"

"We are free of him if we pay him. It is the simplest of bargains. Again we pay him and we are free. We pay him and we are free!" Gabriel said bitterly.

At this Mary clapped her hands, laughed, and skipped a short frolic.

"It's a sour bargain, Mary," Gabriel said, and did not smile and did not appear relieved of the worry as Mary expected. Her recent unmitigated joy had been roughened in the last days.

She had been girding herself for heartbreak and felt a profound relief at Gabriel's news.

Her husband's studied self-possession was the one most durable tenet of his personality. He would stand. He was not easily shaken. In fact, Mary had never seen him shaken, only rising to meet adversity. He had come back and said they were free if they paid Ridley out. What then was causing him to quake so? Mary rubbed her mound absently and wished it to be a boy — for Gabriel — just to please him in this troubled moment. Gabriel brushed away quickly and entered the kitchen.

Mary had given him a good rehearsal. When he entered and faced Annie and Ellen, he was prepared.

"It's a sour bargain," he said. "We are paying him again. As you said, Nanny, it was only money he wanted! If we give him the money we will not stand the examination."

Daniel Joshua had turned up to sit with the women and await the outcome. He detected a further whiff in Gabriel's words but could not identify it. He was patient for the more that was coming and continued eating his beans.

"Well done, Brother," Annie said.

Ellen listened, then questioned timidly, "We are paying, Brother?"

"Yes, Ellen, we are paying again and we escape the examination." Gabriel swept aside more questioning with sitting next to Daniel Joshua. "Mother, do you have a plate of beans or has friend Daniel eaten them all?" he joked.

Mary would have danced to the table with her husband's plate if she'd known a formal step or could stop her stomach from twitching. She put down hoppin' John and chuckled to herself.

It was a cold precedent — keeping troubling news to himself — thinking now that he was the strong one above all and that any big concern was his to tangle alone.

"Husband, husband, husband," Mary said softly, sliding close to Gabriel. She petted the side of his body and tried to put her head against his shoulder. His body resisted her ministrations. His face would not relax. His arms were tense despite her kneading. After gentle moments of urging and wifely appeal to affection, Gabriel brushed her hands aside.

"No. Let me be, Mary," he said.

Mary ducked beneath the covers in embarrassment and Gabriel left the bed to agitate on the floorboards. Nervous that he might set off a tizzy of fretful babies, he went out into the yard.

He sat beside one of Nanny's wooden casks and drummed his fingers upon the wood of it and was lulled. The bile did not rise — he was not ill with the worry. He was resolved, but sickened with dread of the others knowing about it. The turn was damnable!

Gabriel wished to grab Nanny now in this torment and crush her skirts and wring out or tease out a way from this thing. He had always taken his troubles to her. He had never considered standing against her. But if she upbraided him — if she commanded him to go back to Jonathan Ridley and pay for, beg for, bargain for Delia — then he would be in a quandary.

An order to the girl came within a day. Gabriel let the paper spell it out for the women. Delia had been claimed by Jonathan Ridley and sold, and would be taken by the traders.

The force of the words was as a lash to Ellen's face. She threw up her hands and hugged her head. Mary looked at Gabriel in horror and clutched her sobbing sister-in-law. Rather than cry out, Annie slammed her flatirons upon the stove. Ellen and Mary continued to wail in accompaniment with Annie's pounding. The only quiet ones were Gabriel and Delia. She silently accepted that her fate had found her.

It sobered Ellen to realize Nanny and Gabriel had not shared her embrace of the illusion that she was Delia's mother. When the child was given to her, she'd taken her and taken the story. Aye, she had fashioned her own story, with Delia at its center. But Nanny and Gabriel did not see it this way! And Ellen realized that she was at the place that would crush her heart no matter which turn she took.

When the sheriffs came to the tailor shop to seize Delia, a boy called Tillie's Bill cried out, collapsed to the floor, and allowed himself to be dragged away in petticoats and shawls and sobbing loudly. The Coatses maintained the fiction by crying out and attempting to hold on to Tillie's Bill.

The boy had performed this ruse before and commanded a good price for it. He employed an expert disguise as a girl and was practiced at slipping bonds over his thin wrists. Upon Annie's suggestion, Daniel Joshua had contracted him and Annie had looked him over. She had perused his limbs and noted him slim below the waist with long, delicate-looking arms and little hair upon his flesh. He was as well yellow-skinned and had the eyes of a fawn.

Bill, tied loosely in deference to his womanly delicacy and a solemn promise to remain still, worked on his bonds as soon as he was closed into the holding room of the slave agents. He waited for sounds of drunken snoring outside the cell. This was his signal to fly. And since his escape would be on the agents' watch, he would be their loss. A runner was the liability of the one from whom she last had run.

A stinking jailer, set and determined to have a taste of the girl beneath the shawl, also awaited the others falling into drunken sleep. This one entered the shed and pulled away the shawls from Bill. He scuffled with the girl and when he thrust his hand between her legs, he found particulars he did not expect. " 'Tis a ruse!" he growled low, for fear of discovery amid mounting excitement. "Still I can take you as easily, lad — and enjoy it, too!"

A clever coquette, Tillie's Bill did appear to surrender and the jailer loosened his pants.

"But not today," Bill answered with a knife. He worked the blade into the jailer's gut — a deep thrust that preempted a scream. After this he sprang up and ran off toward the Long Bridge, pulling off the skirts and petticoats as he flew.

Delia boarded the train for Philadelphia with a layer of face powder and holding to the arm of William Higgins. They made a lovely, plausible traveling couple and were not thwarted. Nervous, they sat on the train reading prayer books and appeared to be a pious pair who never spoke.

Upon arrival in Philadelphia, William Higgins escorted Delia to the home of abolitionist friends and commended her to them. He was reluctant to leave her to these friends though. He had become fond of the feeling of protection and thrilled a bit to be a part of her adventure. He also explored the rise and fall of his unpracticed member that responded to this fond, soft girl. Young Delia had needed him and had had to sit so close to him that he'd risked being enamored.

Twenty-three

CAME THE MORNING, Winnie Wareham made her way through the streets with much trepidation. She rushed to exchange information with her dear friend Annie. Her eyes spun wildly as she gained the threshold at the back of the shop.

"Lord help us! The secesh is coming. Hunger is coming!" Winnie insisted, for she'd worked herself into a lather on the crossing from threshold to threshold. She struggled to catch her breath, so that her voice was weak and shrill. The poor woman's hands shook and Annie was pained to see her friend in such a state. The two had become boon companions over the secret about Reverend Higgins.

"If the secesh comes runnin' over the capital, then colored will be on a string going deep south. 'Tis what they've promised to do. I ain't young enough!" Winnie exclaimed. "Can we go off from here, Annie? Can we leave?"

Annie tried to soothe her friend. "Where would we go, girl?"

"We could go down by where you all come from — down in Maryland," Winnie said in a soft, pleading voice.

"None of that, girl. We're not rabbits. We can stick here." The two women bumbled and whispered their fears. Their worries kept them rocking and wringing their hands.

The women's ill ease was part of the growing plague of worry in the town. That very night a circle of free Blacks collected at Mount Zion Church to discuss the situation of safety for the capital and themselves. Another frenzied group gathered in the basement in Holy Trinity Church. Daniel Joshua appealed to Gabriel to make the rounds of the secretive meetings. He countered Gabriel's reluctance by pointing out that the Coatses had interests. They should be alert to danger in this atmosphere. Though there was reason to fear being out and abroad, there was also the need of information and resolve.

Some urged calm and hiding for fear of riling the whites. These cautious ones thought it best for colored men in Washington and Georgetown to be careful and to wait and see which way the wind did blow. Caught as they were between the slaveholders in Maryland and the slaveholders in Virginia, they were in a shaky position. Who would defend the city itself? Who would defend free colored?

The firing on Fort Sumter and President Lincoln's declaration of a state of insurrection and calling out militia to defend the city had been the signal for some. Risking recapture in Washington, a good many bondpeople in the surrounding towns and hamlets found courage to take to the road. Clutches of folk from nearby Maryland and Virginia had taken flight while the white folk were tied up with figuring which way they would land.

The newcomers had met with very little sympathy in the city precincts. Pushed into camps set by open sewers, they were hard-pressed to eat or get shelter, and illnesses swept through the encampments. Few reached Washington without carrying fevers.

The fortunate ones were those who could still do a day of work. Arriving contraband were forced to labor on fortifications throughout the town. Daniel Joshua worked alongside the new men with his wagon for shoveling and collecting horse manure. They transported it to dumping spots near the waterfront. Almost daily Daniel Joshua found himself hauling a footsore old grandpa or a woman with several babes in the back of his wagon after he'd dumped a load at the waterfront. He generally deposited the newcomers at an encampment on 12th Street.

"Keep here," Daniel Joshua suggested to the wide-eyed comers with spirits flagging. "The thoroughfares are not for you. There's ruffians and southern agents and a chance for floggings and beatings. Lay low!" was his grim advice.

After Fort Sumter and the rumbling, stumbling fury that followed, there was little chance to rest and no contentment in the edgy capital. Residents and the numerous transients were occupied with gaining news of the conflict.

Would the secesh overrun the town and sell all colored back into slavery? Would they squeeze off the town and starve out the residents?

"We are in a vise, my friends, a trap. We are caught between our enemies. And it appears that our defenders are weakened and far, far off," a brassy speaker at Mount Zion said, calling for colored men to arm themselves. But he spoke softly, furtively, for fear of the neighbors.

"Must we not look to our own safety? Will we not endeavor to protect our hearths, our wives, and our children?" Each speaker at the church meeting exhorted the group of colored to look to defense — to arm himself or herself for fear that none other would take their bond.

Some in Georgetown rightly feared what the city's considerable number of southern sympathizers was liable to do. This alone was reason to stock secret arms — to provision secret cellars.

Winnie Wareham's nervousness was exacerbated by the regiment of federal troops sent from New York City to defend the president and the government that were billeted on Georgetown College's grounds. Greeted with enormous relief at first, their nightly drunken revels had worn their welcome thin on the campus. Their uniforms, emblazoned with green shamrocks to promote an image of Irish fierceness and determination, initially endeared the regiment to the priests, but their whoring and campfires on the college's grounds ruined their luster. On a recent night scalawag soldiers in their number had come to the Trinity Church rectory kitchen to beg flour, a stick of cinnamon, and a snatch of sugar — and left behind a splat of tobacco juice and beery piss in the hedges beside the door. After sundown, Winnie was afraid to budge and had taken to locking herself in with a boning knife.

Political contention did, as usual, roil the town. Followers of each party and faction asserted themselves in speeches and parades and alley fisticuffs. Competition increased and invitations to balls and receptions circulated furiously. The bawdy houses were full and flourishing. In this atmosphere there was increased call for suits of clothing and decorative embellishments to old garments. There was a consistent call for the embroidery of partisan slogans and symbols on colorful cloths for fluttering and hooraw. Embroidery being Ellen's bailiwick, she saw an increase in requests for her work especially. And she came to delight in these commissions. One faction and another bought her work and she cared nothing to take a side.

A woman pushed open the store's door. "I want a banner done to this design. Is it possible you have a girl who does fine embroidery?" she asked, issuing an impatient order to Aaron Ridley's stunned face. He did not answer quickly and she asked again with little blush and no blister, "Do you execute fine embroidery?"

"Madam . . . our girls are the most skilled in town. Of that there is no dispute." Aaron Ridley stammered despite himself. "We can execute any design. Gabriel, bring samples of the girls' work. Madam, you have my assurance that the girls in this establishment are of exemplary character and are circumspect in the preparation of all garments and accoutrements, especially those items unmentionable." Aaron Ridley had begun to adopt a demeanor of service that he had heretofore disdained. He had fallen into the habit from necessity and no longer bothered to resist it. Placed in the business, he was becoming used to it. Though it had not the status to which Aaron Ridley truly aspired, he saw that it did have cachet in the heady, exuberant atmosphere of the city. He snapped his fingers in Gabriel's direction and the tailor brought forth bundles of cloth with intricate designs upon each.

The young woman gasped uninhibitedly and click-clacked her teeth. The design samples were extremely lovely. "Ah. Ah, ah!" she said beneath her breath. The considerable skill was apparent. She looked directly in Aaron Ridley's face and asked, "You have a girl on your premises who does such work?"

"Indeed, mademoiselle," he replied with a growing subservience.

Gabriel was amused and showed it only by the mischievous inclination of his head to his left shoulder. He turned away from the young woman and Aaron Ridley and busied himself with threads and spools.

"This is as good as that obtained in Paris," she said. "I assure you," she added with a fillip of arrogance. She was certain this provincial had never dreamed of the shops where her name was well known.

"Bring her out. I want to see her. I want to have work done — expert needlework — work of the highest caliber. I want to have this seamstress. I will speak to her. I will hire her, sir. I want a banner done. That is nothing! I will pay her a large commission to work solely for me. I must execute a trousseau. You will take your part, I am sure," the young woman added with a hint of sneer. She managed a singular act in taking the wind from Aaron Ridley's sails. He who always had success with women was confused and again stammering.

"Miss . . ."

"Miss Millicent Standard." The young woman spoke more softly than before because she was sensitive at her heart for the discomfort of another. She had stung him with her tone and she was momentarily contrite.

"Miss Standard, we will accept any commission. It would be an honor for us to furnish your trousseau." Aaron noted her retreat and regained his bearings — his ease.

"She can be hired to work for me solely? She will come away with me — just now. Hurry her! I will have many things right away. I will pay whatever is asked." She returned to fingering the made samples.

Having never been brushed aside by a woman, Aaron Ridley stood stock-still in the center of the floor and followed Miss

Standard's movements with his eyes. She walked about and peered at fabrics and only glanced disgustedly at the chairs to which Ridley tried to steer her.

Gabriel turned cautiously, looked at the floor between his feet with great concentration, and rumbled his throat several times. The sound drew attention and he spoke with little animation. "Mistress, the needlewoman is Ellen Coats, my sister. She is a free woman and is at work in the tailoring operation here. She will gladly accept whatever commission you would honor her with. However, she must remain here and attached to this concern. She has a great many commissions for prominent ladies and gentlemen. Is this not so, Master Ridley?" he added obsequiously.

The two whites were able to negotiate Gabriel's impudence in addressing Millicent Standard directly by noting that his eyes had never left the floor. Only the top of his head was visible. Small snips of thread covered his clothes and made them humble. He was a still post except that he spoke.

"Quite true, mademoiselle. Ellen is associated only with this establishment. We will direct her to fulfilling your requests. You will be best served if she remains here," Aaron pronounced in agreement. "It is our firm policy," he added, enjoying his own arrogant self-assurance. "She will accept the commission of your trousseau and will go immediately to your house to measure and receive your dispatches. She will work under supervision of her brother and will execute your commission efficiently. He will keep her hard at it, I assure you."

"I do not believe this woman is your sister, tailor. I believe she is your concubine and you would not lose your comfort," Miss Standard said sharply and viciously, and shocked both men. "I am aware of how things stand in this town. But . . . as you say, she will work under your supervision. I will have none other to touch my commissions, sir." She turned hard eyes on Aaron Ridley after staring hotly at Gabriel's bowed head.

"Miss Standard, you have my solemn promise," Aaron answered.

"Good day then. Send her to this address," the young woman said, ending the business with thrusting her card forth in her hand. Aaron Ridley snatched the card quickly, taking extraordinary care not to touch Millicent Standard's fingers. It was an ungraceful movement. Millicent Standard turned ungracefully also and swept out of the door as if crossing a ballroom floor. The sight was ludicrous and provocative of humor.

"Indeed! No one will touch your commissions to be sure, miss!" Aaron exploded, and turned hot, sarcastic eyes on cautious Gabriel, challenging him to react. The tight rein on reaction that Gabriel had always held kept his demeanor neutral. He showed nothing to Aaron Ridley, who continued. "I pity the unlucky bastard that gets that one!" Aaron Ridley assuaged his fallen pride with a calculated wound to Gabriel. "I should think that one and your Ellen to be a good match," he said, smirking. "Two bitches with nails between their legs, eh?" He waited to read a flinch or a question or a threat, but Gabriel gave him no satisfaction. "Send her to take the measures," Ridley gruffed.

"Sister, you are widely sought," Gabriel crowed upon entering the back room to have his midday meal. He cheerfully announced the doings of the day to the assembled and Ellen. "You are commissioned especially to the trousseau of Miss Millicent Standard, an elegant young lady with particular tastes. You are to go to her home to take measures." At this Gabriel tittered in recollection of Aaron Ridley's pique and cringed to recall his jibes at Ellen.

"Surely not!" Ellen cried out. She was delighted and behaved as though Gabriel, in bringing the news, had created the boon.

"Oh, Brother, is't a good commission? A trousseau! A good commission!"

"Yes, very good. She's a very haughty young woman. She is impatient for you. Go right away."

Ellen gathered up her implements and continued to congratulate Gabriel, though she credited herself privately for accomplishing the commission.

If Millicent Standard had looked into the calmly demure face of her seamstress, she would have seen that her stinging taunts of Gabriel and Aaron Ridley were unfounded. In fact, Ellen was so prim and uncommunicative — only whispering her directions to turn here or there as she took measures — that Miss Standard might have mistaken her for a Catholic nun. She wore a sedate charcoal-colored dress that admitted no view of her flesh but her face and hands. Her hair was covered with a tied cloth of nearly the same color — only slightly lighter and capable of pulling more of daylight toward her complexion. Under this influence her skin was buttery milk chocolate and luminous.

Though frightened of Miss Standard, Ellen managed the young woman's commissions. The future Mrs. Charles W. Beech required handkerchiefs, table linens, napkins, counterpanes, as well as bed jackets, shawls, camisoles, chemises, and a snood, all embroidered with her future monogram. She stammered at explaining to Ellen that she would also require a lacy, diaphanous garment to entice her husband. She impatiently rejected the seamstress's suggested fabrics until Ellen brought a length of silk that Gabriel took from his stores. The beautiful sheer caused rounds and rounds of hearty laughter in the kitchen when Gabriel cut a caper with it drawn over his hand. This beautiful blue cloth would cover a body in name only. It was so transparent that it depended upon the color of skin beneath it to rise to its loveliness.

"Sister, do not be a goose!" Gabriel said laughing. "This young woman is nervous to keep her new husband." Ellen grew warm and perplexed, but executed a garment that would cause excitement in a papist's cell.

Ellen's flawless, spirited embroidery — her knots and whorls and precision — occupied her attention but did not distract her from thoughts of Delia. From beneath the folds of her dress Ellen drew out a snuff pouch and pulled on her bottom lip to form a cup under her tongue. She had picked up the habit during her sojourn at the Warren Plantation. The tobacco-topping gang adopted the practice of grinding fine tobacco, resting it under the tongue, and moving spittle around in their mouths to alleviate the monotony and exhaustion of their work. It was a habit for a gal to cultivate, for it caused no smoke and gave her a whiff of soft dreams. The effect of the snuff fostered a contemplative look. Ellen's graceful face was often caught with a thin trickle of brown spit on her bottom lip and chin while her eyes were focused off and away. But for the snuff she would feel a knife in her chest at the thought of Delia, her dear girl. She dipped up snuff and ruminated on first sight of Delia come bawling through the legs of the gal, Katharine. That event was now so far back and removed from loving the girl. It mattered little now how she'd come or from where.

Ellen dipped and spit. Her industry masked her longings for

Delia. Despite Gabriel's wishes she'd maintained a connection. Reverend William Higgins had brought letters and had forwarded her replies to Delia. The letters from Delia were comforting, for the girl had spoken of succeeding at her lessons and of being busy, but content. Ellen had read the letters in secret, reluctant to displease Gabriel.

Ellen recollected the girl's soft voice at their leave-taking. "Uncle loves you, ma'am. He loves his mother and his wife and his babies. But he loves me not at all. Don't cry," Delia said. Her own cheeks were wet.

"He is wrong about you," Ellen had declared vehemently. "You are a good girl."

Twenty-four

"IF THERE BE something to see I'd as soon see it as another," Daniel Joshua declared against Gabriel's entreaties. Some merriment was in the air along with smoke.

As a worrier, Gabriel was slow to partake in the excitement. He was happy enough to do the work on uniforms, but his feelings were dark on the enterprise of war.

"Certainly there are as many in the town who are for the southern cause as for the Union. In that case we are ducks and should be securing our safety!" Gabriel countered. He and Daniel talked out all sides of the thing.

Annie had surprised them with her decision to accompany Daniel Joshua on a ride out to see the war. Daniel was hired for his wagon and horse and had the chance to see the fighting up close. None other than Mr. Jonathan Ridley had commissioned Daniel's wagon simply because he preferred not to spoil his town carriage on the rutted roads to the battlefield.

Ridley's lady friend had begged prettily for the excursion. She was the one who first suggested the ride out to battle. Day after day of military parades whetted the palates of citizens, and the movement of troops southward promised gay entertainment. The sable brown curls at Bella Strong's temples were expertly dressed and well set off by a be-ribboned, tricolor hat bought for the occasion.

Provisioned with baskets of food and drink, Daniel and Annie sat aboard the front of the wagon and Ridley and Bella Strong rigged soft seats in the bed of the conveyance. A merry cavalcade of citizens followed behind companies of soldiers and army sutlers.

As the four gay travelers straggled back into Georgetown, their faces were soot-blackened and somber. They were all-over weary and looked like owls. On the retreat Ridley had changed places in the wagon and sat beside Daniel at the reins. Something inside the coddled man had wanted to participate in his own deliverance. No matter that he sat on equal terms with an underling. Both men knew that, in this moment, they had their particulars in their hands and must hold and fly. They were braced against each other as Daniel guided the team over the collapsing road. They navigated ruts made by the retreating army's wagons and the passengers were tossed like beans.

The sky blackened quickly with approaching night and profuse smoke from rifles and cannons. The women huddled in the back of the carriage, each with her head down in her skirts. Bella Strong let the contents of her stomach into her kerchief. The ribbons that had sat so jauntily on her hat in the morning were slick with grease and hung drearily.

Annie had shrunk into the back of the wagon when Jonathan Ridley usurped her position at Daniel's side. She peeped intermittently at the passing action, then propped her sock and needles upon the end of her nose and worked to avoid seeing.

When the anxious, retreating cavalcade reached Georgetown, Ridley refused the offer of a hot toddy at the tailor shop and he and the lady were taken directly to the Whilton Hotel.

"Will you rest?" Annie said to open up with Daniel. Both were stunned to silence.

"It would be foolish to come down from this buckboard or leave this animal," Daniel replied. Indeed he dared not leave the wagon and horse. He put a club at hand for pummeling somebody's head who would try for the reins. Annie brought him a toddy to the alley behind the shop where he tied up. She stood at the side of the wagon and sighed as he sighed from the buckboard. They stood a bit longer without talking. Then Annie brought fodder for the horse. She pressed Daniel to wait as she went to the house for a biscuit with meat.

As transport of any kind was a luxury, Daniel returned to the Long Bridge to ferry some wounded and some simply weary to a higher ground. The wealthy paid well to have a ride and the indigent begged loudly. There were many horses running madly across the Long Bridge, having thrown their riders along rutted roads clogged with panicked onlookers and soldiers. The animals were trailing their bridles and some folk tried to rein them. Crying from the loose horses frightened Daniel's usually dull nag and there was trouble to steady him.

Annie recited the tale of the day in a monotone, for she was exhausted and past lively. "They lollygagged getting there — the soldiers. We all lollygagged — we onlookers. We were playful. We saw the soldiers on the road out. They picked berries and worried the countryside. They sang songs and cavorted

with saying they would be Sunday soldiers and would be right
back to home. So the secesh were ready and sore. The Sunday
soldiers were punished bad. We got there when it started and
turned back on the run. Still some of the green soldiers got in
front of us. Daniel and Master Ridley had it to whip 'em back
to keep to the road."

Gabriel brought a basin with cool water, rinsed his mother's
feet, and set them soaking. He rubbed and twisted her feet to
unwind them, screwing them up and releasing them like rags.
Annie wanted to push him off for his presumption, but his
hands were good on her feet. She let him rub her back and lead
her to bed.

"You are shivering, Nanny. Your bones are rattling," Gabriel said.

"Aye, Brother," she answered. "Come." She drew back the
covers and let him come to lie by and warm her. He put his
head on her breasts and hugged her to give her his own warmth.
He stayed cradling her until he slept. Then she woke him and
sent him off to his own bed.

"Bodies floating downstream on the river. Come and see it,"
Daniel urged. He put his head in the door and shouted. Annie
rose to her feet in alarm. Of late, every day brought a sight to
pull a soul from her chair. There was a parade or a boat or a
wagon of wonders of some kind. There were constant sounds of
exploding shells, discharges of firearms, loud animal cries, shouting, and general banter. The small girls seated about the floor
sprang to their grandmother.

" 'Tis not the time for clicking and clacking needles, woman.
There is a fearsome sight on the river."

"Ye, ye," Annie cried, drew up her shawl, and followed Daniel.

The gentleman Gabriel waited upon in the shop twisted like a small boy in a stir and was impatient to fly to the riverbank and see for himself what had so many shouting out about what all. He wriggled free of the measuring tapes.

"Cut the coat." The man tossed coins at Gabriel. "Start the work," he said, and left Gabriel standing in the center of the floor with his tape between his fingers. Rather than watch the running panorama, Gabriel stared at his own hands and the tape. He recorded the figures of the man's physique methodically, then put his equipment neatly into its place. Only then did he turn attention to what was going on. So much had happened and so much had been grim that he was more cautious now than ever. And he felt as if bruised — sore in some spots and fearful of bruising himself more.

Walking through to the workroom, Gabriel saw that all the others had left. He was surprised. He brushed threads from his own coat and went out into the thoroughfare to have a glimpse of the passing show.

Bodies floated like leaves downstream on the river. Word circulated that a great battle upstream had loosed these bodies to drift. Their uniforms, full up with decomposition, were gassed like balloons, and rodents clung to some of the inflated corpses. From shore the rats appeared to be seamen piloting their own skiffs.

The Coatses stood high on Prospect Street overlooking the activities below at the riverside. Figures scurried about the bank launching hooks and nets to snag and haul them in. The gassy bodies resisted capture and some floated past despite all effort and made for the Eastern Branch and the bay toward the open sea. These escaped floating bodies bobbed alongside downed branches and animal carcasses and other flotsam. Altogether the river looked like a pernicious stew pot.

"Cover the children's eyes. T'ain't a good thing for babes to see," Annie said when she came back from dumbness. The small girls were summarily turned into their mother's skirts and held there. A preacher stood on the bank below the prospect and called for repentance, citing evidence of things gone awry — the floating bodies, rats on the march, and highly painted jezebels.

At sight of all this, Washingtonians had been changed. No longer a picnic lark, war became war.

With ever more combatants billeted in the District, skillful navigation of the streets was required, for the thoroughfares were taken up with drilling men and frivolous, excited onlookers. Fortification and provisioning were undertaken around the clock, forcing citizens to become hoarders. Coming and going was a constant. Scavenging opportunities increased and there was someone to want most everything discarded by another. The stream of wagons, buckboards, and goat carts entering and leaving was likely carrying most any kind of contraband. And what was tossed aside by one was plugging a drip hole or cushioning a pallet in an alley for another.

Few dogs remained barking in Georgetown. The dusk was quieter without this small cog of sound. Folks had killed their own pets to have the meat of them before some other purloined the animal. Pet pigs and Sunday horses were likewise going this way.

Washington, the improbable seat of the federal government, was chock-full of southern sympathizers and bold agents working for the Confederacy. The town could not possibly be certain of itself. Every argument was heard expressed. No restraint was shown.

War intoxicated most of the men. Aaron Ridley was not immune. "By God, I'll do what has to be done! No matter what my uncle says, this one Ridley will do what has to be done!" Aaron exclaimed as he packed his belongings to leave Georgetown. Working in the tailor shop as his uncle's functionary and spy had lost its appeal for Aaron Ridley in the climate of war. The glamour of the fighting enticed him. Here was courage, dash, and exhilaration.

Aaron, born in Richmond, the capital of the new Confederacy, coerced himself to defend his mother's honor and fight for the South. Clementine Stern Ridley's blood whispered to him insistently as horses, men, armaments, uniforms, and breathless women came ashore in the District on the tide of the war. Aaron had watched the excitement build and could no longer stand life on the sidelines.

Aaron Ridley's mother saw the conflict as an opportunity to reclaim the South she had lost when she had married and been swallowed up by the Ridley family. The Sterns were Virginians, not ambiguous Marylanders like the Ridleys. And her Aaron had a duty to his Virginia relations to defend the South! Clementine was firmly snagged in the romantic fervor of the Confederate war effort and she had written many breathless letters to her son. She cajoled him toward the war. She was thrilled at the handsome, heroic son defending her way of life. The picture came alive in anticipation.

Miss Violet Anne Marie Bristol also influenced Aaron. In her fast, elite circle the young swains were of the opinion that the war would be over quickly and would offer opportunities for conspicuous valor. Violet constructed a fanciful mental scene that she shared with her impressionable beau. Aaron Ridley, she imagined, would look handsome in his uniform as she fluttered a lace handkerchief embroidered cleverly with violets at his receding figure.

Aaron bade Gabriel, Mary, Annie, and Ellen farewell with warmth and ceremony. The irony of it struck Gabriel over and over like a small hammer. It was Aaron who had talked his uncle into taking Gabriel's cash for the freedom. Jonathan Ridley had been lazy about it, but Aaron had prompted him. Aaron had worked to free the Coats family. Now it was he going off to defend the cause of slavery? Now it was he wringing the hand of his former slave as if both were joined in sentiment about the conflict? More surprising to Gabriel was Aaron Ridley's leave-taking of the shop. Aaron thrust out his hand and colored up around the collar as he grasped Gabriel's hand to pump and say that he would miss them all. He looked around at the bolts of cloth and the forms and needles and sighed wistfully.

"Take care of things, old boy," Aaron said cheerfully. "I'll be back pretty soon and we'll take up where we're leaving it." It would have been a sorrowful parting if Aaron had not been so naively enthused.

"God grant you good fortune, sir," Gabriel called out. He felt a breeze of sympathy for Aaron — hoping he might fall from his horse on the way, break a leg, and be unable to join up. Aaron Ridley was not for fighting. He surely had no business in the fray. He was too much a boy, even if ones much younger had gladly gone and made good use of themselves.

Aaron rode to Scottsboro to take leave of his mother and the Ridley Plantation before joining the Confederate army. He went as well to fortify his arguments. He packed a boyhood penknife and a family Bible in his haversack. Young Ridley, an inadequate horseman at best, left Scottsboro to join up astride a great-grandson of his grandfather's favorite stallion.

Aaron's mother stood on the gallery at Ridley waving him off. She said he was the image of his grandfather. Jonathan Ridley pronounced her a fool as she waggled her fingers and swelled like a toad.

Jonathan had thought his nephew a right fool, too, to join up to fight with the Confederacy. He could as easily have fought with the Union. Ridley sincerely wanted to offer his nephew and heir the opportunity of a wider world away from the plantation lifestyle. It was what he had always wanted for himself — a larger stage. The day was late for the gentleman farmer. Times were changing. Hell, times had changed.

One of the swains in Violet Anne Marie Bristol's circle, Martin Tolbert, seized on fulfilling his obligation to the Confederacy by hiring the soldiering services of another man. He reasoned the Confederacy was getting a fitter man — someone with more vitality and fighting acumen to offer in the contest. Joe Bungate, eager to get free of a Virginia prison at any cost, was the proxy who sold his service to Martin Tolbert and the army of the Confederacy.

Twenty-five

ANNIE HAD BEEN more than dutifully fond of Gabriel and Ellen's father, Bell. He was the man she had chosen. She had worked herself toward him and away from Jonathan Ridley in a plan. She had taken the gamble that the master would not go where his blacksmith had gone when she put herself in the way of Bell. Master might have killed or sold or beaten them both, but his need of their value had mitigated his anger. Both Annie and Bell had presentiment of tragedy from the first. Neither expected they would grow old together.

From the beginning, Annie refused to pull back caring for her boy though. As well as she knew that she toyed with sorrow, she clung to the child. Hope was a feature on his face. She had put it there and she resolved to be clever and keep him. And if he were lost, then it would be her portion to swallow, for she was committed to love him. She later pledged in her heart to Ellen, too, but she was less ardent with her. She had got used to the hurly-burly exercise of love when Ellen came and could easily choose between the two.

Annie guided Gabriel — nay, she had cut him if the truth be told. Here was a man she had shaped. She had trained him to be clever and she guided him to the clever path.

The woman helping her bring Gabriel had been short with her, impatient of Annie's writhing and bucking labor. The woman handled the baby roughly when he emerged and let him squall long minutes before bringing him to Annie. "Don't give him the tit too quick! He's got to learn right off that he'll wait for his vittles like everybody else. He ain't no king on a throne," she growled. But Annie took him up and clutched him, and he latched to her breast and sucked and would not be loosed until his head fell back sleeping and a trickle of milk came from his mouth.

"Ah, you'll cry," the irritable helpmeet pronounced as she left with her bandages and slop pans.

Child Gabriel did come hungry and Annie never pushed him off. The pleasantest moment was him waking up hungry and kicking his small feet against her stomach in the excitement to get at her breast. Her milk let down at his sigh. On this night, in this dark, Annie touched her nipples in pleasurable recollection of the past and palpated them.

Though it had become thin and manly, Gabriel's face began fully round and soft. And in satisfied repose he was a lovely, moonfaced sweet bun. Ellen's little face at the breast was heart-shaped — a perfect idea of a girl. She was a precious bundle and she was delight for Gabriel as much as for the parents. He lifted her and dandled her and cavorted for her entertainment. All of them together — Bell, Annie, Gabriel, and Ellen — that was the highest moment of joy captured in her mind's eye. At the top of the stair was that lovely moment, and all else fell away.

◆◆

Loath to run into the streets like a boy — to follow the parades — Gabriel did secretly enjoy the pomp and march of the men raised from firefighting units in New York City. They were the flavor of excitement, dressed in lobster-colored coats, white gloves, and pants so straight-legged! And their middles were cinched with leather belts of exquisite thickness and burnish —and jaunty caps!

The antics of the Fire Zouaves were like a traveling circus's high-wire aerialists. They shinnied up light poles to delight crowds. Gabriel stood at the window of the shop and brushed at errant threads and lint on his vest. The sight of the marchers thrilled him and he was drawn away from his work. He walked out into the thoroughfare to gape. He had forgotten to remove the measuring strop from his neck, and it lay under his collar as an advertisement of his profession. Some small boys shrieked and pointed to the sky as they ran to the highest prospect along High Street. A startling globe rose into the air and commanded the attention of all.

"Nanny, come and see." Gabriel's voice was excited as he rushed into the kitchen — bursting through the curtain and surprising Annie and the girls. He yelled, but did not wait for her to answer or any other. He clapped his hands and ran back to the street. The loft of the thing took him and he was swept away with it.

The three young nougats had never heard so much exuberance in their father's voice. They were startled and drew back toward their grandmother. They did not follow their father.

When Annie came out to the street, she wore the little girls upon her skirts like decoration. Their heights rose as stairs do: the one oldest, then the next girl a few inches smaller, and the third this same increment smaller. Their faces were much alike, too — a repeating pattern of round faces, molasses-drop eyes, and sunny cheeks.

Out on the avenue the girls clung shyly to their grandmother and used her shawl to cover their faces. Naomi, the eldest, peeped skyward, then giggled into her grandmother's skirt. Each of the others took a turn.

Nanny's patience with these little girls was amusing to Gabriel, for she had always been so firm against his clinging. Ah, she could move so quickly then. Her habit was to swat him away from her path and not be obstructed or slowed.

"Are you able to cut and sew a suit on commission for one as myself, sir?" A handsome, self-possessed colored man broke through Gabriel's reverie. The man assessed him cannily. His voice was well modulated. Seemingly none but Gabriel heard him speak. The two stood shoulder to shoulder in the crowd lining the thoroughfare, watching the military parade.

Jacob Millrace was plum-colored. He had a particularly broad forehead that was unlined and quiescent. His eyes were small, but piercing, and his face belied the obstacles he must have overcome to reach the level of wealth suggested by his clothes. The cloth of his suit was fine. Gabriel inspected it out of the corner of his eye.

Gabriel wondered momentarily why the man was secretive. There was nothing illegal about tailoring. Yet it did behoove a free colored — as this well-dressed man must certainly be — to be cautious with all in all circumstances.

"I take commissions, sir — for tailoring, mending, and laundering. We — my mother, my wife, my sister, and I — produce knitted and embroidered articles also. A gentleman's wardrobe can be augmented at our establishment." Gabriel did not smile as he spoke but bowed his head.

"I would have a suit or two. Come to this house and inquire for me," the gentleman said much more loudly than previously as he handed over a crisp white card embossed with the name *Jacob Millrace.*

Gabriel looked at the snow-white business card. The address was notable if memory served. There was no information as to the profession of Mr. Millrace. The name did not include the honorific of reverend or doctor, so Gabriel guessed that Millrace was neither. What did the man do to earn his rich living?

Gabriel Coats was a quick observer and an accurate estimator. Was the fellow broad or narrow through the shoulders, taller or shorter than himself, weak and birdlike or taut and muscular in the chest and belly or barrel-shaped or beer-belly rounded, long-legged or set on stumpy legs, slumped with age or upright and vigorously youthful? The composite of these measures stamped a durable picture in Gabriel's mind. Jacob Millrace was nearly heroic in his measures.

Among the circle of his acquaintance, Jacob Millrace was viewed as two men. With the community of free colored, he was a proud, wealthy businessman. Jacob Millrace was adequately educated. He could read well and figure and was fond of a spirited exchange on the news of the day. He did not have so much education that he felt comfortable to discuss literature and the arts. Nevertheless he attended the courtly forms of entertainment — parlor concerts at the homes of free people of stature and the gamut of lesser diversions. Essie Millrace, Jacob's daughter, was versed in literature and the arts and held her own quite well with an educated crowd. She served as her father's hostess.

The other half of the shell was Millrace's lucrative profession. Jacob Millrace accumulated his wealth from a curious, unlikely

source. He owned a line of highly prized English springer spaniels bred from an elite pair belonging to his late master, Joseph
Pendleton of St. Mary's County, Maryland. Jacob Millrace was
the undisputed owner of these hounds following the untimely
death of the entire Pendleton family and the slaves they owned —
Joseph, his wife and three young sons, as well as forty-five field
and house workers. All of these had succumbed to a fever in '48.
Colored and white had fallen left and right, with Essie's mother
and two brothers among them. Jacob and his daughter were the
only survivors excepting the pair of hounds, Hercules and Circe.

Jacob had stood to lose his freedom to a relative of Mr. Pendleton, but no relative with claim had turned up. Some said
they existed, but were fearful of the pestilence.

After Jacob buried all of the dead, he and Essie walked off the
Pendleton Main. The two surviving hounds walked behind them.
The four kept together and carried on. The survivors laid claim
to a hunting cabin on the farthest reaches of the Pendleton tract
and settled and improved upon the structure. Jacob groomed and
fed the spaniels and looked after Essie. When the bitch had pups,
Jacob and Essie coddled them and trained them.

The word circulated that Pendleton's prized spaniel bitch
with liver-colored splotches and his dog that matched her point
for point had a litter of pups. Word was they were beautifully
marked and showed real hunting promise. When the dogs ma-
tured, Jacob Millrace built a respectable, lucrative business in
taking out the dogs for gentlemanly hunting of upland birds.
Millrace himself became trusted as a guide and as a hand to tote
and load weapons.

Jacob adopted a humble demeanor in his work with the gentleman hunters. He allowed his dogs to be the true hunting
experts and behaved as though he were at their beck and call.

The pups, utterly devoted to Jacob and attentive to his every mood and movement, nevertheless pretended to consider him beneath their notice when customers were about. Dogs and man worked together to create the fiction.

Jacob maintained cleverly and with suitable awe that the animals were privy to an ancient knowledge of birds and were likely of some royal stock. Thus he claimed to be the honored custodian of royal dogs. Whether or not this was true, people around understood the dogs had been bought in England some months before the fever had struck. In cockeyed local logic, people felt that the fever survivors — both human and canine — were given a special dispensation from illness. Hunters crave a talisman for luck, and upon this, Jacob Millrace built his business.

Millrace's hunting guide and dog commerce was so successful that he and Essie could afford to live in Georgetown in the off-season, these times being the hottest summer months and the dead of winter. Jacob Millrace bought a house in town and arranged that his daughter be schooled at the home of the Dunston sisters, who taught the children of free people in Georgetown.

By comparison with the Coats family's rooms above the tailoring shop, Jacob Millrace's home was palatial. He employed the services of a general man about and a cook/housekeeper. Both of these were free colored persons. They deferred to Mr. Millrace, though they did not kowtow, and seemed a happy household.

Gabriel's preliminary estimates of Mr. Millrace's measures had been largely correct. The gentleman desired two suits of clothing of dark and modest cloth, and he requested that all of the appointments be au courant.

The parlor into which Gabriel was shown had a woman's furnishings. There was the feeling that here lived someone who felt it necessary to add warmth to the domicile. Gabriel thought of Ellen and of his mother as he looked at the lovely pattern work of the antimacassars on the chairs in the parlor. Did Mr. Millrace and his wife entertain a wide circle?

As Gabriel took his leave, he suggested to Mr. Millrace that if there were a need for laundry service, he would gladly send his wife to fetch it and return it.

"Ah, Mr. Coats," Millrace said with a chuckle. "You have guessed it. My Essie does struggle with the laundrywoman. And she is never satisfied."

"My wife will come tomorrow, sir. She subscribes to the syndicates. Your wife, sir, will be pleased," Gabriel trilled, happy to pronounce the possession of so many flowers and eager to impress Jacob Millrace.

"Ah, ah, no, Mr. Coats," Millrace said, and Gabriel felt a jolt of embarrassment. He had jumped too soon! "Mr. Coats, it is my daughter. My Essie is my daughter, sir. Please do send your missus to us." Jacob ended with a warm handshake and Gabriel left with a smile.

As he walked back to the shop, Gabriel felt excitement race back and forth in his veins. The sight of Mr. Millrace's wealth, its display, he a colored man like Gabriel, a self-made, free man! Gabriel was truly jealous for the first time.

Gabriel's warm hearth at the back of the tailor shop was unchanged when he returned from Jacob Millrace's house. All was as it would normally be. Annie, Ellen, and Mary were hard at their tasks. But the picture felt stingy and small and, for a moment, Gabriel was not quite happy. The wide room with a large table put to many a daily task and chairs aplenty around the periphery and food stores and work tools consigned to this, that, or the other place was not quite a parlor — a fit place for a family. Gabriel yearned for something more like the parlor that Jacob Millrace had. Was this next rung so far above him?

Unaware of her husband's tormented thoughts, Mary prepared a strong cup of coffee. She put his vexed air down to weariness and trusted the hot drink to restore his mood. Work generally made Gabriel pleased and he enjoyed beginning a new commission. After he sipped a bit of his coffee, Mary asked, "What of Mr. Millrace's house, Husband? Is it grand?" Annie and Ellen perked their ears as well. They all were curious about Jacob Millrace's house.

Gabriel answered in a tired voice. "His daughter keeps his household. She is young and needs laundry help. Call on her to inquire and you might see his parlor for yourself."

Twenty-six

A NAUSEATING MIASMA composed of the stench of rotted bodies and the accompanying odors of embalming fluids cloaked the air. What little food Mary ate came back as soon as she left the shop to fulfill her laundry circuit. She regurgitated in the trench running next to the path from the back door to the alley at Olive Street. When she relieved herself of the burden of these vittles, she worried that not enough was left for the coming babe.

Mary had hurried to get out of sight of Gabriel — not wanting him to see her retching. He'd begun to look disappointed when she showed fatigue and discomfort. Ellen came upon Mary's heels and wiped her face.

"Shall I fetch your husband, girl?" she asked, though she knew that Mary would say no.

Recovering her equilibrium, Mary answered, "Leave him be, Sister."

Mary had taken on the laundry commission for the Millrace household as pressed to by Gabriel. The Millraces entertained among the town's prominent Negroes and there were fine table linens, as well as monogrammed sheets. Gabriel ordered vinegar and lemon and rainwater and special note of every piece. In fact, Gabriel made Mary nervous over the Millrace commission. He checked and cluck-clucked in a way that peeved and tired her.

The town's laundrywomen were an important cog in the engine for helping the waves of wounded soldiers. Sanitary Commission officers scoured the city and impressed colored women into washing service. The Ladies of Olives put themselves forth as professional laundresses and its members were given contracts for hospital sheets. Even the bawdy houses had surrendered bed linens for bandages. A premium was put on crisp antisepsis and the Sanitary Commission favored the Coats women.

Recovering herself, Mary turned from Ellen and followed the path she was accustomed to take on her rounds. A wave of folk lately off a nearby farm surged toward her at the corner of High Street and Olive. A great wide woman burdened down with belongings tied in bundles and situated atop her head herded a group of children with a rough-cut walking stick. The woman gathered the children by slashing out at their legs if they strayed from her skirts. One of the group, a mud-covered toddling child, grasped Mary's skirt as she passed by and sought to be borne along with her. When Mary moved her leg to walk, this child swung along, riding her.

Mary halted, balanced her laundry load, and pried the babe's stringy fingers from her skirt. His little fingers were wound tight, though his strength and endurance seemed dangerously used up. His facial features were sunken and he bore the look of an old person, with a frosting of light hair at his temples and ashy skin. A young girl with an expectant look on her tobacco-leaf face came to retrieve him.

Mary pressed a penny in this girl's hand and bade her, "Buy

milk for the boy." The girl smiled at her good fortune and kept
onward with the advancing column of contrabands. She hoisted
the child on her hip with bundles tied on her back and some
more bundles tied as a sausage at her waist. The group moved
eastward under press of the provost marshals and headed for the
encampment on 12th Street. Mary wondered at the girl's lighthearted step and hoped the coin would go for milk and not whiskey. Heretofore in her childbearing, Mary had tripped lightly
and energetically. Perhaps this burdensome one was the boy
they were all praying for.

Ellen had been reluctant to break from Mary to pursue her own
customers, for her sister-in-law seemed unsettled with her babe.
She had confided to Ellen that she wanted a boy for Gabriel's
sake. Ellen mused that all and too much was put before Gabriel
these days. Gabriel had decided against Delia long before the
master claimed her. And no plea had ever convinced him that
Ellen was Delia's mam and would always want her.

Ellen was jogged from her reverie by a stern tugging on her
sleeve. The force upset her basket, and some of the precious
whites she carried were tipped up and dumped in the mud at
her feet. She screamed out in shock, turned toward the force
grasping her arm, and set eyes on the mud-covered woman who
held her. Ellen wrestled and lurched to pull herself free and to
retrieve the laundry. The woman's grip was formidable. Ellen
tottered, lost balance, landed on the ground, and struck her
shoulder. She thought to grasp her skirts and guard them from
the gutters, and as she did so the woman snatched the laundry
basket. The piled-high whites spilled out completely and the
woman grunted and sucked her snaggled teeth. The woman
had a hard-set face that was broad, flat, and unyielding. For the

long moment that Ellen looked into her visage to gain an explanation for the woman's actions, she saw only an implacable will. The expression caused Ellen to redouble her efforts to keep the laundry. Both women wallowed on the ground and tugged the basket between them. A small crowd of amused onlookers gathered to observe.

Ellen regained her feet. The woman next sucked in her ribs, set her strength, and pulled. Knocked completely off her feet again and her sleeve hitched on the basket, Ellen was dragged. The women's clothes became saturated with the muddy effluvium of the roads. Ellen's dress was as well ripped from under her left arm to her waist. She was warm with shame to imagine the look of this brawl and had at that second resolved to tear away from the basket and attempt to reclaim her honor.

What finally caused Ellen to break her hold on the basket was a solid, painful kick to her stomach. She let out a yowl. The blow came not from her antagonist but from a mountainous man standing over Ellen. He then kicked viciously at the other woman sprawled on the ground and turned to aim his foot again at Ellen.

Shrieks sounded from ladies passing in a carriage, and a gentleman called out, "You! You there, what is this, sir?" The soldier did not answer.

A woman painted thickly with cosmetic and walking abroad in the fashion of a harlot called out to the vicious kicker, "What! Hold! What's the beef, Irish?"

The marshal loosed his grasp of Ellen then and looked at the woman. Happily, she claimed his attention momentarily and Ellen and her assailant gained their feet in the interval. As they staggered up, the partner of the distracted marshal clamped shackles on their wrists.

"Aye, is some contraband wenches causing a riot on the street, beautiful. Get along with ye!" he replied.

"Careful you don't cause no monkey business right here on the public street," the blond harlot teased him, and caused him to guffaw.

The violent events had happened so quickly that Ellen was unable to make a coherent protest of her arrest. She was grabbed up and forced to follow the marshals along with her attacker. The two were roughly pushed into a jail wagon with some other contraband women. The woman who accompanied Ellen began to sing and Ellen cursed herself for a heathen, for she wished solemnly to throttle this woman.

All were brought to the jail known as the Blue Jug. Thus called because of the peculiar color of its crumbling, dank marl walls, the jail was located north of the city hall. This was a fearfully unfamiliar part of town for Ellen. Her heart sank. The colored — contraband and those protesting their free status — were confined in a large one-room cell. Some few men, more women, and some children were crouched around the periphery of this one room. They sat or lay upon a layer of straw that was dirtier than that used to line a horse stall.

No part of the contents of the laundry basket came to the jail with Ellen. She worried about the laundry more than about herself! The spotless cleans were ruined and now lost. Ellen looked down at her dirty dress and petticoat that had so lately been immaculate. In this cell full of ragged, nearly naked women she became scared for her clothes. Would they be torn from her? She alone had the luxury of a petticoat in this precinct.

The trough running along the south wall of the cell was clogged fully with the nervous waste of the occupants of the cell. There was no curtain of privacy, yet the listless inmates took little interest in one another. They were quiet — mostly ill and disconsolate. Off in the corners facing the walls were women hacking and coughing and expectorating. These were doubtless suffering from the variola and were feared contagious. Forced to the periphery, they had only themselves as helpmeets. Ellen gathered her skirts beneath her seat on the floor. She moved her hands over her body and felt for her sore places. She resolved to keep her head in this place.

In the morning Ellen remembered her papers — the permit she carried to signify she was free and gainfully employed as a laundress. This document lived in the deep pocket of her skirts and could prove her status and gain her freedom! Buoyed at the thought Ellen dug her fingers down to find the permit and came back with nothing. The permit was gone!

Even in daytime the Blue Jug's cells were mostly dark. There was a sliver of light from a stingy opening near the top of one wall. The woman who'd begun the horrible events of the day before had reached the jail with bruises, too. Her left eye, surrounded by dark purple, was closed. Crustiness and blood remained on her face and her hair was dotted with chaff. But her spirits seemed not too much deflated. She approached Ellen with a hint of smile and said, "You'll forgive. Won't you?" Ellen did not reply. She looked at the other warily, not sure whether the woman meant to start up again with fisticuffs.

"'Twas me that got you here. You hurtin' bad?" she said not unkindly. Still Ellen only stared.

When a few moments passed silently and Ellen's courage had built, she asked the woman, "You take my permit? You take my papers, did you, in all the tussling?"

"'Twas after the basket. I'd have sold the laundry though. I'd

not known you had papers," she said sincerely, and Ellen believed her. Some other had taken advantage of the opportunity
the fight had presented.

The cell's occupants were called to attention when two soldiers entered and carried a large vat into the center of the room.
In the bowl, filled to the rim with water and swimming onions,
floated several small potatoes. For these meager vittles the hungry prisoners elbowed one another. Ellen and Eva, the woman
who was arrested with her, stood at the back of the crowd and
satisfied their hunger on what cooled and congealed liquid was
left at the bottom of the pot when the others had finished.

When Ellen hadn't returned home at her accustomed time,
Mary had called out the syndicate, who had circulated to trace
her route. Going abroad herself to look for Ellen, Mary had inquired at the last house upon that day's circuit. Ginnie Claxtor,
the cook at the Beech house — Mrs. Millicent Standard Beech's
house — said the laundrywoman and the load of clean had
never reached them. She said Missus was chagrined that her
sheets had not returned and was already noising about calling a
constable to report them stolen, though she knew Ellen and
trusted her. She said the mistress imagined the precious covers
of Irish linen had been sold to a sutler and taken to Richmond.
It was well known that such commodities were short among
the Confederates and brought a good price. Mary's shoulders
slumped at the news. She protested that she had but to find Ellen to know the fate of the sheets. She implored Ginnie to quiet
her missus's fears. The sheets would be found!

When Mary left the Beech house, a wave of nausea revisited
her. She fingered a knitting needle in her sleeve. It was mate to
the one that held her work and had been left in the kitchen.

This sister to that one was ready in case of trouble. She quailed to think what might have happened to Ellen. Perhaps she had stopped to watch a parade — thrice-daily occurrences now in the town — and had forgotten cares and followed along? Though it was not like Ellen to dawdle, Mary took heart at this possibility. She paused at a junction of streets and looked at the panorama of passersby. She perused faces. Her hopes rose at the approaching form of a woman similar to Ellen, but were dashed as the woman came close. Mary marshaled her remaining strength and returned to the kitchen upon the hopeful wind that Ellen had come home while she was away.

After a frightened supper Gabriel went out to scour the city for his sister. Going abroad on a search through the streets at dusk was a risky business on account of the various patrols. Daniel Joshua, daily driving his wagon transporting night soil, was known well enough to pass unhindered, especially in Georgetown. The frequent constables acknowledged his and Gabriel's passing with a nod. Daniel and Gabriel drove slowly, deliberately, as to seem to be merely plodding homeward after hard labor. In this way they checked the streets, lanes, and many alleys from College Street to Dumbarton Avenue. Gabriel's anxiety increased with each block.

Trading upon acquaintances and favors, Daniel made inquiries at the contraband camp. No information was forthcoming. Then, hemming and hawing, one old fellow with a knotted bandanna at his throat suggested that Ellen had been swooped up and taken to jail as a contraband whore.

" 'Tis a common fate for a colored woman in the streets without papers," he said. The codger narrowly missed Gabriel's fists upside of his head for the information.

"My sister is a free woman!" Gabriel cried out in a great wounded voice. "She has her papers upon her!"

The codger ducked good-naturedly and added there was word circulating that a handful of colored women had been taken in. Daniel pulled against Gabriel's arm and said he thought it a likely explanation. He thanked the man.

The two men plodded up and down the streets throughout the night mostly to occupy themselves. Daniel was sure the old codger was right about Ellen being nabbed by soldiers. If so, there was nothing to be done until the morning. But Gabriel refused to stop looking and Daniel felt it his duty to stay with Gabriel to prevent a further tragedy. It was not likely they would come upon her seated at the side of the road with a broken heel on her shoe. This is what Gabriel seemed to be looking for — a gentle tragedy, a little bit of trouble. But Daniel knew she had been caught and they were going to be up against it to help her.

Around the time that roosters were reporting to their duty, Winnie Wareham came to knock at the back door of the tailor shop. She came breathless to say that Reverend William Higgins had wrung news from a provost marshal. Winnie no longer cared to converse head-on with a person because one of her front teeth had been lost. She preferred to speak over her shoulder while at her work. But this morning she came with urgency and she held her left hand in front of her lips as she spoke.

"They took up some gals yestidy. Is likely Ellen's in with 'em."

"Is likely," Annie conceded.

"Reverend beg a chance to see for hisself — to talk to her. Him short of the mark this time. They don't 'low him in!"

Winnie cried, obscuring the hole amongst her teeth with a cupped hand.

William Higgins's reach wasn't sufficient in the new circumstances. The chain of power in the town was upset and reordered by the war. Authorities, keen to control the numbers of colored on the streets, seized all opportunity to round them up. Though Higgins tried to testify on Ellen's behalf, the marshals refused to hear him. Influence had shifted.

The sheriffs said Ellen was a contraband prostitute and cited and sentenced her for a street brawl. Ellen was ordered to serve thirty days in the filthy confinement of the Blue Jug. Only one concession was given: women would be permitted to visit the jail to bring medicine and vittles for Ellen.

"No visits from men for any o' the fancy girls — period!"

For his part, Gabriel struggled to wait in the wagon beside Daniel Joshua. Though secretly relieved that Annie thought his idea to disguise himself and sneak into the jail was a bad one, he was frustrated with his own impotence. It was a torment to know Ellen to be in this place and not lay eyes on her. Daniel had said it rightly that Gabriel was trussed up with them all — the women. But it was a loving truss, for Nanny and Mary and Ellen and the babes were all that there was. Ah! Friend Daniel was stuck as well, for he sat in the wagon, too.

They needed Ellen to return. The hearth was cold without her. They needed Ellen as ballast. There was a hum — a sweetness in the air when all were there and hard at their tasks — after the dinner with a cup of tea or coffee and a dip of snuff. Without Ellen the biscuits tasted flat.

In dark contemplation of the horrible events that had befallen Sis Ellen, Gabriel sat in a shallow light at his worktable. Curiously he felt he had not earned his rest because he had not come to a solution for this trouble. The one chance might be to call upon the influence of Miss Standard — nay, Mrs. Millicent Standard Beech. The haughty girl, married well, was now a haughty woman. She maintained her especial preference for Ellen's work, and the Beech table linens and monogrammed bed linens executed by Gabriel's sister had earned a place in the Beeches' heirloom blanket chest. Certainly he could beg her to intervene at the jail — to vouch for Ellen. The begging left him cold, but he was resolved to do all and everything to bring Ellen home.

Gabriel scratched up a short note pleading with Mrs. Beech to help Ellen. He tucked the note into a stack of sheets he carried to Mrs. Beech's back door. These sheets were embroidered with a deep border that was similar to the ones Ellen had made for her customer. The border was so intricate and plainly beautiful that if decorated linens were as persuasive of a man as women chose to believe then no man could turn away from these sheets or the girl who came with them.

Mrs. Beech came to the door of the kitchen. Gabriel and Ginnie Claxtor rose quickly. Gabriel held his eyes to the floor, resting his chin full upon his chest. Ginnie took a position that was between Gabriel and the young matron.

Millicent Beech affected an urgent occupation elsewhere and carried Gabriel's letter with the tips of her left hand as if she feared it held a pox. She found it difficult to reconcile the note with her image of the rascal who employed Ellen and called himself her brother. She handed the letter to Ginnie and spoke. "Tailor, your sister, you say — your Ellen — has fallen into the hands of the authorities. We will not press a complaint regarding our linens as you have brought comparable goods to replace them. We are distressed to learn of Ellen's troubles. But we cannot go into these precincts to influence the circumstances. Tailor, I will give her my commissions when she is free. But my position will not allow me to intercede. Tell her that I weep for her and await her return." Millicent Beech turned and left the room in a swift movement. It was her signature departure. It was the same way she had exited the tailor shop on her first visit.

Gabriel wanted to run and grasp the young woman and throttle her for her dismissive manner. If only she would appear and vouch for Ellen his sister might be released to come home! This woman was so covetous of her own comfort! She'd come into the room and demanded attention and deference and that a swath be cut for her — so that her person not be forced up against some unworthy other. Yet poor Ellen was mashed up in the Blue Jug in uncertain, unhappy circumstance! Did she not care one whit for Ellen? As if to give a crumb of comfort to another would take a feather from her own.

Ginnie Claxtor followed Gabriel from the back door of the Beech house. She waited a few moments while he turned on his own heels in the yard. He sought to blow off his anger before heading home and when he collected himself, he looked at Ginnie sheepishly.

"Boy," she commanded, "tell your mama that I say there is a gal named Callie Dodge that is favored by the jailer at the Blue Jug. Money at the right place can shorten your sister's time. Tell her that Dodge's Ginnie says so," she concluded, and stamped her words true. Annie would know her veracity because Annie knew the story of the Dodge place.

Disgusted by Millicent Beech's selfish behavior, Gabriel related Ginnie Claxtor's words to his mother in an offhand manner. It was the least of his news, he thought. He was brought low at his failure. And he was tied up inside with the worry that Mary waited upon a plan from him. She did not say so, but her expectations were palpable. Her trust that he would rise to the challenge of getting Ellen out of the Blue Jug sawed at his gut. Gabriel reflected that Mary was nervous of disappointing him, too. She had no need to be, but she was worried that his love hung upon her bringing a son this time.

"You are bathing her in salt water, Mary. You must stop your crying now," Annie said to her daughter-in-law when the baby girl came forth.

Mary cried out, "Oh! A stone is on her head! Oh, no!" She set to crying buckets of tears and kept it up. She imagined she saw a caul upon the girl's head and was frightened after the long labor. Annie wrapped mother and daughter in clean cloths.

"Another girl! Oh, Gabriel will want a different wife!" Mary whimpered as she took the fat, active baby into her arms.

"Be quiet, girl," Annie answered impatiently. "Gabriel is no bull in the pasture and you are no beast. You bring the child you make and you build your life upon its head. This one is fat and strong. We can use her. We don't need no boy around here pissing on a wall and getting underfoot!" she countered vehemently, as if rehearsing her script for Gabriel.

Mary took her mother-in-law's hand as Annie smoothed and tucked the bedclothes around her. "Mother, I want to please Gabriel." She sounded like a small child and Annie put it down to her great weariness.

"He's a grown man, Mary. He don't need no more pleasing," Annie answered. She was eager to settle Mary's unease before it grew.

◆◆

Aye, Annie was compelled to please Gabriel, too. But her indulgence was tempered with her control of him.

"Brother, we have more proof of you. You have another daughter." Annie came out to the back porch where Gabriel and his others sat on the porch lip.

"Oh!" he cried, and stood up, spilling his lap work. Annie put her body directly in front of him and stopped him with a hand on his chest.

"Your Mary is disappointed not to have a boy for you," she said. "Are you disappointed, Brother?" Annie would know a lie if he told it because her hand was over his heart. She knew this heart from long association with it. She had listened to it and ticked off its regularity from the first.

"I can't say that I am, Nanny. I love my children. I can't think that a bigger joy could be possible," Gabriel said thoughtfully, as if he'd already worked it out.

"Go on, Brother. Be joyful," Annie said. "This one is already fat and saucy."

The next morning Annie pursued Ginnie Claxtor's well-meaning advice. She sought out another one of the Dodge women and this one led her to Callie Dodge, the jailer's wench.

"I don't mind it much, Miz Coats," the short pale gal with a ragged, faded-fancy dress told Annie happily in the alley behind High Street. She offered her right hand as a cup for Annie's coins. "I'm used to him." She laughed. "He an' a mean man. He just got stiff whiskers." She guffawed and spread her mouth wide. "I can get your Ellen out short time. He hungry and he like sweets. He trade his favor for what he likes." She laid it out with shrugging shoulders. "I'm sweet, Miss Jessie say. I don't know no better. I ain't had no ma, Miz Coats."

Was the solution to every problem beneath the skirts of some gal or other? 'Twas no way else but this? Each and every time out of a fix they had to buy a man's favor. Again and again Annie mused, "'Tis a man's town."

Annie pushed forth another coin more. "Don't go hungry. Get a buttered biscuit an' a cup of coffee." The girl laughed heartily. "Thank ye, Miz Coats. I get a drink of whiskey, though, and I like it better." She guffawed again.

Twenty-seven

"I SHOULD PUT shoulder to wheel, Mary, if this fighting will bring about freedom for all the folk." Gabriel explained his position to Mary in the bedroom. "Is't not my duty to muster in — to join them? Those who are in a way to know have said that Black men are being given the opportunity to serve in Massachusetts and Pennsylvania. Literate, skilled men are needed to fill up posts of responsibility with their own. Here is a man — himself — who can read and write and figure. Have I — Black Gabriel Coats — not an obligation to go?" He spoke loudly and pointed at his chest.

"Husband, you are making a speech," Mary replied. She had listened to his arguments with equanimity. She sat on the side of their bed and her fingers traced a pattern on the counterpane. Perhaps he would interpret her calm as uncaring, but she did not want to hold him back if he wanted the war. The men wanted the war. Perhaps it was the Black man's turn at the wheel. Let her excellent husband have the war if he wanted it! She would miss him. She had come to be so pleased with his ways and manners that she knew her innards would ache for him.

Colored men were, at last, allowed to form up regiments! Locals shook their fists and declared it was high time for it and was a good way to get rid of niggers. "Send them to the front lines instead of wasting the lives of white men!" was an oft-repeated, cynical slogan. Colored men cheered the idea, for they wanted to fight.

Reverend Henry M. Turner and Reverend Raymond of Israel Bethel Church dressed trees and boards throughout the Negro neighborhoods of Washington and Georgetown with posters calling out to recruit colored soldiers in the District. Champing at the bit to secure manumission for all colored, Gabriel had become impatient. He felt himself small and getting smaller because he was not in the fray. Should he not be one who leads? He had built a commercial concern. He had accomplished what had been thought impossible for colored. His family was poised on the cusp of this war, and their survival surely depended on his being here to run the business — to look after the women and children. Could he take the risk of joining up?

Gabriel Coats had purchased freedom over and again as if it were quicksilver. As soon as the coin was handed over it seemed that the stuff of it — freedom — disappeared. It became something else that couldn't be had or held. It chafed him. He was not fully free! He was only not as bound as others. For this he resolved to fight the war.

He would go for the girl, Delia, too. A feeling he could not expel from himself was that he'd not done enough to help her case. He had offered the money to free her. Ridley would not have it. Perhaps if Gabriel had pleaded more Ridley would have capitulated. But Nanny and all of them had gotten her free and away. They had done that!

The loose and volatile encampments of contrabands and other transients in every alley and public open area in the town threatened to upset a balance, and in the view of some who had been in town awhile longer, there was danger from these. The new, confused colored congregating in alleys had easily fallen into a tumble of behaviors that brought censure and caused many to cringe and turn sour on them. The free Blacks of long standing in Georgetown were nervous of these and sought to set themselves apart. Ah, a divide was there and Gabriel felt himself on both of its sides. The contrabands would hardly be his patrons for tailoring — bedraggled as they were. But they were a wave he had been awaiting. At long last they were seizing their chances and coming to fill in the crevices and fill up the town with colored. He had known this place to be freer and craved it for these as well. Did these not have a right to breathe this air? Gabriel knew the Union army was driving them and hoped this army would drive the secesh back into the south — into submission. Still it seemed to Gabriel that the free and newly freed in the District were caught together between this millstone and that oh so hard place!

Newspapers were full of discussion of the Black man's role in the conflict and Gabriel and Daniel stoked their passions upon these. Meetings and oratory regarding the formation of colored troops took place around town nightly. Gabriel and Daniel attended the meetings and Gabriel, unbeknownst to the women, verbally sparred with others like himself. Information at the nightly forums was fresher than newspaper reports because the daily influx of contrabands and newsagents brought updates on troops and what lay beyond the District's borders.

Provost officers, secesh sympathizers, and ruffians full of tanglefoot whiskey openly observed the meetings between colored
and their friends. The protection of church sanctuary kept some
violence at bay, but attendees were vulnerable on the streets to
and fro. Many nights Daniel Joshua ran a ferry of attendees between the church and their homes with a couple of fierce clubs
and his "near son" beside him.

At one evening's recruitment meeting, Gabriel was surprised
to see Jacob Millrace seated alone at the back of the room.
Gabriel'd been unsure of Millrace's thoughts on the war. They
did not discuss such in their commerce. Though he was aware of
the respect Millrace afforded and he reciprocated, Gabriel did
not imagine himself Jacob Millrace's friend. The two of them
had not talked of fighting nor had Gabriel overheard any comment. He understood that Millrace was a favorite of southern
gentlemen who liked the hunt. Even watching Mr. Millrace's
face unobserved, Gabriel could not glean the man's opinions.

Gabriel and Daniel swept off their caps and relaxed their coats
as they sat in Mount Zion Church. There were pockets of fellows
they knew from previous meetings and there was a bumble buzz
throughout the room. The looks upon the faces of the men in
the church were emphasized by haunting shadows thrown by
lamplight kept low to disguise the doings. The fervor at previous recruitment meetings had stirred up hostile actions about
town and the potent threat of more. Soldiers were detailed to
keep an eye out for rowdies at the churches, but some inside
doubted that the Union soldiers ringing the building were entirely trustworthy. The whiskey they drank could cause them to
change their minds about what their purpose was this evening.

Into the meeting came an important-looking figure. A journalist for the *Philadelphia Press* — perhaps the only newspaper-

man known to be colored — who reported on battles where the colored soldiers were fighting. The audience had come tonight to see him paint the picture from the colored man's point. What were the conditions for colored troops in this war?

Thomas Chester's verbal pictures ignited flames of glory in the imagination. He spoke with spiraling pride of the valiant colored troops already fighting. As he concluded, he began to sound more like a rabble-rousing preacher than a journalist. He was stirring! Gabriel got beside himself and his natural reticence vanished. After Thomas Chester sat, he stood and applauded heartily.

"I am no man of war nor a man who is wont to fight," Gabriel began, addressing the assembled in a clear voice. "Even I know that the white men are not fighting for our freedom. If we are dependent upon them for our survival, then we have little chance of it. We had better raise the gun in defense of ourselves. We had better earn our freedom with the fighting. Let them give us a chance! While many whites chafe at defending the cause of abolition, Black men are being denied an opportunity they long for. And while the government is eager to take unwilling white men, they are passing on brave Black men more than willing to shoulder arms!"

The men answered him with a full-throated "Hurrah!"

Gabriel was swept with the warmth of the occasion. Until this moment he had never allowed his passion to overwhelm his control of himself. The race of events was shaking him wholly and remaking him. For the first time ever thoughts that came together in his mind were rushing out of his mouth. Gabriel looked around the knot of men gathered shoulder to shoulder in the pews and their eyes were riveted upon him. Their eyes were as enflamed as his were. Daniel Joshua jumped up and clapped Gabriel's back with the force to wind him. They were ready! They had questions and fears, too. But they were ready! All of them!

Jacob Millrace, enigmatic and drawn up straight and proud, was ready, too. Who is to say that his mind had not been firmly made when he entered the church? But Gabriel, the tailor, had convinced. Millrace was now ready to enlist. Now was their time to show. Now was their chance!

When Gabriel returned home and entered the kitchen, he paused near the door. Mary looked at his face. She learned a thing there. Gabriel had an expression of great stimulation. His face was perspiring and Mary was alarmed that he might be ill. But the expression and the lather and the smell of passionate rumination were on him and gave him away. He had made the decision that would plunge them all into the conflict. It was as plain a thing as her nose.

Mary's face was not the same face he was wont to see ordinarily either. Some measure of his mood was spoiled.

The talking to his mother took place in the kitchen workroom in the first light of the next morning.

"It's been a long time coming," Annie said bluntly — simply. "I never expected to hold you, though I think you have stayed with me and worked so hard because of wanting to help me to freedom as well as yourself. You have done a good job for yourself and me and your sister and your wife, too. You have toiled us out of bond several times now. I thank you," Annie said, and looked square in Gabriel's eyes. She took his hands and kissed his palms and folded the hands together. With these hands she drew him to herself and held him awhile. He was docile in her arms. She pushed him away, but held him atether by his fingertips. "You've toughened up nicely. You go and do," Annie said, and turned from him with dry eyes.

"Aye, Nanny, too tough for a stew pot. I'll survive," Gabriel said to lighten her mood after she turned away.

"Do that, pup," Annie replied, unable to relinquish the last word.

Twenty-eight

TEARFUL FAREWELLS WERE daily and fashionable on Washington streets. The streets were lined with handkerchief wavers following the drill of departing soldiers. When the time came for Gabriel to go, Annie reached up to his lapels and pummeled his clothes with her stiff brush until the bristles bit down.

"Come," she said in that way from long ago that compelled him and caused him to smile and submit. Mournful indigo was the color of the suit of clothes upon him — his uniform. He was so vain of it and its color! *Lord, Lord, Lord, it is low-down sad to look at,* Annie thought.

There was a small nut of worry — of sorrow — that rattled around in her skull at the sight of the cloth. When she dug into the back of his coat and scraped and brushed him, it was a feeling to take the place of hugging and kissing.

Gabriel preened before the cheval glass dressed in the uniform he had solemnly sewn for himself while ruminating on his decision to join the combat. When he had been Abraham Pearl's assistant, Gabriel had doubted his image would appear in the glass. For the longest time he had remained the wraith in the background of the oval. His young eyes were trained primarily to close work. When he progressed to measuring and fitting his customers, he began to see differently — in a different relation, but still oblique to the glass. This day Gabriel Coats looked in the glass straight on.

He was vain of his military appearance, though reluctant to let Mary observe his failure of virtue. Before his wife, Gabriel sought to characterize his enlistment in the war as a noble duty. However, it had the pleasure of pomp and march, too. The excitement buoyed Gabriel and worked to carry him off.

The assembly of colored men into the army was cause for riotous behavior in Georgetown and Washington City. There were knots of ruffians who jeered at any colored in a group, with any semblance of uniform and with anything that resembled a weapon. For this reason the recruits were told to report in their civilian clothes to the makeshift ferry at the river's edge that was thrown up to take them to Mason's Island. The isle, heavily wooded, was low-lying and swampy. The main camp was at the middle of the island and out of view of either the Georgetown shore or the Virginia side.

Gabriel wore his uniform only briefly on the streets of Georgetown. When he left the shop — taking it upon himself to walk from the front of the shop in a jaunty manner — he was pursued down Bridge Street by a pack of lobster-colored boys with rocks. They were already in a high state of excitement when Gabriel emerged from the shop. They became more so at the sight of a colored man in a Union soldier's uniform. Gabriel eluded them for most of a block, taking only a small missile to the center of his back. He then stopped in the doorway of a confectionary shop to remove his coat. Reluctantly he turned the proud jacket in upon itself, tucked it under his arm, and continued to the riverside.

Annie pulled back from the group in the absence of Gabriel. She cast herself as grim leader of the band and sternly pronounced on what they must prepare — what to look to around each corner. She formulated plans into bit-sized chores and gave out orders in a steady stream. In truth she was frightened of their fears — Ellen and Mary, Naomi and Ruth and Pearl and tiny Hannah. Survival was perilous without Gabriel, and Annie upbraided them to keep them solid and firm and focused on their duties.

Mary mitigated loneliness by throwing her energies into ever more laundry commissions and working socks through much of the nighttime. Annie's carping directives were little pinch to her. They were an accompaniment — a constant. Oh, how Mary craved a constant now! With Gabriel gone, any a thing to hang a shawl upon! Annie's concise delineation of household duties — "do this, do that" — was just such constancy as Mary looked for.

Ellen emerged as the clerk in the shop in the absence of Gabriel and Aaron Ridley. Less productive in her needlework than before, she enjoyed her new duties.

In the absence of Gabriel, Daniel Joshua made daily visits to the back of the shop. He entered the back door after announcing himself with scraping his shoes, slapping his hat on his clothes to shuck off dirt, and expectorating what his lungs had gathered on his circuits. He checked for chores gone wanting and found little. Annie kept herself and the others hard at it. Lately it had become a regular occupation for him to read out of the newspapers or spin out a tale as the women worked. He enjoyed his role as diversion for the needleworkers around the table. Not wanting to thwart themselves by talking, they happily listened to Daniel Joshua. A bit of tanglefoot whiskey made him hold back less than he might usually do. If there was joy in this precinct without Gabriel, then it was on these evenings of all together — the women's industry set to the sound of Daniel Joshua's voice.

Daniel spread the paper and brushed it smooth as the others waited. "*'Though the government openly declared that it did not want the Negroes in this conflict, I look around me and see hundreds of colored men armed and ready to defend the Government at any moment; and such are my feelings that I can only say, the fetters have fallen — our bondage is over.'* So says George Hatton of North Carolina," he read out. Daniel thumped his own chest and looked away from the newspaper.

"Who have fell, Daniel? What he mean?" Annie asked. "What fellers have fallen, man? Is't our Gabriel?" Her voice was plaintive and frightened.

"No, Mother. He is talking 'bout the freedom. Our Gabriel is ours yet," Mary pronounced with certainty, but was unconvinced. As the least of the needleworkers, she was particularly attentive to the reading. She worked socks to keep busy, but she was keenest for information of the war. She wanted the news of Gabriel. "Brother Daniel, please read it slowly — again — so we can come around again," she asked. And softly, too, she prayed to herself — to savor any mention of the colored men who were fighting.

He read it out again, then paused. "'Tis a grim story that follows, girl," he said.

"Go on," Annie and Mary said together. They fell quiet for

fear of hexing and Annie crossed herself from forehead and across the chest like the papists do.

They threw their arms upwards to surrender, but were shot to death anyway! No quarter was the cry and the solemn vow!

Many colored soldiers threw down their arms, pleaded to be taken captive, and were cruelly shot numerous times while on their knees begging!

Some Negro soldiers feigned themselves dead until Union soldiers came along!

Huts and tents were set on fire with wounded still in them!

Some were shot while in the river and others were shot on the bank and kicked into the river to drown!

Some soldiers that were not dead were made to dig graves and were flung in and covered when they had done it!

Days after of rain and trampling confusion and still the ground around contained heads and arms and legs protruding!

Annie gasped and Mary and Ellen covered their eyes for fear of their imagining. Their heads were bowed. The hands were stilled. Mary rose when Daniel stopped reading and gently took the sheet from his lap to spare the young ones more of the story.

"T'aint a good thing to read long into the nighttime." Annie fussed like a bumblebee, as if the bloody carnage at Fort Pillow would have seemed less in the daylight. Uncharacteristically, she wound and wound her yarn around her index finger in frustration. Daniel came to her and bussed her neck and petted her.

Mary took the turn to put water on the stove. She drew her shawl with a shudder as she left the room for the pump in the

yard. Horrible pictures coursed through her head as she worked
the handle. Colored soldiers standing for tall, raising their hands
above their heads, and them hacked down with vengeance because of their audacity! No quarter! No quarter! Why give no
quarter — to these! They gladly accept it when it is given to
them! The surging pump water made Mary's water come and
she put down her pan and dashed to the toilet. She sat to ruminate that rebel prisoners who surrendered and were spared the
bayonet were regularly paraded through Washington — still
with what was left of their hated uniforms upon them! Why was
it that the same feel for colored to stand firm upon their rights
was so odious to the sense of the Southerner? When these brave
colored men stood to fight, they were given no quarter. They
were cut down where planted like sugarcane! Whither Gabriel —
how was he keeping, he and Mr. Millrace?

Next came a thing the women had not expected. Amidst the
crisis pulse of the town, regiments of colored soldiers marched
under arms through the city streets. The Coats women fluttered
to think of Gabriel, but knew he was not among them. These
soldiers were brilliant in their uniforms. Annie, Ellen, Mary,
Naomi, Ruth, Pearl, infant Hannah, Essie Millrace, and Winnie Wareham assembled along the thoroughfare to bless the
colored troops' passing. Upon these very ones headed south to
secure the freedom rested the turning of the tide.

"Ho there! Hallo!" Bad Eva, Ellen's companion from the
Blue Jug, hailed and waved exuberantly from the back of a sutler's wagon trailing the troops. Only loosely attached to the
town and jittery fearful of the coming battle, Eva had decided
to go off south behind this tide. She had fashioned herself a
laundress and had found work with the moving military.

"Oh, oh," Ellen cried at recognizing Bad Eva in the passing parade. "Farewell!" she called sincerely.

As the city's defenders headed south to fight, rumors of an attack upon Washington flew about. Newsboys hawked extras on the corners of every thoroughfare. Dubious information swirled about and was snatched up by confused citizens. Most folk now wrestled with whether to go or stay and, if go, where to go? Trouble was rumored coming from the north — north of Washington — in precincts held by Confederates. There was no escape for the colored who feared a tide that could carry them southward. Word was the Confederates had drawn around and were tightening a noose about the capital.

Some like Eva had attached themselves as cooks, laborers, and women for pleasure, animal keepers, laundresses, boot-blacks, nurses, and cobblers and moved off south with the soldiers.

"No sense in us runnin' now. We thus planted and we done stood this far." Daniel cut into the quiet of the women around the nighttime table. "We must to provision the cellar and keep our heads down."

"Yes, Brother Daniel," Annie answered him. "Where would our heart look for us if we let our gut take us on a runner?" Annie sat in her accustomed chair as if the hands in her lap were weighed with sinkers. Her thoughts were heavy and ponderous and oppressed with missing Gabriel.

The newspapers that touted the Confederates at the door to the capital proved correct. The flood of country folk coming in from northwest of town carried word of secesh troops as close as Rockville and hard on the city. A great many of the sick and wounded troops in the city's hospitals were roused up and pressed to defend the city. Colored troops and contrabands were rounded up to work on fortifications. Even staunch but peaceable nurses like William Higgins were given arms and put to defense.

◆◆

My mother,

My dear Mary,

My sister,

Daughters,

We have arrived in the Camp. I will not tarry on this page with descriptions of Camp Greene. We are training hard. We are given little free time. We are not to be allowed to return to our homes. We are awakened at 5:00 a.m. by bugle call of reveille. This is followed by roll call, breakfast, sick call, cleanup of the compound, guard duty or picket duty, and much drilling. We drill again after our noon meal then we assemble for a dress parade before we eat our supper. Many of the men have never eaten so much and so often — with so much regularity. Some ignorant ones fear we are being fatted up to feed the white soldiers. In truth our rations are meager. We are allowed a period of free time to attend to wants before the beating of tattoo commands us to our quarters. Our day ends with the bugle call of taps, for we are made to put lights out. This is a difficult time of day for me. It is at this time that my eyes fill with water. I miss all with my heart and soul, especially in the deep dark. I occupy myself with some knitting to pass these long hours of darkness, as I am unaccustomed to sleep so early. Though truly we reach this time of day in a very weary state. As I have little yarn, Mother, I undo and begin again. Mr. Millrace, too, yearns for his home when we reach our cots and try to close our eyes. In the dark he speaks of the young Miss Essie Millrace. He greatly misses her and his dogs.

I am thankful that I am well equipped with warm clothing. Also, I am well able to trade the stores that I brought. We are kept apart from the town and have only our uniforms. Several of the men were amused at the large bundles that I carried. They are now thankful for the socks. The ground is very damp and our feet are often wet.

We have also found that many who are already here have traversed much of the country on foot from the slave states. They have walked long to reach here. Many are without any shoes — let alone socks. I am requesting that you work diligently upon more socks that I may sell some, barter some, and give some away. Will you three jewels work hard on this task? No fancy, dear Ellen. Simply knit.

The one who is devoted to you all,
Pvt. Gabriel Coats

Gabriel imagined the group at table — at work on the socks. He worried about their comfort and safety, as they must be worried about him. But his fears were soothed when he thought of them seated in the kitchen humming about their duties. The picture of Nanny, at head of them all, sitting and knitting, reassured him. If his mam was there, steady at her tasks and ringed by all the others intent upon their work, then all was well. When Gabriel contemplated his mother it was her finished work that he pictured. This "milk of the fingers" was nearly flawless when she wanted it to be. It was distinctive and distinguishable by him from that of any other. He imagined that it was only he who could see the impact of the mother's fingers upon the work. Only a tiny — nearly invisible — bubble was ever there in the fabric of her quilting or a length of her knitting to tell that it had been Annie's needlework. But this tiny bubble was instructive and it stamped a thing as Sewing Annie's own. It was possible to begin here, contemplating his mother's needlework, and dream of them all in turn with heads bowed somewhat and intent upon the growing in Sewing Annie's lap.

The women were hardly ever sitting and ruminating these days as Gabriel imagined them. During the daytime, the kitchen, the yard, and environs of the tailor shop had now been given over to washing laundry. The entire precinct was hung with sheets and what all else that was put to dry. Sweet and fine needlework was pushed aside for brute hauling and churning and punching suds for the Sanitary Commission. Mary applied all worrying energies not spent on Gabriel and the babes to the laundry barrels. Guarding the wooden laundry casks was essential, as the hunt for firewood imperiled any crate, fence, chair, or barrel in the town. It had become common to see a woman walk straight to a slat fence, kick it with her foot, and tear away what would come off to haul to an alley enclave.

Daniel Joshua was a component of the increased commerce of the shop, for he used his wagon to collect wood and gather coal to feed the women's water stoves. His help kept them efficient and, in some measure, safer. In times such as these, clubs like the Ladies of Olives were no better than twigs.

With Gabriel gone at war and heartily missed, there was competition to sit latest in the kitchen — nursing loneliness and the fire. Ellen left the warm first. It was a tumbledown habit for Ellen to put the younger babes on their pallets while their mother worked on. Mary allowed Ellen to fuss with them to assuage her longing for Delia, but this comfort did not distract Ellen from worrying that the girl was safe. It lightened Ellen's heart to know — from the letters she received through Reverend Higgins — that Delia thrived in Philadelphia.

Mary soothed her longing for Gabriel with working late — pressing on to bone tiredness so that sleep would come easily. At very last Annie would send Mary ahead of her to bed with the admonition that she needed the rest to care for her babes. Mary must not, her mother-in-law insisted, fatigue herself with worry. It was a small tug between them that gave Sewing Annie the upper hand. She would be the captain of worry over Gabriel. As well, there were no private missives between husband and wife. All of the letters received from Gabriel were read out by Daniel to be heard by all. Mary keenly suffered the loss of marital intimacy with her Gabriel and was frightened for it — anxious lest it be gone forever. She became covetous of her babes' kisses and huggings at night when they were settled to sleep in their upstairs room. These were Gabriel's and hers!

Twenty-nine

Dear Ones,

You must laugh at this, dear ones. As we colored troops are given little provision, most of the men are without any supplies for mending clothing. These men have recently left off the places they were held and so they have little or nothing belonging to them. It is only himself that each has carried off from one of the places around here — no pocket-knife, no scissors, no tin cup.

I am, as you know, well supplied. Also, I have the skill for mending. I have very little skill for such other as shooting and hunting and marching. So I have taken on the job of mending in spare moments. For this I am heartily appreciated and am called "Housewife" with affection. It is a joke doubly because the sewing kits given to the white soldiers are called "housewife." We colored troops are given none of these. I am kept very warm as I have so many socks and shirts. I have given one pair of socks to each of the barefoot. When a coin circulates, they buy another pair. I am satisfied with this system, loved ones.

Your devoted,
Pvt. Gabriel Coats

◆◆

Dear Ones,

Mr. Millrace and I are the subject of a good deal of fun. Many of the other soldiers are lately off their masters' places and have seen little of a city. They have only the few clothes upon their persons. They think Mr. Millrace and I are popinjays, for our underclothes are clean and show little wear. We have great trouble to keep them so. Mr. Millrace is a rough and hardy fellow to be sure. He is used to the hard tasks of training and handling his dogs and is an expert at hunting and tracking. He is proficient with knives, rifles, and pistols. The fellows are impressed with him and are fond of his skill for snaring small game. Our regiment has had rabbits when others were eating only beans.

I have run afoul of the regimental sutler in our camp. This is the fellow who sells us our goods. He has approached me regarding my socks and other items. He does not like my selling wares. He has the permit to sell exclusively in the camp. I must be wary.

Pvt. Gabriel Coats

Dear Ones,

Oh, how high our spirits were when we left our base camp and boarded transport! At last, we felt ourselves being made good use of. A battle is coming! We have been here in Virginia for some weeks and we chafe at the inactivity. Well, we are not inactive at all. We are only kept from the fighting. And grousing does set in as we are used as mules by the army — and not as soldiers.

We are mostly put to fatigue duty in the camp. That is, we are made to do the heavy labor that white soldiers are not pressed to do. We are put upon the level of the army's animals. We are daily, nay hourly, submitted to insults by white soldiers in other regiments. They taunt us as cowards, saying we will not fight. They curse us as the cause of the fighting and accuse us of responsibility for the bad odors about the camp. At this last we are amused, for none of us — black or white — have had a good washing head to toe, and our clothes are so dirty and inhabited with lice that they would walk away if we dared take them off. We keep still in the face of insults, for our minds are on the battle. Mr. Millrace and I have become good companions. He wishes that I give greetings from him to you all. Mary, on your circuit of the town, please look in on Miss Essie Millrace and assure her that her father is well. Mr. Millrace has letters from her but is eager to know the temper of her countenance. Is she bright and cheerful or sorrowful?

Mary's blood throbbed at the sound of her own name singled out in her husband's letter. "Yes, yes, dear one. I will do as you ask," she murmured, and sealed it on herself as a pledge and a duty.

Daniel read on with no pause.

Mr. Millrace is often melancholy about his dogs. He worries that they are well and have something to eat. I tell him that dogs such as his are well able to look out for themselves. He worries that the old man he put in charge of the animals may have lost courage and abandoned them. He agitates over their care, for they are his livelihood and are like his own children.

We are moving at last! We are transporting via railcars to the fighting!

Your Gabriel

The foot-weary men were forced aboard a train car. There was disgruntled display on the part of the trainmen and the conductor. The commanding officer attempted to quash the discontent by encouraging the colored men to sing as they sat in the train car. The officer thought this singing to be an effective way of calming the men. At first, some were reluctant and were themselves disgruntled at their treatment. Were they not soldiers fighting? But these softened and soon were singing. They began with spirituals. The voices of the troops rose and they sang with vigor. The conductor came into the car — the one who'd taken pleasure in forcing the colored troops to a separate car —and barked.

"Shat up that racket!" he exclaimed, snuff juice trailing down his chin. "Stop that caterwauling! Hear me, Naygurs!"

A quiet did descend on the car in response to the conductor. But he and the uniformed and armed men knew that it was not fear or respect that silenced them. They sat silently, ominously, in their Union blues. All of the troops turned eyes on the blushing conductor, then upon their pale commanding officer. They would not lower their eyes and the two white men realized themselves outnumbered. Raw feelings mounted in the car as the men tensed muscles and girded for conflict. A man called Matthew, one who styled himself a preacher, rose and commenced, in midst of the turmoil, to sing.

> *Hush, hush, somebody's callin' my name*
> *Soon one mornin'*
> *Death come a-creepin'*

The men joined in. All had cut their teeth upon this song and knew it well. They sang verse after verse. The men of the First United States Colored Troops proudly kept to their seats and sang absolutely all of that song. They proceeded through many another piece until they reached the military rail depot south of Petersburg.

◆◆

Gabriel's letter home after the siege of Petersburg was as usual cheerful. It consisted mostly of an account of the company's preparations, their monotonous marching, and the many small things they did to assuage boredom. Gabriel dared not write of the artilleryman whose headless body was dragged from his guns and replaced by another. He did not speak of the wounded men crawling on hands and knees — in circles, in confusion — until their bloodless bodies collapsed still. He did not speak of the fingers, arms, legs lacerated by whizzing minnie balls. Dead and wounded bodies leaked blood into the ground and it became soaked and spongy. What they did not know about would not touch them, he thought.

Guiltily, Gabriel realized after the most grueling part of the battle that the only person whose life meant something to him had likewise survived. Jacob Millrace had not died! Gabriel had been so fearful that he'd been copiously ill in his guts. He'd recognized many of the varied pieces of his comrades — this man's arm that bore the patch he'd sewn or that man's hat or that man's face that still bore a blank, unquestioning expression — but it was only Jacob Millrace that he'd looked about the battlefield for. As he had perused each corpse on the ground before him, he looked feverishly for only that one. For he'd wanted to hear Jacob Millrace speak again — to reiterate the last words they'd shared before the battle.

"We know well who we are if this war be a game — a game of dominoes, let us say. We are the slack black pieces with the spots upon us, my friend. They will aim for us. We are certain . . . we will fall. But we will fall in the service of securing freedom!"

Gabriel had been puzzled as to what to make of Jacob's

words. He was scared — nearly as terrified as he had ever been. His thoughts were thick and husky and he yearned to be back with the group around the kitchen stove. He was here on this battlefield for them — he'd not needed Jacob Millrace to tell him. He had come because he'd felt it was his place to fight this fight. But now he was simply sick to his soul for wanting to be with them. For himself he could dash full-chest into the enemy lines. But he was sick with longing for Mary and the babes and Nanny and Ellen, and yearned to look upon Daniel Joshua. These specters called him. On account of these he wanted to come home — not be left in pieces upon the field. And what of Miss Essie Millrace, the phantom of Jacob's late-night musings? It was for her, too, that Gabriel had searched for Jacob.

The men who'd made their way with pulling and hauling and moving around chafed at waiting and lying about in trenches. Gabriel found it easier to bear the inactivity. He kept his fingers busy with maintaining his weapons and he occupied his mind with counting and figuring as he had kept the habit of. As well to while the time, Gabriel stitched his name inside of his clothes. He stitched in Millrace's uniform, too, and in many of the other men's clothes. It was a hope. The men hoped thus to be identified upon the battlefield should they fall. Some men who could not write asked for help and some others said it was foolish to bother. The men had heard that colored soldiers were not even buried in some campaigns, only plowed under the ground.

They could no longer even raise their heads above the trenches. Confederates were as near as a hairbreadth. The closeness put an especial shiver in the colored troops, for often they could hear the white Union soldiers trading pleasantries with the rebs and they worried about their safety in the precinct. They did not doubt their fellow soldiers. The outcome of any battle, though, held consequences for the colored. Any man would quake to recall what had happened before. The air was rent with the smell of nervous bowels. All the men, regardless of color, were afraid.

"Those that call me say 'Carbon.' That's my name, I 'spect — as much as any other. I don't know how that'd be in letters, but I like to have my name," the young soldier pronounced shyly. This Carbon was one of those who had never spoken to Gabriel or Jacob. Some of the men who had just left their bond and joined up and knew little of going about in a town were in awe of Gabriel Coats and Jacob Millrace. They called them "genelmen" and generally deferred to them.

"I can work your name up and put it in your clothes," Gabriel assured him.

"Just so's the Lord will know to hollar me out. I don't want to miss nothin'," Carbon said, leaning on his weapon. "I'll catch up with my mam there," he added, smiling. "I don't want to miss nothin' that the Lord got in store." There was a look of youth, innocence, and bland bravery that was mitigated only by his resignation to his fate. This boy had come up a soldier in the few months they'd trained and marched and slogged together.

Gabriel sewed dutifully and quickly. He embroidered each of the soldiers' names in their uniform coats. Afraid to omit anyone, he worked furiously and took it as a salvation to complete this token for each man.

In the most recent days, Jacob had begun questioning the usefulness of their efforts. Mired in these siege trenches, were they carrying the day for freedom as they'd hoped — as they'd convinced themselves at the outset? Were their chickens going to see the promised land? It rocked Gabriel to hear his staunch friend speak this way. He was afraid that Jacob was losing his bearings. Jacob insisted upon a pact: that whosoever survived the upcoming battle would be responsible for the care and stability of the other's family. It was a pact from the heart, as each man would have done so in any event.

"Take care of my Essie, Gabriel, and I will care for your mam and your wife and all of the others," Jacob whispered into Gabriel's ear as he brought him close and put a kiss upon his cheek to seal their agreement.

Gabriel said, "Yes, Jacob." But a pall fell upon him. He felt keenly that he was losing the optimism that had supported him thus far. Longing and fear had taken him, and he and Jacob were losing their starch. Gabriel feared that, despite their virtuous pact, neither would survive and all of the chickens would be lost — and maybe the freedom, too.

"Liberty is better than life, Jacob," Gabriel said to his friend, pulled from his embrace, and clasped his hand.

As Gabriel had solemnly promised, he removed the contents of his friend's pockets and held the watch, the pipe, a small book of writing, and a monogrammed handkerchief next to his chest, breathing their aroma. Placed in a pouch, they became Jacob. And these things lay a poultice on Gabriel's chest. They were Jacob journeying home.

When Gabriel reached in to clear Jacob's pocket, he choked on his own spittle to see the embroidered handkerchief that he himself had worked. He had made the handkerchief hastily, more to set off the breast pocket of the suit coat than as a gentleman's accessory. It could not favorably compare to the meticulously executed handkerchiefs done by Ellen. It bore Jacob's monogram and had a border of simple tatting. The handkerchief was but a fillip to flatter a good customer, as Jacob had been. But it was now a souvenir of their friendship — a talisman that Gabriel must surrender to Essie along with the watch that it was wrapped snug around.

In the *National Republican:*

However terrific the fire of the enemy, however fearful the contest, or however much outnumbered by the foe, with all the threats of death, if captured, staring them in the face, they nevertheless stood to their post firm and unbroken, unless when thinned out by the deadly fly of the enemy's missiles.

Regiments on their right and left have flagged and succumbed to the paralyzing effects of battle strife. But the Fighting First, as they have been called, have in no instance dishonored the nation's glorious escutcheon. This has been the proud career of the Fighting First through eleven engagements. And now, as the war is over, it will undoubtedly return when its time expires (next June, unless sooner discharged) to its friends and relatives in Washington, with a name unsullied with cowardice; while it has not escaped the fate common to all regiments, having a few bad men in its ranks, it has to all ordinary considerations escaped the fortune of cowards.

Withal, there is not a man in their midst, officer or private, but feels it a special honor to acknowledge his identity with USCT.

Thirty

THE AIR WAS owned by the sound of concussion. There was little or no escape from the noise and the feel of the booming. The air was brightly colored blue also by the invective shouted by soldiers at recalcitrant and frightened mules collapsed in mud puddles. Daniel Joshua put his hands on Annie's shoulders, squeezed her heartily, and bade her go to ground in the cellar. Armed with a fierce club as well as numerous other iron files and blades to defend his horse and wagon, Daniel put in with a volunteer militia of colored men that was forming to defend the town block by block.

Perhaps it will be cooler below ground, Annie thought. Sheltered from the damnable sun and the putrid air, they might be better off. But Annie feared being trapped and suspected the other women did, too.

They stayed in the darkened back room of the shop listening and speaking quietly. Provision was made and the hide was ready. They kept themselves behind the boarded shop windows and no lamp was brought to the front rooms. All the storefronts along the avenue were poised for the siege.

The Coatses urged Winnie Wareham to join them and she consented. Inactivity fed Winnie's fears. There was no longer a routine of meals at the Holy Trinity rectory. The priests remaining — the committed unionists — were absorbed with nursing, and their meals were had at odd hours. Reverend William Higgins, not the least ambivalent about the rightness of the struggle, was not averse to bearing arms. He no longer slept or ate at the rectory.

"When the city's hands change, it ain't goin' to be nice. We be run over! They'll come like ants over a hill and we be run over and it be a time you won't know hither from thither," Winnie said, and rocked herself for comfort. She'd lost all of her remaining courage in the days anticipating the Confederate raid. The Coats women were shaken by Winnie's collapse. Ellen and Mary hoisted under her arms and walked with her to the rectory to retrieve her possessions. She insisted on getting a Bible to clutch to her breasts when the secesh came.

"If it ain't save me from a bullet, it be my ticket for the glory train!" Mary and Ellen fought not to chuckle at their dear friend's distress.

Winnie had absorbed the teachings of the priests from her proximity and with respect to the charity in them. But she was no true papist. The practice of Catholicism suited her some, for there was pomp to it. But she well enjoyed attending the other churches at which there was more singing of the old, heroic hymns. These she knew by heart, but was always surprised to hear them burst forth from herself, for she had no ordinary consciousness of them. They did burst forth. When she returned to the Coatses' kitchen, she slipped to the floor and crouched near the fireplace. Winnie sang and did sing. And with her singing came tears.

Beyond the Coatses' barricaded back door, the white people's social whirl continued only slightly abated by the war. Though muted, parties went on and outings for entertainment were common for those of means and leisure. The street lamps remained lit. Lights on hilltop mansions blazed with reverie at night and some residents worried that signals were being transmitted to the enemy. Mrs. Millicent Beech refused to curtail her social rounds because of the war. She kept her dinner parties bright. She ordered a stream of decorated shawls and gloves and was a regular, though perennially irritable and impatient, customer of the Coatses.

"At last your indolent brother is where he should be," Mrs. Beech shouted at Ellen in the shop. She seemed to mistake Ellen's reticence with her as deafness. "If they put the niggers on the battlements, this war will soon be over and our boys returned home!" she continued loudly. "Perhaps then you will be shut of your brother once and for all." The young woman turned away with her purchases and walked toward the door.

Ellen stared at Millicent Beech's back, though she'd wanted to look deep into her face. She'd been too frightened to stare, but was curious to know from what place this animus toward her brother sprang. They — the Coats women — all prayed and clutched themselves with worry and harrying angels to keep Gabriel safe, and this young matron would toss his life away.

The swirling, pretty Millicent Beech draped herself up decoratively in a ball gown and accompanied her husband to celebrate President Abraham Lincoln's inauguration. The town had been nervous of the election and concerned for the president's safety and its own self. But the grand ballroom of the Patent Office was doing duty for the festivities. This precinct that housed wounded and held the fascination of scores of tourists was lit to its rafters and glittering. The happy young wife's diamond earrings sparkled near to her chin, though the packed ballroom allowed of no other dancing. Gold frippery and elegant laces, jewelry of all descriptions, and a plethora of feathers and silk crowded out the plain and were worn shamelessly in the battle-weary town.

A month later cannon boom signaled the surrender of Petersburg, Virginia. Twice as much cannon accompanied news that mighty Richmond had fallen to the Union army. Small babes cried out at the booming and the rattling of windows, but all others took the great cracks for a call to jubilation. The throbbing meant the end was upon them. Residents cocked their windows open and stood doors ajar to guard their glass from concussion.

When finally the haughty little general of the Confederates surrendered his starving army at Appomattox Courthouse, the rapid firing in celebration caused a furious thunderstorm. Washingtonians crowded the streets and were drenched and took the rain for a great washing and purging. Annie Coats was sorry for not having more barrels to collect water.

Some five days later when the great man was shot — killed — shouting awakened the Coatses, then shrieks of horrible shock at the news. Early that morning, after the long night of the president's dying, his wife screamed and throughout town church bells sounded. The air all around was torn with the violent tolling.

The Coats women came out the kitchen door peeping around

like turtles to take the temper of the town. After all the weary-
ing revelry of the past several days, the dull thud of this news
struck a devastating blow. A secesh plot had succeeded! How far
did it go? Always conscious of — always fearful of — a large,
more malevolent other who would punish them, the Blacks of
Washington and environs were not surprised that Father Abraham had been killed. They should not have thanked him. They
should not have revered him, for they had sealed his tragic fate!

On the day of the funeral, Annie came out with a dress of
black coal cloth that had been stored away. It had lain like an
infant in the bottom drawer of a chest — cherished above all.
She laid it reverently on the table and sat to a cup of tea and
gazed on it. It was still the finest and blackest piece of cloth
that Annie had seen. In all the years that she'd kept it since her
mentor's death, she had never failed to be impressed with its
simple darkness. It was bombazine and embellished discreetly
with black jet. Over the years the dress was subject to brushing,
conscientious washing, and careful mending. It had persevered.
Rescued from a fire by Knitting Annie, Widow Campbell's discarded mourning dress had become a solemn costume for Annie. Aye, it was beautiful on her. Over the years she was careful
and frugal of wearing it.

People of every hue went about weeping publicly, bawling
in fact. And many raised their fists to curse the conspiring secesh, to revile Jeff Davis, and to call for his hanging. A great
many of these had on previous occasions cursed Abraham Lincoln himself. Now they sang a different tune. Now nothing
would do but to dress the windows of the town in black. Annie
put up a pretty funeral swag on the facade of Ridley & Ridley
Fine Tailoring. A pity that Gabriel was not able to do the cutting, for he was a skilled hand at scissors and setting a bow.

Streets so lately full to overflowing with celebrants at news of the fall of Richmond and Lee's surrender at Appomattox were filled with criers. Cannon fire repeated, and more. The town that celebrated the end of the war with bonfires and drunken dancing, with singing and speeches, now was fallen to tears. Sorrow had seemed nearly stanched but for this additional blow.

On the day of the funeral procession colored folk were determined to line the byways and see Father Abraham off to his glory. Annie Coats applied her brushes to the children's black clothes — to which the girls submitted quietly and the grandmother was hardly gentle. She pounded — was furious to destroy nits and to flick any tiny bit of lint no matter how small that would spoil the solid, mourning black. Mary and Ellen also submitted their garments to Annie's pummeling and picking and fussing over.

Many were fearful and many jostled for a place from which to watch. Regiment after regiment assembled at the head of the funeral cortege leaving on that afternoon to carry the president's body to the Capitol. Word flew through the knots of colored citizens — some who'd bought the spot of ground they sat upon by their ceaseless vigil since the word had come to them — that their own would lead the procession. Most were hopeful, but they were prepared to take whatever role was given, for they were accustomed.

An old woman dressed in dark and dusty clothes stood a spot nearby the Coats family. She was planted on High Street when they took up their places. Her eyes were directed toward the roadway and she seemed to notice nothing else. Her hands were folded across her stomach as if attached with hooks. There was no fidgeting of her body.

A great surge was felt among the assembled when the soldiers came into view. The tremor at the appearance of these colored troops was a potent, electric blend of grief and exhilarated pride. The dark soldiers were crisp. Their uniforms were be-ribboned and they held themselves with exquisite military precision.

When the colored troops marched past sharply at the head of the cortege, the solitary woman dropped to the ground in a swoon. The old woman's heels drummed against the pavement. She lost control of her anus and pungent gas was let loose in the air. Mary and Ellen bent to right the old woman and hoist her to a sitting position. She convulsed at their touch, then ceased and died.

Thirty-one

PRAYERS IN TIME of war are simple: *Please bring him home. Please send him back with both of his arms. Please set him upon his pins and send him walking home!*

Lincoln had been taken home for burial. The thoroughfares were now full of outbound commerce. Combatants in both uniforms stumbled toward their homes in the countryside. Folks carried bits of news from Virginia and told further what they knew about the movement of the troops. They were all said to be coming homeward now. When the joyful victory cannons had fired, the Coats women had thought that their beloved Gabriel would appear next day at their doorstep. But where were the colored troops now? How were Gabriel and Mr. Millrace getting back home?

Most of the soldiers Gabriel passed on his trek home from Richmond were as stunned as he not to be dead. They were not inclined to impede him. He trudged toward Washington in a loosely bonded group of his own company. Much of the order that had kept them upon their duties had fallen. The soldiers' guts were in a quandary. They were used to killing and being ready to die. It was as if only the merest luck, not soldierly skill, had caused one or another to be yet alive. Gabriel had seen men who were far better soldiers fall next to him. Most often they had fallen back on their haunches, grabbed their bellies, and died at the wonder of it. So much blood had run into the ground around these men! What sodden, miserable crops from these fields if people returned to planting in them!

The thing Mary noticed as Gabriel walked over the cobblestone streets of Georgetown and came toward the shop was that he had shrunk inside his coat. If she'd been made to choose him out, she would not have said that this gaunt figure was her husband. With each step, Gabriel took the weight of his haversacks and was pushed down. He had to push back and rise to advance himself. He accomplished this laboring advance with regularity, and his glazed-over eyes brightened at sight of the sign over the store. This was home! He had managed to reach the threshold.

"Nanny!" Gabriel called first. "Mary! Sis Ellen," he said, and dropped his packs to open his arms and collect the four little running girls who came to him. These names he fumbled, calling each one, but not being sure which belonged to which. "Naomi, Ruth, Pearl, Hannah!"

Mary, Annie, and Ellen had been looking out for Gabriel for a month as word of the valorous discharge of colored troops had wafted back to them. There had been one of them posted daily to watch for his arrival through the front window of the shop. Aaron Ridley was known to be dead and the women had assumed operation of the shop. The girls were not reticent in this precinct and they exploded toward Gabriel through the front door. Their grabbing set him off balance and he wobbled to keep upright.

When Annie rushed to catch sight of Gabriel, she hoped he stooped only because he was burdened down with the things he carried. She took a haversack from him and found it to be light. Nevertheless Gabriel revived a bit upon being relieved of it. The pack was burdensome, but not heavy. He stood straighter and clamped his mother's face to look down into her eyes.

It was good the army had moved them back — mustering them out at their "joining up" spot. In their confusion and profound weariness the soldiers might have gone off elsewhere. They might have walked off the edge of the earth. Gabriel had doubted he had the strength left to embrace home, but he came toward it like a pigeon.

Gabriel still wore the faded pool of Jacob Millrace's blood on the front of his shirt. It was the only shirt left to him and the stubborn stain had survived several washings since Mr. Millrace had died.

The regiment had been commanded to hold down in their trenches and be ready to march and meet the enemy. They were to wait for the order to charge, rise as one, and go forward with all that they had.

When the charge was called, within his clothes Gabriel Coats was stewing in a soup of his own sweat and urine. All of the men responded and moved. Jacob came up first, determined to be in front of Gabriel. He shoved Gabriel back into the trench and as he rose above his friend a shot caught him full in the chest and thrust him back collapsing onto Gabriel. Blood shot from Jacob's chest and coated himself and Gabriel. Under Jacob's body, shielded from the vicious fire, Gabriel agitated. In this way he withstood the first volley. However, he forgot to hold to the pact and cover himself and turn to simple survival. His mind did not credit it. He stood and fired his weapon and continued as he'd been instructed. A neophyte with guns, Gabriel had nonetheless mastered the loading and firing. He let off with conviction and fury and pulled down a number of charging Confederates before ducking back into a blind on command.

For Gabriel the cruelest moment on that day was the order to move on. The moment came when he must go forward without friend Jacob. All who survived were ordered onward to another position. All of the company's dead and gravely wounded were left.

Ah, what would become of Jacob's body? The captain had said he would shoot any man who would not march on, for he would not let it be said that he lost all of his men at this spot. Jacob was stiff and sour when Gabriel collected his pockets. In this his friend was more fortunate than those whose last prayers and imprecations could be heard behind the departing soldiers.

Gabriel had walked off counting each of his own steps to keep himself steady. He mourned Jacob with every step and buoyed himself with knowing he would recall exactly how many footfalls would bring him back to his friend. Gabriel had resolved to remember the location of the trench in case he could return and bring Essie to the spot.

Cunning had kept Gabriel safe this far. He had accomplished the long trek home to Georgetown because of his socks. Aye, some had left toes in trenches where they'd squatted. But Gabriel had kept his feet dry and warm and had persevered. It was simply that! His head swooned when even his shoes wore away to flapping five miles from Washington. The stout socks had sustained him!

That which had brought Private Gabriel Coats thus far ran

out of him like sand from a glass. He collapsed in extreme weariness on the threshold of Ridley & Ridley Fine Tailoring and the women maneuvered him into the kitchen. Annie knelt beside him, clutched him to herself, and rose with him. She carried him to be near the stove, and she moved her hands along his body to check for infirmities and wounds. She found him chafed and sore, weary and starved, but all of a piece. She called Mary and Ellen to her and the three of them removed his uniform by gently rolling him back and forth between them.

It was left to Mary to remove Gabriel's grimy long johns. She peeled the garment away with warm water and laved him intimately, but dispassionately.

The garment removed, she noticed it was decorated curiously. Running her fingers over the soiled, smelling cloth, Mary felt knots and ridges and whorls of thread and recognized a pattern of embroidery. This work extended down the front of the garment where Gabriel's hands had been available to it.

Mary's fears had caused her to regress in her book learning as the war progressed — after Gabriel's leave-taking. She was superstitious that, in picking various scraps of events off the broadsheets and letter papers, she would give them life and animation. If the newspapers said a thing, would it more likely occur for them pointing at it?

The pattern on the long johns was clear and comprehensible, but Mary did not understand it. Gabriel had embroidered a pattern — had put a reckoning in thread upon his underclothing. He had made a desperate record. She would ask him about it. She did not put the garment to soak.

❖❖

Gabriel woke from a daylong nap with jerking and fear. He felt his nakedness beneath cool, fragrant covers. His wife and mother and sister had lifted and pulled him upstairs and placed him in bed. He wept as he came to himself, for he was ashamed to feel so comfortable when his companion and friend Jacob Millrace lay in a gulley so far from home.

Gabriel lay in the honeyed bed at the top of the house through several nights and days. The bed was so soft that his body felt more aches with sinking into it. Mary saw the bone weariness in Gabriel and thought he might stay forever in the stuporous sleep. On his second night abed, when she came to the side of the bed to tuck him, he grasped her hand forcefully and pulled her toward him roughly.

"Woman, I have got home," he said in a low, angry voice that she flinched to hear from Gabriel.

"Yes," Mary said. "Yes."

He jerked her to lie on top of his body and held her in a vise splayed on top of him. Her clothes were between them, but both felt each other's body. Mary tried to shift and pull away from Gabriel as his breathing slowed and she thought he had fallen asleep again. But he gripped her and held on to her and she was made to sleep atop him. Small tears fell off her face onto his neck while she was held so tightly.

Gabriel would have walked to the Millrace place to give the news of Jacob to his beloved daughter, Essie. But Daniel pressed him to take a wagon and a lean, tractable mule.

Gabriel should have had accompaniment, but set out alone in a somber mood. He dared not wear his uniform — colored soldiers in military dress were targets still — though he felt

himself naked without it. He plodded along to Millrace's out-
lying place because people in town had said that Essie had gone
there to stay with the hounds.

Jacob Millrace's prized hounds were strikingly beautiful.
They held their heads rigidly when they stood erect. It was a
main feature of their poise and authority. They were intelligent
in the eyes and they were ready to impress with their demeanor.
Beautiful, too, was the fur that covered them — the fur that
was scrupulously groomed by Essie and the hands. There was a
variety between the hounds, but the colors and quality of the
fur was consistent among the sixteen dogs. They had auburn-
to liver-colored patches with chalk-colored bodies. Upon each
were variegated freckles of auburn fur in with the white. No
two had the same patterning and each was instantly known
with a glance. Essie had named all but the original pair, Hercules and Circe. Essie's Matthew was at head of them all now
that his father was slower. Mark, Luke, and John were stalwarts
from the first litter of dogs after the fever, and Dorcas and Sara
were the first bitches. Sheba, Lizzie, Paul, Ham, Noah, Elijah,
Esther, and Shem were the survivors of subsequent litters and
were the core of the hunting business.

Word had come to Essie that hands her father had left to care
for the hounds had gone off and deserted them. Sick with worry,
Essie had left the city and journeyed home to keep the dogs for
Jacob. The news of Jacob's demise had not reached her. No one
had cared to come so far out of town to give her the news.

"Is't Miss Essie Millrace?" Gabriel called from the gate as he
approached.

Essie, her companions ringing her feet, looked at Gabriel
when he hailed her. He was struck to see the change from her

photograph. This woman was likewise sloe-eyed and held herself slim and erect. But the young woman he saw wore a rough hat and patched jacket and her wide shoddy skirt was drawn between her legs and tied to create pantaloons. Her face — the one Gabriel knew so intimately — was only reflected in this visage beneath the hat. It was Essie's elegantly photographed face, but it was not immobile. In defiance of all womanly convention, this face was in constant movement and ranged in expression from hot to cold temper. It had some dirt upon it.

"Ma'am, may I have a word? You have known me as your father's friend, Gabriel Coats."

Essie had no fear of the scraggly stranger, though she could well have. She knew the hounds would put off any interloper and she was coolly confident of them.

"I have word of your father," Gabriel said, and Essie's heart leaped fearfully when he spoke.

"What is your news, sir? Say it plainly please," she demanded warily, not allowing him to come close. The dogs enforced her wishes with staring.

"Lord have mercy, Miss Millrace. Your father is gone to God. He sent me to give you his words," Gabriel said with some agitation.

Essie sank on the news and fell. The dogs put their heads down and licked her. In fact, only some of the animals licked at Essie's face and arms while the others turned their hard eyes toward Gabriel to keep him back from her. Gabriel called out her name again and again, and Essie finally roused herself and stood up. She commanded the dogs with a series of cluckings and tongue-suckings and sent them inside the house. One of them — Matthew —took up position at the window and watched Essie from this post. Essie then walked toward Gabriel, put forth her hand to shake his. "Please come into the house, sir."

The Essie whom Gabriel had so long imagined sitting in her parlor ready to receive him was not the young woman who sat before him now. This woman appeared sturdy, hard-eyed, and flinty, and she seemed a ruler of the subjects arrayed on the floor at her feet. Her authority was unquestioned in this room — on this property.

In a corner of the front room of the large log house was an ornate writing desk. Upon the desk were ledgers and arranged piles of papers and writing implements and accoutrements. Gabriel had interrupted Essie's business occupation, that was clear. And she seemed impatient to have his news and return to her desk.

"Sir, you are my father's friend. But you have no claim or interest in any of these dogs. Of that I can assure you. I know my father."

"Oh, Miss Millrace, I am a tailor. I know nothing of dogs. I have no interest but to bring you word of poor Jacob. He died and I turned out his pockets and collected these things and brought them to you because I pledged to Jacob." Gabriel nervously pulled an embroidered handkerchief with Jacob's monogram from one of his inner pockets — near his heart — where Jacob had commended him to place these things and bear them to Essie: a watch, a pipe, and a small leather book with Jacob's words. Essie let the objects fall into her lap and allowed the cloth to slip from her hand. The small leather-bound journal was the only item of interest to Essie. Gabriel shifted to pick up the handkerchief, but one of the hounds growled and forced him back into his chair.

Thirty-two

A WELL-DRESSED, GRACEFUL young woman descended the streetcar on Bridge Street. She wore spectacles and was a good bit taller than she'd been. Her self-confidence was arresting, for she moved along the street with ease, navigating amongst the crowd with a bearing that Gabriel would never have imagined from their Delia.

"Sister, look here," Gabriel called, looking out at the street through the window.

Ellen bolted from her chair, crying, "Oh!"

"Mary, Nanny, come and see," Gabriel trumpeted to the other women.

Though she was Delia, the young woman approaching the shop was also a young white woman, moving among the other whites with a prim hauteur that the Coatses had never seen.

"Ma'am, Nanny, Mary!" Delia called out excitedly. She spread her arms to draw the surprised women to her, and Ellen, Annie, and Mary ringed her and pulled upon her. She melted into them and all of the women were joyful.

Gabriel observed sullenly that Delia's garments were strictly simple, if embroidered highly — exhibiting fineness he had seen only from Ellen's hand. He could recognize Ellen's work at a glance from any distance. Gabriel realized that Ellen had not done as he'd asked. She'd not cut off from this girl! A quiet, obedient sister was one pillar he had counted on, and Gabriel felt the picture threatened again by this girl.

Delia wore her costumes prettily and had an exuberant, confident demeanor. Gabriel's sour look did not dampen her greeting. She was delighted to mark the changes in all, including Naomi, Ruth, and Pearl. She swung the baby, Hannah, high in her arms with glee and baby talk.

"Sir," Delia called Gabriel when she gave up the baby. "Sir," she said with a jot of a curtsy, though she might have called him "boy" and it might have appeared the more appropriate. "I have relinquished your name, sir. I call myself Miss Delia Cameron," she said pertly as she extended her hand to Gabriel. If passersby stared at the respectable young white woman touching a Negro, they did also remark that many things had changed since the end of the war. Most recognized Miss Cameron for whom she must be. Most would think her clabber color to be of that class of local Negroes of some prominence in the town. She could affect the look of these or seem to be a white woman. In Philadelphia she was a promising young schoolteacher — one who would soon go south to teach the newly freed and their children.

It was Ellen she loved — Ellen that she came for. When all entered the back room of the shop, Delia sat down at her old accustomed place at their table. She came straight out and presented her plan to Ellen. In front of the cups of welcome tea, she implored them to give up Ellen, her mother.

"Take up with me, ma'am. Please go south with me. We go

to teach among our people. Please go with me, ma'am," Delia begged sweetly, and sipped her tea. She cajoled her mother with showing how Ellen's skills were needed. "We might give a leg up to those among the folk who want to rise and make a way."

Ellen turned her face toward the girl, though she did not look up into her eyes. She was too shy to stare into this familiar, beloved face. Ellen feared she would cry — would begin to wail. And Gabriel and her mam would disapprove of her display. "Yes," Ellen said quickly to cover the quiet — to reassure Delia. Behind her head she heard Gabriel's disdainful snort. What of her mam? The silence from her mother was, as always, telling. Did Nanny not have an opinion? Could Nanny never take her bond? Was it that she would always take her Gabriel's side?

"Yes," Ellen said again, and stood abruptly, upsetting a candle. Delia popped up from her seat as well and both stepped away from the table as if preparing to dance a reel.

From such a long time ago these two were pushed at each other — forced to do or not do or wait to be told what they must do. For the first time they looked at each other and realized they would do as they wished. Between them had been sulky, anguished dreams and their own small but quiet spot. Here it was! The girl had gone away and come back with this in her pocket! Ellen did wish to go with Delia to the South. For whatever purpose they would go — to teach, to give this leg up that Delia spoke of so persuasively.

The old woman — the midwife, Meander — would have snuffed out Delia's breath in that first moment as easily as swatting a fly. Meander did set her fingers to pinch off the girl's nose, but Ellen had stopped her hand by catching at it. So Ellen's gesture was taken as application and Meander thrust the baby into her arms. The long-ago solution suited.

"What will you claim, girl?" Annie piped up at last. "You cannot claim to be a white woman and claim she is your mother in that south land. You'll mark yourself and Ellen will bear the brunt."

Delia stood and looked at Annie respectfully, but full of her own vigor. "I will claim myself a colored girl as I am, Nanny. I will claim my mam. 'Twill satisfy the folk we'll live amongst," Delia said.

Again Gabriel made a sound that ridiculed the girl's resolve, but it did not sink her. Her hair was, as always, pulled murderously tight and anchored at her nape as a ball. She reached up and massaged at her scalp in a mannerism left from childhood. She then grasped Annie's hands and kissed and took Ellen's hands and brought them to her forehead in a gesture of reverence. She turned to face Gabriel and asked demurely, "Sir, can I take my mother with me? She wants to go, but is loath to leave you. Sir, she would go if you gave her leave. I will take care of her. Give her your leave to go, sir."

Gabriel would not look full into Delia's eyes either. He was shocked in his own soul that still — this long while and in these circumstances — he disliked and distrusted the girl. He longed to refuse her and turn her away. Though she'd come with a sweet mouth and a chaste, upright bearing, Gabriel continued to doubt her true nature.

"Never make my sister your servant, Miss," Gabriel Coats demanded.

"No, never, sir," Delia promised.

"I will hold you to your vow," he said grimly. Gabriel still did not look up to Delia's face. His eyes were trained on the knitting needles stalled in his hands. He struggled to move them in service of the pattern, but they would not. His shoulders collapsed to countenance the collapse of this tightly dreamed plan — that Ellen would produce more of her finest work, that Ellen would stay a warm and quiet helpmeet for Mary and Nanny and him. He was averse to this change.

The day that Ellen was born had been an unusual one, for Gabriel had been separated from his mam in the early morning and kept at his father's side. He had tagged along with his blacksmith father and smelled the leather and sweat and manure in the barns. In the evening they had returned to their cabin and squatted in the back, leaning against the cabin wall. Sweat ran off them from their exertion in the barns and from Gabriel's fear for his mother. He had heard her intermittent groaning and the midwife cajoling her through each rise. Finally Ellen had come squalling and everyone had sighed and lifted up happily, and some one of the adults — tall trees above his head talking excitedly — had handed him a cake of gingerbread. Its special flavor had arrested him and ever after he had been able to call up the taste of gingerbread and warm thoughts of that day. He'd delighted in training Ellen and coddling her and had never given a thought to cutting her away — to losing her.

Resolved to take it as his own failure of heart, Gabriel realized that all of the others were, as always, convinced of Delia. And Ellen wanted to go with her — that was clear. Ellen would be the ribbon that tags along always, for she did love this girl!

"Take care of my sister and honor her," Gabriel said. "She did save your life once, child."

Thirty-three

✇ ✳ ✤

"THE BIGGEST TRANSGRESSION perpetrated against our race under the banner of racial superiority is that they have taken our good, sweet picture of ourselves and each other from us. They have made our people despise themselves and falter because of it. We must lose no time in educating our people. We have been left behind others and must work hard to catch up!" The speaker's voice sounded like a rusted back door crux in need of oil. It was, however, compelling. Most surprising was that the voice belonged to a woman.

Going home along High Street, Naomi Coats walked alongside her mother's right hand, feeling the pull toward her father. Gabriel Coats walked next to his wife and his leadership was the magnet. Naomi believed that her father created and maintained this pulling toward himself. Lately it irritated her that all of them must defer to her father. Gabriel Coats was the visionary! He was the one whose ideas were gold because he had brought them all out of slavery. The way the family always spoke, it was as if Mother and Granmam and Auntie had not thought of a single thing! What about how they'd struggled during the war when Papa was away in the fighting? They had been grand — all of them! Was it not her mother who had directed them to plant the eyes of potatoes in straw in the root cellar? And had they not all fed on potatoes through months of privation? Instinctive, rebellious Naomi drew away from her father.

Naomi wanted to pull her mother back toward her and very nearly did do so. She put her hand on her mother's arm to turn her — to talk to her about Affinity Dunlap's speech. But her mother's attention was elsewhere.

Mary had been as touched by Miss Dunlap as her daughter. "Husband, did you hear? Is't grand — does it not sound grand and hopeful? A school just for the colored! Hampton Institute — 'tis a school to teach the colored how to make a good way," she said excitedly.

" 'Tis a lot of grand talk all right, Mary." Gabriel's hand patted Mary's forearm authoritatively and shushed her enthusiasm. "There are a great many schemes to help the former bondman. Not many will succeed."

"How could a school not succeed if it will look to the fitness of its students?" Mary pummeled Gabriel's forearm gently and was shocked that he tugged it from her. Mary knew the women had been in the dark about how things had been for the soldiers — especially the colored ones. She knew when she saw her husband's sagging silhouette — when he stood on the threshold — that the truth of the travails was harsher than she had imagined. But the harshness in him was not lessening as she had expected. She'd held the hope that his melancholy would give way to contentment at his own hearth, surrounded with his own children.

Affinity Dunlap's speech had given Mary the seed of an idea for her daughters and she risked floating airborne in her excitement. Gabriel so coolly rejected the lofty dreams of education and equality that Mary had lost much of her gases by the time they arrived at home.

Affinity Dunlap, the woman whose voice and message had held the Coats family in thrall, was an educator and the daughter of a prominent family of free Black Washingtonians. She was passionately committed to the education of her people. A charismatic, inspirational speaker, she made the rounds of the city's colored forums, and her message was an exhortation: education for the newly freed, education for all, education above all.

Affinity's mother, a confidential lady's maid to a rich Washington matron, had become fond of a word she heard spoken in lighthearted conversation between her employer, Mrs. Elizabeth Coyle, and her husband. Affinity — so lovely and diaphanous! The Coyles said the word often and Cora Dunlap simply enjoyed the sound of it. When her child was born, her lovely little girl, Cora chose the name Affinity.

Miss Affinity Dunlap would be noticed in any room. She was tall, and unlike some others of her gender, she drew herself to her full height. She appeared always proud to be head and shoulders above the average. In fact, her habit of engaging the eyes of her mostly male fellow lecturers and audience members was considered impertinent and possible only because she was so tall, of heroic bearing and relatively well-to-do.

Cora Dunlap's little girl had thrived on the advantages of living in at the Coyle mansion, Her tall father wore livery and drove the Coyle carriage, and the girl occasionally rode behind him in masquerade as a wealthy dowager. She grew to be polished in manner and speech. Her educational accomplishments — advanced work at Oberlin College — reflected her parents' and her benefactors' goals. The abolitionists and the ambitious parents molded a good model of intellectual rigor and moral rectitude in the exceptional Miss Affinity Dunlap.

Mount Zion Church hosted Miss Dunlap for a lecture on education and the new Hampton Institute in the spring of 1870. Naomi Coats was so impressed with Miss Dunlap's zealous insistence that education would be essential — especially the education of young colored women — that her breath nearly stopped. Miss Dunlap spoke eloquently and passionately of the Negro people's grand march out of bondage. Her talk had been heart-throbbing in its vehemence. Several times during her talk the men and some of the older women became uncomfortable at the lecturer's strong tone. At these moments Miss Dunlap cleverly softened and won back their love by drawing pictures of the ones dead in bondage. She unequivocally advocated advanced education in the scholarly studies for women so that young women would be able to instruct their children in their own homes. Until such time that they were married, these young women — a veritable army — must go out to teach the race's children.

"We are put behind the other race and must work hard to catch up! Let us give our sons and daughters to the task!" Miss Dunlap said loudly and forthrightly. "We must take their places at the errands and the duties to give them over to their education. There is a great need for teachers and skilled nurses for our people, and expert seamstresses and laundresses are always wanted. Our daughters can go into the cities and labor for their keeping until they are married and settled. For this invaluable work they will be well suited. They will cultivate their homes with distinction and educate their own offspring." She finished on a note to satisfy the churchmen and their wives. But she was for herself not so fond of matrimony.

Spelled out in this fashion, it seemed wrong to Mary to keep their jewels at home. Her daughters were precious and of much more value to the wider circle than to their home only. "Gabriel, these girls might benefit from attending the school. What fine skills they have already would be strengthened at the institute."

Naomi was surprised to hear her mother talk of sending her and Ruth to Hampton Institute. She had been downhearted because she was sure her father would not let her leave his employ. Skill with sums was crucial to the Coatses' work and Naomi was strong in this knowledge and had facility for sewing. During the years of the war, whilst her father had been gone, Naomi had pitched in ably with work in the shop and had, as well, the care of her younger sisters.

"We have trained them up to give their services here — with us. We will build our trade upon them." Gabriel squelched his wife's wild ideas. He would not relent easily. He insisted that the girls were needed at home. Commerce had returned following the war. There was much work they would be leaving.

Mary bartered with Pearl. She convinced her husband that this daughter would easily be the match of the other two. Pearl was growing tall and broad and was able to hoist pots. She was also skilled at fine lap work. And there was young Hannah to train. Mary coyly suggested, too, that another hand might come, which caused Gabriel to soften with his wife's flattery. He capitulated finally. He would permit the girls to go to Hampton. Mary felt a sad triumph.

Gabriel and Mary could have sent them via train, but greatly feared the young women might be ill treated if riding alone.

Thus Mary and Gabriel set out aboard a wagon to take Naomi and Ruth to Hampton Normal and Agricultural Institute down on the coast of Virginia.

The day they set out was bright and quiet and the wooden fence pickets along the roadway were whitewashed as pearly as teeth. Much of the countryside they passed through was still flattened from the war and stripped of luster. The group — partly merry, partly sad — rode along the scarred, rutted country roads in Virginia heading toward Hampton Roads.

When the nervous parents arrived at the Hampton Institute with their daughters, they pressed them to stay close to each other and buoy each other in the school. Gabriel grasped and firmly impressed upon each that she must return home when her education was complete. He meant to insist that he loved and cherished them and wished always to protect them, but rather he said they were his chickens and belonged in his yard. It was a familiar phrase and the girls beamed at their father lovingly. Naomi bade her parents good-bye with more enthusiasm than her sister. Ruth rained tears and pined for her mother and father as soon as their backs retreated from view. Naomi pinched Ruth's arm mischievously and immediately gave her attention over to her studies.

Gabriel and Mary bade the babes good-bye with hope despite their sadness and fears. Gabriel drove the wagon toward Washington feeling a great pull to get back and to doing. His hands were impatient for his needles and unaccustomed to the horse's reins. Upon a rutted road, their wagon pitched near the river's edge and went into the Potomac. They drowned.

Thirty-four

THE RIVER SHIMMERS jewel-like with the full sun. Its colors then are iridescent blues. But it is a dirty jade green when you shade your eyes and look directly down in it. The Potomac is always this way. It is no true-blue body of water.

Gabriel was all and all was gone.

Sorrow is the boon friend of memory — two devoted ones walking hand in hand. They are everywhere together! And Annie saw herself and the boy likewise together in all. At his table and about the tools near the hearth. Upon the rise of the hill at Ridley where, in his childhood years, they climbed to gather herbs. In the town when he became a man and his rhythmic, youthful passions thumped overhead in the loft astride his wife. All was gone! Annie pictured Gabriel at work and mumbling his stitch count to himself and moving his lips so gently. Ah! She tasted his soft, puffy lips with a hint of salt upon them when she moved her tongue across her own lips. No more! Gabriel was all and all was gone.

Again and again Annie saw the rosy times gone and again and again she faced the sight that must have been: Gabriel and Mary smashed on rocks and battered to death against them and drowned. They were close to home and had become careless or unlucky or pompous in their joy of their daughters. They had died so nearby that their bodies were recovered and turned over to their people in complete defiance of the probable.

The horse had misstepped at the Virginia side of the bridge to cross into Georgetown. She, too, had forgotten herself in excitement to be home. The wagon had tipped for being unevenly weighted. On the road to Hampton the wagon was burdened with wares and the girls' belongings. It had become lighter when they left off the daughters at Hampton. Joy and pride had buoyed their return trip, though Mary had cried at leaving the girls. It was her own idea to send them for schooling, but the separation was punishing. Now she was sensitive of Gabriel's annoyance at her crying.

"Clam up, Mary. Quiet yourself. We have done as you wanted. We have left them to their schooling. When you see them again they will be women like yourself," Gabriel had said gruffly. But in the next moment he had pinched her arm and laughed at her crying. "No more, old girl. You have other chickens at home."

Mary's answer had been to nod and sniffle and paw at her own face to dry it.

The wagon had turned over on the slide down to the riverbank. At the bottom of the bridge, the horse had regained her feet and, confused, plunged into the water, pulling the shreds of the buckboard and with it Gabriel and Mary clinging. This dashing had battered the legs of the animal on rocks and had cut the things she towed through the rough, stirring up bloody foam.

Ah! He was cut up! Both were. Annie gave over dressing the bodies to the mortician, for she could not look upon them. The sight rendered her silent — grudging with her words. She then slipped into a narrow precinct as she'd done during the war. She gave out her directives as to the work, but said little more.

Long ago in Gabriel's childhood, Annie had all of him in her hands. Did she think that her first and foremost handling of him meant she could always have him so? Yes, she did. A mother thinks so. She recollected the momentary hardness of his tiny penis when she first put his heels in warm water. She pinched his scrotum and teased him and he kicked his fat legs, splashing water in her face and shushing pee over her neck and breasts. This renegade thought she drove off quickly, but wanted to savor some. If Gabriel were like his father, his member would be shrunk in the laying out. The liveliness gone from it! Huh! Death, the thief! Death will snatch up everything — even what the master covets. Ha! 'Tis a comfort to the hard-suffering ones!

Annie feared herself in danger of being forgetful of Gabriel. A silly panic! His stamp was upon her. She would have mental pictures of him and phantom words and potent hauntings for all her days when she lay down to sleep. This was certain! He had cut her just as she had cut him.

And still the sensation of his little body knifing through her unused womb — opening her up and changing her body forever — returned in memory. The desperate, fearful inevitability of it was what caused her crying and moaning testimony. But, too, there was the twitching of pleasure that seemed as if she were feeling what Bell felt in his shuddering climax and the same as the other one that grunted and sweated. The sullen midwife cut her eyes sideways at Annie, but was occupied to catch the child who worked his way to daylight between Annie's thighs with such agency. This little bitty one changed her body more and more completely than the others.

Annie touched her privacy and thought of her babe. Oh! This one would teach her her own body again at this advanced time? Recollecting Gabriel brought her back to her own body. And the exercise of it puzzled her. The thoughts coming were fearsome. It was confusing to feel herself thinking, dreaming of Gabriel, her son, this way. Beyond the veil what relation is there? Longing for the loved one has no cast — it is only longing, pulling, piercing, and skewering.

And then she feared being forgetful of the time before Gabriel was born — before he had come to change her life. Between these times there was only left the present time of painful loss. Annie was stuck and planted in a hurting present. She felt the pain of it as a knife blade in her chest. She was forfeit of half her life without Son Gabriel! Mary! Mary! Mary! — an afterthought — shameful that Mary was an appendage to her thoughts. Beloved Mary had perished alongside her husband, leaving all of her little chickens! Oh, Mary! Oh, Gabriel! Annie keened their names, but it was Gabriel that she mourned.

He was gone and dead now. The cruel joke had been played. Look here. Look there. Around the corner comes the trouble and for that one brief moment your head is turned and lifelong caring is gone for naught. He was gone. Was there yeast in her to keep on — to gather up these others and go on? Through a bad headland they had all come. Yet it was now — when all was calm and quiet and looking forward — that Gabriel and Mary had died? Now that the cruel turn had come?

Annie had long been a patient bitch alert to trouble, poised to lash out to keep him safe — to come to his defense. For so long she had been caring for Gabriel. She'd shorted Ellen in looking out for Gabriel because she reasoned that the man — because he was a man — needed more of her maternal agency. She had loosed him to come to the city and then she had loosed him to the war and fighting because of the times. She'd had no choice but see him go. He was a man she had made to stand on his own legs and go and do and he followed that trail. She'd suffered without him, but took it as her portion. She put little hope in his survival in the war, for their luck had been so good thus far — in the scheme of things. It surely had been used up. But he'd surprised her — delighted her. Son Gabriel had come up with more luck. He had come back from war with all of himself intact. His survival was the most improbable turn of their lives until this last inexplicable turn.

With once sharp, clear eyes going toward rheumy, Jonathan Ridley came to inventory the shop directly after Gabriel's funeral. Neither an early arrival nor one who stayed to see the dirt cast on the coffins, Ridley waited in the tailor shop for Annie and the others to return. His blurry eyesight and uncertain speech were most often achieved at late afternoon. But this day had begun early and he'd fortified well with ale before the service and the cemetery. He expected to be forced to look at Sewing Annie and her brood. He'd endured the gaudy funeral they concocted for Gabriel and his woman.

The one most distasteful was the one he tried to avoid: Sewing Annie. But she dominated the funeral proceedings. She was central to the mourning. That ugly, old amulet! His silly wife had wailed in sympathy with the old woman. She'd said how she imagined Sewing Annie's heart to be broken to lose her precious Gabriel.

He was happy for the chance to sneer at his wife's idiocy. "'Tis clear you know nothing of these niggers. That old thing will never give over to grief. She will never be like your sister-in-law. She'll never lie abed sniveling for something that can't be changed! She will miss her Gabriel to lean on, but she'll not pine for him." By his account the true cost of war had been just this: gone the fecund loins and the happy women. All that was left were the silly and the weak and the worthless slaves free to do as they wished!

Annie was the first one who turned to leave the cemetery, staying only to witness the first dirt to be thrown. This privilege she gave to Gabriel's own girl, Naomi, the oldest and strongest of them. The girl did rise up firmly and toss a hand of dirt for each of them: Mary, then Gabriel. At this signal Annie turned to walk away and the obedient girls followed. They wore pleated black sashes across their bodices as though they were widows. Annie regretted the exhaustion of her long-preserved black cloth, but she used the last virginal clod of it on these banners and the drapes for the funeral bunting.

Ah, and the funeral dress did live again! The rescued remains of Widow Campbell's mourning dress were brought forth. Annie had been a bigger-sized woman once, too, when last she wore this. Now the garment hung from her.

Annie led them a parade — promenaded from the graveyard without turning her head to note what she passed. Daniel Joshua caught her elbow and tried to guide her, or keep her steady, but his ballast was not needed, for she was firm. She continued on the thoroughfare straight to the front shop window. She stopped and seemed to eye the door, then eye the window. She saw Ridley seated inside the shop and looked at him impertinently. He returned the look and stayed in his seat. She remained looking through the window at him defiantly — contrary to all accepted custom. She saw him sitting — low in the chair — in some measure collapsed. The girls stood behind her, well hidden from view, though they'd not been told to do so. Daniel Joshua was prudent and quiet and smaller in stature in his mourning dress and made himself invisible behind Annie. She turned her head as if considering entering through the front door — as if taking her own counsel on the issue. She watched Ridley's face awhile through the picture glass, but gave up the menace. She turned about and walked to the back of the store. She walked into her precinct and took possession there.

In his state of drunk and resignation, Ridley was easily turned away from the things that Annie coveted — the belongings in the shop that were Gabriel's. He put his hand to a store of linens and quilts and coverlets and his gesture stung her.

"No!" Annie hollered at him because she'd lost all care for caution. She marched about the room pointing and designating which things belonged to the Coatses. The master was so completely affronted that he could not speak. Nothing more important could be lost to her than Gabriel. He was all and all was gone. No more need for caution or care.

And the task was accomplished, for Ridley was put back on his heels and flinched at the vehemence in Annie's voice.

"Don't touch!" she screamed. It stopped him. For the first time some word or movement of hers had stopped this man. The words were simple, emphatic, but they were momentous in her mouth. For the first time a flame of true anger came forth and she braced for a quick, paralyzing reprimand. Annie put her hands on her hips and opened her chest to him, facing for a blow and wanting to take it full on and at once — to be struck and die on the spot.

Ridley's face was dumb. His eyes were puzzled rather than flashing angry. He looked hard at her as if straining to be certain it was Annie who had spoken. She started to belch and snort with stamping her feet, and hot tears came out of her eyes, for it was with great strength that she held from striking him. Ridley's look continued incredulous. He thought he saw froth at her lips. The sight caused him to waver — to pull back his hand. Annie bared her teeth at him and he noted chaff in her hair and that her skirt was soiled and frayed at the hem where it dragged the ground. A puzzling Annie! Just come from the funeral and disheveled. Ridley retreated from her. He left her to her piles of things touched by Gabriel.

"A good thing gone and wasted, your Gabriel," Jonathan Ridley said from the door. "A good effort made and then no fruit. Go off, old woman," he said to her, who was a girl under him the first time he put his full manliness in her mouth. Was he so old now that he did not remember this?

What had been between them came back into her mind in a spit. It was a bestial picture! Him a rigid dowel and rocking her cheeks and pounding her throat — him letting his slop down her throat and over her face.

"If you use your teeth, I will throttle you," he had seethed, though his eyes were bright-flecked. These eyes had danced a tarantella in dark-blue passion as he had plunged himself down her throat.

Slumped and wallowing now, Ridley sneered again, "Take what you want and go off. A pity you pinned all of your hopes on this pup. Now you are old to start again. 'Twould be a kindness to give you the quilts and bed linens and such. 'Tis your boon, old gal," he slung at her. His stomach rested on what used to be his heroic thighs, and Annie thought to kick him or lunge at him and cut his gut open. But she did not. A bone of caution broke through all else. The dog backed off and she, the bitch, crawled forward to take her advantage. She took the linen treasures.

"Waste no water on it. Swab yourself and think no more of it," Knitting Annie had said to her. Because she had followed and watched, the old woman knew the young girl had come to no especial harm from Ridley. She had escaped the fate of another such one with sad little milk teeth that had collapsed and died with his knob in her mouth — choked to death in the midst of the master's pleasure.

Annie credited her stand as her one act of defiance of Jonathan Ridley. But she'd defied him first when she went to Bell with love and permanence. This was the thing he'd robbed the women of — the slave women on his place — a hearth fire and their own children ringing it. Ridley split and splintered children in his speculations and caprice, even children he'd fathered. Annie stole that from him — her Gabriel. Bell was lost, but she'd kept Gabriel beside herself and trained him up some measure. This had been her first defiance.

Annie looked at Ridley's lazy belly now and she remembered him otherwise. He'd been a strong and demanding stallion once. His dangling bits and pieces had some beauty in those youthful days. He was slyly admired by some of his concubines on the place. Vain of his attentions, they competed to brag on him and his endowments and his stamina.

He had done the other for Annie first, too. On one night when she was a girl — a night of big hilarity at the end of putting up a crop of beans — all hands were singing and dancing. She stood at the edge of the crowd of laughers and singers, for she was reticent. She had never been raucously gay and capricious. She was wedded to the solitary work at Knitting Annie's side. She kept away from the circles of big fun. Ridley came behind her and grabbed and clamped on her upper arm. He drew her away from the others and smashed his fist into her chin and stunned her. When she dropped he hoisted her to his shoulder and took her into the loom house. There he lashed her to the spinning mule and had her upon the wheel.

"It's done. It's done now and done. Forget about it," Knitting Annie had said again, and dismissed her from the tale. "Shut your mouth and forget it."

It was all fruit that Annie took from the shop. She was barred from taking the looms; spinning wheels; spindles; knitting needles, excepting the ones sewn among the linens; and the sewing needles, excepting those secreted in the children's clothes.

Annie nearly lost composure again when the sheriff came to seize the water barrels. Jonathan Ridley did not come to the battle over these casks, for he knew that Annie wanted to take him on again — to froth at him angrily. Aches and pains and their remedy had made him soft and averse to quarreling. He conspired to rob her of the chance to see him vexed and thwarted over the barrels. So he delegated the duty to a sheriff. When the sheriff arrived, Annie only rolled her eyes and thumped one of the casks as it passed out of the yard.

She stood before the cheval glass on her last circuit of the shop. At first the oval threw back an image of Gabriel bright and proud in his soldier's uniform. But her mind cleared and she saw her true self. Annie peered upon her self's image and saw a disheveled woman standing amidst piled linens and suits preparing to pack all into trunks.

She would go with Pearl and Hannah to Philadelphia to live

with Sis Ellen and her girl, Delia. Then all would go south together to teach. Naomi, determined to pull away from her grandmother, had claimed Ruth and planned to return to their studies at Hampton Institute. These two eldest girls were buoyed by Naomi's dream of the both of them becoming model women of the race.

Here were all of these that Gabriel made!

The most pregnant time of worry was over, yet their real tribulation had come amidst a sliver of calm. The cruelest part being the shock of it.

Stand the Storm

Oh! stand the storm, it won't be long.
We'll anchor by and by.
Stand the storm, it won't be long
We'll anchor by and by.

My ship is on the ocean
We'll anchor by and by.
My ship is on the ocean
We'll anchor by and by.

She's making for the kingdom
We'll anchor by and by.
She's making for the kingdom
We'll anchor by and by.

My ship is on the ocean
We'll anchor by and by.
My ship is on the ocean
We'll anchor by and by.

I've a mother in the kingdom
We'll anchor by and by.
I've a mother in the kingdom
We'll anchor by and by.

My ship is on the ocean
We'll anchor by and by.
My ship is on the ocean
We'll anchor by and by.

IN MEMORIAM

EDNA HIGGINS PAYNE CLARKE

1916–2003

LUISE HIGGINS JETER

1918–2007

About the Author

BREENA CLARKE grew up in Washington, DC, and was educated at Webster College and Howard University. Her first novel, *River, Cross My Heart,* was a selection of Oprah's Book Club. She lives in New Jersey. For more information, visit www.BreenaClarke.com.

BACK BAY · READERS' PICK

Reading Group Guide

Stand the Storm

A Novel

BREENA CLARKE

A conversation with
Breena Clarke

Your first novel, River, Cross My Heart, *was an Oprah Book Club selection in 1999. Describe your Oprah's Book Club experience. In what ways did it change your life?*

The Oprah's Book Club experience with *River, Cross My Heart* was simply exciting. It is thrilling for a novelist to reach so wide an audience.

Shortly after this success, I left my office job and made a transition to writing full-time. It wasn't as effortless as I thought it would be. I began by structuring my writing around swimming. I took my first swimming lessons in 2000, and the experience changed my life. I began swimming regularly, and a loose structure evolved that helped me figure out my most productive, creative time of day.

What was your starting point for writing your second novel?

Work on *Stand the Storm* began with research — reading books. I cast a wide net and brought back plenty. The subject of the Civil War is vast. I visited museums and historical houses and perused documents. I also collected some historical newspapers from the mid-nineteenth century. These documents were immediate and provocative of ideas. They helped me get into the "flavor" of everyday life in nineteenth-century Washington, DC.

River, Cross My Heart *was also set in Georgetown. Why did you revisit this community in* Stand the Storm?

Well, frankly, I am curious about Washington, DC. It's my hometown. And I am fascinated with Georgetown for all kinds of emotional reasons, as well as simple curiosity.

I believe that Washington, DC, suffers for being the nation's capital. Images of the town are shaped by partisan politics and the machine of the federal government. Like much of the nation, Washington, DC, has a "slave" history, and I chose to consider closely the lives of people who lived in Georgetown and Washington in that time.

What's the meaning of the novel's title, Stand the Storm?

The title is from the lyrics to a traditional African American spiritual. The Coatses are survivors and are determined to meet any challenge to their survival, their freedom, their dignity. They will stand up to any storm that assails them. They are emblematic of the many descendants of enslaved people who have triumphed in their own personal lives, though they go unrecognized in the mainstream.

Novels that focus on slavery rarely portray African Americans as skilled workers, as the Coatses are. How did you come to choose needlework as the occupation for the Coats family?

First and foremost, I wanted to portray a profession that, if not typical of African American slaves and free persons of the time, was plausible for them. Enslaved people who labored in Washington in the eighteenth and nineteenth centuries were occupied in a variety of agricultural and nonagricultural professions.

I selected needlework for the Coatses because the skills can be transmitted in a mundane, utilitarian way or in a culturally significant way. The individual practitioner can interact dynamically with others in quilting, tailoring, and knitting and/or develop highly individual artistic expressions.

Tailoring and dressmaking were commercially viable professions before the wide availability of affordable ready-to-wear clothing. The laundry business was also commercially viable for enslaved and free blacks — especially for women.

I chose to emphasize less the stereotypical image of slavery as only agricultural work, only rural, and only unskilled labor. Perhaps an unlikely spark to my ideas was a nugget I came across while reading. I learned that George and Martha Washington included several male and female knitters in their inventory of slaves. Though far larger than the typical Virginia or Maryland plantation, Mount Vernon is a good model of a self-contained, slave labor agricultural operation. There was textile production at Mount Vernon so that skills in this profession could be acquired.

Traditions in needlework have defied the limitations of literacy and have been preserved through hand-to-hand links. I wanted to put my characters squarely in the line of African Americans who pursued literacy and pursued a highly specialized, creative art.

From the time Gabriel was a little boy he watched his mother sew and knit. How did that shape him as a worker and a person?

Sewing Annie Coats is not a woman who sews and knits in her off-times. She is mandated to the tasks of needlework and textile production on the Ridley Plantation. She has been trained specifically to these tasks through her apprenticeship to Knitting Annie. She decides to apprentice Baby Gabriel to herself — to develop his skills as her own were developed and make him more valuable to Master Ridley for this specialized work rather than for the work of the field, as an agricultural laborer.

Gabriel's father's influences should not be discounted. His specialized skills as a blacksmith made him an important model for his children. Sewing Annie shapes her children's temperament to the work with a view toward self-preservation and, ultimately, self-emancipation.

The road to freedom was never smooth. Gabriel soon experiences this, yet he diligently continues to pursue freedom. How does he manage to remain resilient in the face of adversity?

One of the most important things that I discovered in reading autobiographical narratives of slavery is that it was not a condition of "on/off" — one day a slave and the next a free citizen. Most self-emancipators struggled to get to freedom, and most struggled daily to maintain their status.

Gabriel has been trained to his profession, and the values of patience and determination he has learned in his work are of value to him here as well. He is stalwart. He never loses his vision of his own future: a successful man working as a tailor with his family working alongside. This vision is under constant assault, but Gabriel Coats stands against any threat to it. I suppose his experiences in the Civil War tested his resilience, and Gabriel is something like an exhausted piece of elastic band when he returns home after the war.

What is the significance of quilting in the novel?

It would be hard to overemphasize the importance of quilting to nineteenth-century women (and men). Needlework skills were considered an important component of a young woman's education. For African American women needlework proficiency was often the key to self-sufficiency and freedom. It was always an important "necessary skill" for a woman to build a home.

Also, quilting traditions have long been used to transmit sacred symbols and to document births, deaths, marriages, and other social milestones. For women with superior skills and design ideas, quilting provided one of the few opportunities for artistic expression. And in an era before the mass marketing of ready-made bedding, quilts were made in the home for family use. The popularity of patchwork, also known as crazy quilt, emphasizes the ways that people with limited resources executed beautiful, utilitarian quilts.

The use of quilts by conductors of the Underground Railroad may seem fanciful because there is no incontrovertible proof of it. However, there is anecdotal evidence that quilts were displayed in a variety of ways to signal to escapees and to identify safe houses.

The women in Stand the Storm *play key roles in the family's struggle toward freedom. Can you tell us more about why you made your female characters so strong?*

In my view and in the Coats family, strength and the myriad qualities that we consider signs of strength — i.e., physical prowess, determination, courage — are not gender specific. Strength does not belong to men alone. The women of *Stand the*

Storm are survivors. They could hardly be otherwise, given the threats to their health and welfare. Though enslaved and assailed on all sides by the slave system, African American bondpersons and freedpersons worked mightily to cling together and form families with regard to mutual support and uplift. Because African American slave women have been unacknowledged, unappreciated, and misunderstood, I considered it an important duty to give them voice and agency in my text.

How significant are Daniel Joshua's contributions to the Coatses' journey?

Daniel Joshua's inclusion in the Coats family's orbit is a clear example of "mutual support and uplift." He develops a deep relationship with the group and with Annie in particular because he is motivated to help — to protect. And he has had to break from all whom he previously had known as "friends" and "family" when he left his own bondage. This is an unrecognized toll on the life of the self-emancipators. They must voluntarily leave behind their relations — spouse, children, parents, friends — to liberate themselves. A successful and compassionate person like Daniel would, of course, find a circle — a community to gather with, to love.

Though he is not a needleworker, Daniel Joshua occupies a place in *Stand the Storm* as a "knitter" — one who is creating a whole swatch from different strands — as he did in introducing the Coatses to the traumatized runaway Mary, and in keeping them connected to the Underground Railroad community.

Throughout Stand the Storm *it is evident that there were unspoken rules in the nineteenth century on how blacks were to conduct themselves*

*among whites. To circumvent such rules the Coats family developed
gestural ways of communicating with one another. How did this
strengthen their family bond?*

The Coats family developed their gestures and methods of observation because they needed to communicate in the presence of hostile "others." Sewing Annie's decision to educate Gabriel and develop his intellectual skills was, under the slave system, an audacious and dangerous idea.

The stone, the pit, the heart's core of *Stand the Storm* is that, slave or free, every human being is intelligent and motivated to have agency in her or his own life. No additional explanation need be given for the characters' curiosity, reasoning, cunning, and courage.

Sewing Annie forges a special bond with her son to keep him safe and to help him find "a way from no way." Closely observed by whites, the Coatses developed quiet methods of communicating. And, as all needleworkers know, there are myriad ways that the "work" on/with needles is deeply, intellectually stimulating while cultivating a strong social bond. These are dexterous people with imagination.

Questions and topics for discussion

1. What surprised you most about the novel's depiction of slave life in the mid-nineteenth century? Discuss some of the ways in which the lives of urban slaves differed from the lives of plantation-based slaves.

2. Is Sewing Annie Coats a good mother? Is she a good mother to Gabriel? To Ellen? If in your view Annie favors one child over the other, do you think she's justified in doing so?

3. What special steps did Abraham Pearl take to insure that only Gabriel would read the part of his letter in which he revealed the existence of the chest filled with gold buttons? Do you think Pearl actually forgot to take the chest or did he deliberately leave it behind?

4. *Stand the Storm* is unsparing in its portrayal of the dangers faced by anyone who participated in the Underground Railroad. Discuss the particular case of Emily and Matthew Chester (pages 68–73). Was their murder necessary?

5. When Gabriel suffers a humiliating assault by Master Jonathan Ridley (page 108), he manages to resist fighting back. Is Gabriel's response appropriate? Put yourself in his shoes; how would *you* have reacted? What might the consequences have been for Gabriel if he had responded differently?

6. Discuss the character Katharine Logan. When she first appears in the novel (page 89), she is an indentured servant on

the Warren plantation. She is nominally a free white woman when, years later, she visits the Ridley tailoring shop in Georgetown (page 178) and attempts to reclaim the daughter she gave up at birth. Is Katharine's life any less circumscribed than the Coatses' lives? What opportunities does she enjoy in Civil War–era America that the Coatses do not?

7. What is the Reverend William Higgins's secret? Was it by sheer luck that his life took the path it did? Do you think Reverend Higgins feels a special obligation to help the blacks of Georgetown? Did his experiences in childhood make him a better clergyman than he might otherwise have been?

8. Discuss the significance of the wedding gift bestowed on Gabriel and Mary by Aaron Ridley and his mother (page 155). Why does this gift bring Sewing Annie to tears?

9. Why does Sewing Annie reject Daniel Joshua's overtures (page 169)? Why will she not allow herself to become romantically involved with him?

10. Mary and Sewing Annie hold opposing views on whether to join one of Georgetown's laundry syndicates. What benefits did these syndicates provide their members? Whose side would you have taken? Would you have argued against or in favor of joining a syndicate?

11. How did Ellen end up in the Blue Jug? Does it seem credible to you that an unprovoked incident seemingly so minor could have such dire repercussions?

12. In what ways are Jonathan and Mary Ridley typical slave owners? Do they exhibit any attitudes and behaviors that set them apart from other nineteenth-century slave owners in fiction or in the historical record?

13. In chapter 14 we see Gabriel make a valiant effort to rescue other blacks fleeing slavery: he ferries across the Potomac, at great personal risk and in hazardous conditions, a family who are strangers to him. Yet Gabriel seems willing to allow Delia, the girl his sister claims is her daughter, to be turned back over to Master Ridley and enslaved (page 209). How can Gabriel reconcile his actions in these two circumstances?

14. Identify a moment in *Stand the Storm* when one of the novel's principal characters — Sewing Annie, Gabriel, Ellen, or Mary — feels unmitigated joy. How common was the experience of joy in these characters' lives?

15. Discuss the ways in which the war changed Gabriel. How did it change the other members of the Coats family? Compare the Coatses' experience with the experience of American families touched by war today.

16. "Annie surprised herself with longing for Ridley Plantation" (page 193). How, after buying her freedom, can Sewing Annie look back at plantation life — with its abundant rigors and indignities — with any fondness at all? What about Ridley Plantation do you think she misses?

17. Several months before President Lincoln issued his Emancipation Proclamation, the U.S. government freed the slaves residing in the nation's capital. How were the Coatses, who at the time were living in Georgetown as free persons, endangered by Congress's decree (page 197)? Which members of the Coats family were put most at risk? How were they saved?

18. Were you surprised by the turn of events at the end of chapter 33? Even if such unforeseen tragedy is true to life, does it have a proper place in fiction?

19. Discuss the significance of the rain barrels that Sewing Annie installs in the yard behind the shop and uses to collect water for laundering (page 39). What happens to the rain barrels at the end of the novel?

20. Does slavery still exist in our twenty-first-century world? If so, where? How? And what could or should be done to eradicate it?

Look for Breena Clarke's bestselling first novel,
River, Cross My Heart

"A genuine masterpiece . . . full of grace and beauty and profound insights. . . . It bears traces of Eudora Welty's charm and Toni Morrison's passion."   — Michael Shelden, *Baltimore Sun*

"Breena Clarke's first novel is a sweet read. Sweet like a glass of Southern iced tea on a hot day. Sweet like homemade ice cream from a hand-cranked machine, and just as rich."
— Holly Bass, *Washington Post Book World*

"A compelling novel. . . . Inspired by tales her parents told her about growing up in the 1920s, Clarke brings to life a whole neighborhood of vivid personalities, writing blacks back into Georgetown's history."   — Denise Kersten, *USA Today*

"Seldom do I find a novel that I can recommend to everyone. My aunt likes a book to be both sad and funny. My mother-in-law hates violence and sex. Friends like lyricism and depth of theme. Everyone wants a good story. I'm delighted to say that the debut novel by Breena Clarke fills the bill in all these respects. . . . *River, Cross My Heart* is written with the restraint and affectionate detail I associate with no one so much as Eudora Welty."   — Sandra Scofield, *Chicago Tribune*

Back Bay Books
Available wherever paperbacks are sold

Say You're One of Them
Stories by Uwem Akpan

"One of the year's most exhilarating reads. . . . Awe is the only appropriate response to Akpan's stunning debut, a collection of five stories so ravishing and sad that I regret ever wasting superlatives on fiction that was merely good."
— Jennifer Reese, *Entertainment Weekly*

Beginner's Greek
A novel by James Collins

"While the title of James Collins's comedy of manners might cause Jane Austen to raise an eyebrow, were she to crack it she'd discover a debut novel worthy of her own book club. . . . A satire of modern love that will charm both sexes equally."
— Elissa Schappell, *Vanity Fair*

Girls in Trucks
A novel by Katie Crouch

"Sarah Walters's voice is a funny, slim stiletto to the heart of friendship, desire, and love. Crouch's spare prose and sharp dialogue flay open a universal need to belong, whether to a place, a person, or your own true self."
— Peggy McMullen, *Portland Oregonian*

Back Bay Books
Available wherever paperbacks are sold